the Summer of Sunshine & Margot

SUSAN MALLERY

the Summer of Sunshine & Margot

HQN™

ISBN-13: 978-1-335-65997-2
ISBN-13: 978-1-335-01014-8 (Target Exclusive Edition)
ISBN-13: 978-1-335-00824-4 (International Trade Paperback Edition)

The Summer of Sunshine and Margot

www.HQNBooks.com

Printed in U.S.A.

the Summer
of
Sunshine
&
Margot

chapter
ONE

SOCIAL INTERACTIONS FELL INTO TWO CATEGORIES—EASY or awkward. Easy was knowing what to say and do, and how to act. Easy was witty small talk or an elegant compliment. Awkward social interactions, on the other hand, were things like sneezing in your host's face or stepping on the cat or spilling red wine on a white carpet. Or any carpet, for that matter. Margot Baxter prided herself on knowing how to make any situation fall into the easy category. Professionally, of course. In her professional life, she totally kicked butt. Personally—not so much. If she was being completely honest, she would have to admit that on most days her personal life fell firmly in the awkward category, which was why she never mixed business and pleasure and rarely bothered with pleasure at all. If it wasn't going to go well, why waste the time?

But work was different. Work was where the magic happened and she was the one behind the curtain, moving all the levers. *Not in a bad way*, she added silently. It was just that she was about empowering her clients—helping them realize it was all about confidence, and sometimes finding confidence required a little help.

She turned onto the street where her nav system directed her, then blinked twice as she stared at the huge double gates stretching across a freeway-wide driveway. She'd been told the private residence had originally been a monastery built in the 1800s, but she hadn't expected it to be so *huge*. She'd been thinking more "extra-big house with a guest cottage and maybe a small orchard." What she faced instead was a three-story, Spanish-style former church/monastery with two turrets, acres of gardens and an actual parking lot for at least a dozen cars.

"Who *are* these people?" she asked out loud, even though she already knew the answer. Before interviewing a potential client, she always did her research. Overdid it, some would say, a criticism she could live with. Margot liked being thorough. And on time. And tidy. And, according to some, annoying.

Margot pressed the call button on the electronic pad mounted perpendicular to the gate and waited until a surprisingly clear voice said, "May I help you?"

"I'm Margot Baxter. I have an appointment with Mr. Alec Mcnicol."

"Yes, Ms. Baxter. He's expecting you."

The gates opened smoothly and Margot drove through onto the compound. She parked in one of the marked spots, then took a moment to breathe and collect her thoughts.

She could do this, she told herself. She was good at her job. She liked helping people. Everything was going to be fine. She was a professional, she was trained and she was calm. *Calm-ish*, she added silently, then reached for the glasses she'd put on the seat next to her briefcase.

Margot stepped out of her car and smoothed the front of her slightly too-big jacket. The outfit—gray suit, sensible pumps, minimal makeup—was designed to make her appear professional and competent. The glasses, while unnecessary, did a lot to add gravitas to her appearance. She was thirty-one, but in shorts and a concert T-shirt, she could pass for nineteen. Even more depressing, in said shorts and T-shirt, she looked ditzy and incompetent and just a little bit dumb, and that didn't reassure anyone.

She walked up the stone path to the enormous front door. Although she knew nothing about Spanish architecture, she wanted to trace the heavy carved wood doors where angels watched over Christ as he carried the cross toward a hill. Yup, the big-as-a-stadium building really had once been a monastery and apparently the monks had been sincere in their worship.

Before she could get her fill of the amazing craftsmanship, the doors opened and a tall, broad-shouldered, dark-haired man nodded at her.

"Ms. Baxter? I'm Alec Mcnicol. It's nice to meet you."

"Thank you."

She stepped inside and they shook hands. She had a brief impression of two-story ceilings and intricate stained glass windows before Alec was leading her down a hallway into a large office lined with bookshelves and framed maps of lands long forgotten.

She did her best not to gawk at her surroundings. While she was used to working with the rich and famous, this was different. The books made her want to inhale deeply to capture their musty smell and the maps had her itching to trace a path along the Silk Road.

She'd taken a step to do just that when her host cleared his throat.

She glanced at him and smiled. "Sorry. Your office is incredible. The maps are hand drawn?"

He looked slightly startled, his eyebrows coming together in an attractive frown. "They are."

She looked at them one last time. If she got the job, she would have to ask permission to study the framed drawings. She reluctantly pulled her attention away from the distractions around her and took a seat across from him at the wide desk.

When he was settled, he said, "As I explained on the phone, you're here to help my mother."

"Yes, Mr.—"

"Please call me Alec."

She nodded. "I'm Margot, and yes, I understand she will be my client."

"Excellent. She and I decided it would be easier if I conducted the preliminary interview to see if you and she are suited."

"Of course."

Margot relaxed. Hiring someone like her was often stressful. Her services were only required when something had gone very wrong in a person's life. Or if the potential client was anticipating something going wrong. Or was overwhelmed. Very few people looked around at their happiest moment and thought, *Hey, I should find someone to teach me social etiquette and how not to be odd/uncomfortable/weird or just plain nervous.* There was always a trigger that made a client realize he or she needed Margot's services and it rarely grew out of an uplifting event.

Alec glanced at the papers on his desk. They were arranged in neat piles, which Margot appreciated. How could anyone find anything on a messy desk? Her boss, a man whose desk was always covered with folders and notes and half-eaten sandwiches, was forever sending her articles on how messy desks were a sign of creativity and intelligence, but Margot would not be swayed in her opinion. Disorder was just plain wrong.

"You know who my mother is?" Alec asked, his voice more resigned than curious.

Margot filed away the tone to review later. The dynamic between mother and son could be significant to her work.

"I do. Bianca Wray was born in 1960. Her father died when she was an infant and she was raised by her mother until she was twelve." Margot frowned. "Why she was put in foster care isn't clear, but that's where she ended up."

She flashed Alec a smile. "She was literally discovered while drinking a milk shake with her girlfriends, propagating the myth that in Los Angeles anyone, at any moment, is just one lucky break away from being famous."

"You've discovered my deepest wish in life," Alec said drily.

"Mine, too," Margot said, allowing her mouth to curve slightly at the corners. "After a career in modeling, your mother turned to acting. She preferred quirky roles to the obvious ingenue parts that would have helped her have a more successful career. She had one son—you—when she was twenty-four. She and your father, a Swiss banker, never married, but you were close to both your parents."

As she spoke, she sensed tension in Alec's shoulders as if he were uncomfortable with her reciting the facts of his personal life. He might not be her client, but he was her client's son and therefore of note, she thought, but didn't bother explaining herself. Her methods were excellent and if he couldn't see that, then this was not the job for her.

"Bianca is a free spirit, and despite facing her sixtieth birthday, is still considered a beauty. She acts in the occasional project. From what I could see, there doesn't seem to be a pattern in why she chooses the roles she does. She enjoys remodeling homes and has made a lot of money flipping upscale houses. She gives generously to charity and has had many lovers in her life, but has never married. She is currently dating a man named Wesley Goswick-Chance. Mr. Goswick-Chance is the youngest son of an English earl. His parents divorced when he was an infant and he grew up in both England and the small European country of Cardigania. He is currently their senior attaché to the United States. He is stationed at the consulate here in Los Angeles."

There was a lot more she could have mentioned about Alec's mother. There was the time Bianca had been presenting at the Academy Awards and had dropped her dress on national television. Or her sex tapes that, back in the 1990s, had been quite the scandal, although they were fairly tame by today's standards. Bianca was a colorful protestor, a woman who slept with kings, movie stars, artists and, according to some gossip that was never confirmed, had once had a torrid affair with the wife of the world's largest yacht builder. While Margot would never admit it to anyone, she was equally intrigued and terrified by the idea of working with Bianca.

"That was very thorough," Alec said with a sigh. "And thank you for not mentioning all the salacious bits I'm sure your research uncovered."

Margot nodded. "Of course."

He looked at her. His eyes were very nice—dark, with thick lashes. She could see traces of his mother in his appearance— the eyes she'd admired, the curve of his mouth.

"My mother has recently accepted a proposal of marriage," Alec said, his voice stiff. "From Wesley. He's a nice enough man and he makes her happy, so I have no objection to the union."

Margot waited quietly, not showing her surprise. How unexpected that, after sixty years and countless lovers, Bianca had finally gotten engaged.

Alec's gaze was steady. "If Wesley were a shipping magnate or a movie star, there wouldn't be an issue. But he is a diplomat and as such, he moves in the kind of circles that will not be very accepting of my mother's somewhat, ah, eccentric ways."

"She wants to learn how to fit in."

"Yes. To be clear, hiring you was her idea, not mine. I'm not pushing her into anything. She's worried that her impulsive behavior will be a problem for Wesley and she claims she loves him enough to want to change for him."

"What do you think?" Margot asked.

Alec hesitated, his gaze shifting from hers. "I believe most people are who they are. Asking Bianca to be a staid, polite and unobtrusive person is like asking the sun to shine less brightly. Ambitious, but unlikely."

She'd wondered if he would say it was wrong for Wesley to not accept his fiancée as she was. Interesting that Alec had gone in a different direction. "You're saying she can't change."

"I'm saying it's improbable." He returned his attention to her and leaned forward. "My mother is funny, charming and generous to a fault. I'm confident you will enjoy her company but if you take this job thinking you're going to succeed, I'm concerned you'll be very disappointed."

Margot smiled. "You're warning me off?"

"I'm suggesting you consider the possibility of failure."

"Which only makes me want to take the job more, Alec, if for no other reason than to prove myself."

"Not my intent, but I can see how it would happen."

He relaxed as he spoke. Margot found herself as curious about her client's son as she was about her client. She'd done preliminary research on Alec, in the context of him being Bianca's only family. She knew that Alec was a scholar who studied ancient texts. When he'd inherited the monastery nearly six years ago, he'd done extensive remodeling, turning much of the space into a research center for the study of obscure written works. He was reclusive, had never married and was rarely photographed. A few people had described him as stodgy and boring, but she knew they were wrong on both counts. Alec was a man who kept tight control over his emotions—a trait she could respect. To her mind, order was a kind of meditation that should be embraced by all.

"Shall we?" he asked, coming to his feet.

She rose as well and followed him out of the office and down a long hallway that opened onto the grounds. The hallway ceiling was fifteen feet high and all hand-carved wood. The stone floor was smooth and she could see faint grooves from the thousands of feet that had walked this same path. She wanted to ask about the history of the monastery and what it was like to live here. She wanted to know if sometimes, in the quiet of those hours after midnight, he heard the whispered echoes of so many prayers. Margot didn't consider herself religious but she admired those who were. Faith must be a wonderful thing. She was just a little too pragmatic to believe that any divine force was going to help her with her life. As such, she believed in being self-reliant.

To her right were huge gardens. The well-kept grounds went on for acres—a private paradise in the middle of Pasadena. She recognized several of the flowers and plants but many were unknown to her.

"The grounds are lovely," she said, wishing she had time to explore the paths she could see weaving through hedges and by trees.

"Thank you. They were in disrepair when I inherited the place but I hired a landscape architect to clean things up. He's done a good job."

He paused by a stone path and turned to her. "My mother recently sold her house and has moved in with me until the wedding," he said, his voice carefully neutral. "Should you take the job, she would like you to stay here, as well, for the time you're working together." He glanced at her. "Just to be clear, my mother sometimes keeps odd hours."

"Many clients do," she assured him, thinking of the business executive who had wanted to work on his Chinese etiquette between four and six in the morning.

"She's not—" he began, then pressed his lips together. "My mother is—" He shook his head. "You'll have to see for yourself."

He started across the lawn toward the garden. Margot followed him along the stone path that was just as worn as the open hallway had been. They passed between two flowering trees onto a huge patio created with paving stones. Stone benches lined the perimeter while hundreds of pots of various sizes overflowed with exotic flowering plants.

The scent was divine—sweet without being cloying. If she had to pick a single word, she would have chosen *alive* as the fragrance. She found herself longing to sit on one of the stone benches and turn her face to the sun. Farther on, she spotted a table and chairs and desperately wished for a slow-paced dinner at sunset.

"This is the most incredible garden I've ever seen," she admitted, unable to hold in the comment. "It's magnificent."

"I can't take credit." He gave her a slight smile. "But it is very nice."

Nice? Iced tea was nice. This was stupendous!

She reminded herself that she was here for an interview and reluctantly let go of her garden lust. As they moved toward the table and chairs, Margot saw a woman seated in a small, hidden alcove, reading a magazine. The woman glanced up when she noticed them and waved a greeting.

Margot rarely worked with celebrities. Her area of expertise was the corporate arena. If you had a quick trip down to Argentina, for example, she was the one who could give you a crash course on things like greetings—while the first greeting with a client or customer involved a handshake, in subsequent meetings, the greeting was likely to be a kiss on the cheek, even if the business meeting was between two men. She could advise that good posture was important and that dinner rarely started before nine. She found comfort in rules and knowing the right thing to do in any situation.

Each employee in her company had a profile that was made available to prospective clients. Coming to an understanding of who worked best with whom was a mutual decision. Movie stars and those in the music business rarely picked Margot and she was fine with that. She'd been on a couple of jobs with directors looking to be more successful in obtaining financing in China, but that was different. Which probably explained why she was unprepared to meet Bianca Wray in person.

Oh, she'd seen pictures of the actress and had watched three of her movies the previous weekend. She was familiar with the sound of her voice and the way she moved, but none of that had equipped her for the reality of seeing her up close.

Bianca was far more delicate in person. Slim, but also small boned. There was a glow to her bare skin, a grace to her movements. Her deep blue eyes were wide and her light brown hair was wavy, and just past her shoulders.

Taken individually, the features were nice enough but unremarkable. Yet there was something about the way they were put together. Something…breathtaking. Margot supposed that was the difference between the chosen and the ordinary. An undefinable quality that couldn't be manufactured, only recognized and worshipped.

Her great-grandmother had talked about star power. She couldn't say what it was, but she'd been able to recognize it when she saw it. Bianca had star power. When she smiled, Margot instantly felt like the most special person on earth. Even as she reacted viscerally, the intellectual side of her brain cataloged how Bianca stood, smiled and moved toward them. She was looking for clues to the problem, along with any information that would help her do her job to the best of her ability.

"Have you thought about what I said, Alec?" Bianca asked as she approached. She wore jeans and a loose T-shirt. Nothing out of the ordinary, yet both suited her perfectly. Her feet were bare, her toes painted with little American flags. "I'm sure they would enjoy it."

Alec exhaled. "My mother thinks I should invite a few nuns over for lunch."

Margot glanced at him. "You know nuns?"

"No. She wants me to find a local convent and ask them over."

"Why?"

He looked at her, his expression clearly indicating there was no reasonable explanation and with luck, this, too, would pass.

Bianca stopped in front of them. She was maybe five-four or five-five, at least three inches shorter than Margot.

"Because of what Alec has done with the monastery," she said, her voice light and happy. "They would be delighted to see how you've kept the spirit of the building while modernizing it."

"The master bedroom is in what used to be the church," he said drily. "I doubt the nuns would approve."

Bianca linked arms with him. "Oh, darling, don't worry about that. It's not as if you're having sex there." She winked at Margot. "Alec goes out for that sort of thing. He's a little bit like a groundhog. Once a year he makes an appearance, so to speak, then retreats to his regular world."

Margot wasn't sure if the comment was meant to shock her or test her or humiliate Alec. Given the warm tone and loving expression, she doubted it was the latter. Still, it was an unusual thing to say to a stranger—especially about her own son.

"I'm Margot. It's nice to meet you." Margot held out her hand.

Bianca shook it. "It's nice to be met." Her smile broadened. "I'm a fairly hopeless case, as I'm sure Alec has told you. I'm impulsive and reckless and not the sort of person who should be marrying a professional diplomat. But here we are, trying to make it work." Her smile faltered. "It's just that Wesley is all I've ever wanted. I love him and I don't want to be the reason he loses his job."

For a second her eyes were no longer bright but instead filled with fear and uncertainty. Margot studied the flash of emotions and saw the exact moment self-preservation kicked in.

"Imagine falling in love at my age!" she said with a laugh. "What a ridiculous thing. Until now I've only really loved one person and that's Alec." She smiled up at him. "I'm sure he'll be delighted to have someone else share that burden."

Margot nearly felt dizzy from the emotional ping-pong. Bianca had shifted from the odd comment about Alec's sex life to a flash of honest vulnerability with a quick return to fact, all couched in a protective shield of humor. There was a lot more going on here than the desire to learn which fork to use.

One of the advantages of being socially awkward—not that there were many—was the ability to recognize it in others. Bianca might be more beautiful than 99 percent of the population, but that didn't mean she was comfortable in her own skin. She was obviously afraid of disappointing everyone she cared about. Perhaps she thought she'd been doing it for years. *How intriguing*, Margot thought, suddenly itching to get on her computer and begin working on her development program.

Alec squeezed his mother's hand. "I just want you to be happy."

Bianca flashed him a smile that was brighter than the sun Alec had mentioned earlier, then turned to Margot. "Shall we have a little talk to see if we suit?"

"I'd like that."

Bianca led her to the table in the center of the paved garden while Alec retreated to the house. When they were seated across from each other, Bianca studied her for a second.

"You don't need to wear glasses, do you?"

The question surprised Margot. "No. How did you know?"

"I've worn prop glasses before. Why do you do it? No, don't tell me. Let me guess." Her gaze turned probing. "You want to look smart. Oh, because you're pretty. You must be very serious about your work. I never was. I liked acting but I was never passionate about it." The mega smile returned. "However, they do pay me a ridiculous amount of money for it, so why not?"

One shoulder rose and lowered. "Tell me. Can I be fixed? Do you have the skills to make me just like everyone else?"

Margot saw the trap in the question immediately. She sensed that Bianca was testing her in a hundred different ways and wasn't sure what that meant. If she was the one who had requested assistance, then surely she was motivated to change. Yet the way she phrased the question...

"I can certainly teach you how to behave in formal occasions, whether social or political," she began. "As for fixing you, I'm afraid that's not my job. I want to make you feel comfortable so everyone can get to know who you really are."

"I'm not sure that's a good idea," Bianca said quickly. "They couldn't handle the real me."

"Then the you you want them to know."

"What's your background?"

Margot smiled. "I started in hotel management. I received training to work with our international clients and loved it. I was recruited by my current employer and have moved to helping people deal with our ever-shrinking world."

"Hmm, yes, that's fascinating, but what's your background? Where are you from? Who raised you?"

A different question than "tell me about your parents." It was almost as if Bianca knew there hadn't been parents. "My maternal great-grandmother," she said slowly. "She owned a beauty and charm school for nearly fifty years. She trained pageant contestants."

"Were you in pageants?"

"No. I'm lacking certain skills." Like the ability to speak to a group. Margot still remembered the first time Francine had made her get up on the mock stage they had in the workroom and address the group. She'd barely taken her place when she'd projectile vomited and promptly fainted. It had been a fairly quick end to any hopes her great-grandmother had had about Margot taking the crown.

Margot had forced herself to overcome her deficiency and could now give a decent lecture, but she would never be a natural up on stage. Not that she'd ever aspired to be a beauty queen. She just wanted to do her job and live her life. Oh, and not be dumb about men, because she'd already done that enough already.

"Alec picked you," Bianca said. "He looked over all the people at your agency and he picked you. Now I see why."

Did she? Margot hadn't known he'd been the one to make the decision. Why her? She wasn't an obvious choice, was she?

"Can you do it?" Bianca asked before Margot could question

her statement. "Can you help me be who I need to be so I don't embarrass Wesley?"

"Yes."

"You promise?"

Margot leaned forward. "I will use every technique I have, and if those don't work, I will create new ones. I will work tirelessly to get you to a place where you are comfortable in Wesley's world."

"That's not a promise."

"I know. I don't make promises when I can't be sure of the outcome."

Bianca looked away. "I make promises all the time. I rarely keep them. It's just that in the moment, I want the person to be happy."

"And later?"

Bianca shrugged again. "They always forgive me. Even Alec." The smile returned. "All right. Let's do this. Alec thinks I need about two months of instruction. You'll have to move in here. There are a few guest rooms upstairs. I have the big one and I'm sorry but I'm not moving out for you."

"I wouldn't expect you to." Margot looked at her potential client. "Bianca, I don't live that far from here. I could easily drive over—"

"No. You have to stay here. It'll be like we're on location. Alec doesn't care. He rarely looks up from his work to notice anything. The house is beautiful. You'll love it and I'd feel better if you were close."

Margot nodded slowly. She'd lived in before. She didn't prefer it but when the client insisted, she agreed.

"As you wish. I'll send over the contract as soon as I get back to the office. Once it's signed and you've paid the retainer, I'll be in touch to discuss a start date."

"Monday!" Bianca sprang to her feet and raced around the table. She crouched in front of Margot, took both her hands and smiled. "We'll start Monday. Oh, this is going to be fun. We'll be best friends and have a wonderful time."

Bianca rose and twirled, then ran to the house, her laughter trailing after her.

Margot watched her go. There was something, she thought, some secret driving Bianca. Margot wasn't sure if she was running to something or away from it, but whatever it was, it was the key to the problem. Finding out what it was would be difficult, but she knew in her gut if she could figure out the mystery, she could teach Bianca what she needed to know and be gone in far less time than two months.

She glanced around at the beautiful gardens and the monastery's worn, red-tiled roof and reminded herself that whatever she might have to deal with while helping Bianca, at least her living quarters were going to be extraordinary. Perhaps, if she were lucky, she might even run into a ghost monk or two.

chapter
TWO

SUNSHINE BAXTER WAS DONE WITH LOVE AT FIRST SIGHT.
D. O. N. E. More times than she could count, she'd looked
deeply into a pair of—insert any color here—eyes and immediately given her heart. The relationships had all ended in disaster
and she'd hated herself for being so incredibly stupid over and
over again, so she decided she was finished with the falling in
love concept. Over it. Moving on.

Except…

"I've decided," Connor said, pushing up his glasses, his dark
brown eyes staring intently into hers.

Sunshine leaned close, knowing that once again she'd foolishly fallen for an inappropriate guy. "Tell me."

"Ants."

Sunshine smiled. "Are you sure?"

"Yes. I've read three books on ants and they're very smart and
they work hard. I want to build the world's biggest ant farm."

"Okay, then. That's what we'll do. We should probably start
small," she told him. "Get a regular-size ant farm and see if we
can make it work. Then we'll add on."

His mouth began to curve in the most delightful smile. "I
thought girls didn't like ants."

"I don't want them crawling in my bed, but I think an ant farm is super cool."

The smile fully blossomed. Connor ran toward her. She pulled the eight-year-old close and hugged him, telling herself if adoring her new charge qualified as breaking her no-heart-giving rule, then she was willing to live with the disappointment. Connor was irresistible.

He released her and stepped back, nearly slipping off the path and into a tall, aggressive-looking succulent that no doubt had an impressively long Latin name. Sunshine shifted her weight, gently grabbed his arm and spun him out of the way of impalement. Connor barely noticed.

"You're going to tell me that you have to ask my dad, huh?"

"I am. We're talking about being responsible for several hundred life-forms. That's a big deal."

"You're right." He paused, then giggled. "Can I be their king?"

"Of course. Maybe we can teach them to chant 'All hail Connor.'"

Connor laughed. The desert garden section at The Huntington's acres of gardens was his favorite. Given that Connor's father was a landscape architect, Connor and Sunshine both had memberships and in her three weeks of employment as Connor's nanny, they'd been four times. So far all they'd visited was the desert garden, but she was okay with that. Eventually Connor's interests would broaden.

He squatted in front of a reddish plant apparently called *terrestrial bromeliad* and studied it.

"You start school on Monday," he said.

Something Sunshine didn't want to think about. Part of her plan to avoid bad relationships and shift her life onto a happier and more positive course meant going to college. Not back so much, as that implied she'd been at one in the first place.

"I do."

He glanced at her. "Are you scared?"

"I am. Well, maybe scared is strong. I'm nervous."

"Do you think all the other kids will be smarter than you?"

She grinned. "I wouldn't have put it like that, but yes, in part. And they'll be younger."

He stood up. "As young as me?"

"I think a little older, but certainly not my age."

She was thirty-one and had absolutely nothing noteworthy to show for her years on the planet. How sad was that?

Connor took her hand. "You don't have to be scared. You're smart, too, and we can do homework together."

She touched his nose. "You're in third grade. You don't have much homework."

"I'll sit with you and read about ants."

And this, she thought with a sigh, was why he'd won her heart. Connor was a good kid. He was funny and kind and affectionate. He'd lost his mother to cancer a few months ago and while his father obviously cared about his son, he had a big, impressive job that took a lot of time. Declan had hired a series of nannies, all of whom Connor had rejected within a week. For some reason, the two of them had clicked.

"Come on," she said, wrapping her arms around him. "Let's head home. I'm going to make lasagna roll-ups for dinner."

"What's a roll-up?"

"It's all the lasagna goodness rolled up in a noodle."

His gaze was skeptical. "You're going to put vegetables in the recipe, aren't you?"

She grinned. "Yes. Zucchini. Skinny little zucchini French fries."

"How skinny?"

She thought for a second. "Ant size."

He sighed. "Okay, but I won't like it."

"As long as you eat it."

An hour and a half later, Sunshine put a completed salad into the refrigerator and glanced at the clock. According to a text from Declan, he was planning on joining them for dinner. She'd set the table for three, but honestly, she wasn't holding out much hope. Her boss was in the middle of a big project—something about designing the gardens of a new five-star hotel just north of Malibu. Not only was the job time consuming, there was actually no good way to get to Pasadena from anywhere by the beach without dealing with miles of gridlock and hours stuck in traffic. More than once he'd texted to say he would be home in time for dinner only to call her an hour later to say he was still on the freeway and to start without him.

Sunshine didn't mind when it was just her and Connor, but she knew the boy missed his father when he wasn't around.

Once he got home, Declan spent the rest of the evening with his son and he was the one to get Connor ready for bed. They were obviously close, which was good. Still, the whole situation remained slightly awkward for her. Normally by the three-week mark of a job, she was comfortable in the house and had a set routine. She and Connor were doing great, but she'd barely seen Declan and they hadn't talked and she really had to tell him they should have a sit-down at some point. Maybe in the next couple of days.

The first weekend she'd been employed, Declan and Connor had gone to Sacramento to visit Declan's parents. Last weekend, Declan had been out of town at a conference and this weekend she had no idea what was going on.

"Do you and your dad have plans for tomorrow?" she asked.

"I don't know. He didn't tell me. If he's busy, what do you want to do?"

"I thought we'd go to the Star Eco Station."

Connor finished putting the flatware in place. "Do I have to hold the tarantula?"

"Not if you don't want to."

"Arachnids aren't ants," he said, his tone defensive.

She held up both hands. "You don't have to tell me. I'm perfectly fine with an ant farm but if you told me you wanted to start a spider colony, I'd run screaming into the night."

He grinned. "In your pajamas?"

"Very possibly."

His laughter was interrupted by the sound of the garage door opening.

"Dad's home! Dad's home!"

She watched him race across the kitchen and through the mudroom, then looked back at the table. Looked like there would be three for dinner and wouldn't that be fun.

Not that she was nervous. She wasn't. It was just she barely knew Declan. Which was fine—tonight they would have a conversation over lasagna roll-ups with ant-sized zucchini.

"…and Sunshine's going to help me with the ant farm. We're going to check online tomorrow and it's okay because I read three books and I've checked out two more from the library and I'll read them this weekend so I'm gonna know everything."

Based on the framed photographs she'd seen in Connor's room, Sunshine knew he took after his mother. He was small for his age, with a slight build and dark hair and eyes, so every time she saw Declan, it was something of a shock.

The man was big. Not heavy, but tall with broad shoulders and a lot of muscles. He had sandy-colored hair and green eyes, had to be at least six-two. With her only being five-four, that seemed a little extreme. He wore a suit and tie most days, which somehow made him even more impressive. He also had a presence about him—he was someone who was noticed wherever he went. She didn't know him well enough to have much of an opinion about him, but he seemed like a decent kind of guy. He loved his son and honestly that was all she cared about.

"Good evening, Mr. Dubois," she murmured as he set down his briefcase, then swept Connor up in his arms and turned the boy upside down.

As his son hung there, shrieking with happy laughter, Declan met her gaze. "We talked about this, Sunshine. Call me Declan, please."

"Okay, just checking."

"I want to keep things casual."

She liked casual. Now that she thought about it, casual was probably for the best considering she'd kicked off her shoes when she'd walked into the house and was currently standing barefoot, wearing jeans and an oversize T-shirt advertising a bar in Tahiti.

Declan turned Connor right side up, then glanced at the table. "That looks nice. What are we having?"

"Ant food!" Connor told him gleefully. "Zucchini ant sticks."

"Really?"

"Salad, lasagna roll-ups, garlic knots and zucchini fries," she corrected.

"The garlic knots are bread," Connor told his father. "I tied them all myself."

"Did you?" Declan ruffled his hair. "That's great. Give me five minutes to get changed and I'll be back to help." He picked up his briefcase and started for the hallway, his son at his heels. "Sunshine, do you drink wine?"

"Only on days ending in Y."

"Good. Why don't you pick us out a bottle of red from the wine cellar? You know where it is?"

"I do."

Except for Declan's bedroom, she'd explored the house that first weekend. She knew every place an eight-year-old boy could hide and had moved a bucket full of different bottles of cleaning solutions out to the garage. Yes, Connor was old enough to know not to play with stuff like that, but why tempt fate?

The house was typical for the neighborhood. Built in the 1920s with a strong Spanish influence, the structure was a U shape with a patio at the center. Just past the kitchen was the mudroom. Beyond that was a family room and then her en suite bedroom. Behind the attached garage was a large workout room she really had to start using.

Exiting the kitchen in the opposite direction led to a formal dining room, a formal living room, then the hallway curved. Declan had an office, then Connor's room was next, then the master.

The rooms were oversize, the beams in the ceiling original and the garden was something out of a fantasy. Sunshine didn't know much about plants, but she knew enough to keep her window open so she could smell the night-blooming jasmine just outside.

She walked toward the mudroom, stopping at the walk-in pantry. On the far wall was a wine cellar with glass doors. She figured it must hold at least four hundred bottles of wine, grouped together by type. She pulled out racks, searching for a relatively inexpensive red blend. Dinner was casual and the wine should be, too.

She found a foil cutter and bottle opener in one of the drawers in the pantry and carried the open bottle and two wineglasses back into the kitchen, then opened a bottle of sparkling non-alcoholic apple cider for Connor. If they were going to get fancy, it was nice to share.

While Declan got Connor settled, Sunshine dropped the hot rolls into a large bowl then tossed them with melted butter and garlic. The salad was already in place, as were the plates. She gave Connor and Declan each a roll before putting the extras on the table and taking her chair.

The kitchen table seated six. The three of them were clustered at one end, with her across from Connor. Without thinking, she put salad on his plate, only to realize that might be something his father wanted to do.

"Oh, um, sorry. Did you want to…"

"Go ahead," Declan said easily, pouring them wine.

She nodded, then waited for him to serve himself before taking the bowl from him and putting salad on her own plate. When she was done, she reached for her glass of wine just as Declan started to hand it to her. They bumped and the glass nearly spilled.

Sunshine felt herself flushing. Great. Just great. The awkward first days were supposed to be over by now. Living in someone's home, and being an almost-but-not-quite part of the family wasn't an easy transition.

Declan shook his head. "We have to work on our dinner skills," he said, his voice teasing.

"Apparently."

"The last few weeks have been hectic with my work schedule and we haven't had a chance to get to know each other. If you don't have plans, why don't you join me in my study after Connor goes to bed and we'll talk about how things are going so far."

"That would be nice," she said. "Thank you."

Connor held up his glass of cider. "I want to make a toast."

"Do you?" Declan raised his wineglass. "What is it?"

Sunshine picked up her glass and waited. She had a feeling this wasn't going to be the statesmanlike moment Declan seemed to be expecting.

Connor grinned. "And jelly."

"Toast and jelly," Declan murmured, before taking a sip of his wine. "I couldn't be more proud."

Connor giggled. Sunshine winked at him.

"We went to The Huntington after school today," she said, picking up her fork. "To the desert garden."

"My favorite!" Connor announced.

"One day I'll get to see one of the other gardens. At least I hope so."

Connor raised his shoulders in an exaggerated sigh. "In two more times. I promise."

"Yay! And thank you."

"You're welcome." He turned to his father. "How's the hotel?"

"Good. The building approval has been finalized, so I can get to work on designing the gardens." He looked at Sunshine.

"The decisions about the materials they're using will influence what I suggest."

"Sure. You wouldn't want the flowers to clash with the siding."

"Exactly. Connor, how was school?"

"Good. I got an A on my spelling test. We studied really hard."

"The lesson combined spelling words with different kinds of currency," Sunshine added. "Euro, yen, ruble, the word *currency*."

"That one's hard," Connor said as he finished his salad. "And *ruble* is like *rubble* but only one *b*."

"I'd heard that," Declan told him. "Good for you."

Sunshine had just stood to collect the salad plates when Connor piped up with, "Sunshine starts school on Monday and she's scared."

"Yes, well, no one's interested in that," she murmured, walking into the kitchen and pulling the lasagna roll-ups out of the oven.

"You're going back to college?" Declan asked.

"Back would be a misstatement, but yes." She slid the steaming pasta onto plates and carried them to the table. "I'm at Pasadena City College, studying toward a degree in child psychology. I'm starting with my general education classes."

"Good for you."

"Thanks."

Once she was seated, she sipped her wine and told herself she didn't care what her boss thought of her lack of education. Just because he had an advanced degree and a fancy job and a house and a kid and his life was totally together didn't matter to her.

She sighed. It wasn't Declan, she reminded herself. He simply represented everything she didn't have. Roots. Direction. A plan. Her twenties had raced by in a series of relationships that left her with exactly nothing to show for the time except for a string of bad decisions and broken hearts. Some of those hearts had even been hers.

But that was all behind her now. She'd had a come-to-Jesus moment, she was focused and she had a life plan. And nothing and no one was going to cause her to veer off course. Of that she was sure.

Declan Dubois hadn't had sex in a year. Until a few weeks ago he, honest to God, hadn't cared, but recently he'd started to notice and now he cared a lot and it was becoming a problem.

The dry spell had started when he and Iris had been having trouble—if that was what it could be called. Not knowing if their marriage was going to survive or not, he'd taken to sleeping on the sofa in his study. Later, she'd been sick and sex had been the last thing on either of their minds. After her death, he'd been in shock and dealing with the reality of having the woman he'd assumed he would spend the rest of his life with gone. There'd been Connor and helping him handle the loss of his mother. Sex hadn't been important.

But it sure as hell was now, although he had no idea what he was supposed to do about it. Dating seemed impossible and a few minutes in the shower only got a guy so far. At some point he wanted a woman in his bed, and not just a one-night stand, either. He'd never been that guy. He didn't need love to get it up but some kind of emotional interest was preferred. He hadn't been on a first date in ten years—how was he supposed to start now? Where would he meet women? Not through work—that never went well. Online?

He walked the short distance from Connor's room to his study and told himself he would deal with the problem later. Now that his son was asleep, his more pressing issue was to get to know the woman he'd hired to take care of his kid. Somehow three weeks had sped by. If he wasn't careful, he would turn around and Connor would be graduating from high school and he still wouldn't know anything about Sunshine.

He sat at his desk and opened the file the agency had given him when he'd first interviewed her. She'd been the fifth nanny he'd hired and he'd been desperate to find someone his son would like. Iris's death had been a shock. It had been less than a month from the time he'd found out about the cancer until she'd passed away. There'd been no time to prepare, to be braced, and he was an adult. Connor had a lot less skill to handle the impossibly heartbreaking situation. If Declan's parents hadn't come and stayed with them after the funeral, he wasn't sure either of them would have survived.

He scanned the file. Sunshine was thirty-one. She'd been a nanny on and off from the age of twenty. She had no formal training, no education past high school and a history of walking away from jobs before her contract was finished. He hadn't wanted to hire her, but he'd been desperate and the agency had insisted he at least talk to her. After blowing through four of their best nannies, he'd realized he couldn't refuse, so he'd reluctantly met her.

He didn't remember anything they'd discussed except to insist she and Connor spend a trial afternoon together, supervised by someone from the agency. Connor had come home and announced he liked her and Declan had hired her that evening.

The past three weeks had been a whirlwind of work and travel. He'd wanted to spend more time at home, getting to know her, watching her with Connor, but fate had conspired against him. Still, his son seemed happier than he had in a long time and he sure liked Sunshine.

A knock on his open door brought him back to the present. Sunshine stood in the doorway, her smile tentative.

"Is this a good time?"

He nodded and motioned to the chair on the other side of his desk. Sunshine sat down, then tucked her bare feet under her.

She was nothing like Iris. The thought was unexpected but once formed he couldn't ignore it. His late wife had been tall and willowy. Delicate, with small bones and long fingers. She'd been pale, with dark hair and dark eyes.

Sunshine was several inches shorter and a whole lot more

curvy. Blonde with pale blue eyes. She had full cheeks, large breasts and an ass that… He silently told himself not to go there. Not only wasn't it appropriate, she wasn't his type. And again, not appropriate.

Iris favored tailored clothing in black or taupe. From the little he'd seen of Sunshine, she was a jeans and T-shirt kind of woman. She ate cereal out of the box, had no problem lying on the floor to play checkers with Connor and hadn't protested an ant farm in the house. Again—not Iris.

Not that he wanted anyone to be Iris. His wife had been his first real love and with her gone, he would never be the same. He wasn't thinking he couldn't care about someone again, he had no idea about that, he just knew he didn't want an Iris replacement.

"You and Connor get along well," he said.

She smiled. Two simple words that in no way captured the transformation from reasonably pretty to stunning. Declan hoped he didn't look as stupefied as he felt. After all, he'd seen her smile before. He should be used to it, and yet, he was not.

"He's adorable. How could you not totally fall for him? He's a serious kid, but also funny and kind. I know he misses his mom, but he's dealing. We talk about her whenever he wants to. I know he's going to therapy and I'm hoping it helps. Obviously the therapist doesn't say anything to me, but I would say he's coping well."

Her appreciation of his kid relaxed him. "Connor's special," he said, then looked at the open folder on the desk and decided to be blunt. "I wasn't sure if I should hire you."

Instead of getting defensive, she laughed. "I could say the same thing about you. I was hoping to go to work for a high-powered single mom, but the director at the agency talked me into meeting Connor and then I was a goner."

She pointed to the folder. "Is that about me?"

He nodded.

Her full mouth twisted. "Let me guess. The report says I'm terrific with kids. I like them and they like me. I show up on time, I cook, I help with homework, I'm a safe driver. When there's an emergency, I'm nearly always available. But..." She looked at him. "There's a very good chance one day I'll simply disappear with almost no warning. I'm gone and you're stuck." She shrugged. "Does that about sum it up?"

Her honesty surprised him. Was it a tactic or genuine? He had no idea.

She sighed. "It's true. All of it. I've walked away from at least a half dozen jobs. I would meet a guy and fall for him and he'd want me to go with him and I would. Just like that."

"Go with him?"

The smile returned, although with less gut-hitting power. "I tend to fall for men who have unusual occupations or who don't live wherever I am. A guy in a rock band, a travel photographer, a professional tennis player. One time the family I was working for took me with them to Napa. I met a guy who owned a restaurant and when the family went home, I stayed. On the bright side, he taught me how to cook."

She looked away. "I was young and reckless and I don't want do that anymore." Her gaze returned to him. "I won't bore you with the details. Let's just say I woke up alone in a hotel room in London with no job, no boyfriend, no prospects. I flew home and moved in with my sister, then got a couple of jobs because hey, the nanny thing wasn't working for me or the kids."

He wasn't sure what he'd expected to hear, but it wasn't this. "So why are you back being a nanny now?"

"I'm good at it and I need the money. I want to do something with my life. Get an education, have a retirement account, be normal. Working as a nanny allows me to pay for school, have time to study and not have to worry about rent. I want to keep my head down and be smart. No more loser guys. I don't want to be that girl anymore."

The smile returned, leaving him just as speechless as before.

"More than you wanted to know," she said. "I'm being honest. You have no reason to believe any of this. You don't know me, which is kind of the point of the conversation, right? But I'm committed to Connor. I'm not going to walk away from him."

"Because you're not that girl anymore?"

"That's the reason."

It was too much information and he didn't know what to do with it all. She was right—he had no reason to believe her, and yet he did. Was that dumb on his part or intuition? He had no idea.

"Is that also why you wanted to work for a woman?"

She nodded. "I've had a couple of dads get handsy. It's awkward."

"I assure you I would never—"

She shook her head. "I know. You don't have to say anything."

She knew? How? And what did that mean? Had he become so incredibly sexless that...that... Dear God, he couldn't even formulate the question, let alone answer it.

She laughed. "You look confused. What I meant is you seem to be an honorable person. I appreciate that."

"Good," he said, not sure if it was good or not. Time to change the subject. "About your hours. Are they working for you?"

"They're perfect."

She was supposed to be available from 6:30 a.m. until 9:00 p.m. with the middle of the day off, five days a week. She also owed him every other Saturday and cooked dinner four nights a week.

"I'm sorry you had to work Sunday when I was on my business trip."

"Not a problem. You and Connor were gone the previous weekend, so I had that Saturday. Declan, I'm not keeping track of every single minute. If Connor gets up early or stays up late, that's okay. A lot of my job is being flexible."

"Thank you."

He confirmed she knew where all the local stores were, then pulled a credit card out of his desk drawer.

"I ordered this for you," he said. "It will be easier than giving me receipts and having me reimburse you." He smiled. "Don't go to Tahiti on it."

"Oh darn. And Connor and I were talking about taking a road trip just yesterday." She took the card. "He seems to be outgrowing some of his pants and his athletic shoes are looking really bad. Do you want me to take him shopping or is that something you prefer to do?"

"You can do it. For the next couple of weeks, I'm going to be knee-deep in the preconstruction planning for the hotel. Once that calms down, I'll have more time."

"Okay. Then I'll get what he needs right now and you can handle the rest. Anything else?"

His gaze moved from her mouth to her— He swore silently, telling himself being a jerk wasn't allowed. He had to get a grip or, at the very least, get laid. Assuming he remembered how all that happened. He assumed it was like riding a bike—once he and the lady in question were naked, he would know what to do.

"Declan?"

He blinked. "Ah, that will be all."

She stood and slid the credit card into her back pocket. "Have a good night."

"You, too."

He wasn't sure how good it was going to be but there was a better than even chance he would be taking a shower in a bit. A long one. After he would lie alone in bed both cursing and missing the woman he'd been married to. The one who had betrayed him, then up and died before he could decide if he had forgiven her or not.

chapter
THREE

SUNDAY MORNING, JUST BEFORE ELEVEN, SUNSHINE
walked into the restaurant. She'd curled her hair, put on makeup
and had even worn a dress. Not that she was trying to impress—
she was meeting her sister, not anyone who would judge her.
Instead, her reasons were more about self-preservation. Whatever Margot showed up wearing, she would be gorgeous and
while Sunshine knew she couldn't compete on the beauty front,
she didn't want to be the cautionary tale. Or just the sexy one.

She gave her name to the hostess. There were at least a couple
dozen people waiting for tables, mostly multigenerational families. Sunshine watched grandparents corral toddlers and new
mothers fret over babies.

Most of the families looked happy, which she liked to see.
Kids deserved to be raised in a home where things went right
more often than they went wrong.

Margot walked in and spotted her. The sisters hugged. When
they stepped back, Sunshine held in a sigh. Yup, her fraternal
twin was stunning in a navy short-sleeved sheath dress. The
woven material skimmed her body and fell just to her knee. The
neck was high, the cut conservative. Nothing about the dress,
the midheel navy pumps or her plain clutch screamed *look at me*,
and still people did. Looked and gawked.

Sunshine knew she got her fair share of attention but it was for the wrong reasons. She was all boobs and butt with a little jiggle thrown in for good measure. Margot was the cover of *Vogue* while Sunshine was more like a billboard for a gentleman's club. And people said God didn't have a sense of humor.

Margot linked arms with her. "How are you? How's work? Are you nervous about school starting tomorrow? Don't be. You'll do great. You're smart and determined. I'm so proud of you. Look at how quickly you got your life together."

"*Together* might be a slight overstatement," Sunshine murmured as the hostess waved them over.

"Tables for two are easy today," she said with a smile. "It's tables for eight that are the problem. If you'll follow me, please."

They were shown to a small table tucked in by the window. After they were seated, Margot leaned toward her.

"You're really okay?"

Sunshine smiled. "You take the older sister thing way too seriously. You only beat me into the world by eight minutes."

"I can't help it. You're my family and I love you."

"I love you, too."

Sunshine pulled a slim envelope out of her handbag and passed it over. "Proof that I'm perfectly fine. Installment one."

Margot opened the envelope and wrinkled her nose. She pulled out the check. "You didn't have to do this."

"You loaned me the down payment for my car."

When Sunshine had returned to Los Angeles four months earlier, she'd had zero money but surprisingly good credit. After getting a job as a waitress and a second gig as a clerk at a drugstore, she'd borrowed money from her sister and had managed to swing a car loan. Margot had insisted Sunshine get a couple of thousand into a savings account before paying her back. Thanks to her new nanny job, she was doing much better financially, and could finally start repaying her sister.

Margot sighed. "I didn't want you to pay me back."

"Sorry. That was the deal. I'm not a moocher."

Margot grinned. "You make me crazy."

"That's part of the job description. I'm doing good. I love the kid and I start school tomorrow and this is right. I swear."

"Well, if you swear."

Their server appeared and told them about the specials, then took their drink orders.

"Champagne," Margot said firmly.

When the glasses were delivered, Sunshine reached for hers. "To Francine, on her birthday. We love you and miss you and hope that in heaven you're surrounded by beauty queens."

Margot touched glasses with her. "To Francine. I know we're not exactly what you were hoping for, but we love you and appreciate all you did for us."

They each took a sip in honor of the great-grandmother who had raised them. She'd been gone over a decade, but Sunshine could still hear Francine's voice in her head. *Sit up straight. Don't cross your legs at the knee. Think tall thoughts. Elegance is always the right choice.*

"I was such a disappointment," she said lightly, having long since accepted the inevitable truth.

"We both were," Margot murmured. "At least you tried. I was a trembling, whimpering mess."

"Don't forget the projectile vomiting."

"Always a pretty memory."

They smiled at each other.

"How's work?" Sunshine asked. "Weren't you interviewing for a new client?"

"I was and I got it. Should be an interesting one. She's a mass of contradictions. I have to live in, which I don't usually love, but the house is great."

Sunshine knew better than to ask too many questions. Margot was very discreet about her clients and never talked in specifics.

"Where will you be living?"

"I'm staying in Pasadena, so not far from you."

"Nice. Let me know if you want me to check on your condo. You know my schedule is mostly flexible."

"Thanks."

The server returned and they placed their order. When he was gone, Margot picked up her champagne.

"So how's your newest heartbreaker?"

Sunshine laughed. "Connor is totally adorable. He's such a good kid. He's still dealing with losing his mom, but he's so brave. We're going to be getting an ant farm."

Margot shuddered. "Why?"

"He wants one. I think it'll be fun. Do you know the people who sell them refer to the ants as animals? Connor was right there, so I couldn't laugh, but jeez, really. Animals? So are they ant ranchers or something?"

Margot chuckled. "And the man of the house?"

"I'm still getting to know him. He seems like a good dad. He's involved with Connor."

"A nice change."

"It is."

Too many of the parents she'd worked for were not very engaged. They wanted a nanny for convenience and to pass on the responsibility of raising their children to. From what she could tell, Declan was a concerned parent.

"It must be so hard," she said, fighting sadness. "To lose your spouse when you're both so young. They would have expected to have a lifetime together and she's gone."

"Don't," her sister said, her voice kind. "You were going to say you want that, too."

"Not the dying part. Just the rest of it. You know. Love. The forever kind."

They looked at each other, then Margot slowly shook her head. "You know it's not in our DNA."

"It could be. I want it to be. At least Connor has something to mourn. I don't. Just a dozen or so bad relationships that I knew were never going anywhere, yet there I was, running out on my life at the first sign of interest. Normal, sensible people don't do that."

"Is that what we're going to be?"

"It's a good goal. You're halfway there."

"Oh please." Margot picked up her champagne. "I've spent the better part of five years being stuck because of a man and the last few years trying to avoid him. I spend so much time trying *not* to think about him, I can't seem to think about anyone else. I'm great at my job and sucky at my personal life."

"You're not."

"I am a little."

Sunshine knew that was kind of true. "I want to be proud of myself," she admitted. "I want to be a better person and fall in love with someone great. I want a future, not a fling."

"The normal thing you love so much."

"You mock normal, but you'd like it, too. You're just afraid to try. You don't think you're capable of loving anyone but Dietrich."

Margot winced. "While true, a little hedging wouldn't be out of line."

"Sorry. I'll hedge next time."

Margot thought for a second. "All right, I'll say it. I want to put my past behind me and move on. I would like to find out if I'm capable of loving someone else. Someone who's actually good for me."

"Here's to us being brave," Sunshine said, raising her glass. "Or at the very least, not being rash."

Margot laughed. "To avoiding rashes."

After brunch, Sunshine ran a few errands before returning to the house. She wanted to spend a couple of hours looking over her incredibly huge math textbook. She'd flipped through the first few chapters twice and still wasn't sure any part of it was written in English, but maybe this time it would all make sense.

She tried to tell herself that she was taking the class to learn and if she already understood the material, what was the point, but she wasn't totally convinced. Shouldn't she at least know something?

She parked her used Honda Civic next to Declan's BMW SUV, then went inside. After changing into cropped pants and a T-shirt, she headed for the kitchen. She could hear Connor and Declan outside, playing. She filled two glasses with ice and water, and set them out on the counter. She was about to retreat to her room when Declan walked into the kitchen.

He grinned when he saw her. "You're back. How was your brunch?"

He was casually dressed. His shoulders stretched the seams of his T-shirt and the fabric was soft looking and faded.

"Good. I met my sister. It's my great-grandmother's birthday. She died shortly after we graduated from high school but we always go out on her birthday. She would like that we remembered, then she would scold us, pointing out how much sugar was in champagne and that it would go straight to my thighs. Then she would tell me to sit up straight."

His eyebrows drew together. "She sounds, ah, interesting."

"She was a pistol, as they say. Until she retired well into her eighties, she ran her own business." Sunshine made air quotes. "Mrs. Baxter's School of Charm and Decorum. And no, I'm not kidding."

"I don't even know what that is."

"My great-grandmother helped young women become beauty queens. She desperately wanted to train a Miss America, but the closest she got was a runner-up. We were her last hope, but it wasn't going to happen. I was more than willing, but hardly beauty pageant material."

Declan looked even more confused. "Why not?"

"Men," she said with a grin. "I'm too short and way too curvy. Margot's the beauty in the family. Tall, thin, gorgeous. But she couldn't deal with the whole being on stage thing. She would either faint or barf. Not a winning strategy. When we were four-teen, Francine closed the school and we moved to Las Vegas."

"My head is spinning," Declan told her. "I had no idea you had such a checkered past."

"There are surprising depths. Just let me know if you ever want to learn a three-point runway turn. I'm an expert."

"Now you're scaring me."

Connor ran into the kitchen. "Da-ad! I've been waiting for-ever." He turned. "Sunshine! You're back." He rushed to her, wrapping his arms around her waist. "We're playing outside. Come with us."

"Connor, we've talked about this. It's Sunshine's day off. We need to leave her alone."

Connor pushed up his glasses and nodded slowly as he stepped back. "Sorry, Sunshine."

She knew the importance of keeping to a regular schedule, but it was tough when Connor had such a firm grip on her heartstrings.

She touched his cheek. "I have a couple of things I have to do, but what if I join you for dinner?" She glanced at Declan. "If that's all right with you."

Connor jumped up and down. "Yes! Yes! Dad's barbecuing burgers, and say yes, Dad!"

Declan's expression turned rueful. "It appears I'm no longer the favorite."

"I'm new," Sunshine told him. "And shiny. I'll tarnish in time."

"I'm not holding my breath." He wrapped his arms around Connor. "Come on, you. We're going back outside. Sunshine, you are welcome to join us for dinner."

"Thanks. I will."

She retreated to her room and stared at the massive textbook on her desk. Just carrying it was going to be a workout. But in-stead of sitting down and trying to make sense of the first chapter, she walked to the window where she could watch Declan and Connor. They sat on the grass, drinking the water she'd left out for them.

It was obvious how much they cared about each other. They were a family—still healing from an incredible loss, but connected all the same. She wanted that. Love and belonging, something real. Something more than being the flavor of the month. She was willing to change, to be different and try new things to make that happen. What she didn't know was whether or not she could escape who she was and the Baxter women's four generations of disasters in the love life department.

After brunch with her sister, Margot drove home and finished packing for her stay with Bianca. The job was for about two months, but Margot only packed enough for a couple of weeks. She could easily go back to her place whenever she needed to. Her condo was a fifteen-minute drive from the monastery.

She still couldn't believe she was going to live there. Everything about the glorious old structure appealed to her. She was going to check with her host and get permission to do some exploring. And the garden! The little she'd seen of it was magical.

After cleaning out the refrigerator and double-checking that all the faucets were turned off, Margot loaded her car with two suitcases, a briefcase and a couple of boxes. She was bringing her printer, along with a box of books that might be useful. She made sure the front door was locked, then drove toward the old section of Pasadena, heading north into the foothills.

Once again she pulled into the driveway and stopped in front of the impressive gates that kept out the world. She smiled as she pressed the button on the panel, thinking there should be a secret password.

"It's Margot Baxter," she said.

"Right on time," an unfamiliar woman said. "Come on in and we'll get you settled."

Margot waited for the gates to swing open before driving to one of the parking spaces. Before she'd had a chance to get out of her car, the front door opened and a middle-aged woman walked toward her, pulling a utility cart behind her.

"You must be Margot," the woman said, holding out her hand. "I'm Edna Stojicic, Alec's housekeeper. He told me why you were here. I think we're all in for an interesting time."

Edna wore a simple short-sleeved green blouse over black pants. Her dark hair was short, her eyes brown. She looked sensible and competent, with a friendly smile that made Margot feel welcome.

Edna motioned to the cart. "To help with the unloading process."

Together they emptied the trunk and backseat. Margot wheeled one of her suitcases toward the house while Edna pushed the loaded cart. When they reached the front door, Edna pointed to the keypad by the handle.

"This is how you'll come and go from the house. Your six-digit code is in your bedroom. I've also left you a clicker for the front gate. There's a security system, but it's more about monitoring than alarms. There's no setting it or turning it off." She chuckled. "It's always watching, so no dancing naked in the halls."

"Not really my thing," Margot murmured, then wondered if that was a problem with Bianca. Oh well, she'd known the job would be challenging when she took it.

Once they were inside, they left everything by the front door while Edna took her on a tour of the house. To the right of the foyer was the huge kitchen. Margot saw every appliance known to man and some she didn't recognize.

"My staff and I clean on a schedule," Edna told her. "Alec prefers to know where we're going to be on any given day. You'll find that information up in your bedroom, as well. Scholars come and go, studying the old documents Alec collects. They keep to themselves and won't bother you. Let's see. What else? Ah, meals. A chef is here by six every morning. There's a hot breakfast put out in the dining room at six-thirty. We take it away at eight. You can eat there, or take your meals to your room."

"I'll be taking them to my room."

"I'll let everyone know so there's a tray left out for you." She pointed to the refrigerator. "Help yourself to anything in there. There's a big freezer in the pantry, along with plenty of other supplies. Again, take what you'd like. If you use the last of something, there's a grocery list on the counter in the pantry."

Edna led the way to the formal living room with twenty-foot ceilings. The woodwork was incredible, as were the statues along the east wall. Margot would guess they were original, left behind when the monastery was decommissioned or whatever it was called when a church was no longer sacred.

She saw the staircase leading to the second floor and beyond that a media room with a huge sectional sofa and massive TV mounted on the wall.

"You're welcome to use this anytime," Edna told her. "The remotes are in the coffee table drawers, as are instructions on how to make it all work."

She pointed to a set of double doors just beyond the media room. "That's Alec's private suite. Best not be going in there."

"Of course not."

They walked back the way they'd come. There was a second staircase, far less grand, going into the basement.

"There's an old root cellar and some musty rooms down there," Edna told her. "A portion of it has been converted into a wine cellar."

They stepped outside to the covered walkway that ran the length of the house. The cloisters, Margot thought. Was that the right term? She would have to look it up.

They passed Alec's office and then went back inside. Edna

showed her two archive rooms and a file room where hundreds of ancient documents were stored. At the far end of the hall was a small chapel.

There were beautiful stained glass windows lining two walls, along with wooden pews.

"It's all original," Edna said proudly. "Alec's great-uncle bought the place in the 1930s and started converting it to a private residence. When Alec inherited the property, he updated much of it but they both wanted to leave the chapel in place."

They walked back to the pile of luggage at the front door and carried the first load to the second floor. The landing at the top of the stairs opened up to a large lounge area. It was furnished with a couple of sofas, a big desk against the far wall, a TV, a small refrigerator and a microwave.

"Much more my speed," Margot joked as she glanced around.

"The guest lounge. You're welcome to use this, as well." Edna winked. "I agree. It's nice up here and a lot less complicated than anything in the media room."

Margot followed her to a pleasant guest room with an attached bath. The walls were a pale gray and the queen-size bed looked comfortable.

"This is perfect. Thank you. I'll set up my computer and training materials in the lounge."

"Bianca's room is at the end of the hall. It's the bigger guest room." Edna's tone was apologetic.

"Not to worry. I have everything I need."

They carried up the rest of her luggage.

"Is there anything else before I leave you to get settled?" Edna asked.

Margot had seen the Wi-Fi password next to her door entry code and the clicker for the gate, so she had that. Honestly, this was the most organized household she'd ever been a part of. She was impressed.

"I'd love to explore," she said. "What are the ground rules?"

"Stay out of Alec's study and bedroom and don't disrupt his routine. Otherwise, go where you'd like. Oh, don't touch any of the old papers. Most of them are kept safely away, but if it's paper and it looks ancient, don't touch it. Alec does love his musty old scraps."

Edna thought for a second. "The cleaners will be taking care of your room on the days listed, so don't worry about changing your sheets or washing towels. You can do your personal laundry in the utility room in the basement. You'll see Borys around. He maintains the place, especially the wood. He has a few people who help him with big projects but he does all the woodwork himself."

"I would imagine it takes a village to keep a place like this running. But what an amazing house. I'm looking forward to admiring it all."

"Good. Make yourself at home." Edna pointed to the papers on the dresser. "My cell number is there, if you need to reach me."

"Thank you."

Margot quickly unpacked her clothes. The closet was large and well organized and she had more space than she needed.

She set up her laptop and printer in the lounge, along with the books she'd brought. She'd already put together a preliminary workbook for Bianca, which may or may not be something her client was interested in. Still, she would give it a shot. Everyone was different and Margot did her best to accommodate individual learning styles.

She'd also downloaded a fair amount of research on Cardigania. She'd learned the basic history of the country, the size of the population and which industries provided the most revenue. She knew that Cardiganian wool was famous for being both soft and durable and that their chocolate rivaled the best from Switzerland—but there was more to glean from the country's rich history.

Margot had also done a little more study on Bianca's past. Once she'd accepted the job, she'd requested a detailed background check on her new client. Not that she was expecting to find a couple of felonies or anything earth-shattering, but it was always good to have more information, rather than less.

By four-thirty, she was settled and ready to begin her job in the morning, which meant it was definitely time to start exploring.

chapter
FOUR

ALEC MCNICOL DID NOT LIKE HAVING PEOPLE STAY IN HIS house. When visiting scholars came to study any of the ancient texts, they worked in one of the archive rooms during the day, then retreated to a hotel at night. The same with the household staff. Edna Stojicic, his very sensible housekeeper, brought a team of cleaners to tend to the large building and worked her magic in the kitchen before disappearing long before 5:00 p.m. There were weeks he never saw her at all. The gardeners rarely needed to speak to him and he communicated with Borys, the full-time woodworker/handyman the old Spanish building required, via text.

On a good day, Alec saw no one, spoke to no one, and that was how he preferred things. He loved his life just as it was. His routine was predictable and that made him happy. Only now he was not dealing only with his mother—there was a stranger to contend with.

At least Margot appeared to be a restful sort of person. She wasn't loud or garish, nor did she seem the type to always want his attention. Even now, as she moved her things into one of the guest rooms upstairs, he couldn't hear her at all. Of course, given the solid construction of the monastery, she could be rehearsing with a rock band and if the door was closed, he wouldn't hear her. The thought made him smile. The smile retreated when someone knocked on his half-closed door.

"Yes?" he called, hoping against hope it wasn't Bianca come to discuss how he should create a turtle refuge in his backyard, or help her with an application to join SETI. With his mother, one never really knew what to expect.

He was relieved to find Margot in the cloisters hallway, only this was a different Margot than the businesswoman he'd met the previous week. Gone were the sensible glasses, the gray suit, the plain black pumps. Instead she wore dark jeans and a deep purple twinset. As before, her hair was pulled back into a ponytail, but unlike last time, her face didn't have on a lick of makeup.

He could see freckles on her nose and a soft, natural color staining her cheeks. She looked young and impossibly beautiful. With breasts.

He drew in a breath. What in God's name was wrong with him? He never noticed breasts or any other part of a woman. He wasn't visual and he certainly didn't think about size or shape or nipples. Yet thoughts of all three were firmly stuck in his brain. His mother's trainer, or whatever it was he was supposed to call Margot, had breasts and he had acknowledged them. Only to himself, but still. It was a calamity.

"Hi," Margot said with a smile. "I just wanted to take a second and tell you I've moved in. Edna showed me around. You have a spectacular home. The remodeling job makes the space comfortable while retaining the essence of it being in a monastery. The windows, the carvings around the door. Your home is a wonder."

Her words calmed him. He managed to nod and motioned for her to enter his office. Keeping his gaze anywhere but her chest, he led her to his desk, where they both took a seat.

"Yes, the work was carefully planned and executed. I, too, am pleased with the outcome."

"I wanted to confirm the ground rules," she said. "Edna explained about the door lock code and I've seen both floors."

Her mouth curved up at the corners. "Not the basement yet, but I'm so going to explore that. Edna said I was free to go anywhere in the house with the exception of your office and bedroom, of course."

She put her hands on her lap, resting them calmly. Margot didn't fidget. He liked that.

"The guest lounge upstairs is comfortable and certainly has everything I need," she continued. "I'll use the desk for my work and I'm thinking it would be easier if Bianca and I conducted most of our classes outside."

He nodded, not sure what any of this had to do with him.

"I prefer to take my meals in my room." Margot's tone was firm. "I'm not a member of the family and there's no need to act like I am. I've found it's much easier on everyone if we all remember that. There's no awkward conversation and if I have a bad day with your mother, the last thing she would want would be to have dinner with me."

"Bianca is gone most evenings," he said. "She often goes to see Wesley or to spend time with her friends." In fact, now that he thought about it, he hadn't had dinner with his mother since she moved in nearly two weeks ago. Which was odd considering how it seemed she was always *everywhere*.

"No matter. I'll collect my meals from the kitchen and take them upstairs if it's all the same to you."

"Excellent. Anything else?"

"Your mother and I begin in the morning. As my contract is with her, I won't be providing you with updates."

"I believe I will be the first to notice if you make any progress."

She studied him. "You still don't think I can help."

"I'm not sure anyone can help. My mother answers to no one. She is like a leaf on the wind—she goes where she likes."

"I thought leaves went where the wind said."

"You are correct. A poor analogy." He tried to think of another, but the only thing that came to mind was how much he wanted to look at Margot's breasts and that certainly wasn't anything he could mention.

"Tell me a story from when you were little," she said with a smile. "About your mother."

The request surprised him. "What kind of story? A good story or a bad one? Are you trying to learn something specific?"

"Not really. I'm just curious and I'd like to get a feel for her. Can you give me one of each?"

He nodded. "When I turned seven, she rented out an ice-cream parlor and treated my entire class to an afternoon there. We played games and ate as much ice cream as we wanted."

"That *is* a good story."

"Yes, until all the children started throwing up because they'd had too much."

"Oh. I suppose I can see how that would happen. And the other story?"

"When I was seventeen, she slept with my best friend."

Alec immediately wanted to call back the words, but it was too late. They hung out there in the late afternoon, echoing in his large office. Margot's eyes widened.

"I was away at a Swiss boarding school," he added, realizing he had to explain. "She came to visit and took the two of us to Paris for a long weekend. I went for a walk one afternoon and when I came back, I saw him stepping out of her room."

He remembered the sense of betrayal—that his mother would come between him and a friend. She'd always known he didn't make friends easily and to get in the middle of that, to change it into something uncomfortable, had made him furious. And sad.

"I'm not gay," he said. "It wasn't that I was in love with him, but it wasn't something she should have done."

"No," Margot murmured. "We'll leave the fact that she slept with a minor for another time." Her mouth twisted. "I'm sorry. You must have felt betrayed by both of them."

"I did. He and I never spoke of it." Not a word, he thought. But everything had changed. The next year Alec had gone off to University of Oxford and he and his friend had lost touch.

Until then he'd known his mother was impulsive, but he hadn't realized how the flaw affected other people. He'd always kept fairly tight control on his emotions, but that incident had solidified his determination to let his mind dictate his actions. There would be no hasty decisions, no wild flights of fancy. It was a rule he lived by, regardless of circumstances.

Margot worried her lower lip, drawing his attention to the shape of her mouth.

"My mother abandoned my sister and me when we were little," she said quietly. "Her mother had abandoned her the same way. The Baxter women are not known for their good choices in the men they fall for or how they raise their children."

He appreciated her attempt to level the emotional playing field. It was a nice gesture and spoke well of her character.

"You haven't abandoned any children." His tone was firm.

"No, but I've been unwise about men." She wrinkled her nose. "Or rather, one man." She drew in a breath and met his gaze. "But that's behind me now." Her mouth turned up in an impish smile. "Because unlike you, I believe people can change."

"It's not people so much as my mother. Still, she wants this. She does love Wesley."

"You sound surprised."

"She's never been so devoted to someone. He's not her usual type, so perhaps that's the reason."

"Or he's the one she's been looking for all along."

He raised his eyebrows. "A romantic, Margot? I would not have expected that."

"Not a romantic, but I remain hopeful."

He wondered about the man she'd been foolish with. What did that mean? Alec made it a point to never get involved with a woman. Not seriously. If he let down his barriers, if he gave his heart, well, he didn't know what would happen, but the worry that he could turn into his mother was enough to keep him comfortably solitary. He didn't like a lot of drama and emotion in his world. He'd created the life he wanted and he was content. There were no highs, but also no worries that he would become unhinged.

She rose. "I won't keep you any longer," she said. "I just wanted to say hello and make sure we were both clear with the ground rules."

"Of course." He stood. "Have you discussed them with my mother?"

"I will and I'm confident she'll be in favor of them."

He allowed himself a slight smile. "We'll see."

"I can be stubborn and disciplined."

"I'm sure that's true, but Bianca has a way of making things happen that are more to her liking. She swoops in and rearranges until you're left wondering how exactly things got that way. It's a gift."

She laughed. "You mean it's a curse."

"Not for her. Just us lesser mortals."

"I can't tell you how much I'm looking forward to proving you wrong."

"I am rarely wrong, Margot."

"Neither am I."

By nine-thirty that night, Margot was nearly giddy from her excitement about the house. She'd spent an hour in the small chapel, only leaving when it got dark. She'd checked out the empty guest room, the guest lounge and most of the kitchen. She'd made herself a sandwich for dinner and had discovered that the cookie jar was full of cookies. Homemade cookies with frosting or chocolate chips, all soft and gooey and if this kept up she was going to have to up her exercise routine. Or buy bigger pants.

Later in the week, when she had some free time, she was going to explore the gardens. The grounds were extensive—at least three acres—and she wanted to discover every inch.

It was late enough that she knew she should head to her room, but she just wasn't ready. Bianca had gone out and Alec was somewhere—possibly his office or the media room and she planned to avoid both—so it was as if she had the entire house to herself.

She thought briefly about heading into the basement, but decided that might be too much for her first night. At some point she really did have to get some sleep. Just not quite yet.

She walked to the stairs leading to the second floor and told herself to be a responsible adult and just go to her room, only to hear someone coming up behind her. She turned and saw Alec leaving the kitchen. His gaze met hers and they both froze.

She recovered first and smiled. "It's just me. I've been exploring."

"Did you find anything unusual?"

"Not yet. What would count as unusual?"

"Old documents would be excellent. Artifacts, that sort of thing."

"I doubt there are many hiding spaces left. The guys doing the remodel would have found them all." She laughed. "What about a skeleton?"

"No, thank you."

"Because it would creep you out?"

"Because it would bring too many people here."

"Of course. The police, the coroner, reporters. You want something intriguing that won't set off an invasion. I'll do my best to make that happen."

"Thank you."

She expected him to excuse himself but instead he gestured toward the living room. "Would you care to join me for a cognac?"

She wasn't sure a man had ever invited her "for a cognac"

before. "Thank you," she said, and followed him into the living room.

While Alec walked over to the wet bar against the far wall, Margot took in the high ceiling and clerestory windows across the entire east side. She would guess they had once been stained glass, no doubt removed when the property had been sold. Converting the monastery into a home must have been quite the job.

She took a seat in one of the wingback chairs by the sofa. Alec handed her a glass, then took a seat opposite her.

"Any ghost sightings?" he asked.

"I'm not sure I believe in ghosts. Do you?"

"I have yet to see one."

"And seeing is believing?"

"When it comes to ghosts, yes."

She took a sip of her drink. The cognac was rich and smooth.

"Edna mentioned something about ancient texts," she said. "That if I saw anything that looked like old paper to not touch it."

One corner of his mouth twitched. "I assure you, you will not find ancient texts lying around. They are all cataloged and protected."

"Whew. Because I was really worried. I wouldn't want to get a sweaty glass ring on the one document that could further our understanding of a language."

"That would be a tragedy. Now you can rest easy."

"So is that what you do? Study languages?"

"I'm more interested in what the texts say than the language itself. What was considered so important that it had to be captured in the written word. Five thousand years ago, there weren't any sticky notes. Back then a written message was deliberate. Paper had to be made by hand and it was a laborious process. Ink had to be created and then you had to find someone who knew how to read and write."

"I never thought of it that way, but of course you're right.

Today language is careless. We think nothing of writing something down."

"Exactly. There are still languages that we can't decipher. One of my hobbies is trying to translate Indus script. The civilization existed from about 2600 BC to 1900 BC in the area of what we know as Pakistan and northwestern India. They were a thriving people with an export trade and several large towns, and then they were gone, leaving behind a written language we have yet to understand."

"I didn't know there were any written languages that hadn't been translated."

"There are several. Every year or so I take a few weeks to see if I can make any progress on Indus script."

Okay, that was impressive. Her goal on the hobby front was to learn how to knit.

"Tell me how you do your work."

She smiled. "That's a very generalized question. Every client is different and I do my best to customize my approach for the situation. A businessperson wanting to learn cultural norms for a business trip to China is a very different proposition than someone who might be moving to Argentina for a promotion."

"Do you know much about living in Argentina?"

"No." She laughed. "That was an example. I could teach a basic course on business practices in Argentina, but I don't know the nuances necessary for someone moving there. We have experts."

"On Argentina?"

"On nearly every country. I'm more of a generalist."

"Ah. You get the unusual requests."

"When I'm lucky."

He smiled at her. He had a nice smile and she liked his dark eyes. There was something very pleasant about Alec. He was a deliberate sort of person and she could appreciate that.

"Did my mother tell you she's not one for technology? If

you're hoping she'll do work online, you're going to be disappointed."

"I had a couple of workbooks printed and bound. We'll see how those are received. In her case, I assumed we'd do a lot of talking and some role playing. I'm not sure where we're starting, so until I know that, I can't formulate a complete plan."

"I'm imagining formal place settings at the dining room table."

Margot laughed. "That will happen for sure. You can play along if you'd like. Many a client has been overwhelmed by the fish fork."

"Not the dessert spoon?"

"You know about the dessert spoon?"

"Yes. It's up by the dessert fork. You forget—I went to boarding school in Switzerland. I can handle a fish fork with the best of them."

"Training every young man needs."

He smiled. "I wouldn't go that far but those lessons are ingrained."

"Your father was Swiss?" she asked, already knowing the answer.

"He was. A rich banker who met my mother at a party in London. Theirs was a brief but torrid affair with the unexpected result of her getting pregnant. She was twenty-four at the time and my father was in his early forties."

"That is an age difference."

"Yes, and neither of them wanted to get married. I'm not sure my father was all that interested in having children, although *his* parents were thrilled. My mother returned to LA to prepare for my birth." He smiled. "I will admit that when I was little, she seemed almost magical. We were a team. She took me everywhere. There were no bedtimes, no rules. When I was four, she hired a tutor who traveled with us."

"While no rules sounds nice, it's not always comfortable."

"I agree."

She sipped her cognac. "So you made your own rules."

He nodded.

"What about your father?"

"He never had any other children so I was his only heir. I saw him from time to time, but we weren't all that close. I adored my paternal grandparents. I spent a few weeks with them every summer. By the time I was thirteen, I was ready to go to boarding school. My father told Bianca and that was that."

She was sure Alec had been happy to leave his nomadic life for something more structured, but she couldn't help wondering how Bianca had reacted to her only child living halfway around the world.

"Was that the last time you lived with her?" she asked.

"I would spend time with her on breaks."

Like the trip to Paris where Bianca slept with his best friend.

"Your mother is a complex woman," she said.

"She is. You have your work cut out for you."

She glanced at her watch and was shocked to see it was nearly eleven. She rose.

"It's late. Thank you for the cognac and the conversation."

Alec stood. "You're welcome. Good luck with everything. I'm around if you have any questions."

She nodded. "Good night."

She carried her glass into the kitchen, washed it, then made her way upstairs. When she reached her room, she thought about all she'd learned about Alec and Bianca and knew there was so much more to discover.

chapter
FIVE

TELLING HERSELF THAT EVERYONE WAS SCARED ON THE first day of class wasn't really helping. Sunshine alternated between wanting to throw up and simply turning her car around and heading back to Declan's house. Who was she kidding? She wasn't college material. No one had expectations that she was going to make anything of her life and no one would be surprised if she chickened out now.

All incredibly depressing thoughts that did nothing for her self-confidence, but certainly put her current circumstances in perspective. Was she really going to give up before she'd even started? Was she so pathetic she couldn't face a beginner math class?

"I'm doing this," she muttered to herself as she pulled into the sprawling parking lot at Pasadena City College. "I'm going to be just fine."

That decided, Sunshine grabbed her backpack and slung it over her shoulder, then locked her car and started purposefully for her class.

She'd looked at a map online and had a basic idea of where to go. She joined throngs of other students making their way toward the various buildings. Some were by themselves, but several traveled in groups. She eyed the other women, checking out what they'd decided to wear on the cool, gloomy morning.

She was relieved to see her jeans, sweater and boots fit in just fine. At thirty-one she was older than nearly everyone she saw but at least she wasn't wearing something inappropriate.

She found her building, then made her way to the classroom. She braced herself for she wasn't sure what, then went inside.

There were a lot of desks in rows and nearly half of the desks were occupied. She picked one in the second to the back row and slid into the seat. After pulling out a notebook and a pen, she wasn't sure what to do. Everyone around her was either talking to their neighbor or on their phones. She got out hers and pretended to read an email, all the while fighting nerves.

At exactly nine-thirty, a petite, gray-haired woman walked into the classroom. She wore black pants and a flowy blouse that she'd tucked in. She set her briefcase on the teacher's desk, then looked at the class.

"Settle down. I'm Professor Rejefski," she said, her voice clear and strong. "This is Math 131. You're in this class because you completed the prerequisite or you tested into the class."

Sunshine had no idea if she was supposed to be writing any of this down. She glanced around and saw most of the students were still on their phones, which seemed really rude.

The professor waited a couple of seconds before saying, "If you need to use your cell phone during class, you will step outside. If I catch you using your cell phone during class, you will be required to leave for the rest of the session. If that happens more than twice in the semester, you will be dropped from my class. I honestly don't care how close we are to the end of the semester or what your grade is or how much you need to pass this class. Do I make myself clear?"

Nearly all the students immediately slid their phones into their backpacks or pockets. One girl kept on texting. The professor moved in front of her and waited until the student looked up.

"Enough is enough. We're not going to get along," she said, her voice pleasant. "You should take someone else's class."

The girl's eyes widened. She looked maybe eighteen, although Sunshine would have guessed younger. "But I need this class at this time."

"If I see your cell phone again, you're out. Am I clear?"

The girl nodded and put her phone into her handbag.

Professor Rejefski returned to the front of the classroom. "We have a lot of material to cover. If you want to pass this course, you'll need to keep up. Do your homework and come to class prepared. I have no problem answering questions but if you aren't getting the material, either use the math lab or attend the TA sessions. The times and locations are posted online. This is not high school, people. This is college. You are adults and I will treat you like adults. I don't want to hear about your personal problems, I don't want excuses and if you're just here because your parents are making you, then I suggest you take this class with someone else."

"What a bitch."

The low voice came from somewhere to Sunshine's left. She didn't dare look and see who had spoken—she was too busy fighting nausea. She hadn't expected to be coddled, but this class was sounding more like boot camp than higher education.

"The college has a strict policy on plagiarism and cheating. I'm sure this won't be a surprise, but if you are caught cheating you will be expelled. There are no exceptions. On the day of our tests, you will each bring a blank blue book to class. I will take them from you in exchange for one that I have brought." She smiled. "You will be expected to show your work on every problem. There will be pop quizzes. Please make sure you have blank Scantrons, Form 100, with you at all times."

She paced back and forth in front of the class. "What else? I will randomly collect the homework. If you have completed the homework, you will receive bonus points. At the end of the semester, if you are within ten points of a higher grade, bonus

points will be added to your total points and could push you up
to the higher grade. Any questions?"

No one raised a hand.

"Excellent," Professor Rejefski said. "Then let's get started."

Two and a half hours later, when the class finally ended, Sunshine felt as if she'd run a mental marathon. She was exhausted
and her head was spinning. They'd covered most of the first
chapter. While she understood factors and the order of opera-
tions, she was a little shaky on word problems. She'd made a
note to find out when the TA sessions were, whatever those
were. She was going to have to go to all of those. And maybe
the math lab. Hiring a tutor wasn't out of the question.

She glanced at the test schedule the professor had handed out
and then slipped it into her backpack along with her notes. She
told herself that all she had to do was get to her car and drive
home. She could be overwhelmed there. In private. Having a
breakdown in the classroom was not a good idea.

She settled her backpack over her shoulder and walked to the
classroom door. A tall, lanky guy moved next to her.

"Hey," he said with a nod. "I'm Justin."

"Sunshine."

"Hey."

She offered him a tight smile as they walked outside.

"So I haven't seen you around here." He half moved in front
of her. "Are you new?"

While she heard the words, it took her a second for them to
actually sink in. Someone was talking to her. She needed to
respond. Her freak-out about the class wasn't exactly visible to
anyone but her.

"Hi. Yes. Today's my first day on campus."

"I thought so. I would have noticed you before. You're hot."

What? "Okay. Thanks." She went to step past him. Justin
blocked her effort.

"I'm having a pool party at my house this afternoon. Just

friends and beer. We'll barbecue burgers and stuff. You should definitely be there."

The statement was so at odds with her sense of being completely out of her element that she could only stare at him.

"Excuse me?"

He flashed her a smile. "You'll have fun. I promise."

She shifted her backpack to her other shoulder, then actually turned her attention on Justin. He was good-looking, in a very young, teenage kind of way. He'd yet to fill out and he had the eager air of a happy puppy.

"How old are you?" she asked bluntly.

He grinned. "Old enough."

She waited.

His grin faded. "Twenty-three."

She waited some more.

"Eighteen."

"That's what I thought. Thanks, Justin, but no."

She moved around him and headed for her car. Puppy Justin chose not to follow, which was heartening. Now if only she could get rid of her sense of impending doom. Telling herself she could do it, she could figure out college, wasn't working any kind of magic. She was scared and apprehensive and not the least bit confident about her abilities.

"Change is always hard," she murmured to herself as she drove out of the parking lot. "I have to do this. I have to."

It was the only way for her to be more. If she didn't want to believe herself, she had Justin as an illustration. She wanted to be more than the girl with boobs and an ass. She wanted to be proud of herself. It all started with this math class and by God, she was going to get through it.

Or so she hoped.

Bianca had left a note on Margot's door requesting they start at ten in the morning. Despite her late night, Margot was up

at six, and showered and dressed by six-thirty. She waited until
seven to go down to breakfast where, as promised, a small buffet had been set up in the dining room.

Alec was already there, eating his breakfast and reading the
paper. An actual paper—not a digital version—which made
sense, given what he did for a living. He looked up when she
entered.

"Good morning."

She nodded. "Morning."

And that was it. He returned his attention to his paper, she
collected her breakfast and took it upstairs. When she finished,
she returned her dishes to the kitchen before going over her
lesson plan for the first few days. Mostly she and Bianca would
get to know each other. It was very likely that she would have
to modify her lesson plans as she figured out how Bianca liked
to learn and what she most liked to do.

Promptly at ten, Bianca appeared in the lounge. She wore
yoga pants and a sweatshirt. Her dark blond hair was pulled
back in a ponytail and she wasn't wearing any makeup, yet she
still looked so beautiful as to be otherworldly.

"Good morning," Margot said, standing. "I'm excited to get
started. How are you feeling?"

"Nervous mostly. I'm not sure why I'm doing this. It's really
a ridiculous thing, when you think about it. How can you possibly help me?"

First-day jitters weren't uncommon. Margot smiled reassur-
ingly. "Of course you can always change your mind. Let's try
this for a few days and see how it goes. If it's not working, then
I'll completely understand."

Bianca tilted her head. "You're not going to try to talk me
into staying the course?"

"Not my style."

She relaxed visibly. "Good." She pointed to the window. "It's foggy out. Let's go walk in the garden. We can pretend we're in London and we're spies on a mission for Winston Churchill."

Margot's first thought was that if they were spying for Churchill, they wouldn't be in London. They'd be behind enemy lines somewhere in France or Germany, but she sensed saying that would spoil the moment.

"Let me grab a jacket and we'll head out."

The fog was thick and damp and they could only see a few feet in front of them. Margot knew that on her own she would get lost in a matter of seconds, which might be what Bianca intended. But rather than try to remember which way they'd come, Margot told herself to relax and enjoy the experience. Even if she did get lost, eventually the fog would lift and she would find her way back to the house.

Bianca linked arms with her. "The fog always makes me think of Rod," she said with a laugh. "He never liked it. Said it made him sad, which was always funny to me. The man is from Scotland."

"Rod?"

"Rod Stewart. I met him when I was very young." She thought for a second. "Maybe nineteen or twenty. I was in Saint-Tropez and there was a party. Back then there was always a party. We had a wild week together. He was just so charming."

Margot wasn't sure if the story was informational or meant to impress. They were walking along a stone path lined with plants, bushes and trees. The fog seemed thicker and the dampness seeped into her jeans and through her jacket.

"Let's talk about what we're going to do together," she said.

Bianca immediately stiffened and pulled away. "If we must."

Margot stopped and looked at her. "I'm not here to make you uncomfortable or put you in a situation where you feel foolish. My job is to help you in any way I can. I want this to be enjoyable and informative. Would it help if I told you how I work?"

Bianca's gaze was wary at best. Margot half expected her to bolt.

"It might," Bianca said. "Tell me."

"Maybe we should go inside where it's not so cold."

Bianca surprised her by linking arms again. "I know somewhere better."

They continued walking, then turned onto another path. Up ahead Margot saw a structure. As they got closer, she realized it was a greenhouse filled with exotic flowers. They went in through a glass door.

The first thing she noticed was the fragrance. It was powerful but not overwhelming, as if the scents from the thousands of flowers somehow blended into a beautiful singular perfume. The temperature was comfortable, maybe seventy or seventy-five degrees.

"Over here," Bianca said, leading the way to a seating area in the middle of the greenhouse. Wicker furniture formed a circle. Overstuffed cushions offered comfortable surfaces. There was a low coffee table and a bistro table and chairs.

"What is this place?" she asked. "It's wonderful."

"Isn't it? Alec hired the most amazing landscape architect a few years back. The greenhouse had always been here, but it wasn't used for anything. Now there are all these flowers. I love to come here to read or think. Especially when it's foggy. It's like we have our own special place, away from the rest of the world."

Margot had to agree. She had the thought that she would love to bring a sleeping bag and spend the night in the greenhouse. With the flowers and the night sky, it would be quite the experience.

She returned her attention to the job at hand. Once she and Bianca were seated, she leaned forward, deliberately relaxing her body language.

"I thought we'd begin by talking about Cardigania. The history of its customs as well as what the culture is like today. Their basic industries, areas of growth, demographics. That sort of thing. I'd like for us to brainstorm different events you think you'll be attending with Wesley. We can talk about what you might wear and who you'd meet. During those sessions we'll come up with things for you to talk about and I'll help you become familiar with phrases and strategize ways to incorporate their various customs. None of this is formal. We can switch from topic to topic organically. I do have a workbook I'd like you to consider using. It's more structured and we can go through it together."

Bianca wrinkled her nose. "I hate being flawed. Real life is messy. I prefer pictures where everything can be airbrushed."

"You hardly need airbrushing. You're luminous in person. I'm not sure a photograph can capture that."

Bianca's eyes filled with tears. "What a lovely thing to say." She blinked. "Still, there are flaws. I have to do this for Wesley. The Cardiganian ambassador to China was recalled for having an affair. That's so ordinary a thing to do. I'm not sure I could ever be that ordinary. Wesley says I'll be fine, but what if I'm not? I don't want to cost him his career."

Margot had learned that nearly everyone was apprehensive when she started working with them. "Would you be comfortable taking out my appendix?"

"What? You can't ask me that! It's a ridiculous question."

"Why?"

"I'm not a doctor."

"You're right. Knowing how to perform surgery is something a person has to learn. It's a skill—not intuitive. No one is born knowing how to do something like that." She smiled. "That's all this is. Learning a new skill. I wouldn't know the first thing about acting, but for you, it's easy. You wouldn't have to wonder if you could do it, you'd jump right into the role. You have your process and you're confident in your abilities. My job is to make you confident when it comes to dealing with Wesley's lifestyle. Whether you're meeting a factory worker or a prime minister, there are ways to be appropriate and genuine while still being yourself."

Margot shrugged. "A lot of it is just plain silly. Like the way to set a table for a formal dinner. There are rules that sometimes make no sense. We'll study them so you'll know how to navigate state dinners. None of this is hard. It's time consuming and requires some learning, but only because you haven't had the experiences before."

Bianca relaxed. "Like taking out an appendix."

"Exactly. Now how did you meet Wesley?"

Bianca leaned back in her chair and sighed. "It was just one of those things. I had a meeting downtown. I never go there, but that day I had to. When I was finished, I walked back to the parking garage and on the way, I passed a dog park." Her smile turned impish. "I do love dogs so I went in to pet a few. This cute Boston terrier came running up to me. He was so friendly and handsome."

"You don't have a dog of your own?"

"Oh, I've never had a pet. I wouldn't be a good pet parent. I did all right with Alec, but only until he was a teenager. Then he went to live with his grandparents. It was the best thing for him." Her tone turned wistful.

Margot wondered if Bianca had wanted her son to go, or if she'd been given a choice.

"Was the handsome dog Wesley's?" she asked.

"It was. His name is Bruno and while I was loving on him, Wesley came over and introduced himself to me. We took one look at each other and just knew."

"Love at first sight."

"It was. For both of us."

"Do you experience that a lot?"

"Sometimes." Her smile returned. "The best loves are the ones where you know right away, don't you think? But it's never been like this before. Never so powerful or strong." She laughed.

"I haven't tried to change myself for anyone else." Her laughter faded. "Alec always wanted me to be different. He never said anything, but I could tell. Especially as he got older. I disappointed him."

Margot thought about Bianca sleeping with Alec's best friend when they were both still at boarding school. Not exactly a topic she was going to bring up.

"Why do you think you disappoint him?" she asked instead.

"It's just who I am." Bianca sprang to her feet and spun in a circle. "I didn't eat breakfast and I'm starving. Let's go raid the kitchen. Then you can tell me all about the special Cardiganian sheep."

Before Margot could respond, Bianca was gone, running out the door and into the garden. The fog had mostly lifted by now so she could see her until Bianca turned the corner and was lost from view.

chapter
SIX

DECLAN EXPECTED CLIENTS TO BE DIFFICULT. BUT HIS current clients were doing their best to give him a heart attack. Even if that wasn't their stated goal, they were doing a great job of pushing him closer and closer to the edge.

He left his office early and drove home, arriving a little before four. When he opened the door leading from the garage to the house, he was hit by a blast of music and the smell of chocolate and berries and all things delicious.

He walked into the kitchen only to come to a complete stop as he took in the view. Two pies sat on cooling racks. A tray of brownies was on the kitchen table and frosting dripped off obviously still-warm cinnamon rolls. But what really caught his attention was Sunshine.

Connor's nanny had pinned up her hair, leaving her neck bare. The sweet curve led to nearly bare shoulders. She had on some kind of tank dress that came to her knees. It was shapeless, but she was not, especially not when she was dancing and singing along to "Fixer Upper" from the *Frozen* soundtrack.

Her hips gyrated, her breasts moved and as shameful as it was to admit, he stood there taking it all in like a lusty sixteen-year-old. He was as hard as one, too, he thought, shifting uncomfortably, grateful his suit jacket would cover his inappropriate response to her.

It was the lack of sex thing, he told himself. He wasn't disgusting enough to lust after the woman who took care of his son. It was women in general and his not getting laid that had him wanting to set her on the counter and—

Sunshine saw him and screamed. She pressed a flour-covered hand to her chest. "You scared me! Don't do that."

"Sorry." He set down his briefcase while making sure he stayed safely behind the counter where she wouldn't catch a glimpse of his inappropriately hard dick. "Opening a bakery?"

"What?" She dropped her arms to her side, leaving a white handprint on her dress, then reached for her phone and silenced the music. She smiled at him. "It was kind of loud, huh? Sorry. Connor's fine with the volume as long as he gets to pick what I'm playing. He's in his room reading."

"I didn't know he still liked *Frozen*."

She smiled. "Everyone likes *Frozen* although last week it was the soundtrack from *Hamilton*. One of our favorites."

She'd been working for him for less than a month and already she and Connor had favorites. That was a good sign, he thought, letting a little of the ever-present worry about his son fade. As far as he could tell, Sunshine was an excellent nanny—even if she did have surprising hobbies.

"What's with all this?" he asked.

"Oh." Her smile faded and her expression turned guilty. "Yes, well, I stress bake." Her chin came up. "I stopped at the grocery store after class and I paid for the supplies myself."

"Sunshine, I'm not worried you're overbuying flour and baking soda. I was wondering what brought it on. And what we're going to do with it all."

Her smile returned. "Most of it freezes. There's a bake sale coming up at Connor's school so some of it can go there. Maybe you'd like to take cookies to work."

"Mostly I'd like to quit and go live on an island."

"Bad day?"

"The worst. Tell you what. Let me go say hi to Connor and get changed, then we'll compare notes on our day."

A timer dinged. Sunshine reached for hot pads.

"That's the banana bread."

"Of course it is. I'll be right back."

He grabbed his briefcase and positioned it strategically. Things had mostly calmed down but with her bending over the oven, well, he was a disgusting human being. That was for sure.

He went into his bedroom and changed into jeans and a T-shirt, all the while thinking about how many billions of people didn't have access to safe drinking water. A few minutes later, he was back to normal, so to speak. He went in to check on Connor.

When his son saw him, Connor jumped to his feet and raced toward him. "Dad! Sunshine is baking everything. I think we should have pie for dessert. It's mixed berry and I got to taste the filling and it's delicious."

"Then pie it is."

He swept Connor up in his arms and hugged him. Thin boy arms tightened around his neck. This was right, he thought fiercely. These moments with his child. As long as Connor was happy and healthy, then the rest of it didn't matter all that much. Work would figure itself out.

"What are you reading?" he asked as he set Connor on the floor.

"Another book on ants. It's really good. I can't wait for the farm to get here."

"Me, too. I'm going to go back to the kitchen and talk to Sunshine. Want to come hang out with us?"

Connor's gaze slid toward his book. "I'll wait until dinner."

Declan grinned. "No interest in talking with the old people?"

"Sunshine's not old."

Declan clutched his chest. "Hey, I'm not old, either."

Connor giggled. "You're my dad."

As if that explained everything. Declan supposed it did.

He returned to the kitchen. Sunshine had changed the music to a classical station. She'd also cleared off a spot at the island where he could pull up a stool, and set out all the fixings for a martini.

"You read my mind," he said. "Thanks, but I can make it."

"I'll do it. I need the practice."

"Not a martini drinker?"

"I'm more of a wine with dinner girl."

"Then feel free to pick out a bottle."

"That bad a day?"

He reached for a cooling cookie and took a bite. "My business partner and I have a contract with a new hotel on the north end of Malibu. They've started construction so now we're talking about the grounds. They're extensive, both in the front and back, with several acres heading up into the hills."

She measured vodka and vermouth, then added ice. "Sounds like a challenge."

"It is. We're going to build a walking path through the hills, which is easy enough. It's the rest of it that's the problem."

Sunshine poured the drink into a martini glass, then added three olives on a plastic toothpick and handed him the drink.

He took a sip. "Perfect. Thank you."

"Pie and martinis. I am a miracle. So what about the rest of the grounds?"

"They won't make a decision. No, I take that back. We can't get to the point where they have to make a decision. They want something different. Something special, but so far they hate everything we've suggested. I'm to the point of offering dolphins and elephants."

"I'm not sure they'd get along although they are both intelligent species. They might figure it out."

She poured herself a glass of ice water, then sat across from him at the island.

"They're leaning toward breaking up the space into different gardens. They might want a maze of some kind and that's all we've got. At some point they're going to have to pick a direction or kill us. I'm used to clients needing time and hand-holding but nothing like this."

"The Huntington gardens are all different. I wonder if that would inspire them or make it worse."

"I don't think I could get through a field trip," he admitted. "Not without bloodshed."

"Yours or theirs?"

"I have no idea."

She laughed. "So you connect different gardens with a thing, right? The material used to construct it or the same planters or a type of plant?"

"Exactly. Feel free to suggest something. I'm running out of ideas. Last week they wanted all organic. This week they're wondering about sand because we're close to the beach. I could work with sand. Sand is great. Until I got an email this afternoon saying sand was too obvious."

"Yikes. That's not easy."

"We'll get there. Like I said, I'm used to hand-holding, but sometimes it's wearing. Now tell me about your day. Why are you stress baking?"

Her shoulders slumped and she sighed heavily. "It's dumb."

"No, it's not. It's important. Talk."

"I started my math class today."

"And?"

"And it was awful. Professor Rejefski is seriously intimidating. The students are all younger than me and I couldn't follow the lesson."

"Not any of it?"

"Some. But then it got confusing. I haven't had to study since high school. I never went to college. I signed up but then I met some guy and I took off. I was always an indifferent student at best and I figured when I applied myself, it would be easy or at least doable. But what if it isn't? What if I was a C student because I'm just not smart enough? What if this is the best I can ever be?"

He leaned toward her. "Sunshine, it was one day."

"I know, but—"

"One day. Give yourself a break."

"I'm afraid I've peaked."

He held in a smile. "Tell me about making pie."

"What?"

"I've heard making the crust is the hard part. Why can't you just add the ingredients and have piecrust?"

She frowned. "Weird question but sure. It's not just about ingredients. You have to feel your way. It's a texture thing and it takes practice." Her mouth twisted. "Are you using a pie analogy to make me feel better? Pie?"

"Technically piecrust and yes. Look, no one is good at everything the first time. Riding a bike, singing, learning to read, going back to college."

Sex. The thought came unbidden and he pushed it away. He was enjoying his conversation with Sunshine and he wasn't going to screw it up by being a guy.

"It's been one day," he repeated. "Give yourself a break and some time. How was the professor intimidating?"

"She had a lot of rules. And there was something with blue books I didn't understand."

"Rules are good. You know where you stand and what's expected. You'll buy blue books at the student store and take your tests in them. She probably said she would collect blank ones from you before the tests, then give you back ones she brought."

"Why?"

"To prevent cheating. Otherwise people write notes and formulas in the books."

Sunshine looked shocked. "They do that?" She shook her head. "Of course they do that. I'm so out of touch. Some guy invited me back to his place for a pool party. He's like eighteen. Why?"

Declan took another drink of his martini. "You're asking me why an eighteen-year-old guy wants to go out with you? Is that a serious question?"

"I meant I'm not looking for that kind of thing."

"You've sworn off men?" Knowing that would be a big help, he thought. Or at least he hoped it would be.

"Not exactly. I just don't want to be all boo— Ah, I don't want to be dating guys who are just in it for sex and a fling. I want someone who wants a real relationship. Someone smart and kind and funny who sees me as a person."

There was a lot of information there—information he would have to think about later. "Seems reasonable."

"Maybe. I don't know. Right now I want to do my job and figure out college."

"I was a pretty decent student," he told her. "Here's what I can tell you. Keep up with the material. Try to read ahead so you can ask questions during the lecture. Go to the TA sessions."

"That's what Professor Rejefski said. I wrote down the dates, but what is it?"

"TAs are teacher's assistants. Usually grad students. They have help sessions where they go over the material. You can get more personal attention. There's probably a math lab on campus. Check that out. Sit up front so the professor gets to know you. Be engaged. Show interest in the class."

"Why?"

He smiled. "Because she'll see you're trying. At the end of the semester, if you're on the cusp of getting a higher grade, being engaged can push you over the top."

Sunshine's eyes widened. "They do that?"

"They're human, so yes."

"I'm shocked."

He chuckled. "Get over it."

"There's a whole secret world out there."

"The cliché is true—success is about showing up." He pushed himself away from the counter. "You can do this. It will take a while to get into the rhythm of studying and taking tests, but I have every faith in you."

She smiled. "That's about the nicest thing you could have said. Thank you."

"You're welcome."

They looked at each other. Declan wanted to tell himself there was a bit of tension sizzling between them but he had a feeling that was the martini talking. He slid off the stool.

"I'm going to check on Connor, then come back and help you pack up the baked goods."

"You don't have to. I'll take care of it. Dinner at six?"

"Sure. See you then."

And with that, order was restored to exactly what it should be.

Three days into Bianca's training, Alec had to admit Margot was less of a disruption than he would have expected. She was quiet, unobtrusive and, except for when she was in the dining room to collect her breakfast, he rarely saw her.

From what his mother had told him, they were mostly working in the greenhouse until the temperatures warmed enough for them to be outside. Bianca seemed happy, his house was quiet and that was all Alec required of the situation. He still had his doubts about his mother's ability to adapt to Wesley's lifestyle, but that was not his problem.

He returned to the house and saw Margot standing in the cloisters, a cell phone in her hand.

"You piece of shit. Leave me alone."

He was reasonably confident she wasn't addressing him, so rather than respond, he paused and cleared his throat.

Margot spun to face him, her face flushing with color.

"Sorry," she said, tucking her phone into a pocket. "I'm having a moment."

She wore a sleeveless red dress that fit to her waist before flaring out to just above her knee. Her hair was pulled back in a simple ponytail. She had on flat shoes, no jewelry save a watch, and minimal makeup. She appeared competent and capable and yet he found himself keenly cognizant of the fact that she was both a woman and incredibly beautiful. A combination that seemed to, as his mother would phrase it, rattle his cage.

He shook off his awareness. "Do you need assistance?"

"Thank you, but no. I'm fine." She hesitated. "An old boyfriend is trying to get in touch with me. I've changed cell numbers and moved, all without telling him. One of my friends thinks I should give him a second chance. Which would technically be a fourteenth chance. I said no. She thought I was wrong."

Before he could decide how to respond, she continued.

"It's not him, it's me. I'm a relatively smart person. I know what I want in my life and I make it happen. But when I'm around him, I make absurd choices. I completely accept my responsibility in everything that has gone wrong. It's really me. So the best thing is to avoid him. Which is getting easier. I just don't want to see him."

Alec felt a sudden and unexpected loathing toward a man he'd never met. How peculiar. "I'm sure everyone has someone in their past they wish to avoid."

"Even you?"

"Even me."

She flashed him a smile. "You're very kind, but I suspect you're just trying to make me feel better."

"On the contrary, I'm telling the truth. I was engaged a few years ago. She was also a scholar. That was how we met. We were well suited and I suppose we fell in love."

He paused knowing he could go either way with the rest of the story. He could say what he always said, or he could tell the truth.

He briefly looked out in the garden. No, not the truth. It was too personal, and far too humiliating.

"She was well published, or so I thought. It turns out she had been plagiarizing someone else's work. An obscure historian who had published in the 1940s. She was eventually caught." He returned his attention to Margot. "It wasn't the cheating so much as what it said of her character."

"Of course. If she would lie about that, what else would she lie about?"

"Exactly."

"People are sometimes confusing," she said. "I apologize for my outburst."

"No need. I'm sure he deserved every word."

She laughed. "He did, but still. All right. Change of subject. Things are going well with your mother. I would like to plan a couple of social events."

Alec instinctively stiffened. He didn't enjoy social events. There were too many people he didn't know and he found small talk tiresome. Why did he have to put in the effort to get to know someone he would never meet again? How was that enjoyable? He wanted to say as much but he had a feeling Margot had only mentioned what she did because she wanted him to be there.

"Such as?" he asked, hoping he sounded enthused rather than resigned.

"First I want to meet Wesley. Getting to know him will help me understand the dynamics of their relationship. I was thinking drinks somewhere."

"Oh. Wesley is easy to talk to. Probably the result of his diplomatic training. Invite him here. My mother will be more relaxed and that should help you with your observations."

She smiled. "Thank you, Alec. That's very kind. I'll get going on that right away. The second event is a dinner. I want a combination of people Bianca knows and those she doesn't. The dinner would be fairly formal. Several courses, a lot of passing of plates and choosing the right fork. The purpose is to see how she does with the etiquette and with the stress of the people. I would appreciate if you could be there. I'll ask Wesley, of course. I'm thinking of inviting my sister, if that's all right."

"You have a sister?"

"A fraternal twin. Sunshine." Margot smiled. "She's a nanny for an eight-year-old boy. I'd also like to invite her employer and his son. Children always shift the dynamics. I'll find a restaurant with a private room so we're not dealing with outside influences."

While he would never choose a dinner like she described, he saw the purpose immediately. When working with people, observation was an important tool.

"Have the dinner here," he said impulsively. "Edna will be thrilled to cook something more challenging than food for the freezer. She is forever hinting I should host a party." Something that was never going to happen. He did not, as a rule, like strangers in his house. He didn't like situations where he was not completely in control. But somehow this was different.

Margot touched his arm. "Thank you, Alec. I really appreciate your help in this. Let me check with Bianca and get back to you with dates. You're all right with me inviting my sister and her employer and his son?"

"Of course."

She'd rested her fingers on his forearm for barely a second, yet he felt the imprint as if she'd branded him. How peculiar.

She pointed at the gardens. "Sunshine's boss is a landscape architect. He's going to love what you've done here."

Information clicked into place. The landscape architect, the eight-year-old boy, the nanny possibly hired because...

"Does she work for Declan Dubois?"

"How did you know?"

He nodded toward the gardens. "That's his work. He's been to the house dozens of times. I'd forgotten he lost his wife a few months ago. I know Declan, but my mother's never met him."

Her mouth curved up. "And people say LA is a big town."

"It may be but Pasadena is not. As I said, my mother doesn't know him. She didn't come see the house until my remodels were finished. He and his son will be strangers to her."

"Excellent. Then we have a plan. I'll be in touch with the details. Thank you again, Alec. I appreciate the support."

"Of course."

She walked inside. He watched her go, telling himself that he simply wanted to help his mother. There was no other reason he had agreed. It certainly wasn't to impress Margot. What a ridiculous thing to think.

chapter
SEVEN

"FIVE, FOUR, THREE, TWO, ONE. AND TAKE IT DOWN. YOU have thirty seconds to catch your breath."

Margot lowered her butt to the seat of her bike and adjusted the resistance. Her thighs were on fire and she was breathing heavily, but in a good way. Spin class always got her heart racing.

"I hate you," Sunshine gasped from the bike next to her. "Why would you make me do this?" Her sister was sweating and red faced. "Who thought this up? It's hideous."

Margot laughed. "You said you'd go to an exercise class if we were sitting down. We're sitting."

"Not all the time. The instructor keeps telling us to get our butts off the seats. What's the point of having a seat if you can't use it?"

Before Margot could answer, their rest period was over and they had to crank it up again. Sunshine groaned before increasing the resistance and standing in the pedals. When Margot glanced at her, Sunshine mouthed, "You are dead to me."

Margot grinned.

Twenty minutes later the class was over. Sunshine wiped the sweat from her face and neck as she limped toward the door.

"I'm never coming back," she muttered.

"You say that every time we do this class."

"And I mean it. Later I forget, but this time I'm getting a tattoo so it doesn't slip my mind."

"Wasn't there a movie about that?"

"Someone hating spin class? I don't think so."

Margot smiled. "Using tattoos to remember things. It doesn't matter. Come on, I'll buy you a smoothie."

Sunshine rolled her eyes. "You mean at that juice place, don't you? How about a milk shake from a burger place instead?"

"You just burned a bunch of calories and did something good for your body. Wouldn't you rather have a vegan smoothie?"

"No."

"I think you're just pretending."

"I'm sure that's it."

They walked across the parking lot to the juice store. Margot ordered her usual green drink of spinach, parsley, cucumber and kale with a little red apple tossed in for sweetness. Sunshine chose a protein drink with almond milk, cacao, banana and vegan vanilla protein powder.

"I'd rather have ice cream," she said as they sat with their drinks at one of the outside tables. "You should care about my happiness."

"I care about your health, too."

"I don't mind being fat. I've accepted my body shape. It is what it is."

"You're not fat." *Not in the least*, Margot thought. Sunshine was lush and curvy. She looked vibrant and sexy and alive.

Margot, on the other hand, looked cool and distant. There was something about the way she talked or moved that put off people who didn't know her well. She knew that technically she was considered beautiful, but in an "under glass" kind of way. People didn't see her as approachable or warm.

"How are things?" she asked.

"Okay. Work's good, but school is hard. The second day was slightly less overwhelming than the first. I did the homework and I got most of it right, so that's good. But the professor intimidates me and everyone is a lot younger. I worry they're also smarter than me or at least used to the going to college thing."

"You're feeling out of place," Margot said.

Her sister sighed. "Don't try your Jedi mind tricks on me. I'm immune."

"They're not Jedi mind tricks, they're techniques and they could help you feel more confident."

"Um, no. But thanks for asking."

"You don't respect what I do," Margot said, her tone mild.

"I respect it immensely. I just choose not to participate in it. I need to find my own way. You know that."

"I do."

Sunshine had always been the one to strike out and forge her own path—something she'd inherited from their mother. Margot liked making a plan and then following it. She liked lists and goals and knowing she'd made progress.

"School is big for me," Sunshine said. "I know it's the right thing to do and I'll get through it, but it's a shock to my system."

"I find it intriguing that you're so organized and regimented with the kids you work with but that doesn't translate to your personal life."

"I'm not regimented."

"You keep them on a schedule."

"Yes, but children do better when there's a routine. They need mealtimes and bedtimes and playtimes."

"Maybe you do, too."

"You're saying I should treat myself as if I were one of my charges?"

"I'm saying it might be a fun experiment. You already have to be in class two mornings per week. Maybe plan out when you're going to do homework and when you're going to work out. That sort of thing."

Sunshine glared at her. "Work out? I noticed how you slipped that in there."

"You're the one complaining you don't exercise enough."

"You're not supposed to throw that back in my face."

"I was just pointing out you could make a schedule for yourself."

"You mean like have a milk shake every Monday?" Sunshine's eyes were bright with humor. "I could totally get behind that."

"You're hopeless."

"I've been saying that forever. Now, how are things with you? How's work? How's your sex life?"

"I have no sex life."

"Me, either. Sucks, huh?"

"I don't mind so much."

"Liar."

Margot sighed. "I mind a little, but I'm used to it." She wasn't the type to have a one-night stand and sadly there weren't many men who interested her. Along with destroying her life over and over again, Dietrich had somehow convinced her that he was the only one who could possibly find her attractive. That she was too weird for most. While her head said he was a lying bastard with a temper that sometimes scared her and that she was far better without him, her surprisingly fragile heart wondered if he had a point. It wasn't as if there had ever been a line of men ready to beat down her door. That was more her sister's life.

"Why aren't you having sex?" she asked.

Sunshine nearly choked on her smoothie. "Excuse me?"

"I assume you could get someone in a hot minute. Or a cold one."

"I could, but I'm not going to. I told you—I'm done with that. I want to be normal."

"Normal people have sex."

"Normal people have relationships. I've only ever had flings that, in the end, didn't mean anything to either of us. I've run away from my life and my responsibilities because of the promise of a few weeks of bliss, and then what?" Her mouth twisted. "I wake up with the flu, alone in a hotel room in London with no guy, no job, no anything."

Margot stretched her hand across the small table. Sunshine squeezed her fingers. The situation Sunshine was describing was exactly what had happened four months before, two days after their thirty-first birthday. She'd made her way from London to LA and had moved in with Margot, vowing she was going to change her life for the better. No more random guys, no more meaningless, slightly hedonistic existence. Instead she was going to achieve normality.

"I love you," Margot said.

"I love you, too. Even though you've had your shit together for most of our adult lives."

"Have not." Margot set down her drink and held up one finger. "I nearly flunked out of my sophomore year of college because I went to Thailand with Dietrich." She raised a second finger. "I missed registration and couldn't get any of the classes I wanted because I was in Australia, also with Dietrich." A third finger went up. "I was in Patagonia when I should have been interviewing for my dream job and instead I ended up as assistant manager at a midlevel hotel in San Francisco."

"Which ultimately got you to the job you have now, which you love."

"I think I would have loved managing a Peninsula Hotel, as well."

"Not as much."

"I'm not sure. My point is I could keep going. You've been stupid over a bunch of guys and I've been stupid over and over again about the same one. Neither of us wins an award. Instead we have to keep moving forward. Which we are." She picked up her drink. "Quit being mean to someone I love."

"I'm not being mean to myself." Sunshine sighed. "I'm going

to get through it. College, staying at my job, ignoring inappropriate men. Maybe I should give up on men for a while."

"Or find someone appropriate."

"Where?"

Margot shrugged. "I'm actually not the person to ask. I am appropriate-man free."

Sunshine touched her plastic drink container to Margot's. "Perhaps, but you are also Dietrich-free, and isn't that nice?"

"It is. I'm going to change the subject and talk about my work."

Sunshine raised her eyebrows. "Wow. You never talk about your work. Not in specifics. Or are you teasing me?"

"Bianca Wray is my client."

Sunshine choked for a second time. "You said a client's name out loud. Should I duck so the lightning doesn't strike me, too?"

Margot smiled. She was very protective of the people she worked with and never discussed anything about them with anyone outside of her immediate supervisor.

"I have her permission to tell you."

"To quote our friend Lizzy Bennet, I am all astonishment." Sunshine tilted her head. "Wait a minute. Bianca Wray? The actress?" She sat up straighter. "The one who slept with all those guys and unfastened her halter dress on some award show, letting it drift to the ground, and she was naked underneath? I love her. She's my hero."

"I thought you were going for normal."

"Oh right. Well, she *was* my hero. You're working with her? Why?"

"I can't say."

Sunshine rolled her eyes. "You are a giant pain in my ass. So why did you tell me?"

"Bianca is going to be hosting a dinner party. I thought you'd like to come, along with your boss and Connor."

Her sister leaned toward her. "Um, what? Your client, who

has never met me, wants to invite me, the guy I work for, whom she also hasn't met, and his kid to dinner?"

"Declan knows Bianca's son, Alec, who will also be there. Alec hired Declan to design his gardens."

Her sister's expression turned knowing. "Alec? You haven't mentioned any Alec."

Margot willed herself not to react. "He's Bianca's adult son. He's owns the house I'm staying in. He's a talented scholar and his house is a beautiful, converted monastery. The dinner will be at his place. Bianca's staying with him for a few weeks as we work on things."

"You're living with Alec? Funny how you didn't mention that, nor the man himself. You're keeping secrets."

Margot felt herself flush, even though nothing flushworthy was going on anywhere in her life. Ridiculous pale skin.

"I'm not living with him. You're deliberately misunderstanding me."

"Is he hot?"

"He's very intelligent."

Sunshine simply looked at her.

Margot exhaled sharply. "He's not unattractive."

"Married?"

"What? Of course not. If he was married, he wouldn't be attractive. I don't do that."

"Just checking. I'm trying for normal. With Bianca Wray in your life, who knows what you could be trying for."

"My clients don't influence me. I influence them."

"If half of what I've read about her is true, you may have met your match."

Margot shook her head. "So far she's been very conventional." *Surprisingly so*, she thought. Bianca had begun going through the workbook. She was reading about Cardigania, studying the history and customs. So far, their lessons were uneventful. It was almost disappointing.

A guy in a Mercedes convertible pulled up close to their table.

"Hi," he called, his gaze firmly on Sunshine. "Can I buy you lunch?"

"No, thanks," she said, not even looking at him.

"I have a private jet. We could be in San Francisco in an hour. I know a great place on the wharf."

She flicked her fingers at him. "Move along."

"Baby, I'd be good for you."

Sunshine sighed, then leaned forward and kissed Margot briefly on the lips before looking back at the guy. She smiled brightly.

"Wrong team."

"My loss."

"That is actually true."

He drove off. Margot watched him go.

"You didn't even look at him. He was kind of gorgeous."

Her sister rolled her eyes. "I'm not being picked up by a guy in a parking lot in front of a juice bar. That's a very old-me thing."

"Okay. It's just I'm always your lesbian shill. Just once I want you to be *my* lesbian shill."

"I'm totally open to it. Anytime. Is *shill* the right word?"

"I don't know, but you get my point."

Sunshine grinned. "Yes. My successful, college-educated, incredibly beautiful sister wants to be picked up by some random guy in a parking lot."

"Just once. And he has to be a guy driving a Mercedes and who has a private jet."

"He was lying about the jet."

"How do you know?"

"I just know. It's a line. Believe me."

Margot would have to as she had no personal experience with the subject. There was just the disaster that had been Dietrich and he'd never once tempted her with a private jet. All he'd had to do was ask and she'd been there, regardless of what it cost her.

"We are cursed," she said with a sigh.

"We are the Baxter sisters and we just can't seem to escape our destiny."

Margot wanted to say that wasn't true, but they came from a long line of women who had disastrous relationships and the emotional staying power of snow in July.

Sunshine smiled. "But we have each other and maybe that's enough."

"It is," Margot said firmly.

"Fake it until we make it?"

"Always."

"You'll track the package?" Connor asked, sounding worried.

"I swear I will. I'll check every half hour. Plus, the delivery guy always rings the doorbell."

"And you'll be home?"

"I will be home. I'm going to the grocery store as soon as I drop you off, then I'll go directly home to wait. I promise."

Connor still looked worried, but he nodded. "Okay. I trust you."

"Thank you."

The ant farm had been delivered the previous day and the shipment of ants was on its way.

"I will take them into your room and put them in a safe spot so they can recover from their journey while you're at school. This afternoon you can move them into their new home."

"Do you think they'll like it?" he asked anxiously. "Will they be scared?"

"I think they'll be happy to be in one place. Travel is exhausting."

"It is."

His voice was so serious, she thought, telling herself not to smile. But it was hard. Connor was adorable and his concern for the soon-to-be delivered ants was the cutest thing ever.

She joined the line of cars leading to the school. When it was their turn, she made sure he had his lunch and backpack before telling him to have a good day.

"I'll be here right on time," she told him. "With the ant report."

He laughed. "Bye, Sunshine."

"Bye, Connor."

She pulled up a couple of car lengths to get out of the way, then watched until he was safely inside the building. Once Connor disappeared from sight, she drove to the grocery store.

She'd already planned meals for the next couple of weeks. Sunshine preferred to make large batches of food everyone liked, then freeze the extras for easy dinners. While she separated the portions with the assumption that Declan would be joining them, more often than not, he didn't make it home in time, leaving her with a delicious lunch.

Connor was a pretty easy kid on every front, including food. He was always willing to try something new and even though he complained about vegetables, he mostly ate them. As she pulled into the parking lot at the grocery store, Sunshine thought briefly of Connor's mother. How devastating to have such a wonderful family, such a perfect life, only to find out you were dying. To have loved like that, to have known you had it all, and then have it cruelly snatched from you... There weren't words to describe that kind of pain.

She wanted that, she thought wistfully. Not the losing part, but the love. She wanted to give her heart to someone and accept his heart in return. She wanted to be all in with a future and hope and affection and respect. One day, she promised herself. It would happen one day.

Sunshine grabbed her purse and pulled out her list. They had leftover steak from the weekend. She would use that in quesadillas tomorrow. Tonight she wanted to barbecue enough chicken for at least five meals. There were so many options for the leftovers. Salads and enchiladas or tacos. She had a couple of great casserole dishes that used cooked chicken. Having a freezer full of ready-to-go food made her happy.

When she'd first started working for Declan, the freezer had been as bare as the cupboards. There had been snacks for Connor and a few staples, along with breakfast items, but little else. She was on a mission to change that. The big stand-up freezer in the mudroom was slowly filling up.

She tucked her list into her jeans back pocket then started for the store. After collecting a cart, she headed for the bakery. Her recent stress baking had provided them with plenty of goodies, but they still needed bread.

As she walked to the display of Connor's favorite bread, she passed a tall guy in a suit. She wouldn't have noticed him except for the panic in his voice as he said, "But there are so many. How can there be so many?"

Sunshine glanced at him and saw he was staring at a three-ring binder filled with pictures of decorated cakes. He flipped forward a couple of pages, then looked at the clerk waiting impatiently for him to decide.

"Which one?" he asked desperately.

"Sir, I have bagels I need to take out of the oven. If you could please make your choice by the time I get back, that would be great."

"But it's not really my area of expertise."

The guy was in his midthirties, more quirky looking than handsome. The suit was good quality and his shoes looked expensive, so an executive of some kind, she thought, telling herself to walk away. Instead she pushed her cart closer.

"Do you need help?" she asked.

The man turned to her and nodded vigorously. "Please. My sister is six months pregnant and was unexpectedly put on bed rest. Her husband is out of town and her daughter is turning three in two days. I need to order a princess cake for her. I thought it would be easy." He held up the binder. "There are eight princess cakes. How is that possible?"

Sunshine laughed. "There's more than one princess."

"Why?"

He looked genuinely confused by the whole thing, which was kind of refreshing and she liked that he was helping his sister.

She held out her hand. "I'll text her for you and find out."

"Really? You know what to ask?"

"I'm very princess literate."

She flipped through the binder, then quickly typed the names of the various princesses. When she was done, she handed him back the phone.

He read her text. "You know their names."

"I know. It's an impressive skill set."

"And useful."

His phone chimed. He glanced at the screen. "Belle. We need a Belle cake." He frowned. "Does that help?"

"It does." She turned to the correct page. "You want that one."

"It's *Beauty and the Beast*. That is not a princess cake."

"The beast was a prince."

"I don't think so."

She smiled. "Your niece is turning three. I wouldn't argue that point with her if I were you."

"Excellent advice. I'm Norris, by the way." He grimaced. "I know, I know. It's a family name, don't judge."

"Sunshine." She raised a shoulder. "So not really in a position to judge anyone's name."

Norris held out his hand. "Nice to meet you, Sunshine. Thank you so much for saving me. And the birthday party. The wrong cake would have been a disaster."

"I'm happy to help." She reached for her cart.

"Wait." Norris took a step toward her. "Can I thank you with a cup of coffee?"

"Not necessary."

He hesitated, as if not sure what to do, then he blurted, "I'm a financial planner, divorced for two years, no kids and I'm a really nice guy." He waved toward the cake displays. "Obviously. I'm helping out my sister. Just coffee."

He pulled a small leather case out of his jacket pocket and handed her a business card. She took it and scanned the information. It looked official enough and had both a work and cell number on it.

Was being picked up in a grocery store any better than a random guy stopping her in a parking lot? Or was it really about the location? Maybe the guy was more important. Norris seemed like one of the good ones and he had been willing to pick out a princess cake for his sister. That had to mean something.

She pulled a pen out of her handbag, then held out her hand for another card. She wrote her number on the back and handed it to him.

"Coffee," she said. "Sounds nice."

"Excellent." He beamed at her. "I'll be in touch."

Sunshine waved, then walked away. She wasn't sure if she'd just taken a big step toward something better or had completely screwed up. Again.

chapter
EIGHT

DECLAN FOUND HIMSELF EAGER TO GET HOME. SUN-
shine's text around eleven had made him chuckle. *We have ants!*
Connor would be thrilled and knowing his son was happy made
him happy, as well.

He didn't have to go out to the Malibu job site, so he was able
to leave work at five and be home by five-thirty. He walked in
from the garage and called out that he was back. Connor came
running and flung his arms around Declan's waist.

"Daddy, Daddy, they're here! Sunshine waited for them to arrive and kept them safe until I got home. We moved them into
the ant farm and they're really happy. Come see! Come see!"

Declan allowed his son to drag him into his room where the
ant farm sat on his desk.

"Sunshine says I should wait at least a month before getting
a second one. That I have to prove I can take care of them and
that I don't lose interest."

"Those are excellent points," Declan said, not bothering to
mention that there wasn't actually much to do when it came
to the ant farm. Making sure Connor wanted to pursue his ant
farm dreams was the main thing.

"Sunshine is really smart."

"She is."

And gorgeous and sexy as hell and the stuff sexual dreams were made of, none of which he would ever say and probably shouldn't think.

"I'm going to get changed, then let's check out what's for dinner."

"Okay, Dad. I'm going to watch my ants."

Declan kissed the top of his son's head before going into the master and changing into jeans and a T-shirt. He collected Connor on his way to the kitchen.

"We're having barbecue chicken tonight," Connor said. "And pasta salad. I helped with that. It was fun." He wrinkled his nose. "And roasted vegetables. Sunshine said the barbecue makes them better tasting but I don't know if that's true."

Declan saw the table was already set and Sunshine was indeed outside, at the barbecue. She already had a large platter of cooked chicken beside her, along with a few pieces of raw chicken. Apparently she'd been at the grill for a while.

"I'm going to check on Sunshine," he said. "Do you want—"

"I'm going back to my ants!" Connor yelled as he skipped down the hall.

Declan pulled a couple of beers out of the refrigerator before heading outside. Sunshine smiled when she saw him.

"Hi. How was your day?"

"Good." He handed her a beer. "You do realize barbecuing is man's work."

"I'm breaking down barriers left and right."

He nodded at the impressive pile of cooked chicken. "I'm not sure we're that hungry."

"I'll freeze it."

"That or you'll need to invite the neighborhood." He glanced toward the house. "Connor's very excited about the ants."

"I know. The transfer went very smoothly. I think the ant farm is going to be good for him."

"I agree."

It was something positive for Connor to focus on after the last few difficult months.

Sunshine motioned to the plate of cooked chicken. "Would you please take that inside for me? I'll put them away when they cool off. Dinner's going to be ready in about twenty minutes."

"You want me to barbecue for you?"

"What is it about men and outdoor cooking?"

"It's very primal."

"Apparently. Really, I can handle this. Go unwind from your day. I'll call you when dinner's ready."

"Yes, ma'am."

He carried the chicken inside and left it on the counter, then walked into the living room. The furniture was exactly the same as it had been since he and Iris had bought the house. Almost every room was. The only thing he'd changed had been the master bedroom. After she'd died, he'd hired a decorator to completely redo the room. A piss-poor way to try to exorcise ghosts, but it was the only thing he could think of to do.

Connor was doing better, he reminded himself. That was something. Time was helping him heal but he thought a lot of his improvement was due to Sunshine. She and Connor clicked and it was good to hear his son laughing again. Neither of them had laughed for a long time.

He knew he was still battling anger. Declan had been angry for so long, he wasn't sure who he would be if he let it go. He'd carried his rage around for months before Iris had told him she was sick. He'd had to pretend everything was fine for Connor's sake, but it hadn't been.

Even now he wondered if he should have left her. Would that have been better—a clean break? A divorce? Only what about Connor? There would have been the double blow. No, staying, however hellish, had been the right decision. Their son hadn't known Declan had slept on his home office sofa for months before Iris's diagnosis. He hadn't known his parents' marriage had been shattered to the point that it could never be repaired. At least as far as Declan knew. He'd never had the opportunity to make a decision one way or the other.

Maybe that was what pissed him off the most. There'd been no choice, no opportunity to talk about it, to work it out. Because right when he'd thought he might be willing to try, she'd told him she was dying. That the cancer she'd kept from him, the cancer that she'd assumed could be easily treated, had taken a turn and now she had less than a couple of months to live. A couple of months that had turned out to be three weeks. There had been only shock and disbelief and then she'd been gone.

Declan looked out the window, but saw instead the ridiculously sunny day of Iris's funeral. He'd been numb from shock, aware that while he would have to process his feelings at some point, all that mattered was Connor. Getting his son through his grief. His parents had moved in to help, he'd found a therapist for his son and had taken a couple of weeks off to start the transition.

All these months later, Connor was healing. Declan had no idea where he was on his own journey, but wasn't sure that mattered. Iris was gone and he honestly didn't know if he was sad about that or still angry or just plain exhausted by the whole thing.

"You don't have to help me clean up," Sunshine said as Declan carried dishes to the counter.

"I don't mind. You did all the cooking."

She laughed. "I always do all the cooking. It's part of my job description."

Within a day or two of his hiring her, she'd said she was happy to cook dinner every night but her days off. Declan had been relieved and had immediately increased her salary to reflect the new responsibilities.

"Is the cleaning service working out?" he asked. "Is once a week enough?"

"You and your son are surprisingly tidy, so yes. Once a week is fine."

"Let me know if you want them more often."

"I will."

While she rinsed the dishes and put them in the dishwasher, he wiped down the counters. They both finished at the same time. Declan picked up the bottle of wine.

"Another glass?"

She hesitated a second before nodding. "Sure. Thank you."

They sat on the bar stools at the island. He was careful to keep his distance. While he might find Sunshine the stuff of fantasies, he would never say or do anything to make her uncomfortable. She was great with his son and he didn't want to risk losing her.

"I'm glad the ant farm is a hit," she said.

"Me, too. He was so quiet after his mom died. It's good to hear him laughing and see him interested in things again."

"I'm sure it is. He's healing, Declan. I can see it happening in the few short weeks I've been here."

"Does he talk about his mom with you?"

"Sometimes. I know he misses her. When he seems sad, I ask him to tell me about her." She smiled. "He has some great memories. He's old enough that they should stay with him for the rest of his life."

"I hope so."

She picked up her wine, then put it down. "At the risk of going places I shouldn't, are you laughing much these days?"

"More than I was." An honest answer that avoided his ambivalence.

"Are you seeing anyone?"

He drew back so quickly, he nearly fell off his chair. "Are you asking if I'm dating?" He had to clear his throat and consciously lower his voice. "As in...dating?"

Her mouth twitched as if she were trying to hide a smile. "Yes, that was the question."

"It's only been five months. That's way too soon." Dating? He couldn't imagine it. How would that happen? Where would he meet someone and why would he want to?

"Okay, just checking. My point was going to be you might want to talk to Connor's therapist before introducing him to a new woman in your life. Maybe get some pointers on the best way to do it. I'm great with a barbecue and I can do a killer spelling test study session but I have zero experience with the loss of a parent in these circumstances."

Which meant she had some experience with the loss of a parent, he reasoned. Probably a topic he should follow up on, only he couldn't get the dating question out of his mind.

"Are you seeing someone?" he asked, then held up a hand. "Sorry. Not an appropriate question."

"Why not? Declan, I live in your house and cook your meals and do your laundry. I think it's okay for us to be friends."

"I'm not clear on the nanny rules." Except for the one that said he should in no way think she was hot.

"They're not very complicated. Mine is mostly that you should be a good dad. You're doing that one."

"You probably want the check to clear, as well."

She laughed. "Okay, yes. So those two." She drew in a breath. "I'm not seeing anyone. Things ended with my last boyfriend a few months ago and since then, I've been trying to do things differently."

"What does that mean?"

She looked at him. "I'm trying not to be dumb when it comes to men. I want to be less impulsive, more thoughtful. I want something real."

"Like falling in love?"

"More than that. Falling in love with someone who sees us having a future together. I want a guy who respects me as a person and doesn't just see me as a piece of ass." She winced. "Sorry. Saying that would be an example of my impulsive side."

He was too busy feeling guilty about his sexual feelings toward her to be bothered. "No apologies required. You're saying you want it to be…"

"Not about sex for once."

"I miss sex."

Declan had *not* intended to say that out loud. He was only supposed to think it. Horror swept through him as he frantically tried to figure out a way to call it back or unsay it or apologize.

"I'm sorry," he said quickly. "That was not what I meant."

Sunshine turned toward him, her eyes bright with laughter. "It's okay," she told him, her voice kind and a little amused. "I totally get it. You're saying it's too soon to get involved, but getting laid wouldn't be the end of the world."

"God, that sounds terrible, but yes."

"It sounds real and honest. You know, you can have sex without a relationship."

He stared at her. "Are you suggesting I hire a hooker?"

She burst out laughing. "No. You don't seem the type. I'm saying there are plenty of women who want a weekend fling with no attachments."

"Where?"

"Everywhere."

"Not in my world."

"You'd be surprised."

"I would be. Genuinely." He knew she wasn't one of them. Sunshine wanted more. "To be honest, I'm not sure that's my thing. I always preferred a relationship to go with my sex. Even in college, I wasn't that guy."

Her expression turned wistful. "That's really nice to hear. I like that there are good guys out there."

"Yes, and most of us aren't getting any."

She laughed again. "Try being open to the possibility."

"I think I'll just suffer instead. But what about what you want? You should be able to find anyone you want."

"It's not as easy as you'd think."

That couldn't be true. Not that he could discuss it with her. He'd already said too much. Later he would mull over the depressing fact that she hadn't so much as hinted that she found him to be the kind of man she would want to sleep with. Not that he was, or she would or any of that. Dear God, what was wrong with him?

"I hope we both get what we want," he said, struggling frantically for a way to gracefully change the topic.

She raised her glass. "Me, too. Whatever that turns out to be."

Bianca's bedroom was an architectural marvel. This was the first time Margot had been inside and she couldn't stop staring at the beautiful windows and the wood carvings around the doors. The ceiling was domed, the doorway to the bathroom arched and the combination of old world and modern blended seamlessly. If the main upstairs guest room was this nice, what must the master bedroom be like? Margot had to admit she had her first serious crush on a house.

She forced her attention back to the matter at hand—having Wesley over for cocktails that evening. Margot was very curious about the man who had won Bianca's heart. She had, of course, done her research on him and could easily do five minutes on his history and accomplishments, but that wasn't the same as meeting the man in person. Who was he? What qualities and characteristics had made Bianca fall in love with him and be so willing to change to fit into his world? She had high hopes that tonight many of her questions would be answered, but first they had to choose a wardrobe.

Margot pulled her attention away from the carved four-poster bed and the antique dresser to the woman she was working with. Bianca wore an oversize shirt tied at the waist, and leggings. On anyone else, the outfit was ordinary, even sloppy. But on her petite frame, with her gorgeous face and air of sensual grace, it was stunning in its simplicity.

Margot smiled. "This room suits you. All the drama and elegance are the perfect backdrop."

"That's the nicest thing you've ever said to me. Thank you. I like the room a lot. I'd change it if it was mine, of course, but Alec likes things to be traditional."

A quality Margot appreciated, not that she would say that to Bianca. It was important never to be seen taking sides.

Margot motioned toward the closet. "Shall we?"

"I really don't need your help picking out a dress for drinks at home," Bianca grumbled, even as she led the way.

"It isn't drinks at home," Margot reminded her. "It's drinks with a diplomat and a few friends."

"Same difference."

Bianca sounded like a pouty fourteen-year-old, which was probably the point. Bianca was interested in her lessons and remembered Cardiganian history easily, but there was always an undercurrent of defiance. As if she were going to start spray-painting the walls at any second. Or maybe Margot was just projecting. She'd been told Bianca was a certain way, had read about her antics and now she was looking for rebellion. Maybe Bianca had already changed and there was nothing to worry about.

They moved into a large walk-in closet. Dozens, or maybe hundreds, of dresses, long and short, filled one wall. Blouses, jeans and pants filled another. There were shelves overflowing with folded sweaters, racks and racks of shoes and handbags. Small handbags, totes, bucket bags and boxes with pictures showing elegant evening bags.

"Wow," Margot said, turning in a circle. "I'm speechless."

"I love clothes."

"And you look good in them. It's overwhelming but in a happy way. All right, what would you like to wear tonight?"

Bianca walked over to the wall of dresses and flipped through them. She pulled out three. One was a black bandage dress that dipped low in the front and, based on the thick elastic fabric, would fit as tight as plastic wrap. The second, also black, was a tiny slip dress with spaghetti straps. The third one was see-through black lace.

"All right," Margot said, looking at them then turning to her client. "What is the message you're trying to send tonight?"

"I have no idea what that means."

"It might help to think about events with Wesley as more than simply a social evening. What you'd wear to dinner in Malibu isn't the same thing you'd wear to a formal reception for a visiting dignitary. For our purposes, tonight is a cocktail reception. You're Wesley's fiancée. Based on the fact that we're pretending this is for his work, then he's representing his country. You're with him as the woman in his life, so in a way, you're doing the same. What message do you want to send to other guests?"

"Oh, I see what you're saying. What message?" Bianca thought for a second, then grinned. "That I have a rockin' hot bod."

Margot pressed her lips together. "While that's true, I'm not sure it's helpful to Wesley."

"Sure it is. If he can get the girl with the rockin' hot bod, he has power."

"Doesn't he have power anyway? And if this is a Wesley event, perhaps the attention shouldn't all be on you."

"But I like all the attention. It's who I am."

Margot wasn't sure what to say to that, so she kept quiet. Bianca looked back at the dresses she'd chosen.

"You want something more boring."

"I want something beautiful and appropriate. When it's just you and Wesley, wear what you'd like, but when it's for business, dress for the occasion. You'll still have a rockin' hot bod—but the image you present will be slightly more subtle. Think of this as a performance. You wouldn't wear spandex to play Lady Macbeth."

"I wouldn't ever play Lady Macbeth. Shakespeare was never my thing, but I get your point." One corner of her mouth turned up. "I'll make you a deal. I'll wear whatever you decide and you'll wear whatever I decide. We're about the same size."

Margot didn't like the sound of that. Not only was she several inches taller than Bianca, she was fairly sure she was a size or two larger.

"It will be fun," Bianca coaxed.

"I don't trust you," Margot said bluntly.

Bianca laughed. "You probably shouldn't. All right—I'll go first so you can see I'm playing fair."

She went to the racks of dresses and began to go through them. She started on a second rack, then a third before pulling out a lipstick-red dress.

On the hanger it didn't look like much at all—just skinny straps and a longish skirt. But there was something about the way it hung awkwardly that gave her pause.

"I'm not sure," she began.

Bianca shook it at her. "Try it on. I insist and, up until now, I've been a very cooperative client."

"That's true," Margot murmured, taking the dress and heading for the attached bathroom. "But I know I'm going to regret this."

She walked into the marble and glass bathroom. There was a huge walk-in shower, a soaking tub that could easily host a party, double sinks, a mile of vanity space and an entire wall of mirrors. There was genuinely no escaping her reflection.

Margot placed the hanger on a hook by the shower and immediately realized the reason the dress didn't look right was because it was clipped in place—the straps were in fact little more than strings.

Her stomach sank as she took the dress off the hanger and stared at it. There were cutouts. Bunches of them.

"This is a nightmare," she said aloud, then sighed heavily and unzipped her very plain, light gray sheath and let it slide to the floor. She took off her bra, because there was no way it would work, then slipped on Bianca's dress. Once it was in place, she sucked in her breath and pulled up the zipper. Miraculously, it closed easily. Then Margot faced herself in the mirror.

It wasn't as bad as she thought. The color was vibrant and flattering. The bodice fabric dipped to a deep V between her breasts, but was reinforced so there would be no unexpected wardrobe malfunction. There was a good-size cutout on each side of her waist which looked sexy but actually didn't show much. The skirt wasn't that tight and fell nearly to her knee. If she ignored the fact that she was showing more cleavage than usual, the dress was really okay. She hung up her sheath, then stepped back into the bedroom.

Bianca sat on the edge of the bed, her expression expectant. When she saw Margot, she clapped her hands together. "I love it! You look great. See—show a little skin and the world is your oyster."

"I'm not sure that's how the saying goes, but I get your point. You think I should add a little fun to my wardrobe."

"I think you should add a lot of sex to it. You're young and single. Trust me, you'll be old soon enough and then you'll regret all the wonderful things you didn't wear."

"Do you regret that?"

Bianca laughed. "No. I wasn't sharing an insight, Margot. I was really talking about you. Regrets? Not like that." She laughed again, then bounded to her feet. "So you'll wear it tonight?"

"Yes."

"I'm so glad. All right, a deal's a deal. Dress me for a funeral. I'll try not to complain."

"You're not going to a funeral so that wouldn't be appropriate."

"Now you sound like Alec."

A nice compliment, Margot thought.

She returned to the closet and took her turn at flipping through dozens of dresses. It didn't take long for her to notice a trend—anything not remotely glamorous or revealing still had its tags.

She held up a long-sleeved brown dress that looked frumpy enough to insult a woman in her eighties. "Why did you buy it if you're never going to wear it?"

"I have no idea. Maybe it was a gift."

Margot smiled. "No one who's met you would ever give you this dress."

"You're not going to make me wear it?"

"Of course not. I want you to look as if you belong. I'm not here to punish you."

"Just checking."

Margot looked at ten or fifteen more dresses before pulling out a smoky-blue lace dress. It was sleeveless, with a high neckline. The pattern of the lace was exquisite and the dress looked as if it would flow down to midcalf. She handed it to Bianca.

"This one."

Bianca pouted. "It's so plain."

"It's beautiful and elegant and appropriate." She allowed herself a small smile. "And fitted enough to show off your rockin' hot bod."

Bianca rolled her eyes. "Whatever."

Instead of disappearing into the bathroom, she stepped out of her clothes right there, then slid into the dress. After pulling it up, she turned her back so Margot could fasten the long zipper. Together they walked into the bathroom and its wall of mirrors.

The dress was perfection. It was snug enough to emphasize every curve, yet wasn't tight or overly revealing. The color made

Bianca's blue eyes even darker and turned her skin luminous. The lace would be perfect for a cocktail party.

"Oh." Bianca stared at herself for a couple of seconds. "I suppose it's not *too* hideous."

"Stop it," Margot said mildly. "You look incredible and you know it." She moved behind her and twisted her hair up. "I assume you know how to put your hair up?"

"Yes."

"And you have diamond earrings?"

"Does a bear shit in the woods?"

Margot pressed her lips together. "Let's leave the colloquial expressions at home tonight, shall we?"

Bianca sighed heavily. "You don't have a boyfriend right now, do you? We should work on that."

Margot ignored the statement. "So you'll wear that dress tonight?"

"If you wear yours."

"Fine."

"Double fine."

"I'll see you downstairs as six," Margot said, grabbing her old dress and walking out of the bathroom.

chapter
NINE

I'm going to regret this.

MARGOT SENT THE TEXT TO HER SISTER AND WAITED. Seconds later, she had a reply.

You shouldn't. You look amazing. Even if you take the worst selfies ever. If you weren't my sister, I would back the car over you.

Margot chuckled.

You talk so tough and it's all a total lie.

Only because I love you. Enjoy your faux cocktail party.

I'll do my best.

Margot put away her phone, freshened her makeup, picked out a pair of nude pumps she would put on at the last minute, then made her way downstairs. Once she reached the kitchen, she tucked her shoes in the corner, then walked barefoot to the counter where Edna had left serving dishes and instructions.

The woman was a marvel. Despite the fact that they were having cocktails for four, Edna had prepared a half-dozen food items, along with nuts and olives. After slipping on an apron, Margot read the detailed instructions through before going back to the top.

She turned on both ovens and got the crab puffs and the stuffed mushrooms out of the refrigerator. Both were already on cookie sheets and would simply be popped in the ovens when they reached temperature. She poured nuts and olives into serving bowls and took them out to the table by the wet bar. Glasses, small plates, forks and napkins were already in place.

On her return trip to the kitchen, she paused to admire the ceilings at least twenty feet up. The tower bell was still in place, as was much of the stained glass. Everyone should get the opportunity to stay in an amazing house at least once in their lives, she thought as she returned to the kitchen.

Edna had freshly sliced and toasted bread for the bruschetta. All Margot had to do was put on the toppings. She'd just set out ingredients when Alec walked into the kitchen.

Her first thought was that he looked good. He was always attractive, but the dark suit and contrasting white shirt was especially appealing. When he saw her, he frowned.

"What are you doing?"

"Getting the food ready for our cocktail party."

"That isn't part of your job."

"Yes, it is. Not to worry. I won't be actually cooking. Edna left me instructions on how to assemble. She said it was super easy and even I couldn't mess it up."

He smiled at her. It was a nothing smile—casual and amused. It was the kind of smile you gave a stranger, and yet there was something about it. Something that settled low in her belly and made her think about possibilities. Or if not think about them then certainly hope for them. Which was completely and totally ridiculous. She barely knew the man. Most days their only contact was when they nodded at each other at breakfast. He said good morning, she said the same, then she took her breakfast and left. Alert the media—it was the romance of the century!

"I seriously doubt Edna said anything like that," he told her.

She'd been so busy taking her imagination train to a non-existent destination, she had to figure out what he meant.

"Not in so many words," she admitted. "But the meaning was clear. Edna doubts my cooking ability."

"Is there reason to?"

She laughed. "I have a few skills, but they are nothing when compared to my sister, who can cook anything and make it delicious. Regardless, tonight I will assemble with the best. Oh, and she mentioned you would be acting as bartender. I hope that's all right."

"Of course. It's only the four of us and my mother raised me to be the kind of gentleman who makes an excellent martini."

"Good to know."

He raised an eyebrow. "I detect a lack of enthusiasm. Not a martini drinker?"

"I am, I confess, more of a margarita girl."

His dark gaze met hers. "Excellent. When our guest of honor arrives, I will impress you with my bartending skills."

"I look forward to being impressed. Now if you'll excuse me, I need to tend to the bruschetta."

Alec nodded, then surprised her by taking off his jacket and literally rolling up his shirtsleeves before walking to the sink and washing his hands.

"What are you doing?"

"Preparing to help."

"But I can do it."

"It will go faster this way."

She told herself not to read anything into his actions. He was just being polite. Still, she was more than a little fluttery, which was unexpected and made her nervous, which was probably why she accidently blurted, "I feel as if this is the least I can do.

Helping out with the party, I mean. Your mother is doing so well with her lessons and practice sessions. I'm not totally sure why she hired me."

Alec wiped his hands on a towel, then looked at her. "You mean that?"

"Of course. She's a little eccentric and I worry about her wardrobe choices, but otherwise, she's been attentive and interested in learning about the history of Wesley's country and everything else we've talked about."

As she spoke she got out the toasted bread slices and the toppings.

"Let's give it a couple of weeks before you make any judgments," he told her. "There are still a few things to be worked out."

"If you say so." Margot wondered if Bianca had mellowed more than he'd realized. Sometimes it was hard for adult children to see their parents as people with separate lives.

They went to work on the rest of the appetizers. Margot stirred fresh chopped chives into softened cream cheese, then spread it on the bread and topped it with the mushroom mixture. Alec prepared the more traditional bruschetta, topping the bread with diced fresh tomatoes and feta. They both finished as the oven dinged.

"I'll take care of that and set everything up if you want to take care of the drinks," she said.

"One excellent margarita coming up."

"Now I'm curious."

She pulled the cookie sheets from the ovens and slid the various appetizers onto serving plates, then carried them into the living room. Bianca was already there, waiting while Alec poured her a martini.

"Isn't this lovely," she said, her gaze darting around the room. "Stifling monastery meets munchies. Whatever will people say?"

Bianca's sharp tone surprised Margot. As far she knew, Bianca loved the house so what was up with the "stifling" comment?

Rather than respond, she took in Bianca's appearance. She'd pinned up her hair, had put on dangling diamond earrings and strappy high-heeled sandals. Her makeup was subtle while still bringing attention to her beautiful face.

"You look like a model for *Vogue*," Margot said honestly. "Seriously, Bianca, you take my breath away."

"The dress is frumpy," Bianca grumbled.

"It's classy," Alec corrected, handing her the martini.

"I feel old." Bianca swallowed half her drink in a single gulp. "This was a ridiculous idea. I should text Wesley and tell him to forget it. We'll go get burgers or something. What was I thinking?"

Bianca's tension was palpable and surprising. Margot lightly touched her arm. "We've been working on some breathing exercises. They always make me feel better. Make sure you're inhaling to your stomach. Short shallow breaths increase anxiety."

Bianca finished her drink, then held out her glass to Alec. "One more, please. There's a good boy." She swung her gaze back to Margot. "Anxious? You couldn't be more wrong. I'm fine and you might want to put on some shoes."

Margot had totally forgotten she was still barefoot and wearing an apron. Not exactly the example she wanted to set. She returned to the kitchen and reappeared a few seconds later. Alec was pouring her margarita over ice. When he turned and saw her, his eyes widened slightly, as if taken aback by her appearance.

She felt herself flush. "Yes, well, your mother and I had a deal. I got to pick out her dress and she got to pick out mine. Not that this is something I own because, while it's lovely, it's a designer dress and I've never owned anything... I mean, it's your mother's. But it's really pretty and I should stop talking now."

"Yes, you should," Bianca told her. "You look great. If my monk-like son noticed, then my work here is done. Oh, there's the doorbell. I'll get it."

Margot looked after her. "She's in a mood."

"Still think you're not needed?"

Bianca returned with a tall, thin man at her side. Wesley Goswick-Chance wasn't the most handsome man, but he had an air of confidence that was appealing. He wore glasses and a suit that had obviously been custom-made for him, and when he looked at Bianca, it was as if the sun had finally returned after a six-year absence.

Bianca waved toward Margot. "Here she is, Wesley. The woman who is going to fix me. Or at least try."

Wesley smiled and shook Margot's hand. "Lovely to meet you. I'm sure you'll agree that my darling Bianca is exquisite exactly as she is."

"I do agree. Completely."

Wesley handed over a medium-size gift bag. "Just a little something."

"Thank you. Shall I look inside now?"

"Whatever you'd like."

Margot guided everyone to the seating area. Alec handed Wesley a Scotch and poured one for himself, as well. Margot opened the gift bag and pulled out a beautiful cardigan sweater. The wool was delicate and soft, dyed in what seemed to be a thousand shades of blue.

"It's lovely," she told Wesley. "Thank you so much. You're very thoughtful. I will think of your wonderful country every time I wear it."

"Oh dear God," Bianca grumbled. "Isn't that laying it on a bit thick? I mean it's nice, but it's a sweater."

Alec looked uncomfortable but Wesley only laughed and captured Bianca's hand in his. "My delightful Bianca always speaks her mind. It's so refreshing."

"It is," Alec murmured.

Margot made a mental note to discuss erring on the side of graciousness when in a social situation. She would also have Bianca help her write her thank-you note.

She thought about how this Bianca—sharp, almost brittle— was so different from the woman who had negotiated who wore what and who sometimes insisted on ten-minute dance breaks during her lessons.

"Have you been to Cardigania?" Wesley asked her.

"I haven't," Margot told him. "But I hear it's lovely."

"It is. Bianca visited once, but only for a short time." He squeezed her hand. "We're trying to get something scheduled."

Bianca offered a tight smile. "We are. I can't wait."

The words were right, but the panic in her eyes told Margot that Bianca was terrified to visit Cardigania and Margot had no idea why. The visit wouldn't be for formal state business. No doubt they would do touristy things. Of course she would be meeting Wesley's friends and colleagues and that could be stressful.

"Do you enjoy travel?" Wesley asked Margot.

"I do. Like most people, I have a bucket list of places I'd like to visit. My problem is I don't really enjoy the one-week stay. I like to really get to know a place. Talk to the people and see what their everyday lives are like. Not that I don't love a beautiful sandy beach like everyone else."

Alec took his mother's now-empty glass and rose. "Where have you traveled to?" he asked Margot.

"I spent a month in Thailand while I was in college," she said, leaving out the part where she'd nearly flunked all her classes because of it. "I've been to Germany a few times, and in the *did you really* category, I've hiked through much of Patagonia."

"Very eclectic," Wesley said. "I've never been to Patagonia."

"It's beautiful. Rugged and impressive."

She rose and walked to the food table, then carried several serving plates to the large coffee table in front of the sofa. If Bianca was going to keep downing martinis, she was going to need some food in her stomach.

She offered Bianca the crab puffs. The older woman took two and ate them, but wouldn't meet her gaze. Margot knew there was important information to be had, if only she could figure out what it was. Later, she promised herself. Later she would make some notes and brainstorm what on earth was happening. It was just the four of them—Bianca shouldn't be this nervous.

Conversation shifted to where everyone else had traveled. There was a second round of drinks for the three of them and a fourth round for Bianca. After an hour, Wesley rose and thanked them for the invitation.

"My love and I have dinner reservations."

Margot told him it had been lovely to meet him, then let Alec walk him to the door. She carried the food back into the kitchen, thinking there was enough for twenty and not only would this be her dinner, but her lunch tomorrow and there would still be a ton leftover. Alec joined her a couple of minutes later and set down the platters he'd brought in.

"Your thoughts?" he asked, setting them on the counter.

She hesitated. While she wouldn't discuss her client with him, she could certainly speak in generalities without violating any privacy. After all, he'd been right there.

"She was so much more nervous than I expected," she admitted. "I know having me observing can be nerve-racking but I didn't expect her to be so out of sorts."

"Or drink so much? That happens sometimes. Not often, but it's never a good sign. It means trouble is coming, although tonight that's going to be Wesley's problem."

He sounded more resigned than judgmental. Margot would guess he was long used to Bianca's idiosyncrasies.

"This gave me some material to work with," she said.

"You're very diplomatic."

"Part of the job."

He flashed her another of those sexy-to-her smiles, then opened a cupboard and pulled out a couple of plates. "Want to join me for an appetizer dinner? There's plenty to go round."

"I can see that and thank you for the invitation." She probably should take her food upstairs, as per her policy, but this was just one meal. "As long as you don't mind if I take off my shoes. They're really uncomfortable."

"Then why did you buy them?"

"They're gorgeous."

"That is a thing I will never understand."

"It's because your gender isn't judged on its shoes. You get to be all powerful and successful simply by slapping on a suit." She stepped out of her shoes and then picked up a couple of platters and carried them to the table by the window.

"How exactly does one slap on a suit?" he asked, his voice teasing.

"You know what I mean."

He chuckled.

While she collected flatware and napkins, he pulled a bottle of wine from an under-counter cellar and opened it. She set out glasses and they sat across from each other, the food between them.

Margot put both kinds of bruschetta on her plate, along with a couple of crab puffs, then added a few carrot sticks and slices of red pepper for balance.

"Tell me about the travel," Alec said. "How did you spend a month in Thailand? Just as a tourist?"

"Not exactly." She sipped her wine as she debated what to say before settling on the truth. "I went with the bad boyfriend."

Alec drew his eyebrows together. "Ah, what did you call him? A piece of..."

She laughed. "Yes, that would be him. His name is Dietrich. He's from Germany and was an exchange student in high school. He fell in love with the States and LA in particular and ended up studying film at USC. He'd just graduated when I met him. He was doing documentaries and short films and I got sucked into it all."

Alec leaned back in his chair. "So what's the bad for you part?"

"I was weak and feckless when I was around him. He would say 'come to Thailand with me' and off I would go. For a month.

In the middle of my semester. I nearly flunked all my classes—
it was a disaster. I lost my scholarship, which about killed me
financially. You'd think I'd learn, but nope. Not even a little.
He would show up and off I would go."

"Still?"

His tone was neutral and his expression was friendly enough,
so she had no idea what he was thinking. Some version of "but
she looks so smart" seemed fair, but she doubted he would say
that out loud.

"I'm in recovery," she said lightly. "The last straw was when
I missed my dream-job interview because I didn't get back from
Patagonia in time. Ultimately that screwup led me to the job
I have now, which I love, but still. Missing the interview was
a real wake-up call. I stopped seeing him. He shows up every
couple of years and tries to tempt me to do something wild with
him. Thus far I've resisted."

"At least you didn't marry him."

"Marriage was never on the table. Dietrich isn't the marrying kind." He was more the "let's have hot sex in the backseat
of my car" type, but why say that?

She shrugged. "Regardless, I learned my lesson. I refuse to
make bad decisions based on a man."

"I agree that uncontrolled emotions can be dangerous," he
said. "Or rather, emotions that tempt us to do things not in our
best interest. You have quite the romantic past. By comparison,
my love life is ordinary and rather boring."

"I envy you."

"I doubt that. So tell me about Patagonia. Did you enjoy your
time there?"

Three hours passed in what felt like minutes and it was nearly
ten when they finally left the table. After putting everything
away, they said good-night and Margot headed up the stairs,
her shoes in hand.

Alec was a good guy, she thought. He would never ask a woman to give up her life to follow him on whatever adventure he had in mind. He would never get so angry, she was afraid he would hit her. He would be more thoughtful and caring. Not that it mattered. She doubted he was all that impressed by her. Her relationship with Dietrich put her firmly in the dumb blonde category and he wasn't the kind of man to find that the least bit attractive.

Sunshine signed in at the main office of the elementary school and then was directed to the auditorium.

"Are you going to the meeting, too?" a woman asked as she fell into step with her. "Why do they do this? Hold them at two in the afternoon? It's the middle of the workday and not all of us are stay-at-home moms." She grimaced. "Sorry. It's been one of those days and sometimes I rant. I'm Phoebe Salvia."

"Sunshine. Hi. What grade are your kids in?"

"I just have the one. Elijah. He's in third grade."

Sunshine smiled. "I'm with Connor. He and Elijah are friends."

"Right. They are." Phoebe, a pretty redhead in a power suit, studied her for a second. "You're the nanny?"

"Uh-huh."

"I figured. I remember when Iris died. It was so fast and we were all shocked. Poor Connor. He was so sad. I mean any kid would be. How's Declan doing?"

"He keeps busy with work and being a dad. It's tough on both of them."

They walked into the auditorium and took seats together. Someone came by and handed them a sheet of paper with the agenda for their meeting. Sunshine scanned it.

They were going to talk about the end of year field trip for third graders and the all-school bake sale in a few weeks.

"A bake sale," Phoebe grumbled. "There are days I don't have time to shower, let alone bake. Maybe on the weekend when Elijah is with his dad. It's not like I'm busy dating."

She slapped her hand over her mouth. "Oh my God! Listen

to me. I'm so sorry. I'm actually a very nice person who is kind to animals and doesn't spend her whole life bitching. I'm sorry. Maybe I'm getting my period."

Sunshine laughed. "It's okay. We all have days."

"Thank you for saying that, even if you don't mean it." She sighed. "Let me guess. You'll be baking something from scratch, won't you?"

Sunshine thought about the items in the freezer, left over from her stress baking. "Probably. I'm happy to share, if you'd like. Brownies, or some cookies."

"I might have to take you up on that." She leaned back in her seat. "I used to be a great mom, back when I was married. There was more time. My ex isn't a bad guy, but he's busy with his new social life and sometimes Elijah isn't as interesting to him as his hottie of the week." She looked at Sunshine. "Are you married?"

"No. It would be difficult, given what I do."

"You live in?"

Sunshine nodded.

Phoebe sighed. "A live-in nanny. That sounds like heaven. If I ever win the lotto, I'm so hiring a live-in nanny. And a masseuse. And a chef."

"Sounds like a plan."

The principal walked onto the stage and spoke into the microphone at the lectern. "Thank you so much for coming this afternoon. I'll keep the meeting brief so you can all return to your busy lives."

"Or lotto fantasies," Phoebe whispered.

Sunshine held in a laugh. The other woman was really engaging. Pretty and funny with a kid Connor's age. Maybe she and Declan could…

Sunshine hesitated, not sure exactly how to describe what they could be to each other. Declan had said he missed sex and

Phoebe seemed nice. Not that it was her job to help him get laid, it was just…

Awkward, she told herself. She would keep her mouth shut and stay out of her boss's personal life. Besides, for all his claim of it being too soon, she doubted Declan would be happy with a sex-only relationship. He'd admitted he was a more get-involved type. No doubt he would have the choice of anyone he wanted. He was a great guy—sexy and kind and sweet. Not that she was going there herself. She knew better. Sex with the boss would be a disaster. Great for the night, but really bad in the morning. Besides, she wanted something different. Something real and permanent and emotionally healthy.

Sunshine forced her attention back to the meeting and took a few notes for dates and times. She and Phoebe walked out together and promised to stay in touch. Sunshine had just made it to her car when she got a text. She glanced at the screen.

Thanks again for your help last week. The party was a big hit, as was the cake. I've asked twice and you've put me off, so this is my last attempt. Would you please join me for coffee?

She got into her car, but instead of starting the engine, she considered the invitation. On the surface Norris met her qualifications. He seemed stable, he had a job, he cared about his family and he was divorced, so not married. Why not go out with him? If nothing else, he would be practice. Her instinct was to always be that girl and it would take time to break the pattern.

She texted back a quick Coffee sounds great before pulling out of the parking lot and heading home. She had a date with a normal guy. It was a step in the right direction and therefore progress. So yay her.

chapter
TEN

MARGOT DIDN'T SEE BIANCA ALL DAY MONDAY. AROUND nine-thirty in the morning she got a text from her client saying she was going to spend the day with Wesley. Margot had gotten up early to take a long run to help her think through what she wanted to talk about. Bianca bailing on her was a little disconcerting. She used the time to go check on her apartment, then spent the rest of the day revamping her action plan and, while Alec was helping a visiting scholar, had spent a glorious thirty minutes studying the incredible maps in his office.

Bianca had been on edge while waiting for Wesley and once he'd arrived, things had only gotten worse. The four drinks in less than an hour was a problem, as was the biting tone. For nearly two weeks Bianca had been engaged, funny and easy to work with. Sunday night it had all gone to hell. So why? Margot understood being nervous, but that should have faded fairly quickly. No one was there to judge her or try to make her uncomfortable. But something had happened and until Margot figured out what, she wasn't going to make any progress.

Close to six o'clock, she got up and stretched. She was stiff from too much sitting, she thought. She wasn't hungry enough to want dinner and reading a book was too much like what she'd been doing all day. Perhaps inspired by the maps she'd seen earlier, she grabbed the flashlight she'd brought from home and headed for the small staircase that led to the attic.

She'd only found the stairs by accident while she'd been looking for extra towels. She'd opened what she thought was a cupboard door in the hallway and had discovered the steep, narrow staircase that could almost pass for a ladder. She'd been too busy then to go snooping but now she had an entire evening free to poke around.

She turned on the light at the bottom of the stairs, then made sure she could get out if someone closed the door behind her. Edna and her crew were gone, Bianca was still with Wesley and Alec rarely ventured upstairs, so the odds of her getting locked in were unlikely but she wanted to be sure.

Once she confirmed the door opened from the inside, she scrambled up the stairs only to find herself in front of a locked door. She rattled the handle a couple of times in frustration.

"Not fair," she murmured aloud, thinking she could go ask Alec for a key. Assuming he even knew where it was. She was about to turn around when she impulsively stretched up to run her fingers along the top of the door frame. There was plenty of dust and something that felt a lot like a key.

"Gotcha!"

She blew off the key and put it in the lock. The door opened easily.

The attic was dark and musty, the ambient temperature still warm from the sunny day. She clicked on her flashlight and used it to check for a light switch. She found one on the wall, about three feet from the door. She turned it on, then spun slowly to take in the room.

The attic space was large—probably covering the entire second floor, right up to Bianca's room. There weren't any windows but she saw small grates that would provide some kind of air circulation. Part of the open area was still framed, as if defining incredibly small rooms. For the monks. She would guess the attic would have been used as sleeping quarters for the monks.

There were stacks of old-fashioned school desks piled up against a wall. In one corner were boxes of old robes. She found a metal container filled with medical supplies, most of which were so old she had no idea what they were, and another tin box had a ledger containing neat columns of what the monastery had purchased from local farms from 1912 until 1921.

She spent about a half hour more exploring, then retraced her steps and went back to her room. She brought the ledger with her, thinking she would show it to Alec. While it didn't qualify as an unknown ancient language, it was still a part of his home's history.

Thinking of Alec made her remember the previous night. At first she'd been confused as to why he thought his mother couldn't change. The more she learned about his childhood, the more she understood his reasoning. Her actions at the cocktail party had illustrated that he must have had some challenges with her when he'd been growing up.

She would imagine that his life of solitude and study was in direct reaction to his mother's impulsiveness. Here Alec controlled all he surveyed. And yet he'd let Bianca move in for a couple of months and had helped find someone to work with her. Like most people, he was a mass of contradictions, but on him, those contradictions looked good.

She set the ledger on her dresser, then headed downstairs to make something for dinner. She briefly considered popping into Alec's office and asking if he would like to join her. She'd enjoyed talking to him the previous night. She'd liked getting to know him better and the man was certainly easy to look at.

She paused on the bottom stair, not sure what to do. Her head pointed out that she was an employee of his mother's and it was best if their lives were kept as separate as possible. Her heart was fairly silent on the matter, and her girl bits thought Alec had real potential.

Margot was a believer in the philosophy of *When in doubt, don't,* so she headed purposefully for the kitchen, ignoring the wave of regret that washed over her. Her brain went into sanctimonious mode, pointing out that it wasn't as if Alec had come looking for her, either. There hadn't been a single sign from him that he saw her as anything other than another staff member. At which point Margot thought that maybe it was time to start working on integrating the various parts of her body into a single—

"Hello."

Margot jumped and spun toward the voice. Bianca was sitting on a bar stool by the big island, a bowl of ice cream in front of her.

"You startled me," Margot said, pressing a hand to her chest. "How was your day with Wesley?"

"Wonderful. I've been thinking about the formal dinner party you want to have. Well, let's get it scheduled. The sooner the better."

Margot took a seat at the island. Bianca looked as beautiful as ever. Her eyes were clear, her hair perfectly curled. She had on a silk blouse tucked into tight jeans. There was no hint of the slightly frantic almost-bitch she'd been the night before.

"There are some things we have to work on before the party," she said carefully. "Last night didn't go as smoothly as I'd hoped."

Bianca dismissed her with a wave of her spoon. "Nonsense. It went perfectly. You said you were going to invite your sister and her little boy?"

"Connor is the child she takes care of. Sunshine is a nanny. I thought they could both come, along with the gentleman she works for. Declan. He designed the gardens here at the monastery."

"That sounds perfect." Bianca beamed a million-dollar smile.

"We'll have Edna come up with an exciting menu and you can teach me which fork to use. It will be such fun."

"Bianca, why are you trying to distract me?"

Bianca's eyes widened. "I have no idea what you're talking about. You're the one who wanted the dinner party. I'm saying let's go for it."

"Yes, and I appreciate that. But you're avoiding the conversation about last night. We need to talk about it."

Bianca sighed heavily and dug her spoon into the bowl. "Fine. Talk. I was horrible. What was I thinking? Wrong me. There, are we finished?"

Margot genuinely couldn't process all the information Bianca was throwing at her. Most of it was in code, but it was there, if only she could figure it out.

She leaned toward her client. "You weren't horrible at all. You obviously love Wesley and he seems like such a great guy. I'm glad you're happy with him. And it's wonderful how you want to make sure you fit in so you don't jeopardize his job."

Bianca's gaze was wary. "But? Because there's always a but and it's never good."

"We all react when we're nervous. We all have a default position we take to defend ourselves. But for some people, going on the offense is a stronger position. I think you might be like that."

Margot smiled gently. "If you make the conversation about the other person in a disarming way, you deflect attention and give yourself a chance to regroup. You don't have to think when you lash out, which means you haven't done anything to mitigate your anxiety."

"I don't lash out," Bianca snapped. "Who would I lash out at? Alec? Are you saying I'm a bad mother?"

Her reaction had headed the direction Margot wanted, but it was more intense than expected. Yet something else to mull later.

"You're one of the bravest single mothers I know," Margot said. "You literally gave your son the world. All the places he got to visit when he was young, all the experiences he shared with you. I know you two were a team. Yet when he was a little older, you let him go to boarding school, even knowing he was going to be so far away. I don't think I could have done that. I think I'm way too selfish."

Bianca's entire body relaxed as her expression softened. "I had to let him go. It was what he wanted."

Margot smiled. "Yet more love. I admire that and I'm a little envious. My mom took off when my sister and I were still toddlers."

"Did she really? That's awful. How could—" Bianca's eyes narrowed. "Wait a minute. You did that on purpose. You totally changed the subject."

"Yes. When I did, your energy changed, too. You were able to breathe and be a part of the conversation. You weren't defensive or angry anymore. You felt my interest and empathy. It's something I think you could easily learn. You already have acting skills that would be a big help. When you feel stressed or nervous, energy builds up. One way or another, it's going to dissipate. Why not help that happen in a positive way?"

"Instead of drinking too much?"

"Exactly. Alcohol doesn't really make the situation better. It simply masks the problem."

Some of the wariness returned. "You think you're so smart."

"I think I know what I'm doing, otherwise why hire me?"

"I'll consider it." Bianca rose and carried her melting ice cream to the sink. After setting it down, she turned back to Margot.

"I still want to have the dinner party right away."

"I'll talk to Edna in the morning."

"See that you do."

With that, Bianca flounced out of the room. Margot stared after her. She would guess they'd moved past the easy, pleasant part of the training and into the more difficult work. On the bright side, she did love a challenge.

★ ★ ★

When Margot walked into the dining room for breakfast the next day, she noticed two things at once: that Alec wasn't reading the paper and that there was a second place setting at the table.

She hadn't seen him the previous day—her early morning run had meant she'd missed the simple buffet—so today was the first breakfast since their post–cocktail party dinner.

"Good morning," he said when he saw her. He motioned to the extra place setting. "You're more than welcome to take a tray back up to your room if you'd prefer, but if you'd like to stay and eat at the table, I would enjoy the company."

An odd fluttery sensation set up shop in her belly, making her suddenly not know what to do with her hands. Or her brain.

"I, ah, that would be nice. Can you give me just one minute?"

She hurried out of the room and ran back upstairs. After collecting the ledger, she returned to the dining room and set the old leather-bound book next to him.

"I found this last night," she said as she poured herself coffee. "It dates back to 1912 and details all the purchases made by the monks. There are also some unexpected trades. Did you know the monks raised honey?" She reached for a plate. "I guess I mean they raised bees and harvested honey. Also, they had quite the herd of donkeys that were relatively expensive. Donkeys and honey. Who knew?"

While Bianca got a little outrageous when she was nervous, Margot knew she got too chatty. She scooped eggs onto her plate, added a couple of slices of bacon, along with a croissant, then told herself to stop talking.

Alec flipped through the ledger. "Where did you find this?"

"Up in the attic. There's a lot up there. Some of it is just trash, but there are some historical items that probably should be cataloged. They might be of interest to the local historical society or a university."

He looked at her and smiled. "You're not afraid to go into the attic at night?"

"No. Ghosts aren't my thing. And you'll be pleased to know there wasn't a single skeleton to be found."

"That is lucky."

She picked up her coffee. "The attic needs more exploring. After that, I'm going to be going through the cellar. I'll do my best not to see any bones there, either."

"I appreciate that." He studied her. "I've lived here nearly five years and I've never done much more than go pick out wine in the cellar." He smiled. "I always knew if I got started exploring, I wouldn't stop until I'd combed every inch of the place and I haven't had the time. I see I should have made more of an effort."

"Absolutely. People lived here and died here for centuries. Every inch of it is beautiful. The carvings, the stained glass windows, the bell. Your house is very swoonworthy."

"Is that how we're describing it?" His voice was teasing. "I'll accept the compliment on my house's behalf."

"You should."

They smiled at each other. She felt a little *zing* of tension, which she ignored. It was enough to know Alec saw her as more than an appliance. She wasn't going to push her luck. Still, it was nice to find a man other than Dietrich attractive. It meant there was hope for her after all.

"How are things with my mother?" he asked. "I didn't see her around yesterday."

"She stayed with Wesley until the early evening," Margot admitted. "I got a text in the morning telling me she was skipping our lesson."

"Are you surprised?"

"A little, but I'm trying to understand her more. She wants me to get the formal dinner scheduled as quickly as possible."

"You sound worried."

"I hope she's enthused because she wants the practice and not as a distraction. I just don't know which it is."

"Does it matter?"

"Your mother is an intelligent woman—she could easily learn all the skills and customs she needs to be successful as Wesley's wife. Which fork goes where isn't the problem. It's something deeper. A belief system. I'm starting to think she acts out because she doesn't know what else to do in the moment. But knowing that is only half the battle. If I don't know why, then it's harder to overcome."

"I understand your point, but I'm afraid I have no insight."

"That's okay. Are you still willing to have the dinner here?"

"Of course, but I might need to be schooled in the correct fork to use."

She smiled. "We'll have a refresher course before we head into the meal. I texted my sister last night and she spoke with her boss. They are happy to come. They're bringing Connor, who's eight. So the seven of us. I'll speak to Edna today about a menu." She smiled. "Sunshine said Connor told her icky grown-up food was okay as long as there was a good dessert."

"I'm with Connor. Any dress code? Shall we go black tie?"

As much as she would love to see him in a tux… "I think we can wear regular clothes for the dinner. To be honest, I'm not sure I'm up for another round of what's appropriate to wear with your mother. I've reached the place where I need to pick my battles and right now, that's not one of them."

"Knowing your limitations is the sign of a sound mind."

"I shall embroider that on a pillow."

James and Jessica Neal were earnest, stubborn and unbelievably rich—traits Declan had never had a problem with separately or together. Until today. As the thirtysomething couple changed their minds, yet again, he gazed longingly at the large windows in the conference room at his offices and wondered if the three-story fall would maim him enough to get him off the project.

Heath Harter, his business partner, caught his gaze and nodded toward the windows, as if he, too, were suggesting they risk the consequences.

"It's just we want to use as much acreage as we can," Jessica said, her soft tone insistent. "We're totally invested in making this property the best it can be—for our guests and everyone in the community. We want to be a good business neighbor."

An admirable trait that had absolutely nothing to do with the conversation at hand.

"I'm sure the local residents appreciate that," Declan said, hoping his impatience didn't show in his voice. "It speaks well of you two and the project. However, what we're discussing is whether or not you want us to design a walking trail up into the mountains."

James, a bland-looking man with a receding hairline, smiled at his wife. "He's right, Jess. Let's stay on the walking trails. We like them, right?"

She nodded. "We do. But do we want walking or hiking and if we're talking hiking, aren't there different levels of hikes? Plus, we don't want to scare any wild animals or hurt indigenous plants."

Of course not, Declan thought. *God forbid you disturbed a leaf with a walking trail when you've just ripped out three acres to put up a damned hotel.*

Heath quickly put several large sheets of paper on the conference table, because James and Jessica weren't into PowerPoint presentations. It wasn't organic when it was on a screen.

"Here's what we were thinking," he said, as he pointed to the first sheet. "We start with an easy walking trail from the rear gardens. It will be well marked, lit with solar lights and have benches along the way. Once we reach the end of the manicured gardens, there will be three hiking trails all heading into the mountain. One easy, one moderate and one challenging. We'll have signage explaining how long each trail takes and how difficult it is, along with a map showing the route."

Jessica and James exchanged a look of delight.

"We love it," James said. "It's perfect."

Having been burned by the shifting winds of opinion before, Heath passed them a pen. "Great. If you'd both initial the map please."

As they scrawled their initials, Declan braced himself for his part of the presentation. He, too, had giant sheets of paper, which made no sense. A PowerPoint presentation was clean, easy to change and didn't use resources like paper. Clients—they would be the death of him.

"We've brainstormed options for the rear gardens," he told them. "We're looking at just over an acre of relatively flat land. We can increase that by a bit if we use terraced gardens in the back."

"Terraced rather than sloped?" James asked.

"Terracing makes it easier for us to capture rainwater. We'll build in collection areas so there's less runoff and flooding for those rare winters when we get a couple of inches in a day."

Jessica nodded. "That makes sense. What else?"

He flipped to another sheet of paper. "You could have a produce garden over on the east side. The chef would work with your head gardener to determine what would grow best. The chef could pick the fresh produce at a certain time of day and the guests could either watch or participate."

"Oh, that's good," James said. "We could offer that as part of a package. A true culinary experience. I wonder if we could have a couple of cows and make our own butter and cheese."

"You're still in the city limits," Heath said quickly. "There are strict zoning laws."

"That's true." Jessica pursed her lips together. "Too bad, because we do love cows."

"Who doesn't?" Heath muttered.

Declan cleared his throat to avoid chuckling. "So, ah, in addition to the produce garden, we were thinking some kind of maze. It would take a while to grow the hedges but it could be a real centerpiece of the grounds and fun for guests of all ages."

"Yes, we'll do that," Jessica said.

James nodded. "Absolutely. That's totally our brand."

This was their first hotel, Declan thought. They didn't have a brand yet. They had money and an inability to stay on topic.

"Another alternative is a butterfly garden," he said, pulling out a third sheet. "This is more expensive as it would require a habitat, but it's unique. We could work with one of the local universities, maybe breed an endangered species. If you're interested in that, we'll have to research the costs and find out where they're doing research. UC Irvine for sure."

"A butterfly wedding garden," Jessica said dreamily.

"We could renew our vows there, Jess," her husband told her.

"If you want the butterfly garden, that could be the overarching theme connecting the outdoor space," Heath said.

"We want it all." Jessica's voice was firm. "Everything you've discussed."

Of course they did. Declan spread out the pages. "There's not enough room for everything. You'll have to pick the items you like best." *And hey, decisions are not your strong suit.* But, of course, he didn't say that out loud. Or run toward the window. A big victory all around.

"We can't possibly decide," Jessica said, her voice a whine. "What are we going to do?"

"We'll talk about it."

James collected all the pages. Heath quickly pulled back the one they'd initialed. They would keep that so that later, if—or when—they changed their minds on the hiking trails, the company had proof they'd signed off on the plan.

"We'll need a final decision in the next few weeks," Declan

told them. "We'll have tentative numbers on the butterfly garden to you by this time next week. But until you finalize your
decisions, we can't draw up a plan, tally costs or reserve materials and crew."

"Whatever you decide is going to be extraordinary." Heath
rose as he spoke.

James and Jessica stood. Declan joined them and walked them
toward the door.

"Thanks for coming in."

They all shook hands. When the hemp- and sandal-wearing
couple was on the elevator, Declan sank into a chair by the conference table and looked at his business partner.

"I'm sorry we took the job."

"*You're* sorry? I'm the one who's going to have to figure out
how we price out a butterfly enclosure."

"You'd better talk to the bug people at UC Irvine."

"They're not called bug people. Someone who studies but-
terflies and moths is a lepidopterist. I looked it up online."

"Good. Now you'll sound like you know what you're doing."
He glanced at the initialed drawing of the hiking trails. "How
many times do you think they're going to change their mind
this time?"

"At least a dozen."

"Yeah, that's what I thought, too."

chapter
ELEVEN

MARGOT ALWAYS WORE HER HAIR BACK IN A PONYTAIL. Alec hadn't seen her hair any other way, which had become maddening. He tried to imagine her with her hair down and he couldn't get the image exactly right. He wasn't sure how long her hair would be or how soft it would look, and thinking about her and her hair was both ridiculous yet oddly soothing, assuming he ignored the inevitable ache that accompanied such thoughts.

Margot and her ponytail were beginning to drive him mad. Worse, he was starting to like it.

The afternoon of the formal dinner, he'd helped her set the dining room table. She'd placed a diagram on an easel so they could make sure everything was in the right place. From left to right, napkin, salad fork, dinner fork, service plate with a salad plate on top, dinner knife, teaspoon and soup spoon. There was a bread plate and knife, a water glass, red wineglass, white wineglass and a cup and saucer.

She'd been so intense as she'd set the table, so determined to get it all right. He knew she was doing her job, but it was more than that, he thought. She was on a mission.

Some people might think what she did was silly or without merit, but not him. He knew what it was like to toil away on the obscure when those around him didn't get the point. She was a perfectionist but not to the point of being annoying. She was funny, too, and genuinely cared about his mother.

He liked her, he thought with surprise. And that ponytail...

Alec told himself to ignore it as best he could. He changed into a suit and was in the living room precisely at five minutes before six, just in time to see Margot walk down the stairs.

She wore a knee-length black sheath dress with a high neckline. Her makeup was light, her earrings simple silver hoops. She looked cool and elegant. Beautiful. Sexy. And her hair? Ponytail. He wondered how much effort it would take to liberate her—

He tore his mind away from the image and hoped his thoughts didn't reveal themselves in his expression. This was a professional event. Margot was working. His inexplicable attraction was his problem.

When she reached the main floor, she crossed to him. "You look nice."

"As do you."

They smiled at each other. Alec wanted to say that something crackled between them, but he wasn't sure. He hadn't had a regular relationship with a woman since he and Zina broke up. While he wasn't as much of a groundhog as his mother liked to say, he generally met women when he traveled on business and had brief but physically satisfying affairs. When he returned home, he was able to put his baser needs out of his mind for several months and focus on work.

It was a system that was successful. No messy emotional attachments, no risk of betrayal. But it left him woefully out of practice when it came to dealing with a woman like Margot.

"In keeping with the evening, I put a bottle of Dom Pérignon on ice," he told her. "I hope that meets with your approval."

She laughed. "It does. Very unnecessary, but lovely. Thank you."

"You're welcome. Edna said there's a bottle of nonalcoholic sparkling cider for Connor, if he wants it."

"I'll be sure to tell him." She pointed toward the dining room. "I want to check things one more time."

"Because the wineglasses might have moved?"

"You never know."

He followed her as she confirmed the table was as they'd left it. Exactly at six, his mother descended the stairs. Alec was pleased to see she wore a floral print dress with a full skirt. The neckline wasn't too low, the skirt wasn't too short and she seemed almost relaxed. Tension he hadn't felt until now eased a little. In three hours, four tops, this would all be over, he told himself.

A few seconds later, the doorbell rang. Margot let in Declan, his son and a curvy, blue-eyed blonde who looked nothing like Margot. Introductions were made all around.

"Your garden is looking well," Alec told him. "We should take a quick tour before it gets dark."

"I'd like that. Connor, this is Mr. Mcnicol."

"Oh, call him Alec," Bianca said, joining them. She knelt on the floor in front of Connor. "Otherwise he gets far too pompous. And I'm Bianca. You must be Connor." She leaned close and lowered her voice. "I hope it's all right, but I asked if I could sit next to you at dinner. I think you're going to be the most fun person at the table."

Connor might only be eight, but he was still male, and Bianca's personality had felled far more experienced men. Connor nodded eagerly.

"I'd like that."

"Excellent." Bianca held out her hand. "Come on. I'll go with you and your father to see the gardens. We can talk about stuff that makes us happy."

"I have a new ant farm," Connor said proudly, slipping his hand into hers.

"Do you? That is fascinating. I've always wanted an ant farm. Did it come in the mail?"

"Uh-huh. The farm came first, then the ants. We had to put

them in the refrigerator for ten minutes to make them quiet, then we poured them into the farm. Sunshine helped me."

"Did she? That's excellent. Hmm, the refrigerator. I wonder if I could put Alec there when he's bad."

"You can't," Connor told her, his expression serious. "A closed refrigerator can be dangerous for kids."

"You're right and I'm sorry I said that. Now let's go into the garden."

Alec glanced back at Margot, who was watching the exchange with great interest.

"She's good with kids," he said in a low voice.

"I see that. She's very likable and talks to them in a way that makes them feel heard." She pointed to the doorway. "Go take your garden tour. Sunshine and I will wait for Wesley. I'm sure he'll be here any second, then we'll join you."

"You're not going to check on the kitchen?" he asked, his voice teasing. Edna had arranged for a chef and a server for the evening.

"I don't have to," she said primly. "I know your housekeeper has taken care of every detail."

"I'm surprised you aren't double-checking."

Amusement brightened her eyes. "You have to know when to trust people, Alec. It makes life easier."

"So I've heard."

Sunshine watched with interest. He had the feeling she was mentally taking notes and would later report all to her sister. What that report might be, he had no idea.

He glanced toward the garden where Connor and Bianca were skipping through the grass. "Into the Valley of Death rode the six hundred," he said, quoting Alfred, Lord Tennyson.

"Or the one," Margot murmured. "Fear not, I will join you shortly and all will be well."

If only that were true, he thought, walking toward the storm that was his mother.

★ ★ ★

"Hey, you," Margot said, hugging her sister. "You look great."

"I look nice. *You* look fabulous. So, Alec. He's hunky."

A true factoid, but not one Margot was going to acknowledge. "I work for his mother."

"All that means is you don't work for him." Sunshine grinned. "He seems like a very nice Dietrich distraction."

I wish. "What about you?" she asked, hoping to distract her sister. "You never said Declan was all that."

"It doesn't matter what he is or isn't. He's Connor's dad and my boss."

"So off-limits?" Margot asked, just as the doorbell rang.

"In every way." Sunshine sighed. "And the Baxter curse lives on."

An hour later, Alec had to admit he'd been wrong. Bianca was on her best behavior. She was charming everyone, carrying most of the conversation and keeping the table amused with anecdotes from her acting days. Connor was mesmerized by every word, even when he didn't understand what she was talking about. Wesley couldn't keep his eyes off his fiancée, Sunshine seemed equally intrigued by Bianca, and Margot was keeping track of everything while, no doubt, taking mental notes. Only Declan seemed neutral about Bianca's performance, instead surreptitiously watching his new nanny when he thought no one was looking.

With the salad course behind them, there was only the soup course, the entrée and dessert to get through. Alec glanced at his watch and wished they were already eating *white and dark chocolate mousse in a pastry shell*, according to the elegant menu that had been provided.

Bianca leaned toward Connor. "I have a secret."

His eyes widened behind his glasses. "What is it?"

"The soup is going to be chilled."

"Cold soup?" He sounded delighted. "Really?"

"Cross my heart. It's delicious, I promise, but still… Cold!"

They both giggled at the outrageousness of the concept, then Bianca stood. "Why don't I go get it right now so you can try it?"

Connor nodded vigorously.

Margot looked at Bianca. "I'm sure the course will be here in a moment."

"Oh, I don't mind."

Alec knew Margot was trying to figure out if Bianca was simply interacting with a child or if she was looking for a distraction because she felt uncomfortable. As he had no idea, he doubted Margot understood the motivation, either. With his mother, it was often hard to tell.

Wesley watched her disappear into the kitchen. "She is a delight."

"Very charming," Sunshine said. "And funny. Margot, you must love every second you're here."

"I do," she said, catching Alec's gaze and smiling. He smiled back.

Bianca returned, a large soup tureen in her hands.

The second he saw her, Alec knew the moment wasn't going to go well. He didn't usually have premonitions, but this one was unshakable. With each step she took, his sense of dread grew more powerful until he knew he had to do something to stop whatever it was from happening.

But he was too late. Even as he rose, Bianca's narrow heel caught and she stumbled. While she didn't drop the tureen, it tipped and the thick, creamy green soup sloshed onto the hardwood floor.

There was a second of silence, then Bianca started to laugh. "Well, that's perfect," she said, and kicked off her shoes. She set the tureen on the sideboard and held out her hand to Connor.

"Come on. Take off your shoes and socks. It's a Slip 'N Slide. I'll bet you love those!"

Connor hesitated. He looked at Sunshine, who looked at Margot, who shrugged. No doubt she wanted to see how this played out. Wesley wasn't the least embarrassed, if his beatific smile was anything to go by.

It only took a few seconds for Connor to pull off his shoes and socks and join Bianca in the green soup. They slid around the dining room for several minutes, laughing and shrieking and creating a massive mess that was going to make Edna give him a stern talking-to come morning.

When they were done, Bianca turned to Wesley. "Would you get us a couple of towels so we don't track this everywhere?" She hugged Connor. "When it's safe for us to walk, we'll run upstairs to my bathroom and wash our feet in the bathtub."

Connor looked at the floor. "What about the mess?"

"Oh, don't worry about that. Everyone else will take care of it."

And there it was, Alec thought as he rose to get cleaning supplies. His mother's life philosophy in a nutshell. Someone else was always around to clean up the mess.

The next morning Bianca kept Margot waiting an hour before she finally joined her in the guest lounge. Margot had already decided that her client was either going to be late or a no-show, so she wasn't surprised. She'd used the time to think about how to handle the previous evening's, ah, events.

After the soup incident, Bianca and Connor had returned to the table and the dinner had gone on as if nothing had happened. Despite everyone else pitching in to clean the floor, the faint smell of avocado and cucumber had lingered. Margot had left a note for Edna, explaining what had happened and then had tried to figure out what, if anything, had gone wrong.

She knew a case could be made that Bianca had turned lemons into lemonade by inviting Connor to play with her. While it wasn't appropriate behavior for a formal dinner, it wasn't as if she'd dropped her dress or given a visiting dignitary the middle finger. Still, it wasn't exactly a normal reaction. What she didn't know was how much normal was good for Bianca.

Now her client settled on the sofa opposite Margot and raised her eyebrows.

"Go ahead and yell at me," she said, her tone light. "I can take it."

"Why would I yell?"

"Oh please. I danced in soup. That's hardly allowed."

"Technically you used soup to slide around on the floor. I'm not sure that qualifies as dancing."

Bianca didn't smile. If anything her expression turned wary. "You think what happened last night is funny?"

"What do you think it was?"

"A moment of fun. The unexpected happened and I turned it into a party. That's what I do. Everyone will remember last night and isn't that the point? To be memorable? Connor loved it."

"He did." Margot kept her voice gentle. "He had a terrific time and he adores you. How could he not?"

Bianca wore a loose-knit sweater over a tank top. She had on leggings and her feet were bare. She drew her knees to her chest and wrapped her arms around her legs. The defensive position could not have been more clear.

"But?" she asked. "Because there is an obvious but."

"I just wonder what you were thinking," Margot told her. "Not just with the soup, but before. You latched on to Connor immediately. You're so good with children, by the way."

"I wanted to make sure he was comfortable. Having dinner with a bunch of stuffy adults was going to be boring."

"I think it's great you were concerned about him. Your natural affinity with children is going to be an asset for you as you help Wesley socially."

The arms stayed firmly locked around her drawn knees. "I know that's not a compliment."

"It is one hundred percent a very sincere compliment. However—"

"Here it comes."

Margot smiled. "However, last night was about you and Wesley. We've talked about how you want to be an asset to him and his career, and how you're concerned about being a liability. Our goal was to help you get comfortable with formal dining and an eclectic group of guests. It was about mastering the various forks and glasses and a long evening with different courses and following the conventions of conversation. We'd talked about that—we had a strategy."

Bianca rolled her eyes. "I remember. Spend fifteen minutes talking to the person on my right, then switch to the person on my left. Or I can be like the queen and change with the courses. Whatever. I wanted to have a good time."

"I appreciate that," Margot said calmly. "But if you want to learn the rules, you have to study them and then practice until they're second nature. When you're comfortable with the rules, you don't have to think about them and then the fun happens naturally."

"Rules are boring."

You're boring. Bianca didn't say it, but Margot would swear she heard it all the same. There were always difficult times in what she did, and she had just reached the first one in this relationship.

Bianca shifted so her feet were on the floor, then glared at her. "You don't know what it's like for me. I love Wesley and I want to make him happy, but none of this is easy. People have expectations and I'm not always going to meet them. In my regular life, I don't care, but this is different. I want to get it right, but the rules are so arbitrary."

"Of course they are." Margot relaxed. "Everyone assumes formal place settings come from England, but they are in fact from

Russia. Who would have thought? And how on earth did we decide it was important to have wineglasses in a certain order? What if you don't drink wine or don't like or want white wine?"

"Then what's the point?"

"Rules and social conventions provide order. In diplomatic situations, when tensions are running high about a treaty or a conflict, conventions are a framework in which to work. Everyone knows their place and what's expected. Rules help people avoid making mistakes. You're thinking of all that I'm teaching you as a constraint to who you are as a person. But that's not what they're for. They're meant to help you. Like railings on a staircase, or seat belts. If you need them, they'll be there, even if you're not paying attention to what's going on."

Bianca didn't look convinced.

Margot got up and walked over to the small refrigerator in the bookcase and got them each a bottle of flavored water. "I think I mentioned before that my great-grandmother started a charm school back in the 1960s, in a tiny town you've never heard of. In a matter of a couple of years, she had gotten two of her girls into major pageants and they were making the finals."

"I know all this." Bianca sounded impatient.

Margot ignored her. "All she wanted her entire life was one Miss America winner. It was her dream and why wouldn't it be? To have just one of her students win the crown would have validated her entire life's work. Sunshine and I were her last hope."

Bianca raised her eyebrows. "Sunshine, your sister?"

Margot nodded.

"She's a beautiful woman but she's not..."

Margot grinned. "Beauty queen material? It's okay, you can say it. Sunshine wanted it, but she wasn't the right height or body type. We could all see that. So it fell to me."

Margot still remembered the sense of dread when her great-grandmother had told her what was expected. Margot had been thirteen and still growing. She was socially awkward and shy and the last thing on the planet she wanted was to be in front of any kind of crowd.

"The first time I got up on the practice stage, I threw up," she said cheerfully. "It happened regularly for the better part of a year. I also fainted and broke out in hives more than once. I became incoherent, I had no talent and I couldn't get the bathing suit walk. People think being in a beauty pageant is about nothing more than being pretty and having a great body. That's just plain wrong. You need public speaking skills, a platform, goals, achievements and more determination than I've ever been able to muster in my life. I broke Francine's heart. She kept saying if I really wanted it, I could do it. And she was right."

Bianca looked surprised. "You were throwing up?"

"I was, but I probably could have worked through that. The thing is, I didn't want it at all. It wasn't for me. To be successful at something, you have to want it for yourself, not someone else. You have to be willing to do the work. You have to see the benefit in the hours of practice and you have to be willing to fail over and over again. You need determination and an iron will."

She looked at her client. "Bianca, why are you doing this? You're a beautiful, funny, charming woman who is beloved by everyone who knows you. Why on earth do you want to change?"

Tears filled her eyes. "I love Wesley."

"I know you do and he loves you and he's never once asked you to be anything but who you are."

"You can't know that."

"Yes, I can. I've seen how he looks at you. Last night, with the soup, he was laughing the hardest. He adores you. So why am I here?"

Bianca brushed away tears. "I want to be different. I want to be strong. I want to know what to do around those people. They're going to judge me. All of them. I know they are."

And there it was, Margot thought in relief. The real reason

for the transformation. It wasn't about Wesley losing his job at all—it was about her own fears.

"That's better," she said. "So much better. Now we have something to work with. Doing this kind of work for yourself is so much smarter than doing it for someone else. Let's figure out what you want, what works for you and make it stick. Because I want you strong, too. I want you to dazzle them and make every single person want to be you."

"You can do that?"

"No. But you can. We'll keep working and modifying as we go. We'll work on what you're most nervous about and get you comfortable. It's not that hard. It's just a matter of figuring out the right railing for your staircase."

"I want to believe you. I love Wesley and I know he's fine with who I am, but I really don't want his career to suffer because of me. Plus, it's just so hard when I'm around those people. They all went to college and have five degrees and I'm just some has-been actress with a great body."

Margot held up one finger. "No. You're a beautiful, vibrant woman with a rockin' *hot* body. There's a difference."

Bianca laughed. "Thank you. Okay, let's get started. Last night with the soup, I wasn't thinking. I really did just want to get it for Connor, but when I picked it up, it was really heavy and then I didn't know what to do."

"What could you have done?"

Bianca sighed. "I could have asked for help."

"Yes. You could have. So why was it so important to impress Connor? You were really focused on him from the beginning."

"I love kids."

Margot waited.

"What?" Bianca groaned. "You're a nightmare."

"Yes, I am."

"Fine." Bianca got up and paced the length of the room. When she reached the fireplace, she looked back at Margot.

"I'm good with kids. They always like me. I guess I was nervous, so I knew being with Connor was safe and then I got too focused on him and it spiraled out of control." She shrugged. "I told Edna I'm sorry about the soup."

"I'm sure she appreciated that. Why were you nervous? It was a small group of people and you knew most of us."

"Because the whole evening was about waiting for me to fail. I felt like a performing bear and when I screwed up you were all going to know and laugh at me."

Margot stiffened as the truth of her words sank in. She stood. "Oh no. Bianca, I'm so sorry. You're right—that's exactly what it was. Not us laughing, because that wasn't going to happen, but of course you felt on display. That was wrong of me. I apologize. What a horrible evening for you."

Bianca blinked. "You're apologizing to me?"

"Of course. I handled the evening all wrong. I was trying to keep the numbers small so there was less stress on you but everyone knew what we were doing and you were the subject of the lesson. Of course you felt as if you were being judged by everyone. Connor was your only safe person, wasn't he? I totally messed up and I'm so very sorry."

Bianca giggled. "Wow. That was a really good apology. You should give lessons. I'm not upset anymore. In fact, I just want to give you a hug and tell you everything will be fine."

"I'm more concerned about whether or not you still trust me to help you."

Bianca's eyes filled with tears again. She crossed to Margot and held her tight. "Honestly, there's no one I would trust more."

"Thank you."

Bianca's expression turned sly. "Hmm, so you owe me now. I'm going to have to think of how I want to take advantage of that. Maybe we should have your sister over and we'll do a girls' spa day or something."

Margot hesitated, thinking she didn't want to drag Sunshine

into this. "Or we could keep working together to achieve our ultimate goal."

"You're no fun, but all right. Let's get started."

Margot was still processing her giant blunder. She needed some time to regroup. "If you don't mind, I need a couple of hours to rethink the plan. Can we meet after lunch?"

"Sure. It's cold and foggy outside, so I think I'll just stay in my room and watch a movie. Maybe *Raiders of the Lost Ark*. I was up for Karen Allen's part—did you know that? I think I would have been good in that movie and Harrison Ford was so yummy. Oh well. I'll see you after lunch."

With that she walked out of the room, leaving Margot behind wondering how on earth she could have screwed up so badly at something she was supposed to be good at.

chapter
TWELVE

SUNSHINE WAITED UNTIL CONNOR HAD GONE TO BED
before knocking on the open door of Declan's study. He looked
up from his computer, smiled and waved her in.

"How's it going?" he asked as she took a seat by his desk.
"Please don't tell me you're having second thoughts about the
ant farm. Connor loves that thing."

"I have no problem with the ants except possibly the fact that
they're so industrious, I sometimes feel like a slacker by comparison."

"I know that one. How's school?"

"Still awkward and difficult." She was going to the lectures
and doing her homework and falling a little more behind each
day. "There's a TA session soon. If that doesn't help me enough,
I guess I'll go to the math lab."

"Want me to look over your chapters and see if I can help?"

"Thanks, but I'll deal with it."

She in no way wanted her boss figuring out she was a complete idiot. She adored Connor and really wanted to keep her
job here. She was comfortable in her surroundings. She felt safe
and happy and knew she was making a difference.

"The offer still stands," he told her.

"I appreciate that." She thought about the reason for her visit.

"So, this is a little awkward, but I met the mother of one of Connor's friends. Elijah's mom. Her name is Phoebe, she's divorced and really funny and nice, and well, I think you'd like her."

Declan stared at her, his expression completely blank. "Excuse me?"

"I thought you might like to meet her and maybe go out with her. Because the other day you were talking about—"

"Okay, no." He half came to his feet, then dropped back in his chair. "No. Just no. Why on earth would you try to set me up?"

"I can't help it. I'm nurturing. If there's a problem in the house, I try to fix it. You mentioned that you wanted to—"

He winced. "Can we not talk about it? Or repeat what I said?"

"I was just explaining why I thought you might want to call Phoebe. She's a successful woman with a son Connor knows. I'm pretty sure she would be interested." *How could she not be?* "You have a lot in common and you wouldn't have to worry about where you were going to meet someone. She's local."

He groaned. "You have to let this go. Sunshine, I beg you. I can find my own women."

"Or not."

He laughed. "Point taken, and stop. However nice or smart this Phoebe woman is, I'm going to pass."

"Your loss. She seemed really fun."

He pointed at the door. "You should be going now."

She grinned as she rose. "All right. I'll stop. No more comments about Phoebe's availability. If you'd tell me your type I can be on the lookout for other women."

She paused by the door, expecting him to tell her to mind her own business or make a crack about her not giving up. What she didn't expect was the fiery hunger that flashed in his eyes. It was the heat of a man who wants a woman. A specific woman. *Her.*

She'd wondered if Declan found her attractive or sexy or both, but she'd never considered it was more than that. In the nanosecond before the fire was extinguished, she felt an answering tug low in her belly. A need that shocked her with its existence as much as its intensity.

No, she told herself. *No, no and no. Not Declan.* She loved her job, loved the dynamic the three of them had. Getting involved with him would ruin everything. She wasn't that girl anymore—she refused to be. She wanted more than a quick hump while Connor was sleeping. She wanted something real and lasting and important.

She forced her attention back to the present moment. Declan looked as shocked and concerned as she felt.

"I have Phoebe's number if you change your mind," she said, hoping her fake good humor could pass for the real thing.

"I'm ignoring you."

She waved and left. She hurried toward her bedroom and firmly shut the door behind her. She sat on the edge of the bed and told herself nothing had happened. Absolutely nada. And even if that wasn't true, she was going to pretend it was. Fake it until you make it was a time-honored tradition for her. It had worked in the past and she was determined it would work now. It had to. There was just too much on the line.

"I haven't seen you in a couple of days."

Margot looked up and saw Alec coming into the kitchen. It was dinnertime, two days after her uncomfortable revelation.

"I've been in hiding," she admitted with a shrug. "Licking my wounds, so to speak."

His expression of concern sharpened. "What did my mother do?"

"Nothing but be gracious and forgive me. I was totally wrong about that dinner. Instead of helping her, I turned her into a spectacle. The whole idea was a colossal mistake and it's all on me. We're back on track now, though, and things are going well."

Which was a relief, but didn't erase the previous mistake.

"Maybe you're being a little hard on yourself," he offered.

"No, I'm not, but don't worry. I won't wallow. We're moving forward. In a way, I wonder if messing up the way I did has made your mother trust me more. I don't know. I hope so." She smiled. "And that, I promise, is the end of the emotional dump. I was about to take the casserole Edna defrosted out of the oven. Want to join me for dinner?"

"I'd like that." He grinned. "I'll admit I was drawn to the kitchen by the delicious smell. What are we having?"

"Something with chicken and pasta and a cheese sauce. I've already made a big salad to counteract the richness."

While he opened a bottle of wine, she set the kitchen table, then pulled out the casserole and set it on a trivet. They sat across from each other and she passed him a serving spoon.

It was nearly seven and dark outside. The fog had stuck around all day and caused the temperature to drop into the fifties, which was practically an arctic blast for Los Angeles. Bianca was out, the staff had gone home. It was just the two of them in the huge house.

"I'm impressed my mother stayed to talk to you," Alec said as he slid the casserole dish toward her. "Usually she cuts and runs. I didn't expect to see her for a week."

"I'm glad she did stay so I could figure out what went wrong and my part in it." Margot thought about how she'd changed the lesson plans and what was going to be different going forward. "She's challenging. Such an unexpected combination of competence and insecurity." She pushed the casserole dish in his direction. "How is it having her living in your house?"

He shrugged. "Easier than I thought it was going to be. We're mostly on separate floors and she's gone most evenings." He smiled. "I will admit I was worried about having her here. It's been a long time since we were roommates."

"You were barely a teenager when you went to live with your grandparents, weren't you?"

"Yes. She took me to Australia that summer before boarding school. Winter for them, of course. We must have been gone six or eight weeks. She bought an old used car and we drove everywhere. My job was to constantly tell her 'left, left' so she stayed on the correct side of the road."

"That's right. They drive like the British, don't they? I'm not sure I could do it."

"It would be challenging," he admitted. "But she did fine. When we got home, I packed up my things and flew to Switzerland to stay with my paternal grandparents."

"She must have missed you."

"I'm sure she did."

But she let him go, Margot thought. Was it because she felt she didn't have a choice or was it more that she knew it was the right thing for him?

"She loved me," Alec said. "She was totally supportive of whatever I wanted. Once when I was eight or nine, she was dating a man I didn't like and when I told her, she broke up with him. Just like that. I always felt a little guilty about it. What if he was the one and because of me she lost her chance at happiness?"

"If he'd been the great love of her life, don't you think you would have sensed it and felt better about the guy? Plus, do you really believe there's only one person for each of us?" she asked.

"No. I'm not sure I believe in 'the one' at all."

"Then you couldn't have ruined anything."

"That's very logical. Love doesn't work that way."

"I'm not sure either of us is an expert on the subject," she said with a laugh.

He raised his wineglass. "You're right about that. Tell me about when you were growing up."

"Funny you should ask. I was just talking about my great-grandmother with Bianca. Francine raised Sunshine and me after our mother took off. By then she was in her early seventies and raising two kids was the last thing on her mind. Her charm and beauty pageant school was winding down and she was tired. I've always felt badly for her."

"That she had to raise you two?"

Margot nodded. "First her daughter ran off, then her granddaughter. While neither Sunshine nor I made it to the Miss America pageant, at least we didn't end up pregnant at eighteen. Progress, I suppose."

"When did she shut down her school?"

"We were about fourteen. She'd always wanted to move to Las Vegas. We did that and lived in a double-wide trailer. We could see the lights of the strip at night. Francine constantly warned us about the dangers of gambling and fast-talking men. She worried."

Margot wondered what Francine would think about them now. They'd broken the pattern of being unwed mothers but not the Baxter curse of loving the wrong man. Sunshine had her many and Margot had Dietrich. Maybe biology was destiny after all.

"Yet here you are, free of the evils of gambling, and not a fast-talking man in sight."

Margot smiled. "Oh, I think she would see you as a bit of a danger."

Alec looked so surprised Margot started laughing.

"What?" she asked. "You don't see yourself as a threat to women everywhere?"

"Hardly. I'm too academic. My life is solitary. I don't enjoy going out to nightclubs or parties. I can't remember the last time I saw a movie in a theater."

Personal perception was an interesting phenomenon, she thought. People got ideas of themselves stuck in their heads for reasons that had little to do with reality and everything to do with their emotional past.

"You're looking at the wrong things," she told him. "You're successful, kind, good-looking, knowledgeable and, I suspect underneath the reserve, there's a hidden depth only a very few see." Which was her way of avoiding saying *passion*, because wouldn't that be awkward.

"Is that how you see me?" he asked, sounding surprised.

"That's how everyone sees you." She raised a shoulder. "With the possible exception of the visiting scholars. I doubt they see anything but work."

He looked at her for a long time before murmuring. "Very unexpected."

"You're welcome."

He laughed. "Yes, thank you. Now when are you going to start exploring the root cellars? I want to be braced for the screams."

"There aren't going to be any bodies. I don't believe monks are the hide-a-body type. But I'm still hoping for some kind of exciting treasure."

"The ledger you found is fascinating. I've been through it. You're right—the donkeys they raised were highly prized."

"Don't tell your mother. She'll want you to start raising them."

He groaned. "I'm sure she will. Probably as emotional support animals. Try getting one of those on a plane."

Their conversation continued to flow easily, but Margot was aware of an undercurrent that hadn't been there before. It was her own fault for saying what she had about him. Not that it wasn't true, but somehow her words had shifted things between them.

What if Alec thought she was coming on to him? That would be... Well, she wasn't sure what, but something. Not that he wasn't great—he was. And not that she wouldn't mind finding out if he kissed with the same intensity that he did everything else. Because a few hot kisses would go a long way to brightening her day. Only it wasn't like that between them and she'd never really thought that they would... Not that she wasn't interested, but it was...

The complications and weirdness piled on top of each other

until she barely made it through the rest of dinner. She excused herself as soon as she could and bolted for the stairs. Once she was alone in her room, she realized that she would much rather have spent more time with him, which made her incredibly dumb and just as socially awkward as Francine had always claimed.

In the end, Sunshine agreed to meet Norris for a drink rather than coffee. She traded a Saturday evening off for a Thursday, arranged for Connor to spend the evening with his friend Christopher and confirmed Declan would pick up his son there no later than seven-thirty. Declan had made her swear that Christopher's mother wasn't anyone he had to worry about, which would have been funny if she hadn't been so nervous about her date. She'd assured her boss that Christopher's mom was happily married and that Christopher was a change-of-life baby, so she was well into her fifties and therefore far too much woman for him.

Sunshine spent nearly an hour trying to figure out what to wear. She wanted to look good, but not sexy. Pretty. She'd never been one to use her sexuality to get what she wanted in life— guys just kind of appeared. The difference now was she wanted to make better and smarter choices.

When she was nearly out of time, she settled on a light blue dress with a higher scoop neck and a full skirt. It came to just above her knees. As it was sleeveless, she slipped on a cream-colored, three-quarter-sleeve cropped sweater. She curled her hair, went easy on the makeup and, when she was done, realized she looked much more like she was applying for a choir director job than going on a date. On her drive to the restaurant bar where they were meeting, she would have to develop a sparkling personality and hope for the best.

She handed her keys to the valet and then, ignoring her quivering nerves and the urge to bolt, went inside. Norris was already there, looking handsome and professional in his dark suit.

He saw her and waved her over. As she approached, she saw he'd claimed a small table for the two of them.

"You made it," he said, sounding happy. He took her hand in his, then leaned in and kissed her cheek. "You look beautiful."

"Thank you. You're very powerful yourself."

He chuckled. "It's the suit. Men have it easy. We all look decent in a well-made suit."

They sat across from each other. He motioned for the server to stop by. "Sunshine, what would you like?"

A margarita with a shot of tequila on the side, she thought grimly. She wasn't a dater, she never had been. She met a guy, they fell in lust and that was it. There was no getting to know each other over cocktails or awkward fumbling at the end of the night. She didn't know how to do this and she wasn't sure she wanted to learn.

Only this was what normal people did, she reminded herself. They went on dates and got to know each other.

"I'd love a glass of white wine," she said with a smile.

"Bourbon on the rocks."

When their server had left, Norris shifted closer. "Thanks again for your help with the cake. It was a huge hit."

"I'm glad. How's your sister doing?"

"She's getting cabin fever. She hates the bed rest, but it's only for a few more weeks. Our mom moved in with them and that's helping a lot."

"It's nice that she can do that."

"Oh, my mom would change the rotation of the earth if she thought it would help one of her kids."

Sunshine thought of her own mother walking out on her twins when they were still toddlers. Everyone had a story, she thought, and some of them were bad.

"So it's you and your sister?" she asked.

"I have a younger brother. I'm the oldest. What about you?"

"I have a sister. We're fraternal twins. Our family is gone, so it's just the two of us. She lives nearby and we're pretty close."

The server brought over their drinks. Norris drank from his. "Have you been married?"

"No. You were, though, right?" She remembered he'd mentioned something about being divorced when they'd first met.

"Divorced. Nothing dramatic. We just weren't really right for each other. It's been a couple of years. I dated a lot and then that got old. These days I'm looking for something different."

He stared at her intently as he spoke, as if delivering an important message. The problem was, she had no idea what he was trying to convey.

"And you're in finance?" she asked.

"I am. People don't know anything about money, which is bad for them and good for me. I give them a plan and suddenly they're growing their portfolio. I get to be the hero."

"Then it's a win-win."

"It is. You're a nanny?"

"Uh-huh. I love working with kids. I had no idea what I wanted to do after high school. I sort of fell into the nanny thing and discovered I had a knack for it. Now I'm working on getting my degree in child psychology."

Which sounded so much grander than it was, she thought, not sure why she'd said it like that. She was taking her first class and had yet to figure out what she was doing. Was this what dating was? Telling half-truths to look better to the other person?

Before she could correct what she'd told him, he spoke.

"So you live with a family for a couple of years, then move on? Is that hard?"

"It can be. I don't mind leaving the parents, but a lot of times, I really miss the kids." Especially when she'd simply taken off because of some guy. That was her original sin—leaving her kids behind without a word.

She often wondered if they eventually forgot her, as she'd told herself they would, or if they carried that scar of being abandoned with them. She'd been close to a lot of her charges, especially a set of twins. Did they remember her? Hate her? Wish she'd never been part of their lives? Regardless, she had simply disappeared. Yet another pattern in her past she was determined not to repeat. She was going to be more responsible.

"Do you like the symphony?" Norris asked, changing the subject. "A lot of people don't like that kind of music anymore, but it's one of my favorites."

"I've never been to the symphony," she admitted. "But I do like classical music. Connor—he's the boy I take care of—and I play a lot of music. We alternate who picks and he really loves classical music."

"Good. I have season tickets and I'd love to take you."

"That's perfect because I'd love to go."

"I'm glad."

There it was, she thought happily. The normal date. She wasn't sure how she felt about Norris or if under her agitated nerves there was anything close to attraction, but at least this was what other people did.

Norris leaned close. "So here's the thing. I was thinking we could get dinner and continue the conversation. Or, if you're up for it, we could just go back to my place and take things to the next level."

The words were so unexpected that at first she didn't understand what he was saying. She went cold all over as her stomach sank to her toes and all hope died.

"You want me to go back to your place and have sex with you," she said, wanting to confirm she hadn't misunderstood him. Or maybe hoping he would be shocked and tell her that wasn't what he'd meant at all.

He gave her what she assumed he thought of as a slow, sexy smile. "Absolutely. Jesus, Sunshine, you're a walking, breathing fantasy. How could I not want to have sex with you? It's all I can think about."

Tears burned, but she blinked them away. She pulled twenty dollars out of her small bag and placed it on the table.

"No," she said, her voice firm despite the fact she was shaking. "No. I don't want that."

She rose and headed for the door. Norris came after her and grabbed her by her arm.

"Wait. Look, I'm sorry if I read the signals wrong. I'll buy you dinner first if that's what you want."

Because that was what she was worth? The cost of a salad and an entrée?

She freed herself and walked out. The valet brought around her car. As she got in, she felt the first tear leak out. It was followed by another and another.

She brushed them away so she could see to drive. Once she pulled into traffic, she looked for a safe place to stop. She saw a grocery store up ahead and found a parking space in the back of the lot. Only then did she give in to the tears. She cried out her hurt and disappointment as she wondered what she'd done wrong and how she was ever supposed to be more than she was. She'd dressed conservatively, hadn't teased or been sexual in her conversation. She'd thought he was a nice guy, but he wasn't. Or maybe it was her. Maybe she should stop trying so hard to avoid the inevitable.

When she'd run out of tears, she drove home and made her way inside. Connor and Declan were watching a movie. She waved at them but kept on moving. She changed into leggings and a T-shirt, then curled up on the bed and wished she were anyone else but herself.

chapter
THIRTEEN

A COUPLE OF HOURS LATER, HUNGER DROVE SUNSHINE to the kitchen. There was leftover chicken and a bag of salad, along with some avocado and Mexican blend cheese. It only took a few minutes to make a salad. She'd just taken a seat at the kitchen island when Declan walked in.

"You okay?" he asked, shoving his hands into his jeans front pocket. "You seemed upset when you got home. Did something happen?"

She resisted the urge to push away her salad and start crying again. Declan certainly didn't want that. Instead she smiled brightly.

"I'm great. How was your evening with Connor? Did he have fun with his friend?"

"You don't have to tell me if you don't want to," he told her. "But I am concerned."

So much for distracting him, she thought with a sigh.

"Nothing happened," she told him. "It was just a crummy date."

He took the far seat at the island. "Want to talk about it?"

"No. Yes. Let me ask you a question." She put down her fork. "Did you have sex with Iris on the first date?"

"What? No!" He cleared his throat. "No."

"Did you ask her to? Did you expect it?"

"No. Is that what happened? He expected you to have sex with him?"

The tears threatened as she nodded. "I don't get it. I thought he was a regular guy and I never thought regular guys expected sex after a drink."

"Some might but most of us don't. I'm sorry that happened."

"Me, too." She looked at him. "The thing is I was so careful with what I wore and what I said. I wasn't flirty or anything. I just want to find someone who is as interested in the rest of me as my boobs and my ass."

Declan waved toward her. "And that other part."

He was such an unbelievable combination of embarrassed and earnest that she couldn't help laughing.

"Is the word you're looking for *vagina*?"

"We don't actually think that term, but yes."

"So it's never—" she made air quotes "—'Oh, wow, I want to put my penis in her vagina'?"

"No. It's more basic than that. More visceral." His humor faded. "I'm sorry the guy was a jerk. I'm sorry he disappointed you but that's what jerks do. You're going to meet someone normal and nice who sees you as a whole person."

"I'm not sure those kind of guys exist."

"We do."

She wanted to believe him, but it was difficult. No, it was impossible. "I'm so tired of being a piece of ass. I have a personality. I'm good with kids and I kind of like the ant farm. That should matter. I'm not great at math, but it's early yet and I could get better."

"You have a lot to offer. You really do."

There was something in his tone. "But?"

"But it can be difficult for some men to see past the obvious."

"You think I should give Norris a second chance?"

"No. But I think you might have to give a guy you really

like a second chance. In case he was just overwhelmed in the moment."

She would give Declan a second chance, she thought wistfully. If they were dating, she would give him a lot of chances. Not that she would have to. She knew in her gut, and a whole lot of other places, he would never make her feel bad about herself. He wouldn't ask her to have sex right away. He would wait until they knew each other and it became something they both wanted because…

"I want to fall in love," she whispered, brushing away tears. "I want to be someone's world and I want him to be mine. I want to take care of him and our kids and our pets. I want to have a job I like and do laundry and go bowling and plan a yearly vacation. I want to put up a Christmas tree with Popsicle stick ornaments on it. I want more ant farms."

"You're going to have all that and more."

"I don't know." She sniffed. "I think I'm stuck with what I have until I'm old enough that no one wants to have sex with me anymore."

"That will never happen. Of that I am sure."

"Thank you," she said, wiping her face again. "You've been really nice and I appreciate all your kind words." She managed a smile. "And the vagina insight."

"I really am sorry, Sunshine. He's not worth it."

"I know. I don't care about him—it's just I had such high hopes."

She collected her salad and took it into her room, then closed the door. For a second, she thought about rushing back and asking Declan to hold her. Not for any reason other than the fact that she could use a hug.

She would bet he was a really good hugger—the kind who just grabbed and didn't let go. She'd seen him hug Connor and there was none of that A-frame nonsense.

She thought about her list of what she wanted from a few

minutes ago and mentally added good hugging to it, then she set down her salad and curled up on the bed. She gave in to tears and sadness, as she wondered how much of what she was going through was her own fault and how much of it was the Baxter family curse. After four generations there hadn't been a single successful romantic relationship and didn't that just suck for them all.

"You have a delivery," Edna said. "They're bigger boxes than I want to lift. The delivery guy left them in the foyer."

As always, it took Alec a couple of seconds to travel the mental distance from the ancient world where he spent most of his day to modern times.

"Oh, the documents are here. Excellent. Thank you, Edna. I'll take care of them."

She nodded and left. Alec saved his notes and then glanced at the clock in his office. It was nearly four in the afternoon. He hadn't heard Margot or his mother for some time now, so it was possible they were done for the day.

He got out his phone and quickly texted Margot.

If you've finished with Bianca and have a free moment, I have just taken delivery of several ancient pages. You might want to join me to see how they are handled.

It only took a second for her to respond.

On my way.

Even as he smiled, he acknowledged the ridiculousness of texting someone in his own home, but that was how things were these days. Besides, it wasn't as if she were a friend visiting for a few weeks. She was his mother's consultant. Her staying at his house was simply for convenience.

He thought about how he'd been concerned about the intrusion by both his mother and Margot, but both women were surprisingly unobtrusive. His mother was either with Margot or Wesley and Margot wasn't the kind of person who got in the way.

If he were being honest with himself, he would have to admit that he liked having her in the house. He liked their morning breakfasts where they mostly discussed the news of the day. He liked running into her at odd hours and their impromptu meals together. He liked talking to her and laughing with her and looking at her.

He heard her steps on the stone floor as she made her way to his office. Something like anticipation grew inside of him, bringing him to his feet. He had the oddest thought he should kiss her when he saw her. And not on the cheek. He should pull her into his arms and kiss her with all the passion pent up inside of him.

The thought was so intense, yet so unexpected, he found he couldn't move. Margot came to a stop just inside his office.

"Are you all right?" she asked, sounding concerned. "Are you not feeling well?"

"I'm fine," he said automatically, then reached for the most convenient lie. "Allergies."

"Oh. They can be awful. Are you feeling well enough to look the ancient pages or do you want to wait?"

"I'm fine. It won't be a problem."

"Good. I'm very excited. Are they old, old or just a little old?"

Her enthusiasm made him smile. "I'm not sure. Let's go find out."

She wore a pale gray dress that was fitted to the waist then flared out to just below her knee. Her shoes were flats, her hair once again pulled back in a ponytail. She was the epitome of sensible and yet there was an underlying grace and sensuality that was a constant distraction. She made him feel things and he was a man who preferred to be in control at all times. Not that his reaction to her was anyone's fault but his own. He wasn't the kind of jerk who would blame someone else for his responses.

He led the way to the front of the house. Three packages sat by the door. They were large and marked as fragile.

He opened the coat closet door and pulled out the collapsible hand truck he kept for just this reason, then wrestled the surprisingly heavy boxes in place so they could be wheeled back to the archive room.

"I'm very curious about what we have here," she admitted. "This is going to be so fun."

It took two trips to transport the boxes. One was considerably larger and heavier than the others.

Once the boxes were in the archive room, Alec closed both doors and turned on the built-in air filtration system. Margot's eyes widened.

"That sounds like there's a big fan turning somewhere," she said with a grin. "Should I be worried about ancient spores turning me into a mummy monster?"

"Probably not. Based on the weight and size of the boxes, I'm guessing what we have are previously mounted papyri. They'll need rehousing before any more damage is done."

The archive room was lined with cabinets on two walls, and had a huge worktable in the middle of the room. Special bulbs designed to not do any damage to delicate fibers provided excellent light. There was a sink and all the tools and supplies he would need.

Together they lifted the largest box onto the table. He photographed the box, the delivery label, then noted the date and time for future reference. After opening the box, he pulled out protective packing material before lifting out old-fashioned glass housing units.

"As I thought," he told her. "Papyrus fragments. Papyrus isn't paper as we think of it. Sheets of papyrus are made by laying thin slices of the pith of the plant so that they overlap. Once that's done, the sheets are pounded with a hammer, pressed, left to dry and treated with a sizing. A time-consuming process, as you can imagine."

He placed the housing units along the table. "See how there are two sheets of glass, held together by cloth tape?"

She nodded.

"While this old-fashioned method offers some protection for the papyrus, there are problems, as well. The papyrus can stick to the glass, thereby damaging it and the ink."

He pointed to a grayish smudge inside the glass. "That's caused by sodium chloride, which is basically salt."

"Salt? How did that get in there? Is the Nile salt water or fresh water?" She held up her hand. "Wait. It has to be fresh water. It's a source of drinking water for the area. So where would the salt come from?"

"The papyrus itself and the salt from the earth the artifacts were buried in. There's no one direct source."

"What will you do to protect them?"

"They'll be rehoused. I'll do the more significant pages myself and ship the others off to grad students."

She laughed. "Free labor?"

"Absolutely."

They unpacked the other two boxes. There were more glass panels with papyrus inside, but in the smallest box they found dusty, worn, sealed tin cans.

"What are those?" Margot asked. "They look old."

"About seventy or eighty years old. A few may date back to the 1920s." He handed her a tin. "Papyrus is stored inside. Papyrus no one has seen since it was originally discovered in Egypt and put in these tins to protect the paper. We have no idea what it says or what kingdom it's from."

She smiled at him. "Can I please, please be here when you open one of them? I promise not to get in the way or anything."

"Of course. First I have to go through what they sent me in glass, then we'll open the tins."

"You have the most remarkable career."

"Not many people would agree with you."

"All those people are wrong." She pointed to a piece of papyrus under glass. "Tell me what that says."

He moved around the table until he was in front of it, then studied the ancient hieroglyphics. "See this here? It's the sun god Ra. He was the most worshipped of the gods."

He explained why and talked about the most important of the Egyptian gods.

"Nearly every ancient religion supports a cataclysmic flood legend," he told her. "As told to us in what you would know as the Old Testament. But ancient Egypt has no such story."

"I didn't know that." She touched the dusty glass. "You make this all so exciting. I know you love what you do and I hope you take this in the spirit I mean it, but you would have been a great professor."

"I doubt that. I can ramble on. Ask my mother."

"I don't have to. I've heard you ramble and it's fascinating."

She was standing close enough for him to inhale the scent of her body. There was an underlying note of vanilla. A body lotion perhaps, or her shampoo? Once again he wanted to know what she looked like with her hair down around her shoulders. He wanted to see her naked and leaning over him as they—

He tore his mind away from the image. *Control*, he reminded himself. Control was how he survived. Without control there was chaos and then everything was at risk.

"Thank you for sharing this with me," she told him.

The papyri, he reminded himself. Nothing more. She would be appalled if she knew what he'd been thinking.

"You're welcome. We'll set up a time to open the tins."

"I can't wait. Do I have to wear special gloves and a mask? Please say yes, even if I don't."

He chuckled. "You will need to wear gloves. A mask is optional."

She surprised him by grabbing his hand and squeezing his fingers. "You are showing me the best time ever."

"Then you need to get out more."

"Don't say that. This is wonderful." She released his hand.

For reasons not clear to him he felt compelled to say, "Zina, my former fiancée, found the physical aspect of rehousing tedious."

"She was an idiot."

He glanced down at the glass-covered papyrus, then back at her. "She cheated on me while we were engaged. That's why things ended. She didn't tell me herself. The other man, a grad student, came and told me."

Margot stared at him, her expression stricken. "I'm sorry. How awful. I know everyone says better to know before the wedding, but still, what a terrible thing for her to do." Her mouth twisted. "There's been a lot of betrayal in your life. I wish I had something brilliant to say to make it better, but I don't."

"Thank you. Obviously I broke things off with her immediately. Shortly after that, my great-uncle died and left me the house."

He wanted to say more. He wanted to tell her that he didn't feel any pain about what had happened. That it was long enough ago that he could look back and wonder why he'd thought it would work out in the first place. He wanted to say that he didn't trust many people anymore but he thought maybe Margot might be someone he could allow past the emotional gates he kept firmly in place. Only it had been so long since he'd shared any part of himself, he wasn't sure where to start.

"I'm glad she didn't live here," Margot told him.

"Me, too."

"Too bad neither of us knows how to make a little voodoo doll of her. We could stab it over and over again with a really big pin."

He raised his eyebrows. "You're vindictive. I wouldn't have guessed."

"I have my moments. All right, enough talk of old girlfriends. I saw leftover chicken in the refrigerator and a package of crunchy taco shells in the pantry. I say you make us a big pitcher of margaritas and I'll make tacos. You can sweet-talk me with all you know about ancient Egypt while I listen attentively and marvel at your brilliance. How does that sound?"

"Like I'm getting the better end of the bargain."

"Not really, but I'm glad you think so. Come on. It's tequila time."

She led the way out of the archive room. He carefully locked the door behind them so the cleaning service wouldn't go in and disrupt anything.

Margot was special, he thought. Not just beautiful and smart—she was also kind. There was a goodness in her he knew to be rare. He wanted...

He wanted a lot. Sex, of course, but other things. Intimacy, perhaps. But if he let her in, she could disrupt his world. In fact, she was certain to do so. And disruptions were dangerous. As much as he wanted to believe there was nothing of his mother in him, he knew there had to be some genetic essence of her hiding in some corner, just waiting to destroy his carefully constructed life, and that he would not permit.

Not that he had to be overly concerned about that happening in the near term, he reminded himself. For all that he found Margot a significant temptation, the truth was he had no idea what she thought of him. Considering his lack of luck when it came to women, no doubt she saw him as a doddering old uncle, as sexless as a lamp.

Better to be the brilliant professor. Anything else was too great a risk.

Like most men, Declan didn't want problems he couldn't solve. Figure out how to cross a raging river? Sure. Defeat a fleet of marauding Vikings? Absolutely. But bring laughter back to

Sunshine's beautiful eyes or take away the reason her shoulders were slumped? He had no clue and he didn't like that one bit.

He tried telling himself it wasn't his problem to fix. That she had to get over the asshole Norris had been and move on. But thinking the words didn't make him feel better and with any kind of action out of the question, he was left with too much energy and nowhere to put it.

Saturday morning the easiest solution seemed to be to take out his frustrations on his garden. There were hedges he'd wanted to get rid of for a while. He drove his car to the garage where his company kept their landscaping equipment and came home with a good-size pickup and all the tools he would need.

By nine, he was hard at work. By ten, half the hedge was gone and he had sweated through his clothes, which he didn't care about, but he also couldn't get Sunshine off his mind, which he did.

What was it about her? After over a year of not wanting anyone, why did he have to want her with the kind of desperation that left him feeling both powerful and asinine? Was this what Iris had been talking about when she'd tried to explain her affair?

He still remembered the shock of her telling him there was someone else. He'd had no clue—he'd thought they were happy together. Sure they'd been in one of those down times when they were each busy and Connor required whatever attention they had left over, but didn't that happen to everyone? Not every relationship was perfect every second.

Only she hadn't seen it that way. She'd been so calm, he remembered, as she'd told him she was seeing someone else and it was serious. She wasn't sure it was love, but the passion between them was unlike anything she'd experienced before.

He'd been so angry, so disbelieving she would throw away something as significant as a marriage for the fleeting pleasure of passion. She'd told him her feelings consumed her and he'd reacted with contempt. He'd been disdainful even as he'd fought against a rage he couldn't fully explain.

Later, when they'd tried talking about it again, he'd demanded to know if she was leaving. She'd surprised him by telling him she wasn't sure she wanted to lose her marriage. He'd nearly thrown her out then, but for reasons he still couldn't explain, he hadn't. Probably because he hadn't wanted to put Connor through the trauma, and maybe partly because he didn't want to deal with it, either. Not if things were going to be all right in the end.

So they'd continued with their separate lives for nearly a month. Then she'd come to him and told him it was over. That she and her passionate lover were no longer together. She hoped she and Declan could patch up their marriage and grow stronger from the experience.

He'd still been angry. He'd told her it was going to take him some time to work through everything and she had told him that was fine. What he hadn't known then was she'd already been diagnosed with cancer. What he hadn't known was she had told her lover about her disease and that he'd left her. Rather than be alone, she'd decided to return to Declan. He hadn't known that Iris had chosen the other man and when that hadn't worked out, she'd decided that second best was enough.

He continued to tear through the hedge, digging out roots and tossing them onto the growing pile.

She hadn't said a word about being sick. He'd noticed she was losing weight but had assumed it was because she was missing the other man. Perhaps part of it had been, but he was pretty sure it was mostly the cancer.

More time had passed. A few months. Gradually his rage had faded until he could look at what they'd had and realize it shouldn't have been enough for anyone. He'd seen they weren't in a good place and to make things better, to make their marriage stronger, they were both going to have to change. He'd told her he was willing to give it another try, and in response she told him she was dying.

In his head he understood why she'd waited. She hadn't wanted him to take her back because she was sick. But in his heart and his soul and his gut, her withholding that particular truth was the greatest betrayal. Far more than simply sleeping with someone else. Once she'd known she wasn't going to make it, she should have told him the truth. And she hadn't.

He reached the end of the hedge and turned around to look at the destruction. The soil was dark and rich in contrast with the green grass. He knew what he wanted to plant here. He and Connor would tackle that the following weekend. Just like they'd hung on to each other as Iris had died. Connor had kept him going for months, but Declan was now willing to admit he needed to get on with his life.

The back door opened and Sunshine walked out, a tall plastic glass in each hand. It was maybe seventy-two and sunny. She was dressed in shorts and a T-shirt. Neither were tight, neither were the least bit provocative, and yet all he could think about was how desperately he wanted her. Wanted not only what he couldn't have, but wanted a woman who found pain in the wanting. Life was nothing if not ironic.

She smiled when she reached him. "You've been very busy this morning."

"I've been putting off the job too long. The hedge was taking over."

She handed him the first glass. "Water because you're probably dehydrated. Did you put on sunscreen?"

"Yes, I did."

He took the glass and downed the contents. She handed him the second glass.

"Strawberry lemonade. Connor and I made it together. We used the Vitamix. I've never used one before. It's fantastic. I think I have a crush on it."

"That's weird, even for you."

"I know." She held the empty glass. "Sooo, Connor has a playdate with Elijah. I know what you said, but I still think you should consider meeting his mom. I think you and Phoebe would get along."

He didn't want another woman—he wanted Sunshine. But even ignoring the fact that she wasn't into anything short term and he didn't know what love was anymore, she was his son's nanny and therefore off-limits.

He hadn't had sex in a year. It was probably past time he got himself out there. Honestly, what was the worst that could happen?

He sucked in a breath, then shrugged. "Sure. I'll meet her."

Sunshine flashed him a smile that about drove him to his knees. "Yay! I'm so excited. I'll get something set up right away."

She ran back to the house. Her genuine enthusiasm made it clear that she wasn't the least bit jealous or even concerned. So much for her secretly wanting him. Yup, life was ironic and just a bit of a bitch.

chapter
FOURTEEN

MARGOT STEPPED OFF THE BIKE AND NEARLY COLLAPSED
to the floor. Spin class was always a challenge, but this afternoon
it seemed as if the instructor was out for blood.

As she made her way to her locker, she passed a guy throwing
up in a trash can and felt her own stomach lurch. Water, she promised herself. She would drink the bottle she'd brought with her
and another as soon as she got back to her place. Then she would
make sure everything was all right at her apartment, shower,
change, have lunch with her sister, then pick up more clothes and
head back to the monastery. She knew Bianca was going out with
Wesley so maybe Alec would like to hang out this afternoon.

She put on street shoes and collected her tote. Still smiling at
the thought of spending time with Alec, she made her way to
her car. Her phone rang as she unlocked the door.

She glanced at the screen. "Kiska, hi. I haven't heard from
you in a while. How are things?"

"Good. Busy. Dax is traveling all the time and I'm drowning in homework that needs to be graded. We're talking about
getting a puppy, but I don't know. We both work."

Kiska was an elementary school teacher up in the Bay area
and her husband was in sales. Margot had known both of them
since college.

"A puppy would be a challenge. I hear they pee and poop a lot."

"That's what I hear, too. Maybe a kitten would be easier."

"Maybe." Margot started her car and waited for the Bluetooth to engage. Once the call switched to hands free, she tucked her phone into her purse. "Are you two heading down to LA anytime soon? I'd love to see you."

"I'd love to see you, too. Nothing's planned. Why don't you come hang out with me some weekend? We could plan it when Dax is gone and have a girls' weekend."

"I'd like that. Let's get something on the calendar when my current job is done. I'm living in so it would be hard to get away now."

"Sounds like a plan. So, um, I heard from Dietrich."

Margot had just picked up her water bottle. Now she tucked it back into the cup holder and gripped the steering wheel. She was still in her parking space, so didn't have to worry about focusing on her driving.

"Kiska, no. Just no."

"He misses you. He told me."

"He always says he misses me, then he shows up and destroys my life. I'm done with him. It's over. Please, please don't give him any information about me. I don't want to talk to him."

"He's different now."

"No, he's not."

"He's matured. He has his own business and he's really successful. You two were so cute together."

"We weren't. He's bad for me or I'm bad for myself when we're together. It doesn't really matter which. I mean it, Kiska, don't give him my number. I'm done with him. I've moved on."

"If you're sure."

"I am. Very. Very, very."

"Okay. I won't say anything. But I think he deserves another chance."

"He's had about sixteen. No more chances for him."

"Be that way. I gotta run. Let me know when you have a free weekend and we'll plan something, okay?"

"Perfect. Talk to you soon."

They hung up. Margot took a couple of deep breaths.

Dietrich—what a nightmare. He was exactly the last thing she needed in her life. And come to think of it, she hadn't even been thinking of him much at all. She laughed out loud. Had it finally happened? Was she actually over him once and for all? It was a miracle!

"You know I just sweated out five hundred calories at spin class," Margot grumbled as she reached for a tortilla chip.

"All the more reason to load up on Mexican food." Sunshine grinned. "Besides, it was my turn to pick the restaurant, so just suck it up, missy."

Margot eyed the guacamole, as if she were trying to decide if it was worth it. Sunshine waited, knowing exactly what was going to happen. Her sister would hesitate, groan, then dig in.

"I respect that you make the effort," Sunshine told her.

Margot sighed before scooping up guacamole. "I always give in. One day I'll have the power."

"Not over avocados, honey. Besides, they're supposed to be a good fat."

Margot laughed. "You're in a happy mood."

"I'm not. I'm seriously upset, but I'm pretending. I'm doing good, huh?"

Margot stared at her. "You're not kidding. Why didn't I notice right away? I'm sorry. Tell me what happened."

"Nothing." Sunshine was pleased to know her pitiful acting skills were improving. As her life was currently leaping from low point to low point—her work situation excluded—it was good to know she might be able to pretend things were all right even if they weren't.

"Nothing significant," she amended. "I went out on a date

with a guy I thought was nice, and he was a jerk. I still don't understand my math class, although I have my first TA session coming up so maybe that will help."

"Tell me about the guy."

"No way. He's not worth any conversation. And I'll get the math."

Of that she was certain. Even if she had to take the class fifteen times, she was going to figure it out.

"I love my job," she said firmly. "Connor's a sweetie and Declan's…" She hesitated, not sure what to say about her hunky boss. "Declan's becoming a friend. I respect and admire him."

Which was far more politically correct than saying that every now and then she wished they'd met under other circumstances.

"He seemed great," Margot told her. "I didn't get to talk to him much at the dinner, but my impression was really positive. Any chance you'd want to go out with him?"

Sunshine glared at her sister. "Seriously? I work for him. I'm his nanny. That would be tacky and certainly a violation of my personal code of ethics and just no. What if things went bad? I'd lose him and Connor and my job. Then I'd have nothing and I'd have to start over again. It would be a disaster."

Instead of looking chagrined, Margot simply smiled. "Uh-huh. You never said you weren't interested."

Sunshine felt herself flush. "And I'm not interested."

"Too late."

Sunshine honest to God had no idea what to say. She wasn't interested in Declan that way. She couldn't be. The whole idea had *disaster* written all over it.

"I will show my love for you by changing the subject," Margot said cheerfully. "Guess who's trying to find me."

"No! What is wrong with that man? I'm sorry. What are you going to do?"

"He got in touch with Kiska and she thinks I should give him another chance."

"Did you tell her he's already had twenty?"

"Pretty much, but here's the good part." Margot leaned toward her. "I don't care that he wants to see me. I don't care that I haven't heard from him. I'm not relieved, I'm not upset, I'm not worried, I'm not anything."

"Wow. You're over him."

"So over him."

Margot raised her glass of iced tea. Sunshine did the same. They clinked glasses and smiled at each other.

"Baxter sisters rule," Sunshine said firmly.

"You know it, sister. You know it."

Alec was constantly struck by the similarities between life six thousand years ago and life today. Families, regardless of era, worried about children and the future. Wars threatened, illness and injury took beloved souls without warning and the seasons of humans kept time with the seasons of the earth.

He'd been working a translation that was in dispute. He had a copy of the original text, along with two different translations. Rather than compare them to each other, he first translated the text himself. Later he would compare the three and decide which translation was the best.

The work, a poem from 2232 BC, was simple yet emotional. A man at the end of his years reminiscing about his life, both his mistakes and his victories. He'd been a warrior until an injury had taken that career from him, so he'd started farming. Given his battle experience, he'd looked at crops differently than those *raised on the soil*, as he'd put it in his poem. He'd been the first in his village to suggest what farmers today would call crop rotation. He'd also invented clever ways to keep away the birds, rabbits and other creatures that ate too much and offered little in return.

Life had been simpler then, but it hadn't been that different. Boys still dreamed of becoming strong men and doing brave things. They still sought to win the heart of the fair maiden, however that definition might change over time.

Alec made several notations in the margin of his work, then leaned back in his chair and stretched. When he finished his analysis, he would run the poem through a computer program that would offer a slightly more prosaic translation, giving him a fourth point of reference. While the program often missed the nuances in the ancient works, it sometimes provided a note-worthy word choice that could be a jumping-off point for fur-ther study.

He'd just picked up his pen when Bianca breezed into his of-fice, a large vase filled with flowers in her hands.

"Hello, darling," she said, smiling at him. "Remember when you were a little boy and you used to pick me flowers all the time? I was thinking about that today for some reason. Remem-ber that old lady who lived next to us? Mrs. Pearce? You were forever in her gardens and she would phone me, shrieking about how you'd stolen her flowers. You were maybe five or six and she got so upset."

Bianca set the vase on the credenza, then slipped into one of the chairs opposite his desk. Her smile was conspiratorial.

"I told you that she loved you picking flowers and that you should pick some for her as a thank-you."

"I don't remember any of this." Not that he doubted it had happened. His mother was exactly the type to send him back to the scene of the crime to commit it again.

"The old bag was delighted," she said with a laugh. "So touched by your sweet gesture. After that, we couldn't get rid of her. I began to worry she would sneak in at night and kid-nap you for herself."

"I doubt that was an actual concern."

"You're wrong. You were the sweetest little boy."

Not words designed to make him comfortable. He shifted his gaze to the vase. "They're beautiful. Thank you."

"I made sure not to pick any poisonous ones. At least I'm fairly sure I was careful." She studied her hands, then raised them and showed him both sides. "No rash."

"Declan does have a sense of humor when it comes to plants." Not that anything was actually deadly, but there were a few species one had to be careful with.

He returned his attention to his mother. She sat comfortably in her chair and showed no signs of leaving. He bowed to the inevitable.

"How are you liking your lessons?"

"They're much better now. Margot and I have an understanding. She's taking me to a beauty pageant. I've never been to one. Of course I've seen them on television, but this will be different. The contestants are younger. Junior high age, I think."

"What is the purpose of the exercise?"

Bianca waved her hand. "Something about something. I wasn't really paying attention. She'll explain it to me again when we go. She's very thorough that way. We're also looking for some kind of event where I can practice my social skills. She's trying to get me to go to a charity function but I was thinking it should be edgier than that."

Alec felt the beginning of a headache. "Edgier?"

"Yes, like a political fund-raiser. People aren't on their best behavior there. It would be more appealing to me. Besides, Wesley works for a government, not a nonprofit."

She had a point, which was always terrifying.

"How is Wesley?" he asked, hoping to change the subject.

"Wonderful. The man of my dreams. We're blissfully happy. What do you think of Margot?"

As always, when it came to his mother, it took him a second to catch up. "No," he said firmly, when her meaning sank in. "Just no."

His mother's smile turned smug. "She's very beautiful, in a quiet way, which I imagine would be appealing to you. She's smart and reasonable. I would think you two would be well suited."

"No. Don't meddle in my personal life."

"You don't have a personal life, which is exactly my point. Margot is lovely. As far as I can tell, she isn't seeing anyone. I know this violates your rule about sex in your own house, but darling, please, you need a woman. And you have one, right under your nose." She smiled again. "So to speak."

"Stop. Just stop."

"I'm sure she would say yes. From what I've heard from a couple of your previous lovers, you're actually very considerate in bed and are quite skilled when it comes to the female orgasm, so there's no worry on that front."

He wasn't even shocked. That, he supposed, was nearly the worst of it. Not being shocked at all. This simply was—as it had always been—his mother in action.

"I will not go there with you," he said firmly.

She rose and winked. "That's fine, darling, as long as you go there with someone. I'm just saying, she's right upstairs. Take a risk and see what happens."

He pointed to the door. She laughed as she walked out, leaving him alone. Only the comfort and serenity of that state had been lost. Now all he could think about was Margot and the very likely scenario that his mother had had a similar conversation with her.

Sunshine arrived at the tutoring session fifteen minutes early. It was being held in a small classroom with only about fifteen desks. They'd already been pulled into a circle, so she took one by the door and wrestled out her massive textbook and her homework.

They were in chapter three, studying graphs and functions, and it was not going well. She understood how to rewrite an equation to make it a standard form of a linear equation, but the graphing part still didn't make sense. The professor had already done a surprise homework collection, so Sunshine had passed that, but she'd only gotten a C minus on the first quiz, which had been disheartening. She'd studied for two days and hadn't done better than that?

The room filled up. Two o'clock came and went and there was no TA. Finally at two-ten, a scruffy looking guy in his midtwenties strolled in.

"Whassup?" he asked, slumping into the chair at the last desk and yawning. "Okay, I'm Ron. I'm a grad student at UCLA and I only do this for the money. You have thirty minutes, people, so let's not waste my time. Ask your questions and let's see if we can help you scrape by in what I like to call remedial math."

Sunshine saw shock on all the other students' faces. She was sure she looked as stunned. Ron yawned again.

"Tick, tock," he said. "Questions? Anyone? Bueller? Bueller?" He laughed. "Get it? From *Ferris Bueller's Day Off.* No? All right then." He saw Sunshine. "Hey, there. Who are you?"

"One of your remedial math students," she snapped. "We're here for help."

"I can help you any day of the week, beautiful. Want my number?"

Sunshine felt herself flushing. She turned away and wondered if she should just walk out.

"I have a question," a woman in her class said. "I don't understand graphing very well."

"Of course you don't." Ron stood and walked to the board. "Read me a problem."

When the woman didn't say anything, Ron turned to her and pointed. "Open your book to that chapter and read me a problem. Come on, people, this isn't rocket science or even hard math. Let's go."

The woman looked startled. "Um, $y = 2x + 6$."

Ron walked through the solution. He explained what he did

as he went and Sunshine was able to follow. Before she could figure out if she thought she could do it on her own, he'd moved on to another question.

He repeated his process until the thirty minutes was up. By then, her head was spinning. Yes, she could understand why he did what he did, but there was no chance to practice, no way to know if she understood the concept. Everyone else looked as confused as she felt. Weren't TA sessions supposed to help?

"That's it for me," Ron said, putting down the dry erase marker. "This has been so much fun. I'll be back next week." He crossed to Sunshine and waited until she collected her backpack and stood. "Hey, you. I'm Ron."

"So I heard."

"Want to go get coffee? I'm free right now. You are a fine-looking woman, you know that? A little older, but hey, more experienced." He winked. "At least that's what they say."

She slung her backpack over her shoulder and let her gaze linger over his shaggy hair, his scraggly beard, a stain on his faded T-shirt and his dirty jeans.

On the inside, she was crushed, not sure if she had the ability to get through what he'd referred to as remedial math, but no way she was going to let him see that. Self-preservation was a powerful motivator and someone had to give Ron a kick in the balls.

"You?" She smiled, then let the smile grow until she was laughing. "God, no."

With that, she turned and walked out. She heard a couple of people sniggering, which should have made her feel better, but didn't.

One of the young women from the session caught up with her. "You should report him," she told Sunshine. "That's sexual harassment and it's illegal."

"Thanks. I'll think about it."

"He was just a total jerk, talking down to us like that. He's supposed to help us. Well, screw him."

Sunshine offered a tight smile. "See you in class."

The other student nodded. "See you."

Sunshine headed for her car. She told herself she was going to figure this out. Obviously not with Ron, but somehow. She might not have been to college before, but she wasn't an idiot. Other people got through classes—she could, too. She had to. She was determined to be more than she had been before and there was no way she was going to allow herself to get stalled before she'd even started.

"I'm very excited about this afternoon," Bianca said as Margot pulled into the high school parking lot. "I've never been behind the scenes at a beauty pageant before."

"I'm hoping you'll enjoy the experience. We'll start out in the audience for a while, then move backstage. What we're going to see is the preliminary round for talent and the interview."

"Maybe I'd like to be a judge."

"Let's see how this morning goes, then we can talk about it."

"That's very noncommittal."

Margot smiled. "Yes, well, there's a lot more to being a judge than most people think. Every pageant has different rules and different criteria. The winner is far more than the prettiest girl. She has to have a certain quality that is larger than life and often difficult to define."

"You're saying I don't have the attention span?"

"I'm saying we'll talk after you observe for a while."

Bianca linked arms with Margot. "Such a diplomat. I should ask Wesley if there's a rising young star in his social circles and introduce you two."

"Thank you, but no."

"Because you're already interested in someone else?" Bianca's tone was teasing, but there was a real question in her eyes.

Margot immediately thought of Alec, then pushed the thought away. "Let me explain how the morning is going to go."

Bianca sighed. "Really? That's the best you can do for a deflection?"

"Yes."

"Fine. How is the morning going to go?"

Bianca's cooperation was surprising, but she'd been that way for the past couple of days. When they'd discussed wardrobe for their outing, Bianca had agreed to a pretty but conservative dress and a little extra makeup. Margot had chosen a floral print fit-and-flare dress. She'd put her hair up in a fancy twist, wrestled herself into pantyhose and wore nude pumps that pinched her toes. Her handbag was a small clutch in the same pale pink as the background of the floral print, her earrings were simple pearl studs and she'd made time for a manicure.

When returning to a foreign land, it was important to fit in with the natives, she thought as they walked toward the auditorium.

"This is a pre–Junior Miss," she told Bianca. "You don't have to win here to compete at the Junior Miss level, but it helps. At least, it used to be called Junior Miss when I was growing up. They changed it to Distinguished Young Women. Just competing here gives you a leg up. It's good experience and if you pay attention, you can learn a lot."

"Are you saying I can learn a lot or the girls can?"

"Both."

They walked into the auditorium. Margot guided them to seats in the back, on the side, out of the way of family members taking videos and anyone else who had come just to watch. She wanted to have a clear view of the stage, but also be able to talk without disturbing anyone.

"I still don't get the point of all this," Bianca said as they took their seats.

"You're here to get a feel for what's happening. Watch the

girls and their body language. Who wants to be here and who doesn't? Who has the dream and who is being forced into it because Mom never got the chance to compete when she was little?"

"How will I be able to tell that?"

Margot smiled at her. "You are a very keen observer of people. You'll know before I will, but I'll show you what I mean. When you get nervous, you tighten up and look for a distraction. At some point the need to change the narrative takes over and the results can be—"

"Disastrous?"

"I was thinking more that they spiral out of control. I'm hoping by watching these girls, you'll feel what they're feeling and see how they handle it. Or don't. There will be tears and tantrums and outbursts. Sometimes seeing a situation play out in someone else's life brings us clarity."

Margot shrugged. "I'm winging it, Bianca. So this may be a colossal waste of time."

"I'm excited."

A woman stepped up to the podium. "Kristen Kenneth on the violin."

A small girl moved into the center of the stage. She looked nervous and Margot felt herself tense, remembering how much she hated being onstage. Then she reminded herself she wasn't the point of the exercise and consciously relaxed back into her seat. When the girl lifted her bow and the first note filled the auditorium, she could relax for real. The contestant was an excellent musician.

Music soared and danced. The girl's eyes sank closed as she retreated into the beauty of the piece. Margot leaned toward Bianca.

"Tell me what you're thinking?"

"She's gifted and loves her music. I'm not sure she wants to be in a beauty pageant." She narrowed her gaze. "She's not nearly pretty enough. She might grow into her looks, but I doubt it. She's not naturally elegant. I think someone in the family is making her do this and they should leave her alone to have a musical career."

Margot stared at her. "Wow. That was good. Okay, you're totally getting this."

Several more girls competed in the talent competition. One tap-danced with a lot more enthusiasm than talent. When she slipped and landed on the stage on her butt, she burst into tears and ran off.

"A quitter," Bianca murmured.

Margot winced. "That might be a bit harsh."

"She's chubby and there's no way she's going to be a beauty. In my business they call it a face for radio."

"You need to dial it down."

"I'm telling you what I think."

"Try being less mean."

"Whatever."

They watched a few more girls, then there was a break. Margot stood. "Let's go backstage." She narrowed her gaze. "On the condition you only say nice things."

"It was one comment. You know I'm right about her."

"Actually I don't. I've seen average-looking girls blossom into great beauties and pretty girls who weren't the least bit successful in pageants. My great-grandmother would know. She could look at a seven-year-old and tell you how she was going to grow up. It was a gift."

They made their way down the aisle toward the stage.

"So why do they do this?" Bianca asked. "Why take the chance when you have no idea if you're going to be pageant material?" She made air quotes around the last two words.

"Lots of reasons. At this age, some are doing it for Mom, as we discussed. But for others, it's fun to play with clothes and makeup. You meet people and learn skills. If you want to go into journalism or anything to do with the media, you'll learn how to speak to a group, have poise in nearly any situation. At the upper levels, the scholarship money can make the difference between the school of your dreams and community college. If you win at the state level, you'll have opportunities most people can't even dream of."

Bianca stared at her in surprise. "You believe in all this."

"I've seen what the pageants can do. It's a lot more than a show on cable TV." Margot walked around the stage and opened the door leading to the dressing rooms. "Having said that, there are girls who are here because they have to be and not because they want to be. A lot is on the line. Emotions run high and there is plenty of drama."

She showed her backstage pass to a security guard, then opened another door that led behind the stage. The volume went from quiet to battleworthy shrieks and squeals. Girls ran everywhere, laughing, crying, twirling and texting. Family members—mostly moms but some grandparents and the occasional dad—did their best to corral their girls. A few of them looked at Bianca and did a double take, as if they weren't sure if they recognized her or not, something Margot had worried about. She pulled Bianca to the side.

"We're here to observe," she said, speaking into Bianca's ear. "Just watch them. You'll see the ones who are excited and the ones who hate their moms. The purpose of this is for you to experience a visceral reaction to the dynamics, then think about what you could do to defuse that situation if you were involved. What would you say? Where would you go to take a second to breathe? I'm hoping you'll ride the roller coaster of emotions but also stay above them."

"What are you feeling?" Bianca asked.

Margot looked around at the girls in curlers, the mothers applying mascara and thought of the pressure to be all her great-grandmother wanted her to be.

"It can be tough and I could never have done this."

"But you tried."

"Over and over again."

Bianca nodded, then turned back to the girls.

"What do you think you're doing?" one mother yelled, grabbing her daughter by the arm. "You were eating candy. You're already so fat, you barely fit in your dress. Do you know how much this is costing us? I had to take time off work to come here with you and you're eating candy?"

"I'm hungry."

"I don't care if you're starving to death. Fat girls don't win."

Margot fought down anger. She desperately wanted to march up to that woman and tell her to just stop it. Bianca put out a restraining arm.

"Breathe," she said quietly.

"I always hated that part of things."

"Who wouldn't? We just have to trust in karma."

"Or maybe call Social Services," Margot grumbled.

There were other girls who were excited about the competition. Girls who were laughing and hugging their moms.

"There's the pageant coordinator," Margot said. "I'm going to say hello to her and thank her for letting us come observe. Want to meet her?"

"No thanks. I'll walk around instead. Come find me when you're done."

Margot wondered if that was the best plan, then figured Bianca wasn't going to get into any trouble in a place like this. Or so she hoped.

She wove her way through the contestants and found Paula Turner.

"Margot! How lovely to see you." Paula, a beautiful woman in her forties, hugged her. "You're stunning as always."

Margot smiled. "As are you. I see tablets have replaced clipboards."

"Time marches on. Are you enjoying our future queens?"

"I am. There's a lot of talent here."

A sharp scream cut through the babble of conversation. Paula winced. "And the usual drama. Can I convince you to consider judging?"

"Not right now. It would be more of a commitment than I want to take on."

"I knew you were going to say that, but if you change your mind, you know how to find me."

Margot excused herself and went looking for Bianca. She saw her client rushing out a side door.

"What on earth?"

Margot hurried after her and caught up with her by the car. Tears streamed down Bianca's face as she pulled frantically on the locked car door.

"We have to go! Now! We have to go. How could you? Do you know what they're doing? Do you?"

"Bianca, what's wrong? What happened?"

Bianca turned away from her. "Leave me alone. This was a terrible idea. I just want to go home. I want to go *now*."

The last word came out as a scream. Margot flinched, then opened the car doors. The drive back to the house was silent except for the sound of Bianca's sobs.

When they arrived, Margot turned to her. "I'm sorry. I don't know what went wrong."

She expected Bianca to yell at her, but instead she drew in a breath and shook her head. "You can't know. No one can know. It's just… I can never go back there again. Promise me we won't go back."

"I promise. But please, tell me what happened. I want to help."

"You can't." Tears flowed down Bianca's cheeks. "You can't. No one can. But it's not your fault. It's me. It's in me."

With that, she scrambled out of the car and ran toward the house. Margot stared after her, not sure what had happened or what her words meant. *You can't know. No one can know.* What did that mean? That it was a secret? Or no one else could understand what she'd been through?

Something from Bianca's past had been triggered. Something awful and scary. Something that had left scars on her heart and her soul. Whatever it was, it was a powerful force and it had been with Bianca for a long, long time.

chapter
FIFTEEN

DECLAN COULDN'T REMEMBER THE LAST TIME HE'D BEEN so nervous. The whole situation was ridiculous, and yet there he was, with sweaty palms and a burning desire to bolt. Not that he had any idea where he would go or how running away would make anything better.

His reaction—or overreaction—didn't make sense. Some woman was dropping off her kid for a playdate. It had happened before and it would happen again. There was nothing to be concerned about. Except, she wasn't just some woman, she was Elijah's mother, and for reasons that were no longer clear to him, somehow she had become a viable candidate for him to go out with and possibly, eventually, have sex with.

He couldn't remember all the steps that had gotten him from a need without an obvious solution to an actual woman on his doorstep, but here he was and damned if he wasn't apprehensive that certain things were going to go badly.

Today was Sunshine's day off. At least that was something. He wasn't sure he could have endured her giggling in the background. Not that she would have been giggling, but she would have *known* some measure of what he was thinking and dear God, he needed a drink.

Given that it wasn't even noon, he pushed that thought away.

He was about to retreat to his office in an attempt to distract himself when Connor came running into the kitchen.

"They're here! Elijah's here! I'm going to show him my ant farm before we go for batting practice, okay, Dad? You won't rush us?"

Declan smiled at his son. "You take as much time with the ant farm as you want."

"Thanks, Dad."

His plan was to take the boys to the batting cage for an hour or so, then grab lunch before heading to the gardens at The Huntington where they would spend the rest of the afternoon. Both boys should end the day tired and ready for a quiet evening, which was Declan's understanding of a successful playdate.

Connor ran to the front door to let them in. Declan followed more slowly, more unsure than reluctant.

He'd met Elijah before. The kid was about Connor's height, also on the thin side, with red hair and freckles. His mother was a pretty redhead with short hair and an easy smile. She wore jeans and a T-shirt and had a kid-size backpack over one arm.

He tried to figure out if he was attracted to her, but couldn't get past the weirdness of having to ask the question.

"Hi," she said, holding out her hand. "I'm Phoebe Salvia. You must be Declan. Nice to meet you."

"Likewise."

Connor motioned to Elijah. "Come see the ants. They're really happy in their new home and they're busy all the time."

The boys raced down the hall.

Phoebe shook her head. "All that energy. I just want to crawl back in bed and read for a couple of hours." She handed him the backpack. "His batting helmet is in there, along with a clean T-shirt, just in case."

"Good thinking. So the plan is what Sunshine discussed. I'll drop him off between three and four."

"That's perfect. I have a huge list of errands to get done today." Her smile turned impish. "We can't all have a nanny."

Declan knew she was teasing, but still felt a little uncomfortable with the topic. "We're lucky to have her."

"Yes, you are. Maybe instead of a raise, I could ask my boss for nanny credits."

"What is it you do?"

"I'm a manager at a large insurance company."

"Oh, that's…"

"Don't say *interesting*." She laughed again. "Seriously, it's not, but that's okay. I'm responsible for three call centers and a hundred salespeople, so the work is challenging, but whenever I say insurance, people immediately tune me out."

"I won't do that."

"I'm happy to hear that." She glanced down the hall. "Please don't say anything encouraging about the ant farm to Elijah. There is no way on this earth I'm paying to have ants *in* the house." She shuddered.

"I will discourage any ant farm conversation."

"Thank you. Well, I should probably get going."

She hesitated a second before opening the door. As if waiting for something.

While they'd been talking, Declan had forgotten to be nervous, but as soon as she lingered, he suddenly felt like a fifteen-year-old unable to keep from having an erection at a funeral.

"Good luck with the errands," he said. "I have your cell if I need to get in touch with you."

"Yes, you do." Her tone was pointed.

Crap. Double crap.

Not knowing what else to do, he reached around her and held open the door. "I'll see you this afternoon."

"Have fun with the boys."

She waved and walked out of the house. He closed the door behind her, then shook his head. He was totally and completely hopeless, he thought, unable to shake the sense of having missed something.

He didn't want to deal with any of this, he thought as he started for Connor's room. He didn't want to have to figure out if he liked someone or if she liked him. He wanted things to be easy, like they were with Sunshine. Around her, he was always comfortable—well, except for the wanting her part. Not that it was her fault she was so incredibly hot. But it was more than that. He liked talking to her. They found the same things funny, they never ran out of things to say. If she wasn't his nanny, he would ask her out in a second.

But she was his nanny and he didn't want to lose that or screw up what they had. Which left him with the social graces of a twig and the knowledge that he really wanted to get laid.

Alec saw Bianca sitting out in the garden. There was nothing unusual with that—the afternoon was warm and sunny. However, what caught his attention was the fact that his mother was smoking. He'd never seen her smoke before and went out to investigate.

She looked up as he approached the stone table, but didn't say anything. Sure enough, there was a pack of cigarettes next to her, and an ashtray.

"You're smoking." He tried not to sound accusatory, but wasn't sure he was successful. "You've never been a smoker."

"Oh, Alec, the things you don't know about me could fill volumes."

She sounded sad and resigned, not at all the woman he knew. Her face was lined and she looked much closer to her actual age than he'd ever seen her. He sat next to her.

"What's wrong?"

"Margot tried to quit."

His gut clenched at the words and it was all he could do to keep from running inside to demand that she not leave. An unexpected reaction he would study later.

"What happened?"

Bianca inhaled deeply, then blew out smoke. Her movements were practiced. When had she started smoking and why didn't he know?

"Nothing happened," his mother said. "It's all ridiculous. She took me to a beauty pageant this morning. I was to watch the girls and figure out which ones wanted to be there and which didn't. The point was to help me see what discomfort and awkwardness look like so I could feel the feelings and deal with them. I don't know—maybe it wasn't that at all."

"What happened?"

His mother offered him a humorless smile. "You keep asking that. She did the same. Nothing *happened*. No one said anything to me or even noticed I was there. Nothing happened."

"Then why is Margot quitting and why are you out here smoking?"

"She thinks she's not good for me. She thinks she's failing. I told her it wasn't about her. If she and Wesley were getting married, there would be no problem. She would know exactly what to do in every situation. She would be the perfect wife and he would never have to worry about his career."

Alec was in over his head and drowning. He could feel himself going under and had absolutely no idea how to reach the surface. Or what they were talking about.

"Margot and Wesley have no interest in each other. Why would you think otherwise?"

Her smile turned genuine. "Yes, my love, I know that. I was trying to illustrate a point." The smile faded. "It doesn't matter. Not really. I want to do this. I want to get through the problem or over it or whatever the right word is."

"What's the problem?"

She looked at him for a long time. "I'm not really a smoker. Sometimes, when I don't feel right, I smoke because it centers me. I go through maybe a pack a year. You don't have to worry."

"Maybe you should just take a Valium instead."

She got up and patted his shoulder. "Isn't that still drugging myself?"

"Yes, but it's safer."

"I love you very much, and I love Wesley. You shouldn't worry. Everything is going to work out just fine."

With that, she turned and walked into the house.

Alec knew she meant her words to be reassuring but they were anything but. He followed her inside and took the stairs to the second floor, where he found Margot in the guest lounge. She was curled up in a corner of the sofa. Her face was pale and she looked shaken. When she saw him, she flushed slightly, then turned away.

He sat across from her in a chair. "I spoke to my mother."

"I really should leave."

"Why? What happened?"

"I have no idea. We went to the pageant and everything was fine. We talked about the purpose, the scholarships and hard work. She wanted to walk around by herself while I spoke to someone I knew. Not ten minutes later, she was upset—crying to the point where she could barely speak. She demanded we leave and yelled at me for taking her there."

She finally looked at him. "I don't know what triggered her and I have no idea what *was* triggered. Obviously she was upset, but about what? She told me I couldn't possibly understand but that it wasn't me."

She folded her arms across her chest. "First the dinner and now this. I'm not doing a very good job here. I'm supposed to help, not make things worse."

"You couldn't have known something at a kid's beauty pageant would affect her so strongly."

"Did her mother put her in pageants when she was little? Did she have a bad experience at a talent show or something?"

"Not that I know of."

"If I don't understand the problem, there's no way I can help her," Margot said. "Maybe someone else would do better."

"She doesn't want you to go. If she did, believe me, she would have no trouble telling you."

"That's what she said. It's just…" Margot drew in a breath. "What I should tell you is I'm really good at my job and I hate messing up but what I'm really thinking is I like your mom a lot and I wish I could stop hurting her."

"You didn't hurt her."

Her mouth twisted. "I put her in circumstances that hurt her. It's a fine line, believe me. I'm rethinking my entire plan. Again. It's not usually like this."

"Most clients aren't like my mother."

She managed a shaky smile. "You did try to warn me."

He looked at her. "I think you're helping her. She knows a lot more about Cardigania and she's very excited about the political fund-raiser."

He wanted to say more—he wanted to tell her that he needed her in his house, only that wasn't true. Yes, he liked Margot but *need*? That was completely unreasonable.

"My boss thinks I should stick it out," Margot admitted. "He says it will be good for me, that my plan is sound and all Bianca's reports to the office have been excellent."

"There. You have proof you're doing well."

"Until today. And the whole soup thing."

She shifted so her bare feet were flat on the floor. Until that moment he hadn't realized she wasn't wearing shoes, but now that he'd seen her bare toes, he couldn't seem to look at anything else.

Her toes? He didn't have a foot fetish. It wasn't that her feet were especially erotic, it was that they were bare. There was something vulnerable about that, something that made him want to hold her and tell her everything would be all right. None of which made sense. What if what his mother had was contagious?

"There's something in her past," Margot said firmly.

For a second Alec thought he'd spoken his thoughts out loud, but then he realized Margot was talking about something else.

"Behavior is all on a spectrum," she continued. "Including being impetuous and not caring about what other people think. Most of the time your mother is well in the middle range. What you and I think of as normal. But every now and then she becomes outrageous. From what I've observed, some of that is by design, but some isn't."

"We're back to an incident from her past."

Margot nodded. "You really have no idea what it is?"

"I really have no idea. I would tell you if I knew something but wasn't comfortable discussing it."

She smiled. "I knew you were going to say that. And you're her only family?"

He nodded. "She never knew her father—she's an only child, as was her mother, who has since passed away."

"So we have a mystery and absolutely no way to solve it," Margot said with a sigh. "Not unless we can convince her to tell us what it is."

"Unless *you* can convince her."

She grinned. "Not willing to delve deeply into your mother's psychological past?"

"I'd rather face lions."

"Not even for the key to Indus script?"

He considered her words. "No, not even for that."

"Wow. She is powerful."

"You have no idea."

Sunshine finished squeezing limes into a measuring cup. She had tequila, she had Cointreau, she had ice, she had a glass and absolutely nothing planned for the evening. She was going to put the crappy week behind her, get drunk, then start fresh in the morning. Come dawn, or maybe eight-thirty, she would rise refreshed, hopeful and ready to figure out how to graph linear equations. Barring that, she would check out the math lab on campus. She was not going to be undone by Math 131. She was going to excel—or at the very least, pass.

She poured the ingredients into the Vitamix, added ice, put on the lid and flipped the sucker on. It leaped to life with the power of a jet engine and before she could say *Why, yes, I am sulking*, she had margaritas. She turned off the machine.

"Is this a party for one, or can anyone join?"

The voice came from behind her. She shrieked and jumped, then spun around to see Declan standing in the entrance to the kitchen. She pressed a hand to her chest, as if she could still her thundering heart.

"I thought you were out with Connor," she said breathlessly. "Jeez, don't sneak up on me."

"Sorry. Connor's staying over at Elijah's tonight. I just got back from dropping off his stuff. They were having a lot of fun and Phoebe said she didn't mind, so here I am. I didn't mean to scare you."

"I know. It's okay."

She reached for another glass. "Just so you know, I'm feeling especially pouty tonight. If you hang out with me, I'll whine and be unreasonable."

"I think I can handle it."

She ran a wedge of lime around the rim of both glasses, dipped them in salt, then poured in the slushy mixture. She put the leftovers in the refrigerator—not that she expected them to have to last long. It was definitely a two-margarita kind of night.

Together they carried their drinks out to the patio and took seats in two of the lounge chairs. The late afternoon temperature was a balmy seventy-two degrees and the sun had headed west but was still visible. Sunshine kicked off her shoes and put her bare feet on the ottoman by her comfy chair. Maybe she would just sit here forever. Later, when she'd decomposed, Declan could bury her bones in the garden.

She smiled, thinking there were a lot of steps between right now and being nothing but bones. For one thing, she was going to have to pee in a while.

"What's so funny?" he asked, stretching out in the chair next to hers.

"Nothing you want to hear."

"Okay, then why are you pissy?"

"I said *pouty*, but *pissy* works." She sipped her drink. "I went to a TA session a couple of days ago. The guy was a total jerk. He talked down to everyone, was totally demeaning and then had the balls to practically ask me for sex."

Declan put his feet on the floor. "Did you report him? I worked with the college on several projects and they're supportive of the students. They would not tolerate that kind of behavior. I can get you the name of someone in administration."

"Of course you can," she said, doing her best to keep her tone light. "I'm not going to report him."

"Why not?"

"It's too much like running to my mom after someone's mean to me on the playground. I don't want to start something, I just want to pass my class. It's not even him," she added, telling herself she was fine. Or she would be. "I talked to one of the students in my class. I told her what happened." She closed her eyes. "You know what she asked?"

"What?"

"She wanted to know if I was wearing something that made him think I was asking for that kind of attention." She opened her eyes and looked at him. "What year is this? Is that even relevant? For what it's worth, I was dressed how I always am for school. In jeans and a shirt. Except for the professor, I'm the oldest person in the room. This isn't about me trying to get a guy's attention at a nightclub."

"Report him," Declan repeated. "The college would want to know what happened."

"I'm sure they would, but this isn't about that." She managed a slight smile. "I warned you—I'm being pouty, so this is not the time for reasoned conversation." She looked at him. "Please don't try to fix my problem."

"I really want to."

"I know. It's a guy thing. But you have to let this go."

He exhaled heavily. "Fine. But only because you asked."

"Thank you. Drink your margarita. You'll feel better."

He did as she'd requested, then asked, "What are you going to do?"

"Check out the math lab."

"Do you want me to look over your assignments? I might remember enough to be able to help."

"Don't take this the wrong way, but I'm going to go the math lab route. I think it would be awkward to have you helping me with my homework."

"The offer stands."

"Thank you." She drank more of her margarita. "So did you get to spend much time with Phoebe today?"

"And the next topic?"

She laughed. "Come on. You have to admit she's nice and funny and attractive."

"Then you should date her."

"She's not my type, but you could..."

He looked at her, his expression exasperated. She grinned at him. He had a nice face. Strong and handsome. He was a good guy. Cared about his kid, which she liked best of all.

"Fine." She faced the garden again. "I've been thinking about Connor's birthday. It's coming up fast. We should figure out the party."

"You're right, we should. I never much thought about it. That was one thing Iris handled. What did you have in mind?"

He rarely mentioned his late wife. She almost never came up in conversation and Sunshine had no idea what that meant. Connor talked about her, although less often than he used to.

Sometimes, before bed, he sent up prayers to heaven, asking the angels to get her messages about what was going on in his life. But Declan was mostly silent about his relationship with her.

"I would propose we go with an ant-heavy bug theme. I've been looking around at decorations and there isn't much that is just ant based. I can do some custom things easily enough. Let's see."

She put her margarita on the small table between them and held up one finger. "Food. The bakery at the grocery store will do ant cupcakes. I also have a recipe for an ice cream cake that looks like a watermelon with ants on it. We'd do a green punch and call it bug juice. There's ants on a log, of course and I'm trying to come up with a bug-themed sandwich or wrap, but I haven't had much luck yet."

She held up a second finger. "For decorations I can make caterpillars out of balloons and a couple of places sell small plastic ants by the bag, so we'll have those everywhere. I can get bug paper plates and cups. I'd buy plain goodie bags, then glue on ant cutouts. So far I've found Ant-Man soap, bug stickers and I wanted to talk to you about a flashlight. I found heat resistant stick-ons that I can cut into an ant shape so when they turn on the flashlight, there's an ant on the wall."

She grabbed her margarita and took a drink. "I'm hoping the weather will be nice enough that we can have the whole thing outside. I'd want to rent tables and chairs, if that's okay with you. I have some game ideas, too, but it's probably too soon to discuss those. So what do you think?"

He stared at her. "You've thought of everything. It sounds great. Yes, please, let's do that."

"Yay! What's the budget?"

"Spend whatever you want."

"You can't say that. What if I go wild?"

"Then you go wild. I'm not worried. Sunshine, you use coupons when you do the grocery shopping. Those are not the actions of someone who is going to spend a thousand dollars on a kid's birthday party. Also, a lot of what you're describing is labor heavy, so time you'll have to put in. I want to help. I'm pretty sure I could do some of the cutting and gluing."

"I don't know. It's pretty tricky stuff."

"Try me." He smiled at her. "This is going to be Connor's best party ever. The ones we threw him were much more low-key."

"Is it too much?"

"No. It's exactly right. You're very creative. He'll love everything you have planned for him."

"Okay. Thanks for saying that." She finished her drink and waited for the tequila to do its thing. "Do you mind if I ask you about Iris?"

Declan held her gaze. "Sure. What do you want to know?"

She thought he might have tensed a little as he spoke, but she couldn't tell. "Was she an indoor kind of person? Not very physical or athletic? I don't mean that in a judgy way."

"I know you don't." He leaned back in his chair. "She was very much in her head. She worked in medical research and enjoyed reading and quiet activities."

"That's what I thought. You're not like that and I don't think Connor is, either."

Declan raised his eyebrows. "He's always going off to his room."

"Sure. It's what he knows. But he likes to be outside and run around, too. I think he needs a physical activity, like some kind of sport. I'm not sure what, but an organized team would be good for him. After the games he could hang out with the guys, learn the rules of male hierarchy and all that."

"The rules of male hierarchy?" His voice was teasing. "What does that mean?"

"Oh, you know what I'm talking about. Don't pretend you don't. Guys have rules for how they interact with each other. We all see it. He needs to learn that. I'm not saying he'll play pro ball, but it would be good for him."

His humor faded. "It would. You're right—I should have recognized that myself. Thank you, Sunshine."

His voice was low and sexy. Appealing, she thought, as a little quiver took up residence in her belly. Declan was… He was… Nice. Just nice. As a father, as a man. She liked his smile and the way he talked and his sense of humor and how he was with Connor and…

No, no and no, she told herself. Not going there. She loved her job and she was not going to be that girl anymore. She was better than that.

"Were you into sports in high school?" he asked, drawing her back to the conversation.

"I was a cheerleader."

"Of course you were. Great, now I'm picturing you—" He sat up and turned toward her. "I apologize. I never should have said that."

He sounded horrified. Or maybe mortified. She didn't know exactly what he'd been picturing, but it was fine with her.

"Don't worry about it," she told him.

"I don't want to be like your TA."

"Believe me, you have nothing in common with him." She picked up her glass only to remember it was empty. Hmm, maybe the tequila had kicked in after all. Not that she felt drunk, just relaxed and less whiny.

"You should ask Phoebe out," she said.

"That again?"

"Yes. It would be good for you."

"I never should have discussed my personal life with you."

"Or the lack of one?" she teased.

"That, too."

She sat up and swung her legs down and put her bare feet on the pavers.

"Declan, there's nothing wrong with wanting to be with someone. Sex is a part of the human condition. It's not wanting and needing that's the problem, it's how people go about meeting those needs that screws up things. What happens between two consenting adults is perfectly fine."

He looked at her. She had no idea what he was thinking, but that was okay. Just looking at him made her happy.

"You're holding out for love?" he asked.

She sighed. "At this point I would be thrilled to have someone to take me seriously, but that seems to be a losing battle."

She picked up her glass and stood at the same time he got to his feet. The sun had slipped below the horizon and the air was rapidly cooling. The night was still and she could hear the sound of their breathing.

His dark gaze locked with hers. Something crackled between them—something hot and dangerous and yet full of promise. She knew that if she leaned toward him, he would touch her. He might even kiss her and she found herself longing for the feel of his mouth on hers. Only… Only…

And then what? After they kissed, what was next? Sex? So they did it and she walked from his bed to hers and then in the morning, what did they say to each other? More important, what did she say to herself? If she was ever going to be more than she was, she had to break the cycle of giving in because it felt good. Dammit, she wanted to be a person with a moral compass and a spine.

"I can't," she whispered, before bolting into the house. She ran into her bedroom and closed the door behind her. She didn't lock it—she didn't have to. Declan would never walk in without being invited.

She put down her glass and then flopped on the bed. Later she would be all proud and smug but right now she was lonely, tired and sad. She knew she'd done the right thing, but man, did it suck.

chapter
SIXTEEN

"MARGOT, STOP FROWNING. SERIOUSLY, YOU'RE GIVING yourself wrinkles and I'm not sure you're the type who would allow yourself the thrill of Botox."

"I'm not sure anyone thinks of Botox as a *thrill*."

Bianca smiled. "Only those who haven't tried it, my dear. And I know what I'm talking about."

Margot did her best to relax her expression. Worrying wouldn't help. They were committed now.

She looked past her client to the guests entering the ballroom for the political fund-raiser. They were all well dressed and moneyed. Tickets had been at a thousand-dollar minimum.

Margot returned her attention to Bianca. "You remember our game plan?"

"Of course. Polite conversation about anything innocuous. Avoid politics, which is totally ridiculous when you consider where we are. I'm to look for people standing alone, preferably women. Five minutes with someone, then move on. If I feel nervous, I will excuse myself and come find you. If I can't, I'll head to the bathroom and text you."

Bianca patted her arm. "Don't worry. We had a bit of a stumble at the beginning, but we're working well together now. I'm feeling really good about tonight."

"You look good."

Bianca smiled. "Yes, I do, don't I?"

Bianca was wearing a fairly conservative dark red dress that went to just below her knees. Her hair was loose and curly, her makeup subtle. She looked confident, beautiful and just a little sexy.

Margot linked arms with her. "All right. You're ready. Let's go."

They joined the crowd milling toward the open double doors.

"I hope there aren't going to be a lot of tech guys here tonight," Bianca murmured. "I still remember when Steve and I were seeing each other. He was so fun at first, but after a while all he would talk about was Apple, Apple, Apple."

Margot nearly stumbled. "You don't mean...Steve Jobs?"

"What? Yes. It was years ago. He was so young, but then so was I." She flashed a smile, before handing over her ticket to the person at the door.

Margot did the same and they moved into the ballroom. Before she could offer any last-minute advice, she found herself abandoned by her client.

"Good luck," she said to Bianca's back. She was about to survey the room and figure out her next move when she spotted Alec, a glass of champagne in each hand.

"Good evening," he said, handing her one. "You two made it."

"We did."

She had driven over with Bianca while Alec had come separately. The plan was that Bianca would leave alone to go stay with Wesley, and Alec would take Margot back to the house.

Margot grabbed his hand and pulled him to a relatively quiet corner of the huge room. "Did you know your mother had an affair with Steve Jobs?"

Alec didn't look the least bit shocked by the question. "No, but little from her past surprises me."

"Wasn't he married?"

"I'm sure the affair was before that. Bianca isn't into married men."

"You're so calm. It's Steve Jobs!"

"Are you an Apple fan?"

"I love my iPhone, like millions of others. It's just shocking."

He chuckled. "She's been involved with actors and heads of state and race car drivers and you get in a tizzy about Steve Jobs."

"I have nerd-like qualities. I can't help it."

He held out his arm. "Come on. Let's go lurk in the background and watch my mother. Are you nervous?"

"Terrified and oddly resigned."

"An unexpected combination."

They moved through the ballroom. There were several political candidates working the crowd. Margot and Alec avoided them, then finally spotted Bianca near the bar. She was with a middle-aged woman, talking animatedly and laughing. After a few minutes, Bianca spotted them and excused herself.

"I'm doing fine," she said as she approached. "Stop monitoring me. It's unnerving."

"I get paid to watch you," Margot said, her voice teasing. "I have to do my job."

"I enjoy standing in the light that is your beauty," Alec told her.

His mother smiled. "Darling, while I would love to believe that, I'm wondering how much champagne you've had."

"My first glass," he assured her.

"Then watch and learn."

Bianca strolled toward a young man standing by himself.

"This will be noteworthy," Alec murmured. "He'll be overwhelmed by her in less than thirty seconds. He might faint."

Margot was about to answer when she spotted a man also watching Bianca—which should be nothing to worry about except he had two cameras hanging around his neck.

"There's a reporter," she said, starting toward him.

"It's a political event," Alec said, walking with her. "There were bound to be reporters. However, I suspect this one is a photographer hired by the campaign. Please, allow me. I have experience with this sort of thing."

Alec reached the photographer first. "Good evening. Would you mind not photographing my mother? She's here as a supporter, not as a public figure."

The photographer, a tall guy in his midforties, looked more annoyed than accommodating. "She's the money shot."

"I'm sure the senator's staff would be delighted to know that's your opinion," Alec said easily. "Shall we go tell them? Or are you not being paid to take pictures of the event for the website and possibly mailers?"

"You're threatening me?" the guy asked, sounding incredulous.

"I am," Alec told him. "Now, how do you want to handle this?"

Margot watched him weigh his options. She would guess if the photographer was hired for an event this large that he would be used frequently by the campaigns. She doubted he would want to lose that income for a single sale of a shot of Bianca.

"Fine," he grumbled. "Whatever. She's old. No one cares about her anymore."

Alec smiled. "Enjoy the party."

"You handled that very well," Margot said when they'd walked away. "You do have experience."

They searched for Bianca and found her with yet another man. This one was closer to her age and more into her than made Margot comfortable.

"He's standing close and is too animated," she said. "I think she found a fan."

"Not good. Bianca loves being adored."

Although Bianca was at least twenty feet away, with several people between them, Margot heard her laugh over the other conversations. It had a more frenetic quality than she liked, with a slight edge.

"That doesn't sound good," she murmured. "There's too much energy between them." She hesitated, not sure if she should intervene or let Bianca handle herself. The only way to learn was to do, at least in Bianca's case.

She watched her client lean into the man. Alec didn't offer an opinion, no doubt because he knew this was a training session and she was the expert—not that she felt especially certain at that moment.

When the guy leaned in to whisper in Bianca's ear, Margot started toward her.

"Hi," she said, as she approached. "I'm Margot and this is Alec."

"Brandon," the man said, offering them both an easy smile. "Do you know Bianca?"

"Oh, Alec is my son and Margot is…" Bianca's eyes sparkled with mischief. "Margot is his lover."

Margot did her best to look casual and hoped she didn't blush. Bianca was trying to get to her—not a surprise considering her client frequently chafed at being told what to do.

Margot didn't know what to say—should she refute the claim? Ignore it? Say nothing? Before she could decide, Alec stepped in.

"I doubt anyone finds that of interest," he said easily, before taking a sip of his champagne. "Mother, there are some people I'd like you to meet."

Brandon grabbed Bianca's hand. "Don't go. Please. Just a few more minutes." He grinned at her. "Don't take this wrong, but I had posters of you on my wall when I was growing up. You were the sexiest woman I'd ever seen and you still are."

Bianca preened as her smile turned flirtatious. "Oh, stop. You're embarrassing my son."

"I'm used to it," Alec murmured quietly to Margot. He raised his voice back to conversational level. "If you'll excuse us, please."

Bianca shot him an annoyed look. Margot stepped between them. "It's just this way," she said, pointing across the ballroom.

"Fine." Bianca sighed. "It was lovely to meet you, Brandon."

He nodded, looking stricken at the loss of her company. "Could I just kiss your cheek?"

Bianca smiled. "Of course. I'll even do you one better." She leaned in and kissed him lightly on the mouth. "There. Dream about that tonight."

"You know I will." He stared into her eyes. "I'll give you fifty thousand dollars if I can touch your ass. No, wait. I'll give fifty thousand dollars to your favorite charity. Anything. Kids, pets, those cow people. You name it."

Alec took his mother's hand and pulled her away. "That's it. Nice to meet you, Brandon. Have a good life."

Margot stepped around to Bianca's other side as they walked across the crowded ballroom.

"That was a surprise," she said, not sure what to make of Brandon. Regardless, she was going to have to come up with a lesson plan that dealt with middle-aged men with lingering Bianca fantasies.

Bianca smiled. "It's been a long time since a man wanted to pay me to touch my ass. I still have it."

"You'll still have it a decade after you're gone," Alec told her.

"Oh, that's so sweet." She turned to Margot. "I'm sorry for teasing you back there. I just couldn't help myself."

"You're in your element. I completely understand."

Margot was less concerned about the crack now that she knew Alec wasn't embarrassed or upset by it. She had to admit—Bianca always kept her on her toes.

They circulated through the crowd for another half hour. Bianca chatted with a few more people, making pleasant small talk and avoiding any subject the least bit controversial.

Margot glanced at her watch. "The speeches are due to start in twenty minutes. I assume we want to leave before then?"

"Absolutely." Bianca finished her glass of champagne. "We do, indeed. It's enough that I bought tickets to the event. I'm not willing to stay and listen to a bunch of politicians." She smiled at Margot. "I'll have plenty of that when I marry Wesley."

"Shall we go?" Alec asked.

"I'm going to duck into the ladies' room," his mother told him. "I'll meet you back here in a few minutes."

"Would you like me to go with you?" Margot asked automatically.

Bianca rolled her eyes. "I can make it to the restroom and back without incident. Of that I am sure."

She walked away.

"So the evening was a success," Alec said.

"No, no. Don't say that." Margot pressed a hand to her chest. "Not until we're officially in the car and driving away. I don't want to jinx anything."

"Hello, Alec."

Margot turned toward the low, sultry female voice and saw it belonged to a stunningly beautiful brunette standing behind Alec. The woman was of average height and nearly as curvy as Sunshine. Her gaze, both predatory and possessive, locked on Alec.

"Merelyn." He sounded surprised. "What are you doing here?"

"The same thing as you."

"Oh, I doubt that." He turned to Margot. "This is Merelyn. She was my decorator for the house. Merelyn, this is Margot."

Merelyn barely acknowledged her. She moved close to Alec and put her hand on his forearm. "It's been a long time."

"It has. Two or three years."

Merelyn's gaze locked with his. "I still think about you. About…the decorating project."

Margot did her best to maintain a neutral expression when she really wanted to roll her eyes and point out that Merelyn wasn't being the least bit subtle. Obviously she and Alec had been more than decorator and client. Much more.

Margot started to excuse herself to give them privacy or possibly to pout, she wasn't sure which. Before she'd even taken a step, Alec put his hand on the small of her back, as if asking her to stay where she was.

She could feel the imprint of his fingers and the heat from his body. He applied slight pressure and she found herself leaning into him. He slid his hand from the small of her back to her hip, an intimate gesture that caused her heartbeat to suddenly accelerate.

He and Merelyn talked for a couple more minutes, then the other woman excused herself. As soon as she was gone, Alec released Margot.

"I'm sorry if that was inappropriate," he began. "I reacted without thinking."

While she regretted the loss of his touch, she wasn't going to make a big deal out of it. Not when she was still feeling unexpected desire and longed to throw herself into his arms. The reaction was confusing and a little unsettling. Yes, she liked Alec, but she hadn't noticed that somewhere along the way she'd also started wanting him.

"No, it's totally fine," she said, hoping she sounded normal. "I'm happy to protect you from ex-girlfriends whenever necessary."

"I want to say it wasn't like that, only it was. Thank you for understanding."

"You're welcome."

His dark gaze locked with hers. For a second, she was sure he was going to lean in and kiss her. In fact, she was so convinced that she took a half step toward him in anticipation of—

"What if I make it a hundred thousand dollars?"

The familiar male voice carried over the crowd and had Margot spinning around, searching frantically for Bianca.

"Where are they?"

"Over there." Alec grabbed her hand and led the way.

Margot hoped they got there before Brandon made the offer too tempting. Or too fun.

They maneuvered around a small group of people in time to see Bianca nod her agreement.

"All right. A hundred thousand dollars to Children's Hospital." She turned slightly, offering her backside to Brandon.

He reached out a hand, then pulled it back. "I'll make it two hundred and fifty thousand if I can touch under the dress."

"No," Margot said, trying to make the word loud enough to be heard without yelling and attracting attention. But it was like being in a dream. She opened her mouth and thought she spoke, but there was no sound. No anything.

Time slowed until she knew there was no way to stop it from happening. Whatever "it" was. Bianca tilted her head as she considered, then casually pulled up her skirt. Her thigh came into view, then her hip and her left buttock. Because, of course, she was only wearing a thong.

Brandon groaned and put his hand directly on Bianca's skin. Margot stared in disbelief as she heard an odd clicking sound. Too late she realized the annoying photographer was back and had captured the entire incident. And just like that, the picture of a man touching Bianca Wray's bare ass became a thing.

The next morning the photograph was on the front page of the *Los Angeles Times* and *USA Today*. Margot hadn't bothered to go check where it was online, mostly because she didn't want to know. She sat across from Bianca, at the dining room table, wondering where she'd gone so wrong.

"I still don't see the problem," Bianca said, covering a yawn. "It's no big deal. So a man touched my behind? I raised a quarter-million dollars for charity." Her smile was smug. "You know, a studio once tried to get my behind insured, but no one would do it. I would imagine those executives are feeling a little foolish right about now."

"You let a man touch you on your butt," Margot said, trying to keep her tone reasonable and not shrill. "You pulled up your dress and let him touch your butt while you were wearing a thong."

Bianca studied her. "Are you all right?"

"Not really, no. I've totally failed you. I thought we were making progress. I thought I was getting through to you."

"This isn't your fault," Bianca told her. "And it's not a bad thing."

"It's your bare ass on the front page of the *Los Angeles Times*. I'm pretty sure that's not the kind of publicity you need right now." She looked at her client. "Do you really think this is okay?"

Bianca studied the picture. "I look fabulous, so yes, I'm fine with it."

"And Wesley? Is this what he wants? What about the government back in Cardigania? What are they going to think? Or say? What about the prime minister? How do you meet the prime minster after that? What do you say to him? This picture will live online forever. Wesley has adult children from a previous marriage and they'll see it. His grandchildren will see it. Bianca, this is not acceptable behavior. If you two were married, he could lose his job over this."

"That's ridiculous. I told him about it and he said he was fine."

"You told him there was a picture before it hit the front page of *USA Today*. Knowing it exists and seeing it in color are two very different things."

Bianca went pale. "He won't lose his job. That would be ridiculous. I raised a quarter-million dollars for charity. That has to count for something."

"Sure, it's wonderful, but the money isn't the point. Why can't you see that?" Margot tried to figure out what to say to make her understand, only to realize Bianca wouldn't get it because she didn't want to.

"Bianca, why am I here? What do you want from me? You said it was because you wanted to change yourself, but I don't think this is moving in that direction. And if it's about fitting into Wesley's world, then this was a total disaster." She tapped the picture. "People in his world don't flash their butts at people, even for money."

Bianca stood and glared at her. "Well, maybe they should try it now and then. At least for a good cause. Do you really blame yourself more than me?"

"Of course."

"I don't know what to do with that. You're right. I want you to help me fit into Wesley's world, but I can't do that and not be myself." She sighed. "I really thought it was fine. I thought I was doing a good thing. Now I just don't know. I need to think about this."

"Fine. We can talk later."

"No. I need more time than that. I'll see you in a couple of days."

She walked out before Margot could figure out what to say. A couple of days? What did that mean?

Margot supposed she should assume the obvious—that their work together would pick up in two or three days. In the meantime, she could take the time to go to her office and have a long talk with her boss about the assignment. While she really liked Bianca, she wasn't sure she was the best one to help her. And if she wasn't, then it was time to get someone else to take her place.

"I've never failed a client before," she whispered. She'd always been successful, had always done so well. But Bianca wasn't like her other clients and everything about this situation was rapidly spinning out of control.

chapter
SEVENTEEN

DECLAN FOUND HIS BUSINESS PARTNER WAITING IMPA-
tiently for the Keurig to finish brewing a mug of coffee. While
Heath had on a suit, as per usual, there was something dishev-
eled about his appearance. Or maybe it was simply the dark circles under his eyes.

"Rough night?" Declan asked, trying to remember how long
Heath had been going out with the woman he was dating. Six
months? Eight?

"Brandi and I broke up." Heath grabbed the coffee and cra-
dled it in his hands. "Things have been bad for a while and last
night it all came to a head. We talked until two in the morning and when I suggested we table things so we could get some
sleep, she told me I was an insensitive asshole, that it was over
and she hoped I burned in hell for eternity."

Declan put a pod into the Keurig and slid his mug into place
before starting the machine.

"You okay?"

"Exhausted mostly. A little relieved. Brandi was a lot more
volatile than I expected. The longer we were together, the more,
ah, free she was with her emotions."

"No regrets it's over?"

Heath shrugged. "I don't want to get back together with her, but I did like being in a relationship." He drank his coffee. "Why is it we always hear that it's so easy for guys? Just have a decent job, be a good guy and be slightly more attractive than dirt and women will be throwing themselves at us. But they're not. At least I can't find anyone I want to be with. I'm not looking for a one-night stand—I want a relationship. Why is that so difficult to find?"

"You're asking the wrong guy," Declan told him. "My last date was with Iris."

"You're kidding."

"Nope."

"And not, you know, before?"

When they'd been separated? Because he'd told Heath a little of what had happened back then.

Declan shook his head. "It didn't feel right." Iris might have pulled out of their marriage, but he hadn't. Besides, things had been complicated enough without bringing a third—make that fourth—party into things.

Heath leaned against the door frame of the coffee room. "I just want a nice, normal woman who wants to have a happy, regular kind of life. Minimal drama, lots of laughs and if she liked gardening, that would be a plus." He looked at Declan, his expression hopeful. "Think that's possible?"

"I'm sure it is. You just have to get out there again."

"So says the guy who's never been out there."

"I was. In college."

"That doesn't count. You should start dating. Even if you don't find someone for yourself, you can give me a few names."

Declan immediately thought of Sunshine. She was everything Heath had said he wanted and more. She was beautiful and nurturing and pretty much the sexiest woman ever known to man, and she was looking for a normal relationship.

He opened his mouth to mention her, then decided he couldn't. If that made him a jerk, he could live with the label.

There was no way he could stand to have his business partner dating Sunshine. He didn't want to think about them together. It would make him crazy with jealousy and he was already on the edge where she was concerned.

"I met a single mom who seems nice," he blurted out of guilt. "Phoebe. Her son and Connor are friends. She's pretty and has a good job."

"Then why don't you go out with her?"

"It's too soon."

Heath shook his head. "It's not too soon, Declan. It's time. You need to get yourself out there. We both do, but your need is greater. Not every woman is Iris."

"I know that."

"You sure?" Heath waved his coffee mug. "Come on. Let's go figure out how to make our hotel clients happy."

"That's not possible."

"You're right, but we have to at least try."

Margot signed her name and took the package from the UPS guy. The small box had an international label and a customs sticker, making her wonder if it was more ancient documents for Alec to sort through. The last group had been fascinating. He'd even let her help him remount a few of them.

She let herself into the house and left the package on his desk, then headed upstairs. She dropped her tote in her room and went to see if Bianca was back. The large guest room at the end of the hall was empty and there was no sign of the occupant.

Bianca had said a couple of days, she reminded herself. Today was only day one. Hopefully they would resume their work tomorrow.

Margot took the stairs to the main floor and turned into the kitchen. She came to a stop when she saw Alec dicing tomatoes while humming along to jazz music. He looked up and smiled.

"Oh good. You're back. I was in the mood for a steak tonight and was hoping you'd join me." He pointed to a paper-wrapped package on the counter. "I went to the butcher for filets and I've made salad. Edna defrosted a potato casserole for us and there is a very nice bottle of cabernet, if you're interested."

He looked good, she thought, letting the tension from the day flow out of her. Handsome and sexy and just plain easy to be with. She needed more of that in her life. A good guy who got her insides buzzing and her mind relaxing. It was not an easy combination to find.

"Sounds great," she told him. "What can I do to help?"

He motioned to the stools by the island. "Keep me company. Oh, and if you want a drink, help yourself." He nodded at a glass by the cutting board. "I poured myself a Scotch."

She went to the wet bar and quickly mixed up a vodka and tonic, then returned to the kitchen and sat at the island. Alec had moved on to slicing a cucumber.

"Thank you for this," she said, pointing at the dinner fixings. "It's a great end to my day."

"Tough one?"

"Just complicated. You know your mother took off."

"I suspected. When the going gets tough, she often disappears, although I'll admit I'm surprised. I didn't think she was upset about last night."

"She wasn't, but that's okay. I was upset enough for both of us."

He added the cucumber to the salad. "Why were you upset?"

"Because the training is supposed to be helping and it's not. I can't believe she actually thought letting some guy touch her bare ass was okay. But according to her it's just who she is. I don't know. I wonder if I'm the right person for the job."

Something flickered in Alec's eyes. Before she could figure out what it was, it was gone.

"You don't think she's better than she was?" he asked.

"She's made a lot of progress, but I really thought I understood her and last night proves I don't." She thought about the pictures in the various newspapers and had to hold in a groan. "I went and saw my boss this afternoon."

"For advice?"

"Yes, and to discuss bringing in someone else." Margot smiled at him. "I don't know if this counts as good news, but you're stuck with me. Apparently Bianca has been giving me rave reviews and she flat out told them she wasn't interested in working with anyone else."

"What happened with my mother isn't your fault."

"I know that in my head, but it sure feels like my fault. I don't get it. She was doing incredibly well at the event. She talked to a lot of people, she was funny and charming. Then it all went to hell." She sighed. "Enough of that. How was your day?"

"Quiet."

"Just how you like it."

He chuckled. "That is true." He circled around the island and sat on the stool next to hers. "Bianca will figure it out because she loves Wesley and when Bianca loves, she's all in. When I was ten or so, she was dating a race car driver who was very macho. I was a brainy little kid and we had nothing in common. I remember one day he wanted me to go throw a baseball with him. I wasn't interested and we got into it. Bianca got between us and stood up for me."

One corner of Alec's mouth turned up. "He said if I didn't start acting like a man, I was going to grow up to be some pansy-assed homo and it would all be her fault."

Margot didn't know which slur to address first. "He really said that?"

"He did." The half smile turned into a full one. "My mother clocked him. Hit him right in the face. She told him that I was my own person and if I wanted to throw around a baseball, then fine, but if I didn't, then I should be left alone. As for being gay, she said she didn't care if I fell in love with a sea cucumber. That

I was her son and she loved me and would always support me and welcome anyone I cared about."

"Wow. Good for her."

"That's what I thought. She threw him out and we never saw him again." He raised his glass. "That's my good Bianca story."

"I think we should pass on the bad one today."

"I agree."

Margot smiled. "I would have liked to have seen her punch the guy."

"It was impressive."

"I'll bet. So about Merelyn. She seemed nice."

Alec sighed. "Why did I think I was going to escape without having to talk about her?"

"I have no idea." She smiled. "So—the ex."

"She's not my ex. She was my decorator and we had a couple of weeks together. It was nothing serious."

"She thought it was."

He looked at her. "Yes, she did. How did you know?"

"The way she was looking at you. Like she was lactose intolerant and you were a big ol' bowl of ice cream."

"I'm not sure about that analogy but I get your point. It wasn't like that. I quickly figured out she wasn't my type."

Margot knew she should quit while she was ahead. She liked hanging out with Alec, and teasing him about his ex-girlfriend, while fun, wasn't exactly the smartest thing to do. Did she really want him thinking about another woman while he was with her? Still, she couldn't help asking, "What is your type?"

He took another sip of his Scotch. "It's more emotional than physical. I like a woman who is intelligent and kind, with a sense of humor."

"So Merelyn was a humorless dummy who kicked kittens?" she asked hopefully.

He laughed. "Not exactly. She just wasn't for me."

"I'm glad."

The words popped out involuntarily. Margot immediately wanted to call them back, but it was way too late for that. They just kind of hung there in the air before slowly, so slowly, sinking to the floor.

Alec stared at her, his expression unreadable. She succumbed to panic. Was he mad? Repulsed? Confused? Disinterested? She wasn't sure which of the four would be worse, and if she had time, she would rank them from lowest to highest preference, but there wasn't and, oh dear God, couldn't he say something?

She sprang to her feet as her brain offered her the thinnest of lifelines.

"You have a package! I signed for it when I came in and left it on your desk." She pointed back toward his office. "It's kind of small so maybe not documents, but I had to sign for it, so you should probably go check it out."

He studied her for another second. She was about to bolt when he said, "Why don't you come with me? I think you'll find the contents unexpected."

Which wasn't the same as *Hey, I think you're smart and kind and funny and sexy, which wasn't on my list, but you are and let's go make love*, but it also wasn't him running away from her, so good.

They went into his office, where he opened the small package. Inside the shipping box was another, smaller box, then tissue paper. Alec pulled out a tiny wooden carving of a rabbit. It was obviously very old and detailed. There was an odd open space between the rabbit's front feet.

"What is it?" she asked.

He took her hand in his and then placed the small figurine on her palm.

"Netsuke," he said. "It's Japanese. Men's kimonos didn't have pockets to store things like tobacco or other small items, so the men hung stylish boxes from their sashes or obi. The netsuke attached to the other end of the cord as a counterweight to keep the boxes in place." He nodded at the carving nestled on her palm. "This is a lunar hare."

"It's beautiful. The carving is so intricate. I'm assuming netsuke is an art form?"

"It is."

He crossed to the large cabinet behind his desk and opened it. Dozens of netsuke lined the narrow shelves across the entire length of the cabinet.

"You're a collector," she breathed, moving closer to study the tiny pieces.

"I am. Most netsuke are carved ivory—not a practice that we would approve today, of course. But back in the seventeenth and eighteenth centuries, ivory and wood were popular materials."

He took the rabbit from her and put it on a shelf, then handed her a carving of a dragon. "There were famous netsuke craftsmen who signed their work. Those are the most valuable."

The dragon was coiled in a circle and maybe two inches across, but the details were exquisite. She could see the individual scales and tiny claws. There were even little dragon teeth.

"I love him," she said with a smile, handing him back to Alec. She looked at the cabinet. "You have a wonderful collection."

She examined the different shelves. There were more dragons and rabbits, a few monkeys, even a couple of carved men. She was about to pick up a gourd when she realized there was something off about the cabinet. The depth of the shelves didn't match the depth of the side.

A false front, she thought, immediately looking for the release mechanism. It had to be something accessible. A cabinet this large couldn't be moved easily to reach in from behind.

She studied the construction, especially on the sides, and immediately caught sight of two corner pieces that looked out of place.

"Is this it?" she asked eagerly, pushing first one corner, then the other.

"Wait!"

Alec sounded insistent, but it was too late. The entire front of the cabinet swung forward. Behind it were more shelves, just like the ones in front, and there were more netsuke on display. Carved people who... People who...

Margot stared, not sure she could believe what she was seeing. She reached out and picked up what looked like a couple kissing. But as she studied the carving, she realized they weren't just kissing. And there weren't just two of them. There were in fact four people, um, doing each other in very interesting ways. In fact all the hidden netsuke were people indulging in various erotic exploits.

"Oh," she said, putting the piece back where she'd found it. "It's a different style, isn't it?"

Alec stared at her without speaking. Not that she could blame him. What was there to say that wouldn't make things more awkward?

She started to tell him she wasn't offended. That she got this was art, too, and it was as beautifully carved as the other pieces. She realized that, in a way, he was like the cabinet—all formal and forbidding but with wonderful secrets on the inside.

The longer they stood there, the more stupid she felt until she realized she had no choice but to make her escape.

"They're lovely," she told him. "Very original. If you'll excuse me, I need to get something in my room."

A ludicrous excuse but the best one she could come up with in the moment. She offered him a tight smile, turned and ran from his office. When she reached her room, she closed the door and leaned against it.

Disaster, she thought grimly. That had been a total disaster. For someone who was supposed to be an expert at handling embarrassing or difficult situations, she'd just screwed up that one. Instead of being amused or casual or the least bit sophisticated, she'd taken off like a teenage girl who had accidentally walked into the boys' locker room.

How was she supposed to face him after that? How was she supposed to face herself? She groaned, then sank to the floor and pulled her legs to her chest. She rested her head on her knees and told herself that one day she would be smooth, classy and cultured, but until then, she was only herself and for the most part, that really sucked.

chapter
EIGHTEEN

SUNSHINE FINISHED APPLYING A TOP COAT TO HER TOE-nails. She didn't usually bother to paint them but she'd been in the mood. She walked out of her bathroom, balancing on her heels, the toe spacers making her walk funny. After checking on Connor, who was both watching his ant farm and reading a book, she made her way to the kitchen. She would do a little veggie chopping for dinner while her toes dried.

She rounded the corner and nearly collided with Declan. She was off balance already, and coming to a stop so quickly had her stumbling to maintain her balance. Declan grabbed her upper arms to steady her, then quickly let her go. He smiled and started to speak, then dropped his gaze to her feet.

In an instant his expression shifted from happy to stricken. The transformation was so abrupt, Sunshine felt as if she'd been sideswiped by something cold and dark.

"What's wrong?" she asked.

He did his best to recover, shaking his head and giving her the worst fake smile ever. "Nothing. Are you all right? You nearly fell."

"Declan, what's wrong?"

"It's nothing."

"It's obviously not nothing."

He looked away. "Just Iris."

"Oh." She couldn't quite put the pieces— "I did my toes and it's such a girl thing. Of course. I'm sorry."

He studied her for a second. "Sure. That's it."

With that, he walked past her and went into his office. She stared after him. What was going on? It was like he'd totally blown her off.

She went after him, closing his office door behind her.

"Declan, what's wrong?"

He sat behind his desk, avoiding her gaze. "Iris painted her toes, too. Just not at first. In fact, not until the end. She was a sensible kind of person." He looked at her. "That all changed when Iris had an affair."

Sunshine sank onto the chair in front of his desk. *An affair? How could she?* "I'm sorry. I didn't know."

"Almost no one does. It happened several months before she got sick. I had no idea until she told me. I knew things weren't great, but to do that? To risk everything? I couldn't understand."

"Did you split up?" Connor had never said anything, but maybe the trauma of his mother's death had pushed it from his mind.

"No. I thought about leaving, but I wasn't sure. Mostly because of Connor. I moved out of the bedroom and slept here." He motioned to the worn sofa in his office. "We pretended, all the while she continued seeing the other guy."

"She didn't end things when she told you?"

"No."

"Then why tell you?"

"I honestly have no idea. Maybe she wanted to have me be the one to end things. She talked about how charming he was, how passionate things were between them."

Sunshine so didn't want to hear any of this. She ached for what Declan had gone through. How could his wife have done that to him? He was such a great guy and terrific father. How could she have wanted anyone else?

"When I finally reached the point where I couldn't do it anymore and told her we either had to fix things or be done, she begged me for time. I agreed. What I didn't know then was she'd been diagnosed with cancer. She never said a word. It was supposed to be the easy kind, if there is such a thing. I guess she thought she'd have a few rounds of chemo and be fine. Only she wasn't."

He looked at her. "She told the other guy. Mr. Wonderful. She told him she was really sick and he dumped her. He didn't want anything to do with her, so she came back to me."

"She told you the affair was over and that she was dying?" Sunshine consciously lowered her voice. "Seriously?"

He nodded. "I was furious. How could she have done this to us? I knew I would never forgive her, but what did it matter? She was dying and I had to deal with that, and Connor. She was gone in less than a month."

"I'm so sorry." *For Connor and Declan*, she thought. *Not so much for Iris.* "How awful for you."

"Thanks. Sometimes I think the worst part is we never really talked about it. What was there to say? She'd chosen him over me, so our marriage was over, but I wasn't going to leave. And there was Connor to consider. He was devastated. When my folks came to stay with us, I didn't tell them about any of it, of course. They thought everything was fine."

What a nightmare, she thought. How was he supposed to get over what had happened? There had been no time to make things right, no time to process. One second their marriage had been in trouble and the next Iris was dying. Who could possibly deal with that?

"You must still be angry," she said quietly.

"Less so with time. I don't know why she did what she did, but it happened. I'll never know exactly what went wrong with us, but lately I've decided I only have to figure out my part of it. What I'm responsible for. The rest is on her."

"Still, it's a huge thing." She reached down and pulled out the toe spacers. "Sorry about these."

He smiled. "Don't be. I'm not traumatized. It was just the shock in the moment. I'm fine now. I don't want you to worry about painting your nails around me."

"It is an odd trigger."

He chuckled. "Everyone needs to be special in their own way."

She had a lot of questions about Iris and their marriage and what he was feeling, but none of them were her business. She should probably excuse herself and go start dinner, but instead she said, "You really need to go out with Phoebe. Even if nothing comes of it, you'll have broken the ice, so to speak."

"Time to move on?"

"Past time."

"And you're an expert?" His voice was teasing.

"No, but it's always easier to see what's wrong with other people's lives than our own. How can you not know that?"

"I'll consider your advice."

"Good."

They looked at each other. She felt tension in the room and wasn't sure how much of it was from what they'd just talked about and how much of it was wishful thinking on her part. If only he would kiss her, she thought before she could mentally slap herself. *No kissing. No anything.*

"I won't say anything to Connor," she told him as she got to her feet. "You have my word."

"Sunshine, there are many things I question but you doing what's best for my son isn't one of them."

Alec paced for an hour, trying to decide if he was more embarrassed or humiliated. Not that he owed anyone an explanation about his collection. The netsuke were beautiful art—master carvings, regardless of the subject matter.

But Margot might not understand or appreciate the fine workmanship. She might think he was some kind of perverted creep who—

"Alec?"

He looked up and saw her in the doorway to his office. Her eyes were wide, her expression serious.

"Margot."

That was pretty much all he had. He had no idea what he was supposed to say. Telling her he wasn't weird or into pornography didn't seem designed to help his cause.

Before he could stutter through some ridiculous explanation, she began to speak.

"I want to apologize," she told him, her gaze steady. "I was wrong to open the back of the cabinet. I knew it was a puzzle and completely forgot that you might be keeping something out of public view for a reason. Instead I was all about solving the problem." She cleared her throat and looked away. "I suppose on some level, I wanted to show off."

What? He hadn't been expecting that. "You weren't showing off."

She shrugged. "I kind of was. Plus, the netsuke were so fascinating. I got caught up and violated your privacy. I apologize."

"You don't have to." Now it was his turn to clear his throat. "The erotic netsuke come from a time in Japanese society when baser human desires were suppressed, socially. When that happens, the resulting need often spills out into art." He winced. "I could have phrased that more delicately."

She stepped into the room. "I think you phrased it perfectly."

"Thank you."

Without planning it, he seemed to be moving closer to her. Or maybe she was moving closer to him. Regardless, they were only a foot or so apart.

"I was impressed you figured out the cabinet," he said.

"I like puzzles."

"As do I."

She smiled. "The foursome was, um, curious. I'm not sure it's physically possible."

He smiled, as well. "I'm confident it's not. No one has a tongue that long."

"Or a penis like that. Plus there was only one woman. That surprised me."

Their gazes locked. Her eyes were large and beautiful. He found everything about her appealing. No, not appealing. That was a small, inconsequential word that in no way described his feelings for Margot. She was…magnificent.

"Alec?"

He reached for her. Before his hands settled on her waist, she surged toward him. The space between them disappeared as they clung to each other. His mouth found hers. There was no soft, gentle, slow kiss. Instead there was only heat and tongues and a need to get closer and closer.

Passion swept through him, stealing his breath and his ability to think. Their kisses deepened, igniting a growing craving. The rest of the world faded. She reached for the buttons on his shirt. He undid the zipper on her dress. His task was more successful than hers because while she fumbled, he tugged the dress off her shoulders.

She laughed. "We can't both do this at the same time."

"You're right."

He undid the top two buttons of his shirt, then pulled it over his head and tossed it to the floor. She let her dress fall. He had a quick glimpse of her slim body, narrow hips and small breasts before she flung herself at him, pressing her mouth against his as she rubbed his bare chest.

She thrust her tongue into his mouth. He closed his lips around it and sucked gently. She groaned, then nipped his lower lip. He unfasted her bra and tugged it free. Even as he reached for her breasts, she was pulling his hands to her. When he ran his thumbs across her tight nipples, she sighed her pleasure.

He saw the wanting she felt and watched her pupils dilate. She ran her fingers down his belly and pressed her palm against his erection through the layers of his jeans and briefs. His hand slipped lower until he reached inside her panties and found her wet and swollen. He circled her clit and she gasped.

At that moment, it stopped being a game. He unfastened his belt while she pulled off her panties. While she scrambled to sit on the desk, he pushed down his jeans and briefs, then moved between her open thighs and let himself sink into her waiting warmth. She wrapped her arms around his shoulders, her legs around his hips, and drew him close.

Even as he kissed her, he slipped a hand between them so he could rub her clit, trying desperately not to give in to the building pressure inside of him. He wanted her, needed her, but not just for himself.

She leaned back and braced her arms behind her, her hips pulsing in time with his strokes. He moved his thumb against her swollen center.

"Tell me," he growled.

She opened her eyes and smiled. "Faster and harder."

He did as she requested, pushing down as he rubbed more quickly. The smile disappeared as her breath caught. He felt the first telltale quiver deep inside her and increased the pace of his thumb and his thrusts.

Her nipples tightened. Her breath came in pants. She ground herself against him, then arched her back, and threw back her head as she called out his name.

Her orgasm claimed her in a shuddering, rhythmic vibration that sucked him in and hung on until he had no choice but to surrender. He spilled himself into her, savoring the release. When she was still, he grabbed her hips and went in even deeper until he, too, was spent.

She collapsed onto the desk. He slowly withdrew, then pressed a kiss to her belly. They looked at each other.

"Thoughts?" he asked gently.

She motioned to the open door. "I'm just really hoping your mother doesn't choose this moment to come home."

Alec stared at her for a second, then threw back his head and started to laugh.

Twenty minutes later Margot was cleaned up, dressed and standing outside as Alec put steaks on the barbecue. She felt good. Happy. Content. And maybe just a little surprised.

He closed the lid and then pulled her close and kissed her. She kissed him back, enjoying the passion welling up inside of her.

When the timer dinged, they pulled apart so he could turn the steaks. After closing the lid, he turned to her.

"About what happened," he began.

"The kiss?" She batted her eyes.

He smiled. "And before."

"The sex?"

"That would be it, yes."

"It was nice."

He raised his eyebrows. "Just nice?"

"Very nice?" She laughed. "It was great."

"I agree. I'd like to try it again. In a bed. Perhaps without my pants around my ankles."

There were probably several reasons why getting involved with Alec was complicated. She worked for his mother. She lived in his house. She didn't know where the whole thing was going. And yet…

She liked him. A lot. Just as important, the man turned her on. He was fun to be around and smart and she was so ready to be with someone who was actually good for her.

"I think having both of us naked is something we should explore." Her stomach growled. She sighed. "Maybe after dinner."

"I look forward to it."

"Me, too."

Alec stepped out of his shower, doing his best not to whistle. Although there was no reason to hold back. Margot had left his bed a few minutes before to get ready in her own bathroom.

He dried off, smiling the entire time. The previous evening had been better than he could have imagined. After dinner, they'd retreated to his room where they'd made love twice more before falling asleep in each other's arms. She'd awakened him just before dawn, her mouth bringing him from drowsy to aroused in less than thirty seconds. Before he could figure out what she was doing, he'd lost control with all the finesse of a fourteen-year-old boy. She'd still been laughing when he'd returned the favor, going down on her, loving her with his mouth until she succumbed to her own release.

Margot was fun—something he'd expected, but it was wonderful to have it confirmed. He'd also lived the fantasy of having her on top, her long hair loose and hanging across his body...

His body reacted to his thoughts. He quickly changed mental topics until the manifestation eased. With luck, after breakfast, they could continue to explore each other. Of course Edna might come by, or the cleaners. Perhaps instead they could escape to Margot's apartment.

He was still considering the options as he walked in the kitchen. The first thing he noticed was the smell of coffee. The second was his mother sitting at the kitchen table.

She raised her mug and smiled at him. "Good morning, darling. How are—" She stopped talking as she studied him. A second later, she chuckled. "You've had sex! That's so nice. I assume with Margot? She really is perfect for you, and you for her. I was going to start back up with my lessons today but now I think I'll put it off until later in the week. Do you want some coffee before I head out?"

Alec had no idea how long he stood there, staring at his mother, as his mind went completely blank. No thoughts formed—not even words. When he was finally able to pull himself together, he managed to stammer, "E-excuse me," before ducking out of the room.

He took the stairs two at a time, knocked once on Margot's door, then let himself in.

"It's me."

She walked out from the bathroom, already dressed, her hair pulled back in a ponytail. She laughed. "Really? Again? I have to say I love the enthusiasm, but only if you promise we can have breakfast after. You're wearing me out."

He stared at her. "My mother's back and she knows we had sex. She took one look at me and just knew."

Margot surprised him by laughing again. "Okay, that's both awkward and funny. How on earth did she know?"

"I have no idea. She's always been like that." The numbness was wearing off and panic was taking its place. "What are we going to do?"

She put her hands on his chest. "It's going to be fine. She might tease you a little, but nothing more."

The panic receded. "I worried you'd want to leave."

"Not at all. Unless you want me to."

Not ever. The voice was loud and steady in his head—as if imparting a certain truth. "I don't."

"Then we'll continue on as before." She raised herself on tiptoe and kissed him. "Well, not exactly as before."

He wrapped his arms around her. "Tonight?"

"Absolutely. It's a date."

Sunshine had toyed with the idea of what it would be like to be in Declan's bedroom. She avoided it, as a rule, only going in occasionally to put away linens the cleaning service had left in the dryer. Every now and then, when she was being especially foolish, she thought about them together in his room. No, not in his room, in his bed.

She knew better, of course. She wasn't that girl/woman anymore. She was better and smarter and had a lot more self-control. Still, she had daydreamed, but none of her fantasies had been like this.

"What do you think?" Declan asked looking both hopeful and terrified.

She looked him up and down, taking in the freshly pressed button-down shirt, the dark wash jeans and loafers. He'd showered and shaved and he looked good.

"She'll be dazzled," Sunshine told him, injecting enthusiasm into her voice when what she really wanted to do was stomp her foot and tell him he couldn't go.

"*Dazzled* seems strong." He tugged at his collar. "This was a mistake. I should cancel."

"You're not going to cancel. You're going to take Phoebe to dinner and you're going to have a good time."

Declan looked more miserable than confident. "I don't think that's a given. I barely know the woman. What are we going to talk about?"

"Ask about her work. Tell her about yours. You have lots of funny stories about the hotel clients."

"Those aren't funny, they're disasters."

She smiled. "To you. To the rest of us, they're pretty humorous. If you get stuck, talk about Connor. Talk about his school, how the Rams are going to do next season, whether or not she likes ballet."

"Don't all women like ballet?"

"Of course not. That's like saying all guys like basketball."

"Do you like ballet?"

"I do, but that's not the point. Get to know her. Don't say anything about Iris except she got sick very suddenly and then she died."

He sighed. "Even I know not to tell her about the affair."

"You say that now, but in the heat of the moment, you could blurt out anything." Sunshine told herself that however painful this was, sending Declan out with the kind of advice designed to make his date successful was just plain good karma. "Oh, and if I come up in conversation, be sure to tell her I'm in a committed relationship with a giant of a man who you find just a little intimidating."

"What are you talking about?"

Sunshine shrugged. "She's going to ask about me. I'm not saying I'm all that, I'm saying I know what other women think when they look at me. Boobs and butt. It's not a good combination for a first date. If she asks, and she will, I'm in a relationship, and the guy scares you."

Declan studied her and she had no idea what he was thinking. As long as it wasn't pity, she didn't care. Or so she told herself.

"Do I have to say he scares me?"

"No, but it will help."

Connor ran into the bedroom and skittered to a stop beside Sunshine. She put her arm around him.

"Doesn't your dad look good?"

Connor wrinkled his nose. "You do, Dad. Are you taking her flowers? Ladies like flowers."

"Maybe next time." Declan smiled at his son. "What are you and Sunshine doing for dinner?"

Connor started jumping up and down. "Pizza! Pizza! Pizza!" He wrapped his arms around Sunshine. "We have dough and sauce and cheese and pepperoni. I've never made pizza before. Did you know there's a special stone for pizza? We're gonna use that and watch it bake!"

"Sounds like you'll be having a fun evening," Declan said.

"It's always fun with Sunshine."

She laughed. "I'm the cool nanny. What can I say?"

"You are." He glanced at his watch. "I should get going. We have reservations."

Connor walked with his dad to the garage while Sunshine headed for the kitchen. Tonight, after pizza, they would watch a movie. Once Connor was in bed, she would retreat to her room and not come out until morning. She would distract herself with HGTV and not think about Declan out with another woman. Mostly because it wasn't her business. And she didn't care. Not in the least. Not even a little. Not her. Nope, she was completely and totally fine.

chapter
NINETEEN

DECLAN WALKED INTO THE KITCHEN A LITTLE AFTER MID-night. Sunshine had left on the under-counter lights, but otherwise the house was dark and quiet.

His son would have gone to bed hours ago. It was late so there was no reason to expect Sunshine to still be up, but he had wondered. Not that he should have. They were friends. She worked for him—nothing more. They didn't have anything close to a relationship so it was ridiculous to wonder if she'd thought about his date at all.

He turned on the hall light, then flipped off the under-counter lights. After checking on Connor, he made his way to his bedroom. He crossed into the bathroom and stripped off his clothes, then stepped into the shower.

He'd had sex with Phoebe. He hadn't planned on it, hadn't considered the possibility, but once they'd gotten back from dinner, she'd made it clear she was more than willing and he'd…

He wasn't sure what he'd been thinking, he admitted as he lathered his body. That it had been a long time and she'd been funny and nice and the idea of holding someone, of having sex with someone other than himself, had been appealing. Everything had worked the way it was supposed to, he'd made sure she'd come first, then he'd found his release in her.

He rinsed, then stepped out of the shower and reached for a towel. The mechanics had been fine, but now, he couldn't escape the sense of regret. Nothing about being with Phoebe had been about making love with someone he cared about. Maybe he was too old, but getting laid was not the thrill it had been years ago. He wanted more. He wanted to engage more than his dick.

He wanted Sunshine.

He swore loudly, then pulled on a pair of pajama bottoms. After brushing his teeth, he walked into the bedroom and climbed into bed. He lay on his back in the dark and wished… What? That he hadn't done it? That he didn't have to deal with Phoebe now? That he'd met Sunshine another way and he could have asked her out and gotten to know her as a woman and not his nanny?

The answer to all those questions was yes, he thought glumly. But there was no going back and now he was well and truly stuck with a series of situations he didn't know how to change.

"Good morning," Margot said brightly as she walked into the guest lounge where Bianca was waiting. Thanks to Alec's warning the previous morning, she was braced for whatever was to follow. Well, as braced as one could be when it came to the force of nature that was Bianca.

Her client sat on the sofa, a mug of coffee in her hands, her expression both knowing and smug. Bianca smiled.

"Good morning to you. So, you and Alec. How was that?"

Margot took a seat. "I'm not going to discuss your son with you. Not in that context."

"But he's my son. I have a right to know what's happening in his life."

"Not from me you don't."

Bianca smiled. "An excellent answer. Good for you. Some people have trouble standing up to me. I'm glad you don't."

Her expression turned impish. "I won't ask about your night or mention you look a little tired, so we can get right to work."

"How kind of you." Margot knew that Bianca wanted to see if she could be rattled. She did her best to appear calm. She leaned back in the chair and crossed her legs. "Let's talk about the political event."

"Let's not." Bianca sighed. "It's old news. I helped children."

"You let a man you don't know touch your bare butt in public. You knew it was a ridiculous thing to do and yet you did it anyway. That's what I can't figure out, Bianca. Why? I've been turning it around in my head and I can't come up with a single reason that you would..."

Margot stopped talking as the most obvious answer popped into her brain. She had no idea why she hadn't considered it before. What had happened wasn't about her training methods or Bianca not caring or anything like that at all.

"What was the trigger?" she asked softly. "Someone must have said something or done something at the event. Something that upset you. Of course. I should have figured that out in the moment."

Bianca sipped her coffee. "I have no idea what you're talking about. By the way, you still owe me lunch with your sister."

"What?" She started to ask if lunch with Sunshine was really that important only to realize the point of the statement was to distract her.

"We can discuss that later," she said firmly, putting her feet on the floor. "Please tell me what happened at the event to upset you. I know there was something."

Bianca pressed her lips together. "Fine. It was nothing, really. I wasn't going to let that man touch me at all. What a ridiculous thing to ask. He was a pig, by the way. But then, when I was in the bathroom, I heard two women talking about me."

She turned away. "I don't know why we're discussing this."

Margot moved to the sofa and angled toward Bianca, meeting her troubled gaze. "I will never judge you."

"Unless I let someone touch my bare ass."

"I didn't judge. I was shocked and confused, but that was all."

Bianca's bravado faded. "They said I was a whore and a home-wrecker, which is completely unfair. I never slept with married men. It wasn't my thing. I slept with a spy once, only I didn't know he was a spy. He was a movie producer and very handsome. Once, when we were together in his villa up in the Hollywood Hills, the FBI raided his house and he was dragged off. It was very exciting and a little frightening."

She smiled. "I was naked and the youngest agent just couldn't take his eyes off me. It was like real life combined with a movie. I loved it. We dated for nearly a month."

Margot was having a little trouble keeping up. "You and the producer?"

"What? Yes, we dated, but I meant me and the FBI agent. He was too young for me, but very sweet. The things I taught him." She sighed. "Anyway, my point is I never slept with married men. I've always thought that was beyond foolish. Any man who would cheat on his wife wasn't worth my time. But they upset me."

"Those women? Of course they did. You must have felt awful. The truth is they were jealous, mean bitches. They felt inadequate and because they couldn't deal with that, they had to bring you down. I'm sorry it happened."

Bianca touched her arm. "Thank you, Margot. That's very sweet."

"I mean it. I wish I'd been there. I would have told them off for sure."

Bianca smiled. "You would have been formidable."

"I hope so." Now everything made sense, she thought. "You probably would have been fine if you hadn't run into that guy again. You were feeling vulnerable so you agreed to what he asked because it wasn't like he was going to ask them if he could touch their butts. Instead you got to be wild and the center of attention and just a little bit bad. I get it."

She softened her words with a smile. "How did that strategy work for you?"

"I thought it went well, but you and Alec had a fit."

Margot waited. Bianca groaned.

"Fine. I shouldn't have done it because of Wesley and all."

"You're always going to be a target, Bianca. You know that. We need to come up with some coping mechanisms for when you feel attacked."

"I did like talking to the shy people in the room. They were all so grateful."

"Everyone wants to feel special and no one is better at making someone feel like the center of the universe than you. Something else you can do is simply walk away. You're not going to be by yourself at these events. Find Wesley. Maybe the two of you could come up with a code word so he'll know you're upset."

Bianca laughed. "We already have code words. You know for when—"

Margot held up her hand. "No. Do not tell me that."

"You and Alec might want to—"

"Stop."

Bianca pouted. "You're not very fun."

"I'm not here to be fun. I'm here to help you be comfortable in Wesley's world. Talk to him about this. Work on a plan together. He loves you and wants to help."

Bianca's eyes filled with tears. "I don't want to be broken."

"You're not broken. You're..." Margot searched for an analogy. "Remember how we talked about you not being a surgeon? That's still true. You might have an innate ability but without training, you would be dangerous in the operating room, talent or not. That's all we're doing here—learning new skills."

"You do love your medical analogies."

"I've used them maybe twice."

"Still, new material, my dear. It's always helpful."

Margot threw herself against the sofa back. "You're impossible."

Bianca smiled and said nothing.

Saturday morning, Sunshine woke up way earlier than she wanted to. She hadn't slept well at all. Despite leaving on the TV so she couldn't hear anything outside of her room, she'd still found herself listening for Declan. Eventually she'd fallen asleep but she had no idea what time he'd gotten home or what had happened on his date or why she cared or what she was going to do with her day off.

The second to the last one was a total lie, but she ignored it, along with a sense of dread in the pit of her stomach. The obvious solution for all that ailed her was a plan for her day, including something fun. She had homework to do but maybe after that she could get a facial or go shopping or text Margot to see if she wanted to hang out. Assuming she wasn't spending the day with Alec because, according to the text she'd gotten yesterday, things had certainly heated up between them.

She told herself that at least one of the Baxter sisters was having fun and later, it would be her turn. With that positive statement, she got dressed, then went to start coffee. She was still waiting for the pot to do its thing when Connor walked in looking all sleepy and adorable in his car pajamas. He crossed to her and hugged her tight.

"Morning." She rubbed his back. "Did you sleep well?"

"Uh-huh. Can I have pancakes?"

"You can."

Connor released her and scrambled onto a stool at the island while Sunshine got out the ingredients for pancakes. As it was her day off, she wasn't required to make breakfast, but she wasn't going to tell Connor no. Not only did she like taking care of him, she wasn't sure how late Declan would be sleeping.

Or if he was even home!

The thought was equally unwelcome and upsetting. What if he'd stayed the night at Phoebe's? She told herself he wouldn't, or couldn't. He would be worried about Connor, and Phoebe had Elijah, so even if they'd had sex, he would still come home.

She didn't want to think about them together or anything else, but the image was in her brain and didn't want to leave.

"We're going to the zoo," Connor told her. "Come with us."

She cracked eggs into a bowl. "It's my day off, Connor."

"But it's the zoo! Come on. It'll be fun."

"You need to spend time with just you and your dad."

"Why?"

"We've talked about this," Declan said as he walked into the kitchen. He kept his gaze on his son. "Morning, Sunshine."

"Good morning."

Declan hugged Connor. "Sunshine needs her time off. She has things she has to do."

Connor shot her a glance. "Like what?"

"Like none of your business," his dad said as he walked over to the pot and poured a mug of coffee. He added milk and then set it in front of her before pouring a second mug for himself.

Connor sighed heavily. "It'll be better if Sunshine comes with us."

"I'm sure that's true, but we'll have to struggle through it as best we can."

Sunshine added the pancake mix and stirred. Was it just her or was Declan avoiding her gaze? Did he feel as awkward as she did? Was there tension or was it her imagination?

"I'm going to go make a list of all the animals I want to see," Connor said as he slid off the stool. "Call me when breakfast is ready."

He ran down the hall, leaving her alone with her boss. Sunshine wasn't sure if she should start preheating the griddle or simply bolt for her bedroom. Settling on middle ground, she picked up her coffee.

"So, how was your date?"

As she spoke, she glanced at him and he finally met her gaze. His expression was two parts stricken and one part guilty. Their gazes locked.

"I slept with her."

Sunshine felt the kick land squarely in her gut. She knew it wasn't her business, that she shouldn't care, that in the scheme of things, there was no way it could matter, but she still felt stunned by the news. Betrayal joined shock, both of which made her feel hurt and uncomfortable. *All this before breakfast,* she thought grimly.

She took another sip of coffee, hoping to buy herself time and hide any visible reaction.

"Good for you," she said as lightly as she could. "The dry spell is over."

She offered a fake smile he didn't return.

"You're not happy?" she asked.

"It wasn't great." He turned away.

"You mean the sex was—"

He leaned against the counter and swore softly. "No, the sex was fine. It's everything else. I thought I wanted to get laid and she was certainly up for it but when we were done, it wasn't what I wanted. Jesus, I sound like a woman."

"Not really. Your voice is too low."

He looked at her. "Humor?"

"Too soon?"

He managed a smile. "No. It's not too soon. I thought I'd feel great, but I don't. I feel like shit and now I'm stuck with what happened."

Sunshine's discomfort faded enough for her to relax. Not that Declan's sex life was any of her business, but if he hadn't had a great time with Phoebe then maybe he wouldn't want to see her again and—

And what? They would start dating? Hardly.

"She's texted me twice already," he said. "Maybe Connor and I should move to Bora Bora."

"That seems like an extreme reaction to a couple of texts," she said gently. "An alternative solution would be to meet her for coffee."

"What?" He stared at her. "I don't want to see her. What if she expects us to do it again?"

Sunshine did her best not to laugh. "Or you could meet her for coffee," she repeated. "In a public place where your virtue would be safe."

"You're mocking me."

"A little. My point is you can tell her that your night together was great, but you're not ready to see anyone right now."

"She's going to yell at me."

"Possibly, but it won't be awful and you'll be the great guy who was willing to face her."

"Why can't I just be the jerk who ends things with a text?"

"Because deep down inside, you're not a jerk. Plus, you need the practice with women."

"Is it that obvious?"

"Kinda."

They smiled at each other. Tension returned, but this was a different kind. This was about awareness and the whole man-woman thing and the fact that they wanted each other but couldn't go there, or maybe she wanted him and the rest was wishful thinking but regardless, there was tension.

Declan took a step toward her. Every part of her wanted her to move closer to him. Every part of her wanted to hold and be held and get lost in his kiss and his touch and...

Somewhere in the back of her head a siren blared. The last sensible synapse in her brain went on alert and warned her not to be stupid. There was so much more on the line than fleeting pleasure.

Indecision held her in check as she battled what was easy with what she claimed she wanted. No, what she *knew* she wanted. She stepped back.

"I can't."

He immediately retreated. "You're right. I'm sorry."

She pointed to the bowl. "It's pancake batter. If you could—"

"Yes. I'll make them."

There was so much more to say and yet there was nothing left to discuss. Sunshine did the only thing that made sense. She turned on her heel and ran.

Alec hung on to Margot as they both struggled to catch their breath. They were in his office, in the middle of the afternoon. Somehow her stopping by to say hi had turned into something much more appealing.

He stepped back and picked up her panties. She took them, grinned and slid off the desk. Except for his unfastened jeans and her panties, they were completely dressed.

He glanced at the clock on the wall and shook his head. "Three minutes. I'll make it up to you tonight."

She pulled up her panties, then smoothed her dress into place. "Oh, don't worry about the speed," she teased. "When my orgasm is that good, I genuinely don't care that it only took me eight or nine seconds to get there. But we probably should start locking the door."

He followed her gaze and saw that they had left his office door unlocked. It was a weekday. Not only was his mother in the house, so was Edna, the cleaning team and woodworker Borys doing his repair thing on various columns and carvings. Anyone could have walked in.

"I should have thought of it," he said, knowing he was normally so careful. But Margot had breezed in and the rest of the world had disappeared.

"Me, too." She smiled. "Next time for sure."

He pulled her close and kissed her. For a long time they simply hung on to each other.

He drew back far enough to be able to see her face. "I'm not seeing anyone else. I'm sure you assumed that, but I want to make it clear that there's only you."

Her gaze locked with his. "The same with me."

"Good." He liked this, he thought. Liked her, liked what they had. "Let's go out to dinner."

She raised her eyebrows in mock surprise. "You mean leave the property? Together?"

"Yes. We'll have dinner. On a date."

"Oh, so we're dating now, are we?" She put her hands on his chest. "Dating is much more serious than sex."

She wasn't being funny, he realized. She was stating a fact because she understood him. From what he'd told her and no doubt from what his mother had mentioned, Margot knew that he wasn't one for relationships. Trusting someone was difficult and there were other considerations. Usually he insisted on casual, short-term encounters, but being with Margot was different.

"I'll make reservations," he said. "Any preferences?"

"Just that I'm with you." She lightly kissed him. "Now I really have to get back to work or there are going to be too many questions."

"I'll see you later."

She waved and left.

Alec sat at his desk and struggled to gather his thoughts. He'd been working on something when Margot had arrived with her delightful interruption. Something about a—

He stared at his desk, horror sweeping through him. He'd been reading a French-Spanish trading treaty from the 1600s. An original document. Nothing overly rare or unique, but still a piece of history he'd been asked to review. A professor had entrusted him with the painstakingly handwritten pages, believing Alec would protect them and handle them carefully.

Alec looked at the mess that was his desk. Yes, he'd cleaned the surface before removing the papers from their protective box. Yes, he'd worn gloves, but when Margot had arrived, he'd simply dropped the pages on his desk and *left them there*!

They'd started making love and he'd pulled off her panties. Impatient to be inside of her and claim her, he'd been the one to help her settle on the desk. He'd never once thought about the precious sheets or what might happen to them. They'd had sex on a sixteenth-century French-Spanish treaty.

He swore as he slipped on gloves he didn't remember removing and studied the individual sheets. There weren't any stains or wet spots, but there were a couple of creases and a torn corner he was sure hadn't been there before.

It wasn't even a rookie mistake. A rookie would have followed protocol. Instead he'd been careless with a five-hundred-year-old document and he had no idea how he was going to explain the damage.

He put down the pages and leaned back in his chair. What had happened? How could he have forgotten he was working? This wasn't like him at all.

chapter
TWENTY

"THIS IS NOT A GOOD IDEA," MARGOT MUTTERED AS SHE met her sister at the entrance to the restaurant.

"I thought I was the one who lived on the emotional roller coaster," Sunshine teased. "You're the ever calm, nonreactive twin, or did you forget?"

"I'm not reacting and I am calm. I'm also certain disaster lurks."

Sunshine hugged her. "It's lunch with Bianca. Seriously, it's going to be completely fine."

"You say that now."

Margot knew the potential for disaster was nearly limitless. Bianca could want to talk about Alex and Margot having sex, or ask Sunshine something embarrassing or start a conga line. There was literally no telling. She never should have agreed to the three of them having lunch, and yet here they were. Bianca's power could never be underestimated.

Margot led her sister back to the table where Bianca was already seated. She saw that in the two or three minutes she'd been gone, Bianca had ordered a bottle of champagne. Because that was how she rolled.

"Sunshine, so nice to see you again." Bianca stood and kissed Sunshine on both cheeks before patting the space next to her in the booth. "Come and sit by me."

"Two against one?" Margot asked lightly. "I think it should be Sunshine and me as a team. Even then we won't have a fighting chance against you."

Bianca dimpled. "While that's true, I still want Sunshine next to me."

They took their seats. The server, a guy in his early twenties, kept looking at all of them, as if unable to believe his luck.

"Are you all related?" he asked. "Is this your mom?" The question was asked of Sunshine.

Margot was surprised the server didn't recognize Bianca. Later, when he put the pieces together, he was going to kick himself for not figuring out he'd had a movie star at one of his tables.

Bianca smiled. "Why yes, these are my girls. Aren't they beautiful? I made them myself, with a little help from God." She reached across the table, her hand extended.

Margot did the same. Bianca squeezed her fingers, then smiled up at the server. "They are a blessing to me every day."

"Oh, Mom," Sunshine said, batting her eyes. "You're such a tease."

Champagne was poured. Bianca shooed away the server so they "could chitchat before ordering," then held up her glass. "To the men who want us but can never have us. May there always be many."

"So not world peace?" Margot asked.

Bianca winked. "Next time, darling. Next time." She set down her glass and looked at Sunshine. "Now I want to know all about you. I recall from our dinner that you're a nanny and you've gone back to college. Is that right?"

Sunshine looked a little surprised Bianca had remembered so much. "That's right."

"Curious. Because with your looks and body, you could take a much easier road in life."

"I've tried going that way. It never works out. I think I'm

better off trusting hard work and my better instincts than letting it all ride on my boobs."

"That is the correct moral choice, I'm sure. What are you studying?"

"I haven't fully decided. Early childhood development or child psychology. Right now I'm taking my general education classes."

Bianca looked at Margot. "You should go into business with her."

Margot opened her mouth, then closed it, mostly because she had no idea what to say to that. "I'd love to work with Sunshine," she finally offered, then realized it was true. Working with her sister would be great fun, but doing what?

"Margot has a degree in hotel management," Sunshine said quickly. "I want to work with children. Besides, we're at different stages of our careers. I'm barely getting started. College is a lot harder than I thought it would be."

"Pish posh." Bianca finished her glass of champagne and held it out for more. "You have street skills, my love. That's worth five degrees." She touched Sunshine's hand. "Margot has told me a little about what it was like growing up with your great-grandmother. Margot had the looks and body to earn the crown, but you're the one who wanted it, weren't you?"

Sunshine looked at Margot as if to say, *You're right—she is scary insightful*, then smiled at Bianca.

"I did. Obviously that was never going to happen. Now a job at Hooters was certainly an option."

Bianca glanced between them. "You had difficult childhoods. Believe me, I know all about that. You either build character or you're crushed. Neither of you were crushed. Yes, you should be working together. Maybe a nonprofit. Something with young girls in unfortunate circumstances. Oh, I could be your seed money and your front person. I can still draw a crowd."

"That is a suggestion, isn't it?" Margot reached for her champagne, thinking she was so glad they'd Ubered to the restaurant because she was definitely having a second glass.

"Dismiss me all you want," Bianca told her. "But one day you'll figure out I'm right. In the meantime, let's change the subject. Sunshine, did you know your sister is sleeping with my son? They make a charming couple and they're very careful to make sure I never walk in on them doing the deed."

Sunshine did her best not to laugh. "Margot has always been thoughtful that way."

Margot looked around and wondered if it was too late to go directly for the hard liquor or if she should trust the champagne to get her drunk enough that she would completely forget this lunch had ever happened.

Sunshine signed in at the math lab and took a seat to wait. She was careful not to look at anyone, afraid they would be able to see her shame. Despite the hours of study, despite trying desperately to understand the material, she'd gotten another C minus on a test. Not even just a C. She honestly didn't think she could work any harder. It was just one class and she was already studying over fifteen hours a week, not counting class. At this rate, she could never take more than one class a semester and she would be close to retirement age by the time she finally graduated—probably with a C minus average.

Tears burned, but she blinked them away. She wasn't going to cry—not here. She would wait until she got home.

To think, just a couple of days ago, she'd been feeling so good about herself. She'd thought she'd done okay on the test, she'd had a fun lunch with Margot and Bianca, she liked her job. Everything had been on track and now this.

A few minutes later Sunshine heard her name called. She stood and walked toward a gray-haired woman wearing jeans and an "I'm with the Band" T-shirt.

"I'm Ann Lambert," the woman said. "You're having trouble with your math class?"

"Uh-huh."

"Just checking. You'd be amazed how many history students we get in here. I don't know what part of 'math lab' is confusing, but you would be shocked by the number."

Ann led her into a small office with a desk and two chairs, where they sat next to each other.

"Show me what you're working on," Ann said.

Sunshine opened her backpack and her test fell out. When she saw the large C minus in bright red, tears filled her eyes.

"I just don't get it," she said, feeling her frustration welling up along with the tears. "I'm studying so much and I'm not making any progress. I never applied myself before. I didn't go to college, and in high school I didn't care. I just assumed I was smart, but maybe I'm not. I should accept I can't do it."

Ann opened a desk drawer and pulled out a box of tissues. She waited until Sunshine took one to say, "If you're here for help with your math class, then great. If you're here because you expect me to feel sorry for you, then get out. We need the space for someone who actually plans to get through their class."

Sunshine stared at her. "What?"

"You heard me. Do you want to do this? The whole college thing? Because if it's hard now, it's only going to get harder. You're not even taking a class you're getting credit for, honey. You're taking a prerequisite. Are you sure you don't want to go back to whatever you were doing before? You're a pretty girl. Do you really want to work this hard?"

The shock of the words dried up her tears. "You can't talk to me like that."

"All evidence to the contrary," Ann muttered.

"No. It's not right. I'm trying here. I'm doing my homework and I'm prepared for class and, no, I don't want to go back to what I was before. I'm done being a piece of ass. I mean it. I don't care what you say, lady. I'm going to figure this out and I'm going to complete this class and I'm getting my degree, with or without your help, and since helping me is *your job*, you could try being a little more cooperative."

Ann surprised her by smiling. "There we go. Anger is a lot more useful and energizing. Feeling sorry for yourself just wastes time. When it's not your fault, you have nowhere to go. Remember that. Now, when was the last time you actually studied?"

"High school."

"And you're what now? Twenty-three?"

"Thirty-one."

Ann raised her eyebrows. "You have really good genes. Okay, so it's been maybe thirteen years since you were in a classroom. That's a long time. Here's the thing—it takes your brain about eight weeks to figure out what's going on. Right now you're not absorbing what's being taught. That's why when you read a page and go back an hour later, you don't remember anything. The lectures seem endlessly long and the homework takes forever. Give yourself another month and that will get better."

Ann opened another drawer and pulled out a brochure. "This has a lot of good tips on how to study. I'm sure you're doing it all wrong."

"Gee, thanks."

"No problem." Ann grinned. "There are easy things to do to help you along. Adult women are the most successful demographic in any college. It's because they have felt the fear and they are determined. You don't get to screw up that statistic, hear me?"

"Yes, ma'am."

"Good. Before you leave today, make study appointments with me twice a week. I was a math teacher for thirty-four years and then I retired. It was boring, so now I'm here. If you have half a brain, you should be able to figure this out in three or four weeks and then we can go to once a week appointments. How does that sound?"

Ann was direct and a little harsh, but Sunshine liked her. At least she was going to get the truth.

"It's a good plan," she said. "Thank you."

"Happy to help. Now let's get started. Tell me what's confusing you."

Sunshine bit her lower lip. "You really think I can do this?"

"Honey, a monkey could do this, so yes. Let's get you where you need to be."

Sunshine opened the book. Connor would have laughed about the monkey comment and Declan... Well, this wasn't the time to think about him. Despite the C minus, she actually felt a little hopeful.

"I understood linear equations and even the fractions. Everything fell apart when I started trying to do the graphs."

Ann nodded. "Graphs are hard. Okay, let's begin there."

Margot knew she was more of doer than a relaxer but even she liked restorative yoga. There was something calming about the various poses and the focus on breathing. She smiled. It was the kind of exercise her sister would enjoy, she thought. When Bianca had suggested a class, Margot had assumed they would go to a studio but instead an instructor had shown up at the house and had taken them through the fifty-minute session out in the garden. When they were done, Margot was so relaxed, she was practically liquid. She barely made it to the table and chairs in the gazebo, where Edna had brought out herbal tea and scones.

"That was incredible," she said, pouring tea into two cups. "I could do that every day."

"I'm sure you needed it," Bianca said with a sly smile. "What with all the sex. Your muscles are being used in ways they aren't used to."

Margot should have known there would be a price for the class, but she told herself it was worth it.

"Not playing that game," she said mildly, reaching for a scone.

"But we talk about my personal life all the time!"

"Your personal life is why I'm here," she reminded her client. "I won't discuss Alec with you."

"Fine. Then let's talk about the old boyfriend. The one you've been avoiding. What was his name? Dietrich?"

Margot considered herself fairly skilled at hiding her emotions. It was part of her job—but wow, did Bianca test her on a regular basis. Still, Dietrich was a safer subject than Alec.

"What do you want to know?" she asked.

"Why was it so awful?"

Margot considered all the stories she could tell, all the examples of how her life had been messed up because Dietrich was in it only to realize he hadn't been the problem at all.

"I wasn't my best self when I was with him," she said with a shrug. "In truth, I was my worst self, and that's on me, not him. Loving someone should make us better. It should lift us up, not drown us."

She thought maybe she was her best self with Alec. At least she thought it might be possible. When she was around him, she felt good. He never tried to distract her from what was important or make her feel less than.

"What does that even mean?" Bianca asked.

"I suppose I'm saying that loving someone should be a positive experience for both parties. That being around the person you love shouldn't make your life worse. That when you're with that person, you are seeking to be better than you would be without him. Is that too vague?"

"A little, but I think I understand it. I do love being around Wesley."

"Why?"

Bianca frowned. "What a strange question. Because he's perfect. He's kind and he loves me. He always has fun things to talk about." She smiled. "The sex is fabulous."

"This isn't about sex."

"Nearly everything is about sex."

"I don't believe that."

"Whatever. My point is, I love Wesley. He's nothing like some of the other men I've been with. I thought I'd found my best love with Sebastian but was I wrong."

Margot had no idea who Sebastian was, but before she could ask, Bianca continued.

"He was a famous model and we did a shoot together. This was years ago. He left the business and ended up making a fortune trading stocks. We met up, oh, fifteen years later, and it was like we'd never been apart." Her smiled turned nostalgic.

"We got engaged, then we broke up, but it wasn't horrible, you know? Just one of those things." She pressed her lips together. "Three years ago he wrote a biography and he didn't mention me even once."

She looked at Margot. "Can you believe it? I was supposed to be his great love and I didn't even get a footnote. Then he had the balls to invite me to the launch party. Well, I didn't go. I can tell you that!"

"What does that have to do with Wesley?"

"What? Nothing. Were we talking about him?"

"We were talking about love being a path to our best self. Love isn't about what the other person does for you, Bianca, it's about what we do for that person. It's about giving. We aren't changed by what is done to us, rather we are transformed by the act of loving someone else."

She felt herself getting annoyed, which was not going to be helpful, nor could she actually explain her reaction. Maybe it was because in her mind, she was thinking Alec rather than Wesley. Bianca could be charming and fun but she was also self-absorbed and thoughtless. What must it have been like to not know which mother you were going to have to deal with on any given day?

"Are you even in love with Wesley?" she asked bluntly. "Are you going to be there for him, no matter what? Are you going to take care of him, in sickness and in health? What if he ends up in a wheelchair? Will you be there, then? Or is it all about being mentioned in a biography?"

Bianca stood and glared at her. "I can't believe you're even asking me that."

"Someone has to."

"It's not your job, though, is it?"

"My job is to help you be the best wife possible for a man in Wesley's position. I was so careful when I did my research, but I never thought to ask if you genuinely loved him or if this was just another role for you."

"Of course I love him. I do!"

Margot didn't say anything. She wasn't sure how Bianca felt about anyone but herself. Still, she wasn't sure her opinion mattered one way or the other.

"All right. We were going to spend the afternoon discussing the cultural differences between European countries. Would you like to get started on that?"

Bianca was silent for nearly a minute. Finally she nodded. "Yes, let's talk about that."

"There are so many ants that if you took all the ants and weighed them and all the people and weighed them, it would be the same!"

Connor sounded both impressed and scandalized by the information as he lay on the grass, reading from a book on ants.

"That's a lot of ants," Declan agreed.

"It is."

Declan had ripped out the old hedges a few weeks ago. Now he carefully dug out holes to plant the new hedges. The morning was already warm and sunny. The afternoon would get well into the eighties and it was still a couple of months until summer. One of the reasons he loved Southern California.

"Scientists think there are over a million ants alive for every single person alive." Connor giggled. "I want to name my million ants."

"Do you know a million names or will you just call them Ant One, Ant Two, Ant Three?"

Connor laughed. "I'd call them Connor Ant One," he joked.

"So you want a kingdom of ants."

"Uh-huh." He turned the page. "Here it is. There are super colonies, Dad. The ants are all connected and they share the same chemical makeup so they're related." He frowned and turned the page. "Oh, I remember. They're Argentine ants and they're supposed to be native to South America but they're all over the world. The super colonies go for thousands of miles."

"That's a serious pest problem."

"Dad, it's not a problem. It's cool. I wish I had a super colony of ants." He sat up. "I've taken really good care of my ant farm."

"You have."

"Maybe I could get a second one."

More ants? They weren't a lot of trouble and so far the farm hadn't leaked or expelled or whatever it was an ant farm did when the residents escaped, but more of them? In the house?

He looked at his son's eager face and thought about all he'd been through in the past eight or nine months. If he wanted another ant farm, what was the big deal?

"Sure," he said. "Do some research online and then we'll talk about it. I'll let Sunshine know."

"She won't mind, Dad. She loves my ants."

Declan doubted that was true, but knew she wouldn't make a fuss. Very little rattled her, which was one of many things he liked about her. She was down-to-earth and accepting. He knew she cared about Connor.

"I'm going to go tell her right now," Connor said, scrambling to his feet, grabbing his book and racing into the house.

Declan returned his attention to the series of holes he'd been digging. Just three more, he told himself. Then he would start planting.

The physical work felt good. He'd had a difficult week at work—Jessica and James were still annoying him with their inability to make a decision. In theory most of the garden was planned, but all it would take was one distraction and they would be starting over. He and Heath weren't losing money on the job because they'd been careful with the pay structure. Every time there was a deviation from the initial, approved plan, the company billed by the hour until they were back on track. So his frustration wasn't financial, it was that he didn't want a single job to suck up so much of his time. There were other jobs with people who knew what they wanted, and right now he and Heath were forced to turn them away.

"Soon," he said aloud. It would be done soon. Or so he hoped.

He started on another hole, digging deep enough to give the new plant plenty of room for the roots to expand. He'd always liked working in the garden. Iris hadn't shared his love of working outdoors. She'd preferred to watch from the house.

He thought about what Sunshine had said about getting Connor into sports. It was something he should have thought of himself, only Iris hadn't liked organized sports and he had figured there was plenty of time to take on that fight.

He and Connor had already talked and agreed that Connor would go to a summer baseball camp. In the fall he wanted to try soccer and basketball. The baseball camp was three mornings a week, which meant he needed something for the afternoons. There was a park program with a lot of general activities. Sunshine had surprised him by suggesting music camp. They had both full- and half-day programs. Declan had no idea if his son had any aptitude for music, but it might be something for him to explore.

Iris would have pushed for some kind of science camp, he thought. Last summer Connor had been enrolled in an intensive science program but he hadn't enjoyed himself at all. Iris had told him he wasn't trying hard enough but Declan had said he needed other activities. They'd argued about it, then Iris had told him to do what he wanted. As if she hadn't cared anymore. Had that been when she'd started the affair?

He didn't think their fight had been that significant or that any one thing he'd done had driven her into the arms of another man. It might not have been about him at all, although he knew he shared the blame for at least half of what had gone on in their marriage. But while he might have responsibility for setting up a situation where she was unhappy, he knew that her falling in love with someone else was on her. She'd chosen another man over him and Connor. She'd been willing to leave them both. While she hadn't admitted as much, when he'd asked what her plans were for their son, she'd told him it was complicated. Shouldn't she have been a mother first and a lover second?

He moved on to the last hole and dug his shovel into the ground. Even as he thought about Iris and what had gone wrong, he recognized that he had a lot less energy to put into the questions. He would never get all the answers, but the not knowing was now more a curiosity than anything else. While he regretted what had happened, the past no longer tore him apart. Pain had faded into sadness. He knew even that wound would heal over. Time had done its thing and he'd moved on.

Involuntarily he glanced at the house. Although he couldn't see Sunshine, he knew she was there. Wanting uncoiled, but he ignored it, along with the growing need to spend time with her, talk to her, laugh with her. It was enough that he trusted her with his son. Everything else was simply background noise.

chapter
TWENTY-ONE

MARGOT WALKED INTO THE DINING ROOM AT BREAKFAST.
The small buffet was laid out, as it always was, with a hot dish
of some kind, fresh fruit, an assortment of pastries and croissants
along with coffee, juice and water.

Alec was sitting in his usual place, a newspaper open, because
he believed in supporting the local press and had the *Los Angeles
Times* delivered every morning.

In that second before he looked up and saw her, she studied
him. The way his dark hair had a bit of a wave to it, how his
shirt fit across his broad shoulders and the shape of his hands
and fingers.

She knew him intimately now—every inch of him. She'd
touched and tasted all of him enough times that she would easily recognize him by feel alone. She knew the sound of his voice
and what he found funny. She liked his intensity and understood
his need to create a fortress where he could disappear and live
in his head, discovering the secrets of those long dead and gone.

He was an honorable man and when she was with him, she
felt as if she belonged. She had no idea where their relationship
was going, but if she had her way, the feelings between them
would only grow and expand until all the empty places they'd
both carried around were happily filled.

He looked up, saw her and smiled. "Good morning. Did you sleep well?"

She grinned. "I was awake around three, but otherwise, I did sleep well."

"Yes, I should probably apologize for that."

"Do you really think so?" she asked, remembering how he awakened her by kissing her all over, arousing her until she was frantic with need, before bringing her to an earth-shattering orgasm.

"No, I don't, but it seemed the polite thing to say."

She laughed. "Thank you for the effort."

She picked up a plate and served herself breakfast. After setting the plate across from his, she picked up his coffee cup and filled it, then filled another for herself and took her seat.

"How is the world?" she asked, motioning to the paper.

"About where it was yesterday. The bigger issue is my mother thinks you're still angry with her."

Margot dug her fork into the fluffy scrambled eggs. "And she's coming to you about it? That's unusual. She doesn't seem to have a problem being direct with me. I wonder what that's about."

"She wants to see if I'll side with her," he said.

"Oh, that makes sense. Do you love her more than you—" Margot stumbled to a verbal stop. "What I meant was…"

Alec smiled. "I know what you meant and yes, I suspect that's what she's worried about."

"I am the new shiny thing in your world."

"While she's allowed to have new, shiny things all the time, I am not." He shrugged. "Those have always been the rules. It's how she is."

"Did you reassure her?"

"I told her if she had a problem with you to talk to you directly."

"You're such a guy," she teased. "How did she take it?"

"She pouted."

"Thanks for the warning. I'll be prepared."

Conversation shifted to the movie they'd watched the previous evening and plans they had for the weekend after she finished helping her sister with a birthday party for Sunshine's charge. Margot wished it could be like this always but there were going to be changes. Her contract with Bianca was nearly finished. She'd already broached the subject of ending their lessons, but Bianca had refused to discuss it. In a few more weeks, Margot was going to have to insist.

And then what? Would Alec still want to see her or was this simply a relationship of convenience? Assuming he wanted things to continue, how would living in separate houses affect things, and at what point did she start admitting to herself that this was way more than casual, at least for her?

Before she could decide any of that, Alec stunned her by asking, "Is everything all right sexually?"

She put down the piece of toast she'd been holding and stared at him. "I don't understand the question."

"I want to make sure you're, ah, satisfied. If there was something else you'd like us to try or be doing or..." He gestured vaguely with his hand.

The question was confusing enough, but so was the timing. It was barely seven in the morning. They'd just spent the night together and had made love at three in the morning. She'd needed to use a pillow to muffle her cries of delight.

"I still don't understand the question."

He looked away, then back at her. His eyes and pretty much every other part of him was unreadable.

"One of the complaints my ex-fiancée had was about our sex life," he admitted, his voice flat. "She said sex with me was boring."

Margot tried to absorb the statement. *Boring? Boring?* They had sex in his office, the kitchen, the shower, and, sure, in their respective beds. They did it standing, sitting, sideways, in positions she wasn't sure had names but had been immortalized in his erotic netsuke. They played, they talked, they touched and they teased. They were masters at the three-minute encounter with a minimum of fuss and often spent hours enjoying each other, slowly, sensually until they were both shaking with exhaustion.

She opened her mouth to tell him all that and more only to burst out laughing. Once she started, she couldn't stop. She laughed until tears filled her eyes, then she laughed a little more. When she caught her breath enough to speak, she managed a gasping, "No. No, you're not boring." Then the laughter claimed her again.

Alec waited patiently, his expression slightly pained. When she finally got control of herself, she sighed. "Alec, you have many flaws, we all do, but boring in bed isn't one of them. You're not even close. Seriously, the woman was an idiot. You should let that go."

One corner of his mouth turned up. "Thank you. I wanted to be sure you were satisfied."

"I am. Completely. Totally. In every way possible."

His gaze locked with hers. "I am, as well."

"That is very good to know."

Sunshine tried to think of a polite way to say no.

"Come on," Phoebe cajoled over the phone. "It'll be fun. We'll get dressed up and then go have drinks. A girls' night out. Say yes."

Sunshine really didn't want to. She preferred her girls' nights out with her sister. With Margot she could totally relax and be herself. With Phoebe, she was less sure. Did the other woman actually want to spend time with her or did she want to grill her about Declan?

She knew he'd taken her advice and had gone to coffee with Phoebe so he could tell her where he stood, which made it very likely that Phoebe's overture of friendship was more about Declan than wanting Sunshine to be friends with her.

"I'm begging," Phoebe told her. "Say yes, or I'll be devastated."

"*Devastated* seems strong," Sunshine murmured, feeling herself start to cave. "But all right. Drinks would be fun."

"Great. I'm in my car and can't get to my calendar. Let me text you later and we'll set something up. Bye."

And with that, she was gone. Sunshine dropped her phone onto her bed and groaned. She should have just said no, she told herself. It wasn't a hard word. According to her great-grandmother, it had been the first word she'd ever spoken.

"I'll deal with that later," she murmured, heading to the kitchen. She had a busy day planned. Her math class had been canceled which gave her more time to get ready for Connor's birthday party tomorrow. While she felt organized, there was still a lot to get done. Declan had insisted on taking the day off to help her and if she was going to be honest with herself, she was way more excited about hanging out with him than prepping for the party. Not that she had to admit that to anyone. Still, the thought of being together for the day made her feel just a little squishy inside.

Declan met her in the kitchen. He looked strong and capable and more than a little sexy.

"Ready?" he asked.

"I am."

They walked to the spare bedroom and he unlocked the door. Inside were all the party supplies including the items for the goodie bags and equipment for the games. There were also wrapped presents including the custom-made ant-patterned comforter Sunshine had ordered for Connor on Etsy.

It took four trips to carry what they needed to the kitchen.

"I want to save the game setup until the morning," she said, grabbing the goodie bags along with the tote containing her craft supplies. "It's not going to rain, but there's still morning dew to contend with and I don't want anything getting wet."

"Not a problem. I've already turned off the sprinklers so they won't go on tomorrow. That way the grass will be dry."

The birthday party would be held outside. Sunshine had ordered long tables and plenty of chairs. She had game areas, a giant ant piñata and separate tables for presents along with food and drinks.

She pulled out her party to-do list.

"Today we're going to cut out the ants for the goodie bags and glue them on, then load them up. I want to cut out the ants for the flashlights, run through the supplies for the games, confirm the backyard layout and get started on some of the food."

"That's a lot."

She smiled. "Not with you helping me. Margot is coming tomorrow and she'll help with serving the food and generally run interference."

"Won't the other parents be sticking around to help?"

"Oh, Declan, seriously? A kid's birthday party is a chance to have a few hours without worry. That's the deal. Trust me, the parents are going to drop off their kids and bolt."

"I guess I hadn't noticed that before." He frowned. "Actually, I think we never bothered with much of a party for Connor before. Iris wasn't the party type, so we kept it mostly family."

Sunshine knew there was nothing she could say that wouldn't be considered snarky so she offered him a smile and said, "My love of planning parties is only surpassed by the thrill of throwing them. So thanks for letting me do this." She waved her papers. "Let's get started."

They cut large ants out of construction paper and glued them onto the bags. Nine boys were coming to the party, giving them an even ten. Sunshine had ten bags, the last of which she would tuck away until everyone was gone and the postparty letdown had started. Then she would give Connor his bag.

While Declan applied bug stickers to the bags and filled them with the toys and candy, she put a fresh blade into her X-Acto knife and went to work on the heat resistant tape she'd found. Her plan was to cut out an ant silhouette and apply it to the lens of the flashlight, thereby creating a custom beam. She'd just finished two of them when the knife slipped and the sharp blade sliced through the edge of her left palm.

In the nanosecond that followed, Sunshine tried to figure out what she'd done. Nothing hurt and there didn't seem to be anything wrong. Then blood began to gush onto the table and nerve endings lit on fire. She started to stand, only to realize that might be a bad idea.

"Declan!"

He glanced at her, swore and jumped to his feet. "What happened?" he asked as he grabbed a dish towel and wrapped it around her hand. In seconds, the towel was red with blood.

"I cut myself with the knife."

She felt sick to her stomach and the pain was intense.

Declan grabbed three more towels from the drawer and hustled her into the car. He ran back to the house for her bag so she would have ID, then quickly drove out of the neighborhood and to the local hospital. Quicker than she would have thought, she was in a small room in the ER, sitting upright in a hospital bed. Her nurse, who had introduced herself as Nikki, put on a pressure bandage that hurt like hell, while Declan hovered.

"You're going to need stitches," Nikki told her. "Let me get the paperwork started. Are you right-handed?"

Sunshine nodded, trying to ignore her wooziness.

"That's good because you won't be able to use your left hand for a while. Still, have your husband fill out the paperwork. You can just sign it at the end."

She handed a clipboard to Declan before stepping out of the room.

Sunshine leaned her head back and closed her eyes. "You should tell her we're not married," she said quietly, wondering if she really was going to throw up. Blood wasn't her favorite, but it didn't usually bother her. Of course she could be in shock or maybe she'd lost a lot of blood. Either way, her hand was throbbing something fierce.

"I think that's kind of the least of it," he said, taking a seat. "Let me get this filled out."

He wrote in the basic information, then asked her if she was allergic to any medications and about any past medical conditions.

"There's nothing," she said, her head spinning a little. "And no family history of anything." Not that she knew about. Her great-grandmother had been well into her nineties before she'd died quietly in her sleep. As for Sunshine's father, well, they didn't know anything about him. Which was a stupid thing to be thinking about right now, she told herself, even as she tried not to cry.

Nikki returned with several pillows so Sunshine could keep her hand elevated. She put in an IV.

"Fluids and something for the pain," she said. "Do you remember your last tetanus shot?"

"No. I think I was a kid."

Nikki smiled. "You want to keep up with that. The guidelines are for every ten years. We'll get you a booster."

Great. A shot *and* stitches. Of course she already had an IV in her arm, so maybe that was the worst of it. She looked at Declan. "What about the party?"

"Don't worry about it. Let's get you fixed up and then I'll deal with the prep work."

"You can't do it all yourself. This is Connor's birthday party. It's huge."

"I'll manage."

He sounded confident, but she was less sure. "Margot was going to help tomorrow anyway. I can call and ask her to come early or even today," she began.

"Stop," he told her. "Let's get you through this first and then we'll assess, okay?" His voice was gentle but firm. "Sunshine, you're my main concern. If Connor were here, he would completely agree with me. The party will happen. Let it go."

Nikki smiled. "Honey, you've got yourself a keeper."

Sunshine turned to the nurse, ready to correct her. Declan shook his head, then winked.

"You're right," he said cheerfully. "She is one lucky lady to have me."

Before Sunshine could respond or even acknowledge the sudden and powerful wish that she really was that lucky, the sliding door to her room opened and a tall, attractive, dark-haired woman stepped in, a tablet in her hand. She smiled and said, "Hello, Sunshine. I'm Dr. Kumar. You seem to have had a bit of an accident."

"I'd wave but it would get messy," she said, hoping she didn't look like she was about to cry.

Dr. Kumar laughed. "We don't want that. Let me take a quick look, then we'll fix you right up."

Several stitches, a prescription for mild painkillers and some discharge papers later, Sunshine found herself back at home. Her hand was still numb from the local anesthetic, but she had a bad feeling it was going to hurt like crazy once that wore off.

"You should go lie down," Declan told her as they walked into the kitchen. "You need to take it easy."

"I cut my hand. I didn't get in a car accident. I'm completely fine."

"You have no color in your face and you look like you're going to pass out any second. Lie down for a couple of hours and then we'll see how you feel."

"No. We have to get ready for the party. We have nine kids arriving at eleven tomorrow morning. There's too much to do."

"You wrote out a master list. I can follow it."

"No. My notes won't make sense to you."

She had more to say but suddenly felt a little light-headed. She swayed in place, thinking she should probably sit down. She'd barely taken a step toward the stools by the island when Declan jumped to her side and put his arm around her waist.

"Thank you for demonstrating my point," he said, his voice gentle. "Come on, Sunshine. You have to take care of yourself."

"I'm fine."

He looked at her and raised his eyebrows. "Seriously? You're fine?"

He was standing so close, she could see all the colors in his irises. He was a lot taller than her, and strong, and having him hold her felt really good. Like she was safe and taken care of. She wanted to lean against him, she wanted to have him just hang on forever and…

She pushed away the ridiculous thoughts, telling herself she was injured and not at her best and any warm fuzzies were simply the result of the trauma and not the least bit real. She had to get a grip.

She turned and sagged onto the stool.

"Please bring in one of the lounge chairs from the patio," she said. "You can move the kitchen table to the side and put the lounge chair next to it. Once I'm settled there, you can bring in a couple of pillows from my bedroom so I can prop up my hand." She shrugged. "It's a compromise. You need me to help you figure out what to do and you want me to rest. This way we both get what we want."

Something hot and fiery flashed in his eyes. It faded as quickly as it had flared but not before she felt an answering jolt way down low in her belly.

"You promise not to do anything but supervise?" he asked, his voice skeptical.

"I promise."

He flashed her a smile. "Okay then. We have ourselves a deal."

chapter
TWENTY-TWO

THE SATURDAY MORNING PREP FOR THE PARTY COULDN'T have gone more smoothly, Declan thought with relief. Margot arrived just before eight and declared herself more than ready to step in and do what needed to be done. By then Declan had already set up the rented tables and chairs on the covered patio and used construction caution tape to rope off the game area of the backyard. Sunshine, still pale but less shaky, supervised, while an excited Connor bounced from person to person, checking to see that all would be ready for his party. The third time Declan turned and nearly fell over his son, his patience reached the snapping point.

"You've got to stay out of the way," he said, knowing he sounded exasperated, but unable to help himself.

"But Da–ad!"

Sunshine stepped between them. She hugged Connor. "I know you're excited, but if you keep getting in our way, we can't be ready for your friends and you wouldn't want that. Why don't you run into my room and look at what's on the bed?"

Connor tore out of the kitchen. Declan turned to Sunshine. "What did you get him?"

"You'll see."

Seconds later Connor was back with a large, flat, wrapped package in his hands.

"It's really heavy," he said eagerly. "Can I open it now? Can I?"

There was a family dinner that night, something low-key, following the party. Connor would open Declan's presents then, plus whatever Sunshine had bought him. Not that she was expected to buy his kid a present, but he knew she would.

"You can," she told him.

He ripped the bug-themed birthday paper and shrieked when he saw the title of the book. *The World of Ants*. The book was thick, with lots of glossy pictures and more information than the average person wanted to know about ants. Connor beamed at her.

"This is the best! Thank you." He hugged Sunshine, then clutched the book to his chest. "Can I go read it now?"

"You can. We'll call you when your guests arrive."

"Okay." He ran out of the kitchen, leaving the ripped paper behind.

"Well played," Margot said. "You knew he would be excited and in the way, so you planned on giving him the gift."

"I thought it might help."

"Imagine what you could do if you weren't injured," her sister teased.

Declan watched the exchange. Physically the sisters couldn't have been more different. Oh sure, they were both blonde and had similar eyes and shared a smile, but otherwise, they looked nothing alike. Yet they were both kind and giving. He'd seen Margot eyeing her sister, as if making sure she was doing all right with her injury. Margot had given up a day off to help with a party for a kid she barely knew. The Baxter sisters were special, he thought, and whoever won their respective hearts would be damned lucky.

He allowed himself a brief moment to play a mental game of pretend, then pushed the thoughts away. Sunshine was in his house, under his protection. He would not repay her devotion and friendship by coming on to her like some sleazy asshole.

At ten-thirty there was a final meeting to make sure all the prep work was done.

"The ice-cream cake has been moved to the kitchen freezer," Margot said, checking off an item on the list. "Plates and forks are ready to go for that. The sandwiches and finger foods are all prepared and in the refrigerator or in the pantry."

Declan looked at his list. "Goodie bags are finished and safely behind closed doors. I'll get them out at two-thirty. The hall bathroom is stocked with plenty of liquid hand soap and a stack of paper hand towels. I'll check supplies every half hour and make sure nothing gross has happened."

Margot looked sympathetic. "Good luck with that."

"It's the least I can do," he told her, then winked at Sunshine.

She smiled at him, then read from her list. "Game supplies are all in place. You two have the rules of the games. Guests are due to arrive at eleven. We'll go right into the *What Am I?* game, then have lunch with the movie *Ants* playing. After that we'll do the sword relay followed by presents. We'll wrap up with the piñata."

She looked at them. "That's all of it. I'll be supervising from my chair, although there's really no reason I can't—"

"Please," Margot said, rolling her eyes. "You have dozens of stitches in your hand, I know it still hurts and you barely slept. You may be the queen of all things child, but we can handle the details of the party."

Sunshine looked at Declan. "She's always been bossy. Sometimes you just have to go with it."

"I can't help it," Margot told her. "I'm the firstborn. Responsibility is my middle name."

"You're firstborn by eight minutes."

Margot sighed. "I did love being an only child."

They laughed. Sunshine caught Declan's gaze and smiled

at him. Desire exploded, but he had plenty of practice ignoring the sensation. Instead he enjoyed their sense of connection. They were a good team and he didn't want to do anything to screw that up.

Sunday, Margot decided to do some exploring in the monastery cellar. The area under the former church was huge. Part of the old root cellar had been converted into a large wine cellar with shelves and racks and good lighting. The rest of the root cellar was still intact and at first she'd thought that was as much underground as there was.

A couple of weeks before, Margot had found a small door at the back. She'd opened it and discovered dozens of small rooms and winding hallways with stone flooring and wooden support beams. Although there were electric lights in the hallway, there weren't a lot of bulbs, so she'd brought along a bright flashlight.

The ceiling was low enough that she had to hunch a little as she walked. Despite there being no windows or obvious ways to get outside, the air was relatively fresh, so there had to be vents or something. The whole space was perfectly dry, which made sense. This was Southern California—a semiarid region of the country. There wasn't much of a water table to dampen anything, and less than nine inches of rain a year wasn't going to impact the cellar.

She'd walked the whole area and kept coming back to the stone wall on the north end of the building. There was just something about it. Something intriguing. Several of the stones didn't have grout around them and she would swear she felt a breeze blowing between them.

When she'd told Alec about the wall and her hopes that there was a secret door, he'd joked that she was still hoping for old bones. Margot didn't mind what was there, as long as it was something exciting.

She looked for a lever but didn't see one anywhere. She pushed at random stones. A few of them moved, but only a quarter of an inch or so. It wasn't enough to work a mechanism.

Rather than get frustrated, she turned away from the wall and closed her eyes. After taking a couple of deep breaths, she thought about how much she'd enjoyed helping at Connor's birthday party the previous day. He'd had so much fun and his friends seemed to, as well. Sunshine had done a great job planning everything. Every bit of the party had been filled with thoughtful touches—from the way the food had been styled to the decorations to the goodie bags.

Her sister was like that, she thought, smiling. All about the details. It was a part of who she was. She loved children and being a part of a family. She always gave of herself—maybe too much. Margot hoped Sunshine's new plan—to not fall for the wrong guy—worked. She thought she'd sensed a little attraction between Sunshine and Declan, but she wasn't sure. Sunshine couldn't help connecting with the children she cared about. She always had because it was part of who she was. People were defined by what they believed and hoped and dreamed.

Monks were men of God, she thought, turning back to the wall. Their lives were about devotion.

She studied the stones again. Widthwise there was an odd number of stones. She found the middle row and pressed the top one, then one maybe two feet down. Neither stone moved even a little. The key had to be the sign of the cross, she thought. So where was the top?

She pressed each of the stones, starting at the top, and just below the middle, one moved back a little.

She stared at the stones, trying to make sense of it. If she was right, how could that be the top of the cross? Yes, she was tall, certainly for a woman in the eighteenth century, but if that stone was the top of the cross, the monks would have to have been—

"Kneeling," she breathed. "They'd been kneeling!"

She dropped to the stone floor and began pushing the stones

in line with the one that had moved. She found the second one easily. It only took a few minutes to figure out the other two. She was so excited to have solved the puzzle that she nearly forgot her purpose. It was only when the stone door swung open that she realized she'd found, well, whatever it was!

She turned on the flashlight and moved it to illuminate the darkness. From what she could tell, she'd found a huge storage area. There were the usual stacked tables and baskets, a few chests, along with bolts of what she would guess was very old fabric. But what most caught her attention were the statues lined up on several shelves. They were between one and three feet tall, all of saints, and all made of gold and encrusted with large jewels.

Margot jumped to her feet and raced back the way she'd come. She bolted up the stairs and ran into Alec's office. He looked up from his desk and grinned.

"Old bones?" he asked, his voice teasing. "You promised you wouldn't."

"Better. Come see."

He followed her downstairs and through the root cellar.

"Watch your head," she told him. "The ceiling gets lower."

She led the way to the back of the underground area before pressing herself against the wall so he could go ahead of her. She handed him the flashlight.

He glanced at her. "Now I'm intrigued."

"Good. You should be."

They began walking again, turning the last corner with him in the lead. She couldn't see past him but knew the exact second he saw the open secret door.

"Damn, you did find something," he said, his tone respectful. "I should never have doubted you."

"While that's true, let's talk about it later. Go look."

He pushed the door open and shone the light inside.

"Do you see them?" she asked eagerly. "The statues on the shelf? Aren't they amazing? I'm not sure we should touch them.

I don't think anyone's seen them in what? Two hundred years? Obviously whoever was running the church hadn't been told about them. They never would have left them behind. Not only are they valuable on their own, but they probably have religious significance. I told you there was something."

Alec swore under his breath.

"What?" she asked. "Are you mad?"

"Of course not. It's an exciting find. It's just..." He looked at her. "Now they have to be dealt with."

She gazed into his eyes and realized what he was thinking. "Oh no. You're right. Legally they came with the property, so they're yours and you could simply leave them where they are or display them, but you won't do that, will you? You're going to call whoever is in charge of the Catholic church in this area and let them come claim their property. Which means everything will have to be documented and photographed before it's removed. What a mess. I found bones, huh?"

"Better than bones. It won't take them but a few days."

"Still. You didn't want an invasion. I'm sorry."

"Don't be." He put his arm around her and kissed her. "It'll pass. This is a very significant discovery. You said there was something down here and you were right. Good for you."

She smiled. "You should keep one of the statues. Just a little one. Come on, they are so cool and you'd appreciate their historical significance more than most."

One corner of his mouth turned up. "I'll do some research and keep the least valuable of the lot." He led her back toward the stairs. "Any other areas you have a burning need to explore?"

"I think I've seen it all."

"Good."

She laughed. "I promise not to find any more treasure."

"Thank you, but even so, I do have one favor to ask."

"I can guess what it is."

"Yes?"

"Don't tell your mother."

"That would be it."

She leaned against him. "You have my word."

"That's all I need."

Alec found himself pulled forward a couple of hundred centuries by the sound of voices in the hallway. Normally he would have tuned them out but when he recognized they belonged to Margot and his mother, he moved quickly to open the door so he could listen better and decide if he had to intervene.

"This isn't right," Margot said, her tone firm.

"You don't know what you're talking about."

He would guess they were standing on the stairs. The sharpness of Margot's tone surprised him. As far as he knew, she and his mother were getting along well and the lessons were progressing to the point that Margot wouldn't be needed much longer—something he didn't want to think about. Once she left, well, he wasn't sure what was going to happen. He liked having her in his house and in his bed.

"Alec would want this," his mother insisted, getting his attention. "I believe I'm a better judge of that than you are."

"Under most circumstances, I'm sure you're right, but not this time."

"His house is beautiful and now with the treasure," Bianca said. "Shouldn't the world get to admire it?"

The treasure? How had his mother found out?

"No, the world shouldn't," Margot insisted. "This is his home, his refuge. He isn't the kind of person who wants to have pictures of it plastered in some magazine."

"It's not *some magazine*! It's a prestigious publication and being asked to be part of a photo shoot is an honor."

"For you," Margot told her. "But not for him."

"We'll just see about that!"

His mother started down the stairs, while Margot stayed

where she was. Alec debated racing back to his desk so he could pretend he hadn't been listening, but decided there was no point. He pushed open the door wider and waited. Seconds later, Bianca swept in, a glossy magazine in her hand.

She looked at him, her eyes narrowed. "You heard?"

"I did."

She waved the magazine. "Being invited to be a featured home is a huge honor. I can't imagine what Margot was thinking to say you wouldn't be interested." Her gaze was pointed.

"I'm sorry," he began.

"No!" His mother glared at him. "Alec, you will not refuse them. How can you not want recognition for your beautiful house? And the treasure should be seen by all. Not that I would have known about it from you or Margot. I had to hear about it when I ran into that Cardinal who visited and he only told me because I asked what he was doing here."

Alec grimaced. "When you say you 'ran into him' you mean—"

"Oh for heaven's sake. I parked *next* to him. I didn't actually hit him. You are more annoying than usual today. You have a beautiful house and you found some fabulous artifacts that you are returning to the Catholic church and you won't let one measly little writer in here to talk about it and take some pictures?"

"Mother, this is my home and it's private."

"So you're taking her side over mine? I am so disappointed in you."

"I'm not taking anyone's side. I'm telling you what I want, and you shouldn't be surprised. You know how I value my privacy."

She sniffed. "I thought I could count on you. I thought we were a team. I should have known that one a day a woman would rip us apart, leaving us with nothing."

Later he would mull over the fact that Margot knew him as well as she did, and that she had stood up for him, but right now he had a very angry, possibly hurt woman standing in front of him. He thought of a dozen responses, casting each of them

aside. There was no way to convince Bianca he hadn't deliberately set out to disappoint her. And saying that her reaction to
his refusal was over-the-top wouldn't help, either. Since when
were they a—

He replayed the words in his mind, then hid a smile.

"'I should have known that one day a woman would rip us
apart, leaving us with nothing'?" he asked. "What movie is that
line from? It's familiar, but I can't place it."

She turned away. "I have no idea what you're talking about."

"*Gardens of Snow*. That's it, isn't it?"

Bianca's choices in movie roles had never been conventional
or expected. She'd played a lesbian in *Gardens of Snow* decades
ago, long before that lifestyle had gained much acceptance.

"It's what you said to your partner when you found out she
was cheating on you."

The glare returned. "Your excellent memory is annoying
and inconvenient."

"Too bad." He put his hands on her shoulders and kissed her
forehead. "I love you, but there will be no photo shoot."

"You never let me have any fun."

"By now you should be used to that."

chapter
TWENTY-THREE

SUNSHINE FINISHED GETTING READY FOR HER GIRLS'
night out with Phoebe. Despite liking the idea of having more
friends in her life, she would really have preferred to stay home.
Her tutoring sessions with Ann were starting to make a big difference and she wanted to go over her homework again. There
was also the fact that she still had to wear a large bandage on her
hand. But she'd promised to be there when Phoebe had texted
to confirm and remind Sunshine "to wear something pretty so
they could both feel special."

Right on time, Sunshine walked into the Italian bistro in
downtown Pasadena. Phoebe had said she would be waiting in
the bar. Sunshine looked around, spotted Phoebe, then froze
when she saw the other woman sitting at a table with two guys.

What on earth? Why would Phoebe be with two guys? Sunshine
had assumed the evening out was a ruse so Phoebe could find
out what was going on with Declan. She'd expected to be grilled
and possibly to have to deal with tears.

Phoebe saw her, stood and hurried to greet her.

"Don't be mad," she said by way of greeting. "I know I said
girls' night out, but a double date will be more fun. It's not like
you're seeing anyone."

"Didn't Declan tell you I was in a relationship?" She'd told him to mention that on his date with Phoebe.

"Maybe. I don't remember. You just didn't seem like you were."

"But I thought you wanted to hang out so you could ask me about Declan."

Phoebe dismissed that thought with a wave. "We had a night, it was great and then I moved on. What's the big deal?" She turned back to the table. "The guy on the right is Marcus. Isn't he yummy? He's with me. You're with Steven. He's divorced, a movie producer maybe and super nice." She linked arms with Sunshine. "Come on. Let's go say hi."

Sunshine resisted moving. "So you're not interested in Declan?"

"No. Does he think I am? It's always so hard when guys are needy. Oh well. Tonight is going to be fun. It's two guys, a couple of drinks and a good time. What's not to like?"

Sunshine looked back at the table. Marcus was a big guy— broad shoulders with plenty of muscle. He had dark skin and gorgeous eyes. Steven had an olive complexion and short, dark hair. Sunshine had no idea what to do. Leaving made the most sense but felt so dramatic.

"One drink," she said.

"Perfect."

Phoebe dragged her to the table. Both men stood as they approached.

"Marcus, Steven, this is my friend Sunshine."

They all sat down.

The server came over and took their drink orders. Sunshine ordered a glass of white wine that she wouldn't drink and promised herself on her way home she was so going by Taco Bell. After Phoebe's setup, she deserved some comfort food.

Sunshine pushed away thoughts of tacos and burritos and smiled at Steven. "So, Phoebe mentioned you're in the movie business. What do you do?"

Steven gave her a self-satisfied smile. "Wouldn't you like to know?"

"Um, yes. That's why I asked."

His expression turned serious. "I don't like to talk about it."

"Okay. So are you from around here?"

"You mean Pasadena? No. Of course not."

"Then Los Angeles?"

"I moved here a while back."

"From where?"

He frowned. "What's with all the questions?"

Sunshine held up both hands. "Sorry. Just making polite conversation. I'll be quiet and let you talk."

"Traffic was terrible getting here. I usually don't like to go east of I5 if I can help it. There's nothing out here."

"Not counting entire communities," she murmured.

"What? You mean people live out here? Sure, but who are they? What's important to them?" He leaned toward her. "One thing I like about making movies is telling a story. That's the secret to success, you know. Telling a story."

"Good to know."

The server returned with her wine. At some point while Sunshine had been having her scintillating conversation with Steven, Phoebe and Marcus had started making out. Seriously making out, with tongue and everything. The table wasn't big to begin with so there wasn't much space between her and the going-for-it couple. It was kind of like "porn in the round" and to be honest, it was a little off-putting.

She turned back to Steven, then found she couldn't think of anything to say. Thank goodness he was observant.

"What happened to your hand?" he asked.

"I cut myself."

"How long have you been an actress?"

"I'm not an actress."

Steven frowned. "You should be. You're the right age, you

have the body. I could probably make something happen, if you're interested."

She frowned. "You're willing to help me get a job as an actress, but you won't talk about being in the business?"

"I like to be mysterious."

Phoebe and Marcus broke apart. Phoebe grabbed her handbag. "We're leaving. Thank goodness my ex has Elijah tonight, but only until eight, so we have to hurry. See ya."

With that, they were gone, leaving Sunshine alone with Steven.

"Did they just—" She stopped herself, realizing there was no good way to ask "Did they just leave to go have sex?"

"So," Steven said, leaning uncomfortably close to her and smiling. "Want to do the same?"

"The same?"

"Come back to my place. We can talk about your career."

She knew there would be no career talk, no anything but him getting a piece of ass. Not that she wanted to be an actress, which was perfect because she would guess Steven was a whole lot less connected than he wanted her to believe.

Exhaustion flooded her. The man-woman thing had never been a problem before, but lately it was just one disaster after another. She looked at him and knew she didn't have it in her to fight him. From her perspective, there was only one surefire way to get him to back off.

She offered a regretful smile and lightly touched his arm. "I would love to, only things are a little contagious..." She waved her fingers toward her crotch. "Down there, if you get my meaning. It's not horrible but the rash can really burn."

Steven shifted away from her so quickly he nearly lost his balance and fell off his chair.

"All right then," he said, coming to his feet. "We should probably call it a night."

"I think that's a really good idea."

Just then the server appeared with the bill. Sunshine let Steven take care of it and made her way to her car. Twenty minutes later she was sitting on a molded plastic chair at her local Taco Bell, her dinner on a tray. As she unwrapped her crunchy taco supreme, a teenage guy approached.

"Hey, beautiful," he began, as he offered her a smile.

"I'm married and he's a Marine."

His eyes widened. "For real?"

"Yup. He could squish you like a bug."

He sighed and walked away. She finished her dinner, took her soda with her and headed home. When she walked into the house, she went directly to Declan's office.

He was focused on his computer and didn't notice her at first. He looked as good as always, she thought wistfully, liking how his worn T-shirt stretched a little at the shoulders. She could hear the TV in the family room and guessed Connor was watching a movie.

If she wanted, she could close the door behind her, walk over to Declan and… And what? Kiss him? Offer him sex? Hadn't there been enough of that for one night?

Truthfully, she didn't even want sex. Okay, she did want sex, but not *just* sex. She wanted more. She wanted love and a commitment and the promise of years with someone. She wanted forever, not just one night, and while she might see potential in Declan, she had a feeling what he saw was what Steven had seen. Boobs and an ass and nothing else.

"Hey," she said.

Declan looked up. "Hey, yourself. What are you doing back? I thought you and Phoebe had a night planned."

She waved her Taco Bell cup. "Not exactly. She lied. It was a setup for a double date."

"You're kidding?"

"Nope."

She tried to figure out what he was thinking, only she couldn't. His expression was carefully neutral, damn him.

"You didn't like the other guy?" he asked.

"I didn't like being lied to and no, I didn't like Steven. However, Phoebe went home with her gentleman friend. I would say she's completely over you, so you can let that one go."

"Thank you for clarifying."

"Tell me you wore a condom."

He flushed. "What? Why would you ask—" He grimaced. "I see your point. Phoebe seems to be, ah, friendly with many men."

"Exactly. She was with you and Marcus in the past couple of weeks. If we extrapolate from that, it's a heady number."

"I wore a condom, which I hadn't done in years. It was more complicated than I remembered."

"Everything is easy at seventeen," she teased. "Anyway, I wanted to let you know that she has recovered from your breaking up with her."

"I appreciate the information."

They looked at each other. She once again thought about closing and locking the door, but while the next step was really clear, the step after that wasn't. She'd promised herself not to be that girl anymore. She'd promised herself she was growing and changing. Giving in would mean she'd been lying this whole time. Worse, it would mean she wasn't capable of changing.

"I'm going to go study," she said. "There is the slightest of chances I'm beginning to master algebra and I don't want to take that for granted."

"Good luck."

"Thank you."

She offered him a quick smile, then made her escape before she could say or do something that would be amazing in the moment, but disastrous in the long term.

Alec perused the shelves of the upscale wine shop. While he had plenty of wine at home, Margot was cooking coq au vin for dinner and he wanted to get something…unexpected to pair with the meal. He generally favored California and Washington wines, but perhaps a French-inspired dish deserved a French wine. Maybe a nice red Bordeaux.

As he studied the tasting notes from the staff, he thought about how much he was enjoying Margot's company. Being with her was easy—something he wouldn't have thought was possible. In the past, relationships had always been difficult and awkward. Once the sex was over, there wasn't all that much to talk about. At the end of the evening, he'd always been eager to be alone. But with Margot it was different. He found himself missing her when she wasn't there. In the morning, he wanted to stand and talk with her while she got ready for work. He looked forward to spending time with her, regardless of how much of the day they'd already spent together.

"Curiouser and curiouser," he murmured with a smile as he made his wine selection.

The Bordeaux, an old vine wine made in the traditional style that had brought fame to the region, should go nicely with her dinner.

He was nearly at his car when he heard someone calling his name. He turned and saw the manager of the store hurrying after him.

"Mr. Mcnicol, Mr. Mcnicol, wait! Please wait!"

Alec stopped and stared at the man, wondering what on earth he was so frantic about.

"Good afternoon, Nathan. How can I help you?"

The man pointed at the bottle in Alec's hand. "Mr. Mcnicol, you forgot to pay for the wine. If you could take care of that before you leave, please?"

Alec stared at him, disbelief blending with humiliation. He mentally retraced his steps and realized that he had been so caught up in his musings about Margot that he had simply walked out of the store without paying.

"I apologize," he said swiftly, turning around and walking back the way he'd come. "I wasn't thinking. I never intended—"

Nathan fell into step beside him. "Of course not. I understand completely. It happens. You're a brilliant man with so much on his mind. You're also an excellent customer. I never thought it was anything but momentary forgetfulness."

He entered the store and walked to the cashier. No one said anything, but he felt all eyes on him. He'd nearly stolen a bottle of wine. It was unimaginable.

He made the payment and drove home, all the while trying to figure out what had gone wrong. Yes, he'd been thinking about Margot, but he thought about her all the time and nothing untoward happened. Why had today been different?

He walked into the house and put the wine away in the rack in the kitchen. His mother breezed in.

"There you are, darling. I wanted to ask you—" She frowned. "What on earth happened? You look like you've seen the wandering spirit of the Indian god Kali. Or maybe I mean Vishnu. I get them confused."

"What? They're completely different gods."

She smiled. "Oh, I know. I'm just messing with you. So what went wrong?"

He told her about the incident with the wine. "I don't know how it happened."

His mother laughed. "You were distracted. It's just one of those things, Alec, at least for those of us not so rigid as to always be in control. Once, when I was in Italy, I accidentally walked out of the Prada store with a ten-thousand-Euro handbag. No one thought that was funny, let me tell you. I just hadn't been thinking."

"But that sort of thing happens to you all the time. It doesn't happen to me."

Or it hadn't, he realized. Until recently. There had been the priceless, fragile document that had been damaged because he hadn't thought to move it before making love with Margot. Today, he'd nearly shoplifted. What was next?

Although the question was rhetorical, as he asked it of himself, he felt a cold knot form in his stomach.

"You'll be fine," his mother told him. "Just relax and accept that you, too, are human."

He nodded and excused himself, all the while feeling the chill spread. Although he would never admit it to anyone, he knew his greatest fear was that one day he would turn into his mother—that he would not care about doing the right thing or convention or rules or other people. He'd always prided himself on being in control. If he lost that…

He hadn't, he told himself. It was a momentary lapse, nothing more. He would be more vigilant. He would stay in control. He would not, under any circumstances, do anything remotely Bianca-like, no matter what.

Declan was beginning to think there was no solution to the problem. He had impossible clients and he should simply accept it. Jessica and James wanted some way to connect the gardens at the hotel. Something unique. He'd gone so far as to get samples of an artist who worked in stone, thinking some custom pattern or design would excite them but they hadn't been inspired. That was their word—*inspired*.

He tried not to work from home on the weekend, but this Sunday morning he'd wanted to take an hour or so to see if he could come up with something to show them the next time they met. So far he had exactly nothing.

Zen space, he thought, then grinned. He was about to do a Google search on Zen gardens when Connor walked into his office. Instead of settling on the sofa, Connor walked around the desk and leaned against him.

"What's up, buddy?" he asked, putting his arm around his son. "Feeling let down because you had the big party last weekend?"

"No." Connor pushed up his glasses and looked at him. "I want to go see Mom."

Declan immediately shut down his computer, then stood and held out his hand. "Sure thing. Let me grab my car keys and we'll head out."

The first few weeks after Iris's death, they'd visited the grave site every Sunday morning. After that, Declan had let Connor tell him when he felt the need. This would be the first visit since Sunshine had started working for them.

Forest Lawn–Hollywood Hills was a sprawling place with manicured grounds and lots of trees. Declan was more a "be cremated and scatter the ashes" kind of guy, but this was what Iris had wanted. She'd left detailed instructions and had, in fact, chosen her plot before she died.

Declan stopped at a florist and let Connor pick out the bouquet of flowers he liked, then they went into the cemetery and parked.

Together they walked along the path before making their way to Iris's small headstone. Connor put the flowers at the base of the stone before dropping cross-legged to the grass.

"Hi, Mom," he began. "It was my birthday last week. I'm nine. I had a party and it was really fun. Did I tell you I got an ant farm? It's really cool and Sunshine ordered me a second one that's even bigger and it should be here this week."

Declan realized this was going to be a lengthy visit. Sometimes Connor wanted to talk and sometimes he just wanted to drop off flowers. He settled at the base of a nearby tree, prepared to wait for however long it took.

"Sunshine's my nanny," Connor continued, plucking at a blade of grass. "She's really nice. She knows how to cook and make stuff for a party and we laugh a lot. I want her to stay forever. You'd like her."

Declan didn't react outwardly to his son's comment, but he wasn't sure what to make of it. Was Connor getting too close to Sunshine? Not that there was a way to keep them apart. Her entire job revolved around Connor. It made sense that they would be tight.

Life was never easy, he thought. Or straightforward. He glanced at the gravestone. When Iris had died, he'd been so angry. Furious about the affair, devastated she'd chosen someone else over him, enraged that she'd waited to tell him she was sick and beyond pissed that she'd gone and died. He'd had so much emotion and nowhere to put it. But the cliché was true and time did heal.

Looking back he could see that neither of them had been happy in the marriage for a long time. While her way of dealing or not dealing with the problems hadn't been good for either of them, he wasn't angry about it anymore. He could see now that they'd drifted apart and at some point getting back together would have required more than either of them had been willing to put into the marriage.

He saw now that, rather than confront her or do something about her affair, he'd chosen to simply let things drift. Not exactly healthy for either of them. He should have insisted she move on while he stayed and got custody of Connor. He should have divorced her. Except...

He listened as his son talked about school and his friends and learning to play baseball this summer. Except a divorce would have been hard on Connor. His life would have been shattered and then a few months later, Iris still would have had cancer and she still would have died. The irony didn't escape him. His inability to accept what Iris had done had trapped him in indecision. While it had been a crappy move for him, it had been the best thing for Connor.

"I miss you, Mom." Connor said, coming to his feet. He turned to Declan. "I'm ready to go, Dad."

"Okay." Declan stood. He looked at the headstone. After a second, he walked over and lightly touched it. "Goodbye, Iris."

He took Connor's hand and together they walked away.

★ ★ ★

"I'll have the chicken nachos, please," Margot said, passing the menu to the server. She probably should have ordered a salad, but it seemed like a nacho kind of evening.

"Make that a double order." Sunshine watched until the server left, then pointed her finger at Margot. "Okay, start talking. What's up?"

"I have no idea what you mean."

"It's your turn to pick the restaurant and you picked Mexican, which you never do. Then you ordered nachos which you only do when you're unsettled about something."

"That's not true."

Sunshine raised her eyebrows but didn't speak.

The Mexican restaurant was casually tacky, decorated in bright colors and a worn tile floor. It had been in the same location for at least forty years and Margot hoped it lasted another hundred. She stirred the straw in her margarita, then finally sighed.

"Maybe. I'm not so much unsettled as confused."

"I knew it!" Sunshine wiggled in her seat. "Work or man?"

"Both."

"Wow, that's a surprise. You never have problems with work."

"It's not a problem, exactly. Bianca is progressing nicely. I keep telling her it's time to cut me loose, but she says she's not ready."

"What does your boss say?"

"To give it another couple of weeks, then insist we're done."

"And?"

"And that's what I'm going to do."

Sunshine sipped her margarita. "So what's the problem?"

"I don't know. I guess there's nothing." She faked a smile. "This has been a wonderful assignment. Bianca is going to do great with Wesley, and I'm considering working with a group of women coming here from Chile. They sell textiles. It would be a four-week assignment but I wouldn't live in or anything. I'm ready to be back in my own place. So how are things with you?"

"Uh-huh. Nice try. You left out the Alec part of things. What's going on there?"

A simple enough question and Margot had absolutely no answer.

"I don't know."

"What does that mean?"

Margot held in a groan and wished the nachos would arrive. She needed crunch and cheese and a dollop of guacamole.

"I'm confused," she admitted.

"Then let me ask a series of questions to get things started. How's the sex?"

Margot grinned. "Excellent."

"Does he have any weird habits that annoy you?"

"Not really. He's funny and smart and thoughtful. The other night I made coq au vin and he bought a French Bordeaux." She frowned. "Saying French is redundant, isn't it? Doesn't a Bordeaux have to be from France? It's a region so—"

Sunshine slapped both hands on the table. "Stop. Just stop trying to distract me from the main point."

"I haven't made a main point."

"Of course you have." Her sister leaned toward her. "Honey, you're totally and completely in love with him and that has you freaked out and in need of nachos."

Margot shook her head. *No. No way.* She wasn't in love with anyone. "It's not like that. Really. It's not. We're just dating and, well, I guess, semi living together, but that's only because I'm working for his mom and it's super convenient. Okay, that's not the *only* reason. We get along really well. Alec has some unique qualities that other people might find off-putting, but I like them. He's very dependable and solid. That's nice for a change. And his work is remarkable. But it's not love."

The server arrived with a huge platter of nachos. As soon as she set it down, Margot grabbed a chip. "So how are things with your class? You said you were doing better."

Sunshine studied her. "So you're in love with him."

Margot glared at her sister. "Yes! Fine. I'm in love with him."

She closed her eyes as the truth sank in. She was in love with Alec. She probably had been for a while. She hadn't recognized what had happened because it was so different than it had been with Dietrich. Her life wasn't uprooted. She didn't feel foolish or know he was bad for her. When she was around Alec she felt good. Happy.

She opened her eyes. "Oh God. Now what?"

Sunshine's smile was smug. "I love being right, especially with you. You're supposed to be the smart one and you didn't even see it coming."

"That isn't helpful. I'm panicking here. What do I do?"

"What do you want to do?"

"Repeating the question isn't helping."

"I didn't repeat the question. I changed it by at least two words. Calm down and eat a nacho. You don't have to *do* anything."

"I have to do something. In a couple of weeks, I won't be living there anymore. Then what? Are we dating? Does it end? Do I say something? Hope he says something? I should probably say something, but that's an awkward conversation to have. How do you tee it up? 'Hey, beautiful weather we're having. By the way, I'm desperately in love with you so can we keep seeing each other?' You know, he doesn't like messy things and love is often messy. What if he doesn't love me back? What if he does, but he doesn't want to admit it? What if he laughs?"

Sunshine reached for another chip.

Margot glared at her. "This is where you offer advice."

"Hey, I'm not good at relationships. I mean I'm totally team Margot and I wish you the best, but it's not like I have experience making things work. I usually find a guy, sleep with him and then if he invites me to fly around the world, I disrupt my life for the next six or eight weeks, get dumped or leave, then start all over again. Do you really want me telling you what to do when it comes to your love life?"

"I guess not." Margot sighed. "I blame our mother."

"I do, too, but seeing as she died and, before that, neither of us had seen her since we were toddlers, it's not particularly helpful. Although you should probably tell Alec you love him."

"Why?"

"Because falling for someone who isn't Dietrich is a really big step and acknowledging your feelings sends a message to the universe."

"I'd rather win his heart," she muttered, then tilted her head. "Wait. Should I want to win his heart? Or should he offer his heart? Are there rules for any of this?"

"Again, asking the wrong person."

"We're hopeless," Margot said with a sigh.

"Yes, but we look good and seriously, what else matters?"

chapter
TWENTY-FOUR

THE FOLLOWING SATURDAY MORNING, SUNSHINE HEADED for Santa Monica. It was early—barely after seven. Morning fog had rolled in so she knew the beach would be deserted and the sidewalks empty. No one purposefully went to the beach on a foggy morning—except her.

She had a plan—she was going to have breakfast at a cute little coffee shop she'd always liked, read the paper, then walk on the beach. Today was going to be about relaxing and recharging. Not that her schedule was especially difficult, but a little "me time" was always welcome. Plus, Declan was leaving on a business trip and would be gone about ten days. While he was away, she would be on Connor duty 24-7.

She exited the freeway and quickly found parking. She walked into the coffee shop and was immediately seated at a small table by the window. She glanced at the menu to see if it was as she remembered and saw nothing had changed. Her California Scramble was still front and center. The kids' section was also the same.

Her gaze dropped to the smiling cartoon zoo animals in the margin and lingered on the second item from the bottom: Pancake-orama. The twins had always loved that breakfast, one with blueberries and one with bananas. How many Sunday mornings had she and the twins walked over to have breakfast while their parents slept in? Parents with high-powered careers and little time for or interest in their daughters.

Sunshine had done her best with the girls, right up until she met a guy on a motorcycle who had offered to take her to Texas and teach her to rope a steer. A couple of drinks, a good time in bed and before she'd thought things through, she'd quit her job and she'd been gone.

She'd left with almost no warning, texting Elle, the twins' mother, who'd been in Paris at the time. Or was it Rome? Their father had called to scream at her that he couldn't get out of a meeting to go get his daughters and that he had plans for the night. He'd threatened to sue her. Each of the girls had texted to ask where she was and when the guilt had gotten too bad, she'd dumped the phone in a trash can in Arizona and had never looked back.

Sunshine realized she hadn't anticipated the memories joining her for breakfast. She probably should have thought that through before driving down here. Or maybe she'd subconsciously known what would happen and had accepted she had to deal with her past, the ugly moments that she couldn't atone for. She'd been wrong to leave the way she had. Not just the twins but the other kids she'd looked after. She'd left Texas for London nearly a year after she'd left Santa Monica for Texas. All that might be behind her, but the shattered lives still bore scars.

She realized she couldn't stay for breakfast. Not now. She was too embarrassed, too ashamed. She should have picked a different beach and a different coffee shop. She collected her bag and as she stood, she came face-to-face with a furious woman on the other side of the plate glass window.

"It *is* you!" Elle screamed. "Oh my God!"

She started to open the restaurant door but Sunshine hurried to meet her outside where at least the conversation wouldn't disrupt everyone's breakfast.

"How dare you show up here?" Elle demanded as Sunshine

approached. "You're disgusting, you whore. You left them. You left my daughters—you disappeared with no warning. You didn't even have the courtesy to tell them yourself. You never answered their texts or explained. They were devastated. They cried for weeks. I had to put them in therapy to get over the fucking nanny."

Elle's eyes were wild. Saliva flew with each word. She was small, but still appeared threatening. "I had to fly home from my business trip and their father missed work because of you. I will hate you forever. You're a horrible, selfish person and I hope you die alone. It's one thing to screw with my life, but you hurt my children and for that you should suffer."

Before Sunshine could figure out what to say or if it would be better to simply bolt, Elle slapped her hard across the face, then stalked away.

Sunshine stood alone on the sidewalk. She knew everyone in the restaurant was watching her, everyone had heard. She wanted to say it wasn't that bad, but everything Elle had said was true. She had left the girls with no warning, hadn't gotten in touch with them. She'd left children before, but not like that. Never so cruelly.

She walked to her car and got inside, then rested her forehead on the steering wheel and began to cry.

By nine-thirty in the evening, Declan started to get worried. He hadn't seen Sunshine all day and while she was welcome to do what she would like on her days off, she usually made an appearance.

He told himself she could come and go as she liked. That it was possible she was spending the evening with her sister, or maybe she was out on a date. Or possibly right this second she was in some guy's bed, having the time of her life. It wasn't his business—not any of it. Only he didn't want to think about her out on a date and he sure as hell didn't want her doing it with a random stranger, or even someone she knew, for that matter, unless that someone was him, which it couldn't be and, damn, was he messed up.

Connor was in bed, the house was quiet and Declan didn't know what to do with himself. He paced the long hallway leading to his bedroom, then decided to check the garage one more time. Maybe she'd come home when he'd been putting Connor to bed or something.

He pushed open the door and saw that her car was parked next to his. The cracks and pings of cooling metal told him she hadn't been back very long. Relief eased some of his concern. She was home and therefore all right. Fine. He would read for a bit before calling it a night himself.

Only he couldn't seem to make his way back to his bedroom. Something in his gut said there was a problem, although he had no idea why. He had never been very emotionally intuitive.

Still, he found himself heading for the kitchen. Sunshine wasn't there, nor was she in the family room. That left her bedroom which was completely off-limits. He didn't go in there, ever, and he wasn't going to start now.

He turned to walk purposefully toward his room, only as he went by the windows, he saw her in the backyard. She was stretched out in one of the chaises on the patio. It was dark, it was cool and she'd never done anything like that before. Even knowing he should stay out of whatever it was, he opened the back door and stepped outside.

"Hey," he said as he approached. "Did you just get back?"

"I did."

Her voice was low and soft and he couldn't tell anything from her tone.

He hesitated for a second, then sat on the chaise beside hers, angled to face her, his feet on the concrete. It was dark enough that he couldn't see much of her face so he had no idea what she was thinking.

"Did you have a good day off?" he asked, really wanting to know that she was okay so he could retreat to his room and entertain himself with inappropriate fantasies about what could never be.

"It was peachy."

She turned as she spoke and the light caught her profile. She was crying.

Concern almost had him pulling her into his arms before he reminded himself to stay where he was and communicate through his words.

"What's wrong? What happened?"

"Oh, you know. The usual. My past caught up with me and slapped me really hard." She touched her cheek. "In this case, literally."

He couldn't figure out what she was saying. "Someone hit you?"

She looked away. "I'm fine, Declan. Or I will be."

Now he could hear the tears in her voice, the thickness of the pain, whatever it was.

"What happened? Tell me. Or tell me to go away and I'll leave you alone. Sunshine, I want to help but I don't know what to do."

She drew in a breath. "You really don't want to know. Trust me. I'm not who you think. I'm a terrible person. You should fire me. I know that sounds dramatic, but it's true. I can't be trusted with anyone's kids."

"Now you're not making sense."

She looked at him. "Do you remember when you interviewed me and asked about my references? How everyone said I was the best nanny ever, if only you could get me to stay?"

He nodded, not sure what this had to do with whatever was bothering her.

"That's not the half of it. That in no way describes what I've done." She pulled herself forward on the chaise, so she was sitting facing him, their knees nearly touching.

"I'm good with kids," she said, staring at her lap, her hair hanging down, shielding her face. "Really good. Probably because I like hanging out with them. I enjoy their company and being involved with their lives. When you're a nanny, that's the job description—to get involved. Most contracts are for a year and everyone knows that. But telling a kid you'll be gone in a year doesn't mean anything to them. When you're five or eight or ten, a year is a lifetime. It's a faraway place and it's not today so it doesn't matter."

She brushed away tears. "There are ways to handle leaving. You start having the conversation about a month before. You get them ready. You deal with the acting up, the crying, the begging. Or so I've been told. Because I've never done it. I've never left the way you're supposed to."

She looked at him, her expression stark. "I leave. That's what I do, Declan. What I've always done. I meet some guy and decide he's the one and take off, usually with nothing more than a quick note or a phone call. My grandmother left my mother. My mother left us. And I leave them."

She turned away. "It's the worst part of me. It's the dark ugly side everyone wants to keep hidden, but it's right there for all to see. It's in my personnel file, for God's sake."

He tried to make sense of everything she was saying. He heard the words but couldn't reconcile them with the woman he knew. "What happened today?"

"I went to Santa Monica. There's a breakfast place I know—it's a silly little coffee shop, but I always loved it. I used to live with a family nearby. They had twin girls. They were only seven and so adorable. Elle, their mother, is a lawyer who does a lot of international work. Their father's in banking. They were this power couple who were never home and had little or nothing to do with their kids."

She looked at him. "That makes it worse, you know. The parents who aren't involved, because then I'm all the kids have. I'd never experienced it before, until the twins. They were so lonely and sad and they bonded with me instantly. I stayed for nearly eight months and then I met a guy."

She twisted her hands together and shook her head. "It happened like it always happened. He was great and I fell for him. After a couple of nights he invited me to go with him to Texas. He was going to teach me to rope a steer. I thought it was love, so why not? I wrote the girls a note and I left."

The tears returned, slipping down her cheeks. "Just like that. I walked out on them and broke their hearts. I ran into Elle today and she said they were so devastated, they needed therapy. She called me names and she's right. I was so thoughtless and awful."

She wiped her face. "That's why I'm trying so hard to be different. I don't want to be that person anymore. It's wrong—I know it's wrong. I get it now and I'm trying, but how do I make it right from before?"

"Do you want to talk to the twins?" he asked.

"No. I mean of course I do, but it would be selfish. I'd feel better, but I suspect they'd only feel worse. I don't want that."

He didn't know what to do with all that she'd told him. While he knew she was telling the truth, he couldn't reconcile the woman in front of him with the stories she told.

"Would you walk out on Connor?" he asked.

"What? No! Of course not. I love him." The tears flowed faster.

"But one day you'll have to leave."

Something he didn't want to think about, but it was the truth. She wasn't going to work for him forever.

"I'll do it the right way." She grabbed his hands and stared into his eyes. "Declan, I swear to you. I swear. I won't hurt him. No matter what."

"I believe you."

Without thinking he reached for her. He meant to maybe hug her or something but what he did instead was pull her onto his lap. She came willingly, settling on his thighs and burying her head in the crook of his neck where she cried so hard, her body shook. He rested one hand on her hip and rubbed her back with the other. He ignored the heat of her, the curves, the scent and thought only of her pain.

"I want to be better," she told him, raising her head and sniffing. "I want to be proud of myself."

"How are you doing on that?"

"I don't know. I thought I was making progress until today. I'm trying to be a better person, with college and not dating inappropriate men and working to be the best nanny I can be."

"You're doing all those things."

"But what I did before. I can't fix that."

"We've all done things we're ashamed of. The point is to do better when we know better."

"I think for a lot of people the point is to not screw up in the first place."

"Very few of us have that luxury."

She sighed. Her breath was warm against his neck. He became less aware of her emotional pain and more aware of how she felt in his arms. It wouldn't take much to shift her so she was straddling him. He wanted that—the feel of her hot crotch against his dick, her arms around him, her mouth on his.

He wanted her naked, in his bed. He wanted to touch her and taste her and pleasure her, and then he wanted to fill her until she came and then he wanted to do it all again. Yup, he was an asshole. Here she was, baring her soul to him, and all he could think about was getting laid. His gender sucked and he was the suckiest member.

She straightened and slid off his lap. For one heart-stopping second he thought she was going to hold out her hand and invite him into her bed.

But instead, she gave him a trembling smile. "Thank you for listening to me and not judging me."

He carefully stayed where he was, needing the darkness to hide the physical proof of what he'd been thinking. "I would never judge you."

"I know and I appreciate that. Good night, Declan."

"Good night."

He waited a good two minutes after she'd gone inside. He wanted her in her room with the door closed before he moved. His erection throbbed as desire pulsed through him. He told himself he was bigger than the need but he knew he was lying. Once again he would head to his room, get in the shower and do the deed. If he couldn't have Sunshine, then he needed to find someone else he could fall for. Someone who could be a part of his life. He was the kind of guy who wanted a partner, not a party. Enough time had passed and he was ready to move on. He had to—starting now.

"I never thought of learning more languages," Bianca said, sounding both intrigued and apprehensive. "I speak passable Spanish and about the same amount of Japanese."

Margot looked at her client. "You speak Japanese?"

"Some. Basic conversation."

"You speak Japanese and you never thought to mention it to me?"

"Why would you want to know?"

"I don't know—it's an unexpected factoid."

"Oh, if you say so. I picked it up while I was working in Japan for a few months. I did a series of commercials. I took Alec with me, of course. We had such a wonderful time together."

After all these weeks, Bianca still had the ability to surprise her, Margot thought, both impressed and bemused. They sat on the sofa in the guest room, her laptop on the coffee table where they could both see the screen.

"Any other languages?" she asked with a laugh. "Or odd skills I should know about?"

Bianca laughed. "I don't think so." She pointed at the screen on Margot's laptop. "So you think I should learn German and French."

"They would be the most useful, given where you'll be living in Europe. With your acting skills and your ear for accents, you'll probably pick them up quickly. You could impress everyone by learning Russian, but only if you want to. I don't think it's really going to be that helpful."

"Maybe Italian," Bianca said. "Italy is so romantic."

They'd spent the morning going over the cultural norms of various European countries. Bianca had memorized expectations for punctuality, how close to stand, how formal the greeting and a few key facts about every country.

"Bianca," Margot began. "We are genuinely running out of things to talk about."

Bianca raised her hand. "Tut, tut. We agreed not to discuss that until next week."

"I'm not cheap. You're spending a lot of money to keep me here and it's not necessary."

"It is to me. Now I don't want to talk about it until next week. Is that clear?"

Margot thought about pushing back, but she'd learned that Bianca couldn't be rushed. With a sigh, she said, "Sure."

"Good. Now help me decide what language program I should use."

"You can download a sample from a couple of them onto your tablet. Do the practice lessons and see which you like best."

"Let's do that now," Bianca said, coming to her feet. "I'll go get it and you can show me how to load everything."

But before Bianca could walk to her bedroom, Edna appeared in the doorway.

"There's a gentleman to see you," she said, looking a little flustered.

"You mean Wesley?" Bianca asked. "I thought he was in meetings today."

"Not him." Edna turned to Margot. "A gentleman to see *you.*"

Who on earth? she thought, then mentally slammed on the brakes. No. No! It couldn't be.

"Did he give his name?" she asked, hoping she sounded calmer than she felt.

"Dietrich. He didn't offer a last name. He said you would know who he was."

Oh, she knew. But how had he found her? She figured out the answer as soon as she thought the question. One of her friends had caved.

"Dietrich? *Oh*, the ex-lover." Bianca's tone was arch, her expression inquisitive. "This is going to be exciting, isn't it? I do love unexpected drama."

Margot couldn't figure out what to say to that, so she ignored the comment. She rose and headed for the stairs, aware of the other women following her. How lovely—an audience.

At the bottom of the stairs she found Dietrich in the foyer. He looked as he always had—tall, thin, blond. There was a studied casualness about him, as if he had more important things to do than worry about his clothes or how he looked. He was a filmmaker. An artist. The mores of the ordinary world were not his problem.

He smiled when he saw her. "Margot. At last! I've been trying to reach you, but you are hard to find these days, aren't you." He put his hands on her upper arms, then leaned in and kissed each cheek before settling his mouth on hers.

She let him, wanting to know what she would feel. Regret? Longing? Desperate hope that this time it would be different, that this time it would be forever? She held her breath, braced for any emotion.

His mouth lingered. She didn't respond, mostly because she really didn't want to be kissing him. In fact, as she checked in with her heart and girl parts, she realized she felt exactly nothing. No anticipation, no passion, not even interest. If she had to define any emotion it was a sense of inevitability at the tiresomeness that was to follow. Getting rid of Dietrich before he was ready to be gone had never been easy.

He stepped back and smiled at her. "Oh, I know what you're doing. Playing hard to get so I want you more. Well, it's working, my love. How I have missed you. I've missed us. I have so many ideas for films, but without you, everything is meaningless. I thought we could start in Bali. A week at the St. Regis, yes? Then to work." He smiled. "Do you want to go start packing?"

She didn't have to turn around to know Bianca and Edna were right behind her, taking in every word.

"Just like that?" she asked. "You show up uninvited and expect me to drop everything so I can be with you?"

He frowned. "Of course. You always have."

She always had. She wanted to ask why he would say that or even think it, only she knew the answer. She really always had.

She touched her lips. She'd felt nothing when he kissed her and looking at him, she continued to feel nothing. They were done. Completely and totally over. At one time he'd been her world and wasn't that just sad?

"No," she said with a smile. "Absolutely not. To quote my girl Taylor, we are never ever, *ever* getting back together."

"Margot, please." He raised both hands, palms up. "I shouldn't have left the way I did. You are still angry, yes? I understand. But come on. You know we belong together."

"We don't. It's not the leaving I object to, it's the coming back. You need to stop that. I don't want to be with you anymore. Dietrich, we're done." She pointed to the door. "It's time for you to go."

He smiled at her. "Not without you. You want me to fight

for you. I understand that. I stayed away too long." He winked. "You want to punish me and I would like that, too."

She flushed and wished she could bolt, but first she had to take out the trash.

"Margot," he said, his smile fading. "I need you. You're my muse."

"You heard the lady, Dietrich. It's time to go."

The voice came from behind her. Margot held in a groan. She'd hoped to get through this conversation without Alec hearing any part of it but her luck just wasn't that good. She glanced over her shoulder and saw him glowering at Dietrich.

"It's okay," she said quickly, not wanting things to escalate.

"It's not okay." He moved to stand next to her. "He's not listening."

"Who is this?" Dietrich demanded. "Who are you?"

"I'm the owner of this house and I'm telling you to leave."

Dietrich glared at her. "You live with him? You live with another man? How could you? Our love was forever."

She felt the beginnings of a headache. "Apparently not." She walked to the door and held it open. "Goodbye, Dietrich."

"No." He sounded petulant and for a second she thought he was going to stomp his foot on the floor. "It's not fair. I love you."

"You only love yourself. I should have seen that a long time ago."

"While I hate to repeat myself," Alec told him, "you heard the lady."

Dietrich looked between them. Margot had no idea what he was thinking so she wasn't expecting him to lunge at her. Before he even got close, Alec grabbed him by his shirtfront, spun him and shoved him face-first into the wall. Hard. Alec held him, with an arm twisted behind his back.

"Now, are you leaving or are you going to make this difficult?" he asked calmly.

"I'm leaving, I'm leaving!" Dietrich's voice was a squeak. "Stop! You're hurting me."

Alec held on for another second before releasing him. Dietrich scampered toward the front steps. As he passed Margot, he glared at her. "You could have just said you weren't interested."

He ran to his rental car and in a second was gone.

"Bravo," Bianca said, clapping her hands together. "Oh, Alec, that was magnificent. You were so strong and determined. My heart is fluttering just thinking about it."

Instead of answering his mother, he looked at Margot. "Are you all right?"

She nodded.

He turned and walked away. When he was out of sight, she closed the door and leaned against it. Bianca went off with Edna, the two women discussing what had just happened. Margot stayed where she was.

While she appreciated the save, she had a bad feeling about what had just occurred. Not Dietrich—he didn't matter anymore. But Alec's reaction. It had been wonderful but very out of character and something inside of her told her there would be consequences—for all of them.

chapter
TWENTY-FIVE

SUNSHINE'S SAD MOOD LASTED UNTIL THE END OF CLASS
when her professor passed back the results of their most recent
test. She stared at the bright red B plus and nearly whooped out
loud. Professor Rejefski smiled at her.

"A nice improvement, Ms. Baxter. Keep it up."

"I will."

Sunshine gathered her backpack and raced out of the building,
heading for the math lab. When she got there for her standing
appointment with Ann she bounced from foot to foot until the
older woman walked out to get her.

"Look! Look!" She waved the test. "I got a B plus! Can you
believe it? Do you know how close that is to an A? OMG, I'm
so happy."

Ann smiled at her. "You worked hard and now you're seeing the results of that. Come on back and we'll go over your
homework."

"I knew I'd done better, but not like this," Sunshine told her.
"There's been so much crap in my life lately. No, that's not true.
It's my own fault and I've been dealing with—"

Ann turned to her. "Stop. Just stop. If you have a problem,
talk to a friend. If you need emotional support, find a therapist.
I do math. It's my thing."

The words were so harsh, Sunshine thought, feeling emotions rise to the surface.

As they walked into the small study room where they held their sessions, Sunshine fought against tears. She was about to complain when she realized Ann was right. This was the math lab, not group counseling. Ann was a tutor, not a friend or support buddy. Sunshine's emotional state wasn't her job.

"Are there counselors on campus?" she asked.

"You mean like therapists? I don't know. Google it and find out. Now show me your homework."

Tough love, Sunshine thought. If she wanted answers to dealing with her past, then she should do the work of finding them herself. If that meant getting professional help, then she should do that. Sulking and feeling bad accomplished nothing. Hard work got results—and she had the test score to prove it!

Declan had to admit, he was a big city guy at heart. Not a New York kind of city where high-rises dominated and museums were around every corner. He supposed he was more an LA or San Diego kind of city guy where the suburbs sprawled for miles, strip malls were high-class, and in the right part of town, there really was a taco truck on every corner.

He missed those tacos, along with the sun and his son and his bed and, what the hell, no one was going to hear him think this, he missed Sunshine most of all.

He'd been gone four days already and it felt like a lifetime. He and Heath were looking for ways to connect the hotel gardens. Still. It was the project that would never end, he thought grimly. So far they'd spent two days in Napa where they'd discussed using vineyards as the connecting element and then two days in Seattle. Salmon, it turned out, were not the answer. They required more space to swim than the hotel could offer. That led to an entire discussion on koi, but Jessica thought they were too common.

Their next stop was a miniature horse farm in Idaho, because why not miniature horses? He'd tried to explain that, much like the salmon, the small horses would need more space than was available, not to mention care and a zoning modification, but his clients were determined.

He poured himself a cup of coffee from the carafe in the small conference room he and Heath had reserved for their meeting with Jessica and James before the four of them headed for the airport to fly to Idaho. If the horses didn't work—and they wouldn't—the next stop on their never-ending journey was a rock quarry in some place he honestly couldn't remember.

He crossed to the window and looked out at the gray skies and damp garden. From what he'd seen, it had literally rained every second they'd been in Seattle. The town was beautiful, but the rain got to him. He wasn't sure how the locals survived winter.

He wanted to go home. He wanted to hang out with his son and talk to Sunshine. He wanted to do a lot more than talk, but thinking about anything else left him with a dilemma he had no idea how to solve.

"Where is the rock place?" Heath asked as he walked into the conference room.

"I was just trying to remember. It's on our tickets."

"I think I'd rather be surprised." His business partner put down his briefcase and poured himself coffee. "The horse idea isn't going to work."

"I know."

"Whatever it is, it has to be small and preferably not alive."

"So the rocks."

Heath swore and joined him at the window. "What's going on?"

Declan frowned. "What do you mean?"

"There's something. You've been distracted and not just by our clients' inane conversation. Everything okay at home?"

Declan opened his mouth to say it was all good but what came out was, "I can't stop thinking about Sunshine."

"The nanny?"

"That's her."

"You want to bang the nanny?"

"Hey." Declan glared at him. "It's not like that."

Heath was unimpressed by the glare. "Really? Not even a little?"

Declan returned his attention to the hotel garden. "I don't want to bang her. That's wrong."

"But you would like to have sex with her."

"Yes, but it's more than that. It's… I don't know. I like her."

"Oh man, you're screwed." Heath slapped him on the back. "You can't date her because she's the nanny and you can't really try to get to know her better without things getting uncomfortable. I mean, how do you have *that* conversation? You sure as hell can't sleep with her. If you want to find out where things are going romantically, the obvious solution is to fire her so you can have a relationship but once you fire her, she's not exactly going to want to date you. Plus she's going to be gone and who knows where her next job is. And talking about all this with her flirts with the inappropriate and mentioning sex makes you a jerk and possibly the defendant in a lawsuit. Like I said, you're screwed."

"Thank you for clarifying," Declan said, his voice thick with sarcasm.

"I didn't say anything you didn't already know."

"No, you didn't."

Just then, their clients breezed into the conference room. Jessica smiled at them.

"What an amazing hotel. There were so many vegan choices for breakfast. Most places don't offer that."

They sat at the table in the center of the room. He and Heath joined them.

"Disappointing about the salmon," James said regretfully.

"Miniature horses are going to be the same problem." Declan raised a shoulder. "If you still want to go see them, we will, but I don't see them as the solution."

"We were talking about that over breakfast." Jessica sighed. "We should cancel the Idaho leg of our trip. I suppose the rock quarry has possibility."

"It could if we had something unique," James mused. "Maybe different textures or colors. Or rocks from different parts of the country. Maybe tell a story of what the continent was like before man first stepped foot on it."

Declan saw a muscle twitch in Heath's jaw and nearly laughed out loud. He knew exactly what his partner was thinking—some version of "Kill me now." Rocks telling a story? In a place like The Huntington maybe, but not in a hotel garden.

"I wonder if we could do anything with fossils," James asked. "That would be interesting."

"But not unique." Jessica pouted. "A lot of places have fossils and even rock gardens. I want something special. Something no one has ever seen before."

And I want to go home, Declan thought. He wanted to be in his house, or even his yard, listening to Connor go on and on about his new ant farm. The one that—

"Ants," he said, putting down his coffee mug.

All three of them looked at him with identically blank expressions.

"Ants," he repeated, and pulled his tablet out of his briefcase. "Ants have been around for millions of years. The weight of the ant population equals the weight of the human population. There are super colonies of ants that stretch thousands of miles, across entire continents." His son would be so proud, he thought happily.

He typed into the search bar of his laptop, then waited until the photo of an ant farm appeared on the screen. He turned the tablet so everyone else could see the picture.

"Ants," he said again. "They're hardworking, familiar and small. They're low maintenance and no one else has the world's biggest ant farm at their hotel."

He pointed to the tubing. "We could make it beautiful, have lighting for evening strolls. There could be different species and signage with facts." He wasn't sure if he'd just solved the problem or gotten himself thrown off the job. He supposed if he got fired, at least he could go home.

Jessica and James looked at each other.

"I like it, Jess," James said. "Ants are ubiquitous and that is perfect. We need to figure out the design, but as Declan pointed out, ants are small. Imagine how the ant farm could twist and turn."

"No one else has one." Jessica's voice was eager. "I love it." She laughed. "Yes, let's do ants. What's the next step?"

Heath cleared his throat. "I guess we find an ant expert and go talk to him."

"Or her," Jessica corrected.

"Yes. Or her." Heath typed on his tablet, then turned to Declan. "Looks like we're going to Texas."

Alec wasn't sure he'd ever been to the Glendale Galleria. It was a perfectly nice shopping center, with lots of stores and people. It was well lit, open and friendly—the antithesis of how he was feeling.

As he walked the length of the mall, ignoring the stores and shoppers, he tried to reconcile who he had always considered himself to be with who he had obviously become. He'd worked hard to create a life that was orderly and purposeful. There were those who wouldn't see the value in what he did, those who thought the ancient scraps of papyrus should go undeciphered, but their opinions didn't matter. He preferred the opinions of other scholars, university professors and fellows, and his peers. He was well respected, admired even. He had created a perfect life in a wonderful home and somehow it had all gone to shit.

After a lifetime of reining in his emotions, after years of training to keep himself orderly and responsible, after carefully considering every action, he'd become impulsive and unpredictable. He'd physically attacked another man—he'd nearly hit him. The need to come between Margot and her ex-boyfriend had grown until he'd reacted without thinking. It was the incident with the wine, but on steroids. He wanted to say his life was out of control, but it wasn't his life—it was him. *He* was the problem.

He knew the cause—he understood how one small act had led to another and another until he had spiraled out of control. While he only blamed himself for the results, the catalyst came in the form of a beautiful woman, a warm and intriguing laugh, a sharp mind with a unique worldview. He had seen her, wanted her, developed a relationship with her and had entwined himself with her. He'd allowed himself to experience a connection and in doing so he had lowered his carefully erected barriers until emotions were free to come and go, grow and wane. He'd allowed that side of him, the dangerous, impulsive part of him he feared and sought to control, to run amok and now there was a price to be paid.

He started for the parking garage. The decision had been made. He'd known what he had to do long before he'd left the house, but he'd needed to be sure he was willing to do what was necessary to restore world order. There was a price for everything—his relationship with Margot had reminded him of that. And now the bill had come due.

Sunshine was surprised when her cell phone rang about nine-thirty in the evening and she saw Declan's name on the screen. He'd already called earlier to talk to Connor and check in with her. Foolishly, she considered those brief conversations the highlight of her day. The man was traveling on business—of course he wanted to check in. It wasn't as if he were calling because he missed her.

"Hi," she said, putting down her magazine. "How's it going?"

"Good. I'm in Texas."

"So you mentioned before. Connor can't get over the fact that his ant farm saved the day. He's so excited to be able to see the construction of the hotel's ant farm."

"We're getting plenty of information from the bug guy." Declan groaned. "There's a word for him and I can't remember what it is."

There was something about his voice. A tone or a looseness that had her—

"You're drunk!" She did the math and realized it was eleven-thirty in Texas, then laughed. "You went out drinking!"

"What? No. Okay, buzzed but not drunk. There were shots. Heath and I needed a break from our clients."

"At least you're not in a rock quarry examining fossils."

"That would be grim. I miss you."

The unexpected statement caught her off guard. She waited, wondering if he would take it back and when he didn't, she said, "I miss you, too."

"No. You're busy with your regular life. How's school?"

School? He wanted to talk about her math class? Couldn't they talk about the missing more?

"Good. The tutoring is helping. I've signed up for a summer class. It's going to be brutal. Four days a week for three hours a day, plus the homework. It's a general education class. Sociology—so lots of reading. I'm nervous and excited."

"Good for you. It's just you're so easy to be around. And beautiful." He swore. "Sorry. I guess I'm more buzzed than I thought."

Beautiful? "It's okay."

"You sure? I think we're heading into dangerous territory."

She shifted so she was lying on the bed rather than sitting up, and smiled. "What does that mean?"

"You being beautiful? I'm pretty sure that's self-explanatory. But it's not just how you look. I want to be clear about that, although I will admit there are things about your body that drive me wild. It's the rest of it. The you part. I miss that most. Sorry—I'm not making any sense."

Too much information crammed into her head, but what really caught her attention was *The you part*. Being missed for herself rather than her ass was kind of a big deal.

"You're making sense," she said softly.

"I hope so. When you smile, when you laugh—I like that. And you with Connor. You're good for him."

"He's a great kid."

"I know. I'm lucky to have him. Anyway, I just want to be clear it's more than just wanting to make love with you."

Before she could react or even know how those words made her feel, he started backtracking.

"No. I'm sorry. Dammit, Sunshine. I apologize. That was wrong and I didn't mean to go there. You must be so uncomfortable. I never meant to—"

"It's okay," she whispered. "Declan, it's fine."

He winced. "You're very kind to say that, but I crossed the line. I blame the tequila."

He had crossed the line and she'd let him. She'd encouraged a conversation that was dangerous. The right thing to do was to tell him they would go back to normal and pretend this never happened and then hang up. He would feel like crap for at least three days and that would make her feel guilty, but at least order would be restored.

"I think about it, too." The words were soft, barely audible and the first step on the slick road to hell. Yet she didn't want to turn back.

"You do?"

"Uh-huh."

"When? How? Really?"

She laughed. "I'm not immune to normal human emotions."

"I know but you're...you. You could have anyone. I'm just, you know, me."

Warmth spread through her, leaving her achy and restless. It had been a long time, she thought wistfully. Months, really, since she'd been with a man. She missed the touching, the teasing, the tension and the release. Only she didn't just want a guy and an orgasm. She wanted Declan there with her, his hands everywhere. She wanted him naked and hard and looming over her.

As she imagined him pushing into her, she instinctively spread her legs, only there was no man. There was nothing but her rapidly swelling clit and a burning need to have him make her come. But he was a couple of thousand miles away and they were both alone.

"Sunshine?"

"Are you in bed?" she asked, unfastening her jeans and pushing them off.

"Yes, it's late here and—" His breath caught. "You're not asking what I think you're asking."

She pushed off her panties and shifted the phone to her left hand.

"Too soon?" she asked, closing her eyes.

"Not soon enough."

She smiled and dipped her fingers inside to get wet and slippery, then circled her clit. "Are you naked?"

"I am now."

"Good. Are you hard?"

"Pretty much if I'm talking to you, yes."

"I'm wet and swollen. I took my panties off, but I left my shirt on. While I like a guy touching my breasts, I don't enjoy it when I do it myself, which is strange because if I'm in the right mood and he really sucks on my nipples, I can come that way. He has to take his time, though, and most guys can't be bothered."

Declan swore. "You're killing me."

"I'm nervous. I talk when I'm nervous. I'm still touching myself and getting closer and closer, but I'm nervous."

"Are you going to come?"

"Yes. Are you?"

"I'm a guy, Sunshine. My orgasm is the result of friction and fantasy."

"Am I your fantasy?"

"You have no idea how much."

"Good. You're mine."

He inhaled sharply. "Tell me what you're doing. Describe it."

"I'm using two fingers." She closed her eyes to think about what she was doing. "Apparently I go clockwise. I never knew that."

"Hard or soft?"

"Hard. Harder than you could do it because you'd be scared of hurting me, but I like it hard."

"I could work on that," he said, his voice slightly strangled. "You there yet?"

"I'm there."

She was. The heat and need had grown until her coming was inevitable. She could hold back, she could change course, but there was a climax in her future.

"Want to come together?" he asked.

They were asking each other to trust, she thought, dipping her fingers inside again before returning to the pressing, circling movement. One of them could stop and the other would always be vulnerable. They were throwing themselves out into the darkness and asking to be caught.

"I do," she murmured. "You ready?"

"Yes."

She rubbed harder and faster until she was panting with need.

"Now," she breathed and threw herself over the edge. Her body surrendered and she called out his name, wishing he were with her, wishing he could hold her and feel what he'd done to her.

She surfaced in time to hear him groaning out his release. The sound made her smile. So they'd caught each other, she thought happily.

"I need a second," he said.

When he picked up the phone again, she laughed. "Did we forget our box of tissues?"

"We did."

"Female orgasm is much tidier."

"Your gender has many advantages. You okay?"

"I am. You?"

"I'm great." He chuckled. "The truth is, that was the best sex I've ever had and you weren't even here. What does that say about the state of things?"

She smiled. "I'm not sure. We'll have to discuss it when you get home."

"I look forward to that." He yawned. "Sorry."

"No. It's late there and you have to talk about ants in the morning. Go to bed. I'll see you in a couple of days."

"Okay. Thank you, Sunshine. That was amazing."

"It was. Good night."

"'Night."

They both hung up. She was still smiling when she fell asleep.

chapter
TWENTY-SIX

MARGOT TOLD HERSELF THAT THE FACT THAT SHE HADN'T seen Alec in a couple of days didn't mean anything. He was busy, she was busy... Still, she worried. He hadn't once knocked on her door to invite her to join him for anything. Not a drink or conversation or sex. As far as she could tell, he was barely around. While she knew he was probably wrestling with what had happened with Dietrich a couple of days ago, the longer they went without talking, the more she was concerned.

They had to talk. What he'd done had been so amazing and wonderful. Surely he knew that. He had to see that how he'd come to her defense was the stuff of dreams. If she hadn't already been in love with him—something she wasn't really admitting to anyone but herself just yet—that single act would have pushed her over the edge. Only she was terrified he wouldn't see it that way. Given who he was, his past, his mother and pretty much everything else in his life, she was concerned he would find a way to turn his heroic act into something bad.

This morning, she promised herself as she went downstairs. If he wasn't at breakfast, she would find him and insist they talk it out. What they had was practically perfect and she wasn't going to lose it. Not when they'd barely found each other.

She walked purposefully into the dining room. She expected

his chair to be empty. She thought she would have to confront him in his office or bathroom or wherever else he might be. Only Alec was where, until two days ago, he had always been. In his seat, reading the newspaper. Everything was exactly as it had always been, she thought in relief. Only then she saw it wasn't at all.

There was no place setting for her. No neat napkin, no knife and fork, no coffee cup or juice glass. Instead, there was a tray—as if she was expected, once again, to take her meals in her room. As if their time together had never happened.

Alec put down his paper and cleared his throat. She looked at him, saw the careful blankness of his expression, recognized the firm set of his jaw and knew that whatever they'd had, it was now lost. He was done. There was only the horrible, painfully awkward, heartbreaking goodbye.

"I hope you can understand that this has been a mistake," he began. "All of it. While on the surface we were a good match, in truth I have no room in my life for someone like you." He frowned. "Not you, exactly. For a relationship."

Even as her heart shattered and she began to bleed from the broken pieces cutting through every part of her, she knew exactly what he was trying to say. That was the hell of it, she thought grimly. She knew him, understood him, so while what they had was life affirming and fun and amazing, there was a price to be paid. Emotions had to be engaged. And to feel the way he had was to lower the barriers he kept in place. The very act that had made her love him more had been the single moment when he'd been forced to walk away.

"I'm sorry," he said.

She believed him. He was sorry, but not for the reasons she was. She was sorry that they would never have a chance. She was sorry that she had finally found the one man who appreciated her quirks, who delighted her as much with his conversation as his skill in bed, the man who had shown her the best version of herself, and that she had lost him. For years she had given her heart to an unworthy man and when she finally found a worthy one, he couldn't be bothered.

Because that was what it came down to. Feeling was too hard. Loving required too much. He would rather be alone, and how could she fight that?

She looked for anger, only there wasn't any. There was just the gaping hole and the knowledge that he had forever changed her in a thousand ways.

She had no idea what to say to him, so she nodded and walked back the way she'd come. She made her way to her bedroom where she began to pack her things. After a few minutes, she had to stop because she couldn't see through the tears. She collapsed on the edge of the bed, covering her face with her hands as she cried.

She was aware of someone coming into the room, sitting beside her and holding her tight. Sadly it wasn't Alec. She inhaled the scent of Bianca's light perfume and forced herself to get something close to a grip on herself.

She wiped her eyes and faced her client. "I apologize. This is very unprofessional."

Bianca hugged her. "Screw being professional. I was afraid Alec would snap. It was the Dietrich thing, wasn't it? Stupid man. Doesn't he understand how many fantasies he fulfilled in a single moment? I don't care if it's politically correct or not— every woman wants to have her man fight for her."

Bianca released her. "All right. Let's figure this out. You obviously need to leave. I understand. I'll help you pack."

"Thank you." Margot pressed a hand to her chest. "I just need a moment to think. Where will we continue your lessons?" She couldn't come back here. She just couldn't—it would hurt too much. Maybe a hotel would work.

Bianca shook her head. "You've been trying to dump me for weeks now. We both know I need to get on with my life. I've been afraid not to have you around to tell me what to do, but it's time for me to be brave."

"Are you sure?"

"If I don't know the right fork, I'll let someone else pick up theirs first. If I feel pressured or nervous, I'll excuse myself." She offered a wry smile. "If a man wants to touch my ass, I'll tell him no. I'm ready and even if I'm not, Wesley loves me and despite the arguments you and I have had on the subject, I do genuinely love him."

"I know you do." Margot took her hands and squeezed them. "You have a warm, giving heart. You're going to do great."

"As are you. I'm sorry my son is acting like this. He's always had trouble with strong emotions. He thinks they make him weak." She grimaced. "Or maybe it's that he thinks they make him like me. Either way, it's difficult for him. He needs time. He'll come around. He'll see you're the best thing that ever happened to him."

Margot nodded because it was expected, but she knew it wasn't true—not the promise that he would come around, and that was the only part she cared about.

"Tell me we'll stay friends," Bianca said.

"Of course. I'd like that very much."

"Good. Me, too."

Margot collected her belongings and Bianca put them in the suitcase. In less time than she would have thought, she was ready to leave.

As they carried her suitcases to the car, she kept hoping Alec would burst out of his office and tell her not to go. That he would sweep her into his arms and confess that he loved her and swear that they belonged together forever. Only he didn't and, after Bianca went back in the house, there was nothing for her to do but get in her car and drive away.

When Math 131 had started, Sunshine hadn't been sure she could last a week, let alone the entire semester. But here she was, sitting through the review session, going over material for the final exam and she understood it. All of it.

She and Ann had scheduled a couple of extra sessions and they had made all the difference. Now, as the professor reminded them of what they'd studied, Sunshine was able to keep up easily.

She was going to do it, she thought happily. She was going to pass the class, and with a good grade. She had confirmation for her summer school class and had already signed up for a study group. Yes, she had miles to go before earning her degree, but she'd taken the first steps and she was proud of herself.

As she walked through the pretty campus on the way to her car, she admitted that she was less excited about other aspects of her life. Declan would be home in a couple of days and she honestly had no idea what she was going to say to him.

There was no taking back what had happened and she didn't think ignoring it was going to work, either. While the phone sex had been fun and exciting and had made her feel closer to him, she also knew it had changed everything, and not for the better. Her brief morning-after text of That was great, but we should probably not do that again had been met with a return text of nothing more than I agree. A response that left her with a lot more questions than answers.

She got to her car and tossed her backpack in the rear seat before getting behind the wheel. But instead of driving away, she sat there, confused and scared.

She'd crossed the line. In that single phone call she'd gone from professional nanny to what she'd always been. The girl out for the good time, the flighty, irresponsible pleasure-seeker willing to ignore her responsibilities and run off with some guy.

Declan wasn't asking her to get on the back of a motorcycle and ride away, but that didn't change her part in things. She'd made herself a promise and she'd broken it. Her issues weren't about his behavior but about her own.

What if she couldn't change? What if she was always going to be that girl? She wanted to say this time was different because her feelings were different. She didn't just think Declan would be a good time—she cared about him. She was probably in love with him.

Sunshine let that sink in, prepared to turn the information over and see how it resonated, only she didn't have to. As soon as the thought formed, she knew it was true. She was in love with Declan. She probably had been for a while. And why wouldn't she be? He was loveworthy. As for Connor, well, she'd been a goner from day one.

Great. So she loved them both. Now what? If she was going to be a different and better person, what did that different and better person think she should do? Leave? Stay? And if she stayed, how would that work? Would she have a torrid affair with Declan? Let things run their natural course and then when it was over, they would go back to what they had been?

Unlikely. They could start by pretending that call hadn't occurred, but that wasn't going to work, either. All it would take was a look or a touch and they would be all over each other. He obviously found her attractive and wanted her in his bed and she wasn't sure how long she could say no. Which made her what? The slutty nanny sleeping with the boss?

And if staying wasn't an option, didn't that just leave walking away? She leaned back against the headrest and closed her eyes. She didn't want to go. She didn't want to not see Connor anymore. She didn't want to not be a part of his life. He needed her and she needed him. Even if she could run away from Declan, she wasn't sure she could disappear on Connor.

Even saying goodbye the right way would be impossible. Was she supposed to sit him down and tell him that in a few days he would have a new nanny? Was she going to interview other women for the job, knowing they would be staying in her room, cooking for her family, picking up Connor from school and helping him with his ant farm?

She opened her eyes and stared out the windshield. There was no good answer. The worst part was the problem was of her own making. She had no one else to blame. She supposed the best, albeit temporary, solution was to go on as before and see if they were able to fake their way through the first few awkward days. Maybe it wouldn't be so horrible. Maybe they could pretend to forget that single phone call and nothing would have to change.

She knew she was wishing for the moon, but didn't know what else to do. The situation was impossible. If only she'd fallen for someone else, someone she could meet and date and have a real relationship with. But she hadn't and now she was stuck not only with her concerns about the future, but her fears about Declan. Because in all of this, she had no idea what he thought of her and what he expected when he got home. She could make all the plans she wanted, but except for simply walking away, she didn't get to execute any of them in a vacuum. For all she knew, Declan had used her to get off and thought of her as little more than a piece of ass. And if that were true, then she was about to experience a heartbreak, the likes of which she'd never seen before.

Alec told himself he liked the quiet. With Margot gone, there were no more daily lessons, no extra set of footsteps on the stairs, no conversation in the evening, no interruptions at all. It was pleasant. Once his mother moved out, his life would return to what it had always been and he would be content.

He had to admit, if only to himself, that he'd expected Bianca to seek him out. He felt sure she would want to talk to him about Margot, but for the past two days, he hadn't seen her, either. Her car was still parked outside, so he knew she was somewhere, but she kept to herself. Which was what he preferred.

Alec crossed to the window and looked out at the garden. All right—he would admit to some...restlessness. He'd grown used to having Margot in his life. It was possible he missed her more than he'd thought he would. It had been nearly three days and he'd yet to sleep. Getting in his bed reminded him too much of her, and his office couch was not that comfortable. Plus, every time he turned around, he saw another spot where they had made love. His desk, the kitchen counter, his bed, his bathroom, her bed, the living room, outside.

Still, the quiet was pleasant and in time he would be able to focus on his work again. And eat. Eventually the dull ache in his chest would fade. It wasn't as if he'd been in love with her. He'd enjoyed her company—that was all. She'd been different from other women he'd known with her sharp mind and accepting nature. It made sense he might regret the loss of her companionship. Biologically he would miss the sexual release. Everything he was feeling was totally normal.

Without thinking, he reached into his jeans pocket and pulled out his cell phone. It would be so easy to call her, to tell her he'd made a mistake, that he wanted her back.

He thought about hearing her voice and wished she was with him, quiet be damned. Only it wasn't possible. It couldn't be. The price was too high. She had changed him. Or maybe he'd changed himself. Regardless, he was different and he didn't like that. What was next? He would stop paying his bills on time? He would start making a spectacle of himself wherever he went?

He returned to his desk and opened his laptop. He would lose himself in work, just as he had always done. Eventually memories of her would fade and he would go on as before. After all, his life was better when it was quiet.

Declan accepted that he'd totally screwed up everything with Sunshine. That one night had changed everything between them and now he worried that there was no going back.

It was his own damn fault, he thought grimly as he waited outside the elementary school for Connor to get out of class. He knew Sunshine, knew what she wanted, knew what she feared.

She wanted to be taken seriously, to be respected. She wanted normal and he'd given her phone sex.

Even as he thought about that night, he winced. What the hell had he been thinking? They weren't dating. They weren't lovers. In the right context, phone sex could be fun, but they weren't involved that way. He'd treated her like some 900 number and now there would be consequences.

She'd trusted him enough to tell him personal things about her life. She'd trusted him with her hopes and dreams and he'd violated that trust. He knew her well enough to know she was feeling as lost and confused as he was. Their phone calls had gone from easy to awkward. The last two days of his trip, they'd only communicated by text.

Kids started walking out of the school. Declan looked for Connor, then laughed when his son spotted him and raced toward him.

"You're really back!" Connor yelled, and threw himself into Declan's arms. "You're back!"

"Hey, buddy. How's it going?"

They hugged, then Declan walked him to the car.

"When did you get home?" Connor asked, dropping his backpack in the trunk and getting into the car.

"Just a little bit ago. I came straight from the airport. I missed you."

"I missed you, too, Dad. Did you tell Sunshine you were picking me up? Otherwise, she'll worry."

He looked at his son, his young face, the earnestness of his expression. "I did tell her."

"Good. It's the right thing to do."

Connor was growing up, he thought, both happy and sad at the prospect of his boy becoming a man. Happy because that was what was supposed to happen. Sad because he couldn't hold on to young Connor forever.

He started the car. "I thought we'd go get ice cream before heading home."

Connor grinned. "That could ruin our dinner, Dad."

"I know, but let's risk it."

Connor beamed. "Tell me about Texas and the ants. Are you really building a giant ant farm?"

"I am, so I'm going to need you to help me learn about ants. We're still working out the details but I have sketches I can show you and when we start construction, I want you to see what we're doing."

"Me, too! Sunshine says I saved the day. Is that true?"

"It is."

Connor talked the whole way to the strip mall. Every third or fourth sentence mentioned Sunshine. She'd become a big part of both their lives.

They walked inside and ordered ice-cream cones. When they were seated at one of the small bistro tables by the window, Connor said, "We should get some ice cream to take home to Sunshine."

"That's really thoughtful and you're right, we should."

"It's important to show people we love them, Dad. You always told me that about Mom."

He licked his cone, and talked about staying over with Elijah next weekend. As Declan listened to his son, he thought about what Connor had said. It was important to show people they were loved. Something he hadn't done in a long time—mostly because there hadn't been anyone he loved outside of his family. Not in a long time.

But there was now.

He loved Sunshine. It wasn't just about sex or how beautiful she was. It was about who she was—her hopes and dreams and fears. It was how she took care of Connor and planned birthday parties. It was her. All this time he'd been so focused on figuring out what had happened with Iris that he hadn't been paying attention to what was right in front of him. He loved Sunshine. So what was he going to do about it?

"Dad, can I come with you next time you to go Texas?"

"It was a business trip and you wouldn't find it very fun. But you know what? We need to plan a family vacation for this summer."

Connor's eyes widened behind his glasses. "We do?"

"Uh-huh."

They hadn't gone away the previous year because he and Iris had been dealing with her infidelity. And the year before, well, Declan couldn't remember if they'd done anything then, either.

"When we get home, let's go online and figure out a few places we could go."

"I get to help?"

"You do. This is your vacation, too."

"I want to go to the Grand Canyon. Or Legoland. Can we go to Florida and see the Universal Studios there? Or Disney World?"

Declan laughed. "We'll make a list and then decide."

"We have to ask Sunshine where she wants to go because it wouldn't be a vacation without her."

Declan thought of all he had to discuss with her and hoped at the end, taking a vacation together was the next logical step.

"Why don't you let me talk to her first, Connor? Then we can talk about our vacation."

"Okay." Connor finished his cone, then grinned. "You know, Dad, when we get back from our trip, we should think about getting a dog."

"We should?"

"Uh-huh. It's kind of a thing."

Declan laughed. "All right. We'll think about it."

A dog? He supposed they had a yard and plenty of room in the house. He wondered if Sunshine liked dogs. She certainly liked kids. Now if only he could figure out how she felt about him.

chapter
TWENTY-SEVEN

SUNSHINE HAD DEFINITELY DECIDED SHE HAD TO TELL
Declan she was leaving. It was the only thing that made sense.
She would do it right, with plenty of planning and time for
Connor to get used to the idea. She would be responsible and
mature and then she would get the hell out of his house and
figure out how to start over with a shattered heart.

She wanted to stay. She belonged here, with the two of them.
She loved them both, but if she stayed, she would be what she'd
always been. She wouldn't have grown as a person at all. She
would be ashamed and sad and eventually that would destroy her.

Her plan was to explain to Declan that she thought they had
something special and that she hoped he would want them to
date and get to know each other and see where things ended
up. Which was the weaselly way of avoiding saying she wanted
him to figure out if he could love her back. Because that was
her ultimate goal.

She'd gone looking for normal. She wanted a husband and
kids and a degree and she wanted to be just like everyone else.
For once in her life, she was going to do the right thing.

Her determination lasted right up until he walked in the door
with Connor wheeling his dad's large suitcase. The second she
saw him, her heart whimpered, her determination crumbled and

she desperately wanted to throw herself at him and beg him to see if it was possible for him to fall in love with her.

He looked at her and smiled. "Hi. It's really good to see you."

His kind words totally unnerved her. She folded her arms across her chest, then unfolded them and shoved her hands in her back pockets which immediately made her wonder if he thought she was thrusting out her breasts, which made her hunch over and oh dear God this was worse than she'd thought.

"It's, ah, good to see, you, too."

They stared at each other. She had no idea what he was thinking, which was probably okay as she had no idea what she was thinking, either.

He looked good. Tired, but good. Connor had taken his suitcase down the hall, leaving them alone.

She stayed where she was but what she wanted to do was go to him and hold him. She wanted to feel his body against hers and kiss him until they were both senseless.

Ridiculous, she told herself. She had to remember what was important.

"We need to talk," he said quietly. "This isn't a good time, though."

"Right. Later is fine."

"After Connor goes to bed?" He handed her a small container. "We brought you ice cream."

She nodded as she took it. "I'll meet you in your office."

She went into the kitchen to put away the ice cream and start dinner. *Only a few hours*, she told herself. She would enjoy the evening, then explain to Declan that there was no way to go back to what they'd been before and that she had no idea how they were going to go forward.

Sunshine got through the evening. She'd planned a simple dinner of barbecued turkey burgers and a salad. She'd made a welcome home cake with the sprinkle mix Connor liked. Once they'd cleaned up the kitchen, she said good-night to Connor and excused herself to hang out in her room until it was time to talk to Declan.

She made a few notes, paced, tried to watch TV, then gave up on pretending she was all right. She spent the last half hour curled up on her bed, wishing she could go back a week and undo what had been done.

A little after nine, her phone buzzed.

He's in bed and asleep.

She appreciated the impersonal contact. Having him come to her bedroom door would have been five kinds of awkward. Not at all sure what was going to happen and genuinely not sure what the realistic best outcome would be, she walked through the kitchen and down the hall, then entered his office. She closed the door behind her, just in case Connor woke up and came to see his dad.

Declan motioned for her to take the sofa while he settled in a chair across from her. When they were both seated, they looked at each other, then away.

"I thought we should—"

"If you don't mind—"

They both stopped talking.

"I'll go first, if that's all right," he said.

She nodded, both grateful for the brief reprieve and terrified about what he was going to say.

He studied her for a few seconds, then drew in a breath.

"Sunshine, what happened while I was gone is my fault. I'd had too much to drink and I gave in when I shouldn't have. I knew better and I did it anyway."

He shrugged. "I think we both know I have an, uh, admiration for you, but that's my problem, not yours. I apologize for disrespecting you and your position in our household. This is a place where you should feel safe. I'm deeply sorry."

"It's my fault, too," she told him. "Obviously. I started it and I wanted to do it just as much."

His gaze was steady, so she forced herself to keep looking at him when what she really wanted to do was curl up and scream into a pillow. Heat burned on her cheeks, but she ignored it.

"In the moment," he corrected, his voice gentle. "You've made your wishes very clear." He gave her a slight smile. "You're not that girl."

She dropped her gaze to her clenched fingers. "Apparently I am."

"No, you're not. As your employer and your friend, I was dead wrong. Again, I apologize. I hope you can see past what I did to the person I strive to be."

"You don't have to keep apologizing. I know you feel bad. I do, too. Everything is different now. I don't know how to go back. I don't know what you want and if we can't go back, then is there any point in going forward?" She looked at him. "I don't know how to fix this."

"I don't, either, but I have a couple of ideas, although I'm not exactly sure how to say this."

He hesitated. In that second, she realized he was going to fire her. Nicely, of course, with a good severance. He was going to tell her that they'd crossed a line and that while she'd been great, it was over and she should move on.

Her chest tightened and she couldn't breathe, couldn't speak. *No. No!* She loved him, loved Connor. She didn't want to go. They were great together. Why couldn't he see that?

"I'm in love with you."

She heard the words but didn't understand them. At least not at first. "I'm sorry, what did you just say?"

He raised a shoulder. "I'm in love with you. I love how you are with my son. I love that you went back to college and you're making it work. You're honorable and funny and you have the biggest heart of anyone I've ever known. So there we are. And

I know it's complicated. Believe me, I've thought of little else. Do you quit and then we date? Do I fire you and then we date? I know you can't work for me while we date, so that's a problem, but Sunshine, I love you and I don't want to lose you, so just tell me what you want and that's what we'll do."

He looked hopeful and nervous, as he spoke. "Oh, and if it's too soon, then I'm just suggesting but if it's not, will you marry me?"

He was in love with her? As in he loved her? Wait! He wanted to marry her?

Her mind went blank, then slowly started filling in the pieces. He had told her why he loved her and he'd never once mentioned how she looked.

She stood up. He did the same. They stared at each other, then she ran to him and wrapped her arms around him. He drew her close and pressed his mouth to hers.

Their kiss, their *first* kiss, was sweet and tender, filled with love and promise and everything she could want. She tilted her head and parted her lips. He deepened the kiss, igniting passion in every part of her.

She leaned into him, wanting to feel his body against hers. He was as strong as she had imagined and she fit him perfectly. This, she thought happily, was where she belonged.

"I love you, too," she said, easing back enough to look into his eyes. "That's what made everything so awful. I didn't want to leave, but it was all so different and I was scared you didn't see me as more than a convenience."

He chuckled. "You're many things, Sunshine, but easy isn't one of them."

"Easy isn't the same as convenient."

"Yes, but they're close enough. So what do we do? Tell me what makes you happy and I'll do everything in my power to make that happen."

"Is the reason you think I can't stay here and still be Connor's nanny while seeing you is because I'll feel used?"

"Yes."

She smiled. "Of course it is."

She stared into his eyes and thought about the wonder of a man who had been through what he had with Iris and yet was still open and willing to get married again. She thought about how he respected what she wanted and was willing to do whatever it took to make her feel whole. Every day he'd shown her what a great guy he was. He loved her and he wanted to give her the world. She was in love with him and could easily imagine spending the rest of her life with him. What, exactly, was she waiting for?

"Marry me," she said, resting her hands on his chest. "Marry me, Declan. Let me help with Connor, have babies with me, grow old with me."

He whooped and grabbed her around the waist, lifting her into the air. As she eased back to the floor, she leaned into him and kissed him.

He kissed her back, then laughed. "Looks like we're getting married. I should probably warn you I promised Connor a vacation this summer, and he wants to get a dog."

"Sounds good to me."

"You really want to have kids? Because I think that would be great."

"I do want children," she said. "With you." She took his hand in hers. "We done talking?"

"We can be."

She smiled. "Excellent. Your place or mine?"

"Mine is closer."

"I like how you think."

Time did not heal and Alec was pissed about it. Margot had been gone over a week and he was still missing her as much as he had the first day. Maybe more. The entire situation was ridiculous and frustrating and he had no idea what to do about it.

He went down to breakfast, determined that today he would

eat something and that it wouldn't sit like a rock in his stomach, only to find his mother already at the table. She had a cup of coffee in front of her and looked tired. For once she wasn't wearing makeup, which made her look older than she usually did.

"Good morning, Mother. Are you feeling well?"

She smiled. "I'm not sick, if that's what you're asking." She pointed to the carafe sitting out. "Get yourself some coffee. We need to talk."

He didn't like the sound of that, but knew there was no point in trying to avoid the conversation. She would simply stalk him until he was cornered. Better to get it over with and get on with his day.

When he was seated across from her, she looked at him.

"I'll admit at first I thought what was happening was charming. You were falling in love with Margot and really coming out of your shell. I enjoyed seeing that side of you. I thought the change was permanent. But as you grew to care about her more, you started to worry about your new behaviors. What if you were turning into me?"

Alec couldn't have moved if the building had caught fire. He considered himself self-contained, intelligent and relatively inscrutable. In a handful of sentences, his mother had laid him bare, exposing his deepest, darkest secrets as if she'd known all along. Which, apparently, she had.

"Before you tell me I'm wrong," she continued, "you are in love with her. That's the problem. Or do you want to argue about that?"

In love with Margot? He couldn't— He wasn't— Dammit all to hell, she was right.

He picked up his coffee. "Go on."

"Alec, you have always been my first and greatest love. When I found out I was pregnant, I was so excited. I didn't ever really want to get married, but I loved the idea of being a mother. I thought we would be a team. I wanted so much for you—mostly that you would be happy."

"I have been happy. And we were a team." Bianca had her flaws, but when he'd been young, she'd looked out for him, had cared for him. She might not have believed in rules, but she had believed in love. Later, things had gotten complicated, but not while he'd been a kid.

"Alec, you'll never turn into me. You don't have to worry about that." Her gaze was steady. "You can't. Margot was right—there is a secret from my past, one I've never wanted to tell you. I've been thinking about it and I now believe the only way to convince you is to explain why I'm broken and you're not."

Dread coiled in his belly. Whatever she was going to say, he didn't want to hear. With an intuition he didn't believe in, he knew her truth, her secret, was bad. Worse than anything he could imagine.

"You don't have to tell me anything."

"I do." Her smile quivered a little. "I worked very hard to keep you whole. To give you confidence and to make sure you knew, no matter what, you were loved."

"I always knew that."

"I'm glad." She drew in a breath. "My mother, your grandmother, was a very stern woman and extremely religious. She didn't believe like regular people believe. Her view of God was vengeful and ritualist. Her beliefs were cruel and absolute. I don't know if she never wanted me or if she hated me after I was born, but by the time I was four, I knew she resented me with every breath she took."

He wanted to run, only there was nowhere to go. "I'm sorry," he said automatically, loathing the uselessness of the words.

She shrugged. "I tried to make her happy but I couldn't. Eventually I figured out she hated that I was pretty. As I got older, she slipped into madness. By the time I was nine, she was convinced the devil lived in me. She said only the devil would make a child so beautiful. She locked me in a closet. She beat me and starved me. She would scream at me that the only way to get the devil out of me was to kill me and when God told her it was time, she would do just that."

He couldn't imagine. Even though her words painted a picture, it wasn't real to him. No child should go through that.

"I told a few adults what was happening but no one believed me until I was twelve and she tried to strangle me. I was put into foster care." She sighed. "They were mostly in it for the money but they were so much kinder than my mother, I didn't care. You know the rest. I was discovered when I was fourteen and an emancipated minor by the time I was fifteen."

"I'm sorry," he repeated, too stunned to think of anything else to say.

"I know. It's done. I never saw my mother again. I got word that she'd been committed and, shortly thereafter, killed herself."

She picked up her coffee, then put it down. "I never told you because I didn't want you to know. Some of it was because I was ashamed and some of it was I never wanted you touched by her evil. I wanted to protect you."

He pushed back his chair, circled the table, then pulled her to her feet and held on to her. She hugged him back, her grip fierce.

"You did protect me," he whispered. "I never knew. Never suspected."

She released him and stepped back. "I try to forget but I can't always. Sometimes I worry she was right. Maybe the devil does live inside of me. When I get scared or nervous, the past gets close and I act out. Being outrageous reminds me I'm my own person and then I win. But there can be a cost to that." She touched his face. "I'm sorry I slept with your roommate when you were in boarding school. I was so shocked at how grown-up you were and I thought I was losing you and then I got scared, and well, you know what happened."

"Mom, it's all right. That doesn't matter."

"It does matter. I hurt you. Worse, I betrayed you. I'm not making excuses, Alec. I'm explaining. I hope you can see that. You're not like me. You'll never be like me. You can stop worrying about that."

He hugged her again, his mind unable to grasp all she'd said. "I love you so much. You're the strongest woman I know." He stepped back so he could see her. "Wesley is a damn lucky man, and if he doesn't love you for exactly who you are, then he doesn't deserve you. Don't change, Mom. Don't you ever change. You're exactly who you should be and if he doesn't see that, dump his sorry ass."

For the first time since she'd started talking, tears filled her eyes. She brushed them away and laughed.

"He never wanted me to change, Alec. I wanted it for a lot of reasons, but he was happy with me exactly as I was." She took his hands in hers. "You never call me Mom. It's always Bianca or Mother. I like hearing it."

Before he could respond, not that he had a clue about that, either, she said, "Now, about Margot. It's perfectly safe to love her. Whatever you're feeling is not bad. You won't suddenly take your clothes off in public or do anything else to embarrass yourself."

"I nearly shoplifted a bottle of wine. That's not nothing. I attacked Dietrich."

"The wine was an accident and Dietrich deserved what happened. You were protecting your own. That's something to be proud of." She squeezed his hands. "She's good for you. You know that. And even more important, you're good for her."

With that, she released him and walked out of the dining room.

He slumped into a chair. It was going to take a long time to process everything she'd told him. Her past had been a nightmare and he'd never suspected, but now that he knew, so much made sense.

She was stronger than he'd ever imagined, and if loving Margot meant turning into his mother, then he was one lucky guy.

chapter
TWENTY-EIGHT

MARGOT'S NEW CLIENTS—THREE SISTERS FROM CHILE who had beautiful textiles to sell to the fashion industry—were exactly what she needed. As part of a team, Margot was helping the women find their way through the maze of venture capitalists, industry meetings and LA traffic. The short-term assignment was more fun than challenging and allowed her to decompress from what she'd just gone through.

She was looking forward to a quiet evening at home. Some kind of frozen dinner, a couple of hours of HGTV, then off to bed where, hopefully, she would actually sleep instead of lying there, missing Alec and trying to figure what, if anything, she could have done differently.

She parked in her spot and walked into the lobby to pick up her mail before taking the elevator to her third-floor apartment.

She knew what had gone wrong with Alec—that part was totally clear. It was fixing it that had her unable to sleep. Or maybe it was just missing him. She'd gone into the relationship thinking of him as little more than her client's son. Then they'd become friends and lovers and somewhere when she hadn't been paying attention, she'd fallen in love with him.

She hadn't known she was in danger, so she hadn't protected

herself. She hadn't thought he could become so much a part of her that being without him was like losing half of herself.

She ached for him, for them, for what they'd been together. She wanted another chance. She'd thought of calling him a thousand times, only she hadn't. There was no point. She genuinely wasn't the problem. Until Alec could embrace every part of himself, until he understood that life was messy and sometimes people were, too, there was no hope. She couldn't be with someone who was unwilling to give his whole heart on the off chance he might do something that made him uncomfortable. Unfortunately knowing what was wrong didn't make dealing with it any easier.

She inserted the key in her front door. When she stepped into her apartment, the first thing she noticed was the delicious and familiar smell of coq au vin simmering on the stove, something that under other circumstances would have been welcome but, considering she pretty much lived alone, was unsettling.

"Sunshine?" she called, wondering if her sister had stopped by for something. Not that she expected to see her anytime soon. She and Declan had declared their feelings and were both in the throes of young love and planning a late August wedding at Universal Studios in Florida. Given the median temperature and humidity level that time of year, Sunshine was hoping for something indoors.

Someone stepped out of her kitchen. Someone tall and handsome and who made her heart beat faster and her mouth go dry.

"Not Sunshine," Alec told her. "Sorry to disappoint."

"What are you doing here?"

"Waiting for you."

"In my apartment?"

"So it seems."

"You broke into my apartment?"

She was having trouble grasping the fact that he was here and he was cooking.

The big kitchen windows were behind him so she couldn't see much beyond his silhouette. She had no idea what he was thinking, but figured it couldn't be bad. He'd hardly break into her place and heat leftovers so he could hurt her again.

He leaned against the door frame and raised and lowered one shoulder. "One of my mother's boyfriends was a cat burglar. He taught me a few basic skills. I never thought I'd use them, but it turns out they came in handy."

"You broke into my apartment?" she repeated, then shook her head. "Wait. That's not like you at all."

"You're right. It's not. It's something my mother would do, though."

Now Margot was confused. Kind of hopeful, but confused. "I don't understand. Is Bianca here?"

"No. Just me."

He walked toward her, his stride just a little bit predatory. As if he was going to... What? Claim her? No, that wasn't his style, but neither was an early evening B&E.

He stopped in front of her. At last she could see his face. His expression was warm, his eyes filled with affection as he smiled at her.

"I screwed up," he told her. "I was wrong to end things the way I did. Actually I was wrong to end things at all. My feelings for you terrified me."

"You didn't want to turn into your mother."

He raised his eyebrows. "You knew that?"

"Everyone knew that. The gardeners knew that. Why else would you keep yourself so tightly wound and your world so controlled?"

"And I did want to be that man of mystery."

"Sorry. That's not going to happen."

He touched her cheek. "I love you, Margot. I have from the first day you walked into my office, although it took me a while to figure it out."

She forced herself to stay silent. She wanted to hear all he had to say and not just the highlights.

"I don't trust easily," he said. "You know many of the reasons. Bianca can be wonderful, but she can also be difficult and there were times when she downright terrified me. I was determined to be nothing like her. I defined my life by that credo and built up walls."

"Literal and figurative," she murmured.

He smiled. "Exactly. But what I didn't notice while doing all that is that my mother is strong and passionate and brave. We all have flaws, but few of us have her courage. I didn't until now."

He stared into her eyes. "You are my world, Margot. My one true love. I hope you can forgive me for reacting so poorly to my ridiculous fears. We're good together and I'd like the chance to spend the rest of my life proving that to you."

"I'd like that, too."

The smile returned. "You would? And why is that?"

"I love you, too."

He cupped her face and kissed her. "Thank you for giving me a second chance."

"I couldn't help myself. I was lost without you."

"And I was a fool to push you away."

She nodded. "You were. And now you owe me."

"It's why I made dinner."

"You heated up something I'd already cooked."

"I brought a loaf of French bread and a bottle of good wine."

"Oh, then it's okay." She wrapped her arms around his neck. "You really broke into my apartment."

"I did."

"What other skills do you have that I don't know about?"

He grinned. Right before he kissed her, he said, "Let's go find out."

★ ★ ★ ★ ★

The Summer of Sunshine & Margot
Reader Discussion Guide

Book Club Menu Suggestion:
Margot's Shortcut Coq au Vin (recipe follows)

Author's Note

WHILE I WAS WRITING THIS BOOK, I HAPPENED UPON AN article in which my name was mentioned as one of the favorite authors of a woman who was celebrating her 100th birthday. That woman is Bunny Rejefski, and Professor Rejefski is named in her honor. And the statements "Settle down" and "Enough is enough" were something Bunny used to say to her children when they got too rambunctious. Thank you for being a fan, Bunny, and thank you for letting me use your last name.

Questions for Discussion

Note: These questions contain spoilers, so it's recommended that you wait to read them until after you have finished the story.

1. Margot and Sunshine had each made a decision to change before the start of the book. In what way did each character want to change? How did the events of the story challenge their goals?

2. How did you feel about Bianca? Did your feelings about her change as the story progressed? Why or why not? What were some of the highlights and lowlights of Bianca's behavior? (By the way, Bianca's physical appearance was inspired by an incredibly beautiful real-life actress. If you're curious, you can message Susan Mallery via her Facebook page, Facebook.com/susanmallery, and she'll tell you the actress's name.)

3. Which hero appealed to you more—Alec or Declan? Why? What made each hero the right match for the Baxter sister with whom he fell in love?

4. Margot had a very unusual job as an etiquette coach. What qualities and experiences made her perfect for this job?

5. Something happened backstage at the beauty pageant to send Bianca into a tailspin, but the reader never truly learns what Bianca saw. Now that you know about her childhood, what do you think might have caused her to react that way at the pageant?

6. How did Declan's complicated relationship with his late wife affect him? How would you feel if your spouse cheated on you and then died before you could deal with the betrayal? Did you admire Declan's handling of the situation, or did you think he should have done something different? Why? Did it surprise you when he had sex with Phoebe? How do you think that made Sunshine feel?

7. What did you think of Alec's secret collection of erotic netsuke? Why do you think he kept them hidden? What do you think this revealed about his character? How is the collection itself a metaphor for his personality?

8. Discuss the setting of *The Summer of Sunshine & Margot*, particularly the monastery-turned-private home.

9. Many women have body image issues, but Sunshine's had an interesting twist—she felt too sexy, and it negatively impacted the way people treated her. How did you react to this as you read the story?

10. In the original draft of this manuscript, Sunshine's name was Sandrine, but Mallery changed it because she liked the title *The Summer of Sunshine & Margot*. Do you think you would have felt differently about the story if the character's name had been Sandrine? Why or why not? (One of the title suggestions was *The Summer of Sunshine and Merlot*, but Mallery refused to change Margot's name.)

11. Every story needs a black moment. What was Margot's? Sunshine's? How did you feel about the resolution of each sister's story line?

12. Did this book make you think about getting an ant farm? Why or why not?

Margot's
Shortcut Coq au Vin

"Coq au vin" translates to "chicken in wine." When done the traditional way, it can take many hours, but if you want to work that hard for your book club meeting, you're a better woman than I am. This recipe takes several shortcuts to cut that time down to less than an hour, but with full-impact flavor!

1 bottle of cabernet sauvignon or other dry red wine
2 14 oz. cans of chicken broth
4 slices of bacon, in 1-inch pieces
1 large carrot, in chunks
8 oz. mushrooms, quartered (or 8 oz. of presliced mushrooms)
8 oz. pearl onions, whole (or roughly chunk a large onion)
4 cups cooked chicken, or 1 rotisserie chicken, skin and bones removed
1 Tbsp. dried herbes de Provence (or any combination of dried basil, thyme, oregano, rosemary)
salt and pepper to taste

Combine wine and broth in a saucepan. Heat to a boil, then lower heat and simmer, uncovered, until the mixture is reduced by about half, about 15 minutes. Meanwhile, cook the bacon in a large sauté pan. Drain the bacon pieces on paper towels. Discard all but 2 tablespoons of bacon drippings. Cook the vegetables in the drippings until carrots and mushrooms are a bit browned. Cut the chicken into rough chunks and add to vegetable mixture along with the herbs, then pour in the reduced wine mixture. Simmer about 10 minutes longer. Serve with potatoes.